THE FORGOTTEN COLONY

A ZACH CROFT NOVEL

J.B. RYDER

To Mom and Dad

INTRODUCTION

I was an arrogant twelve-year-old.

I don't know why, but with every book I read, I thought to myself—*Pfft. I can do better than this.*

Again. Arrogant.

Nevertheless, I was determined to make good on my word. So, in June 2019, at the ripe age of twelve, I started writing the first draft of *The Forgotten Colony*.

I did not, in fact, do better than those other authors.

Shocker.

But I didn't give up. I still thought I could do better. It would just take a little more work. When November rolled around, I took advantage of National Novel Writing Month and pumped out 30,000 words of absolute garbage. By the end of the year, I had a 50,000-word first draft and very little desire to go on.

But once again, I had to be a man of my word.

For my thirteenth birthday, my father made me a cake resembling an irogen crystal (you'll know what that is later on) and applauded me for writing a novel instead of playing video games. I wouldn't call it a novel, exactly—it was more like the incoherent ramblings of a sci-fi-obsessed child. But I had something to work with. I just had to make it good.

Around this time, COVID-19 hit, and I was *deeply, deeply* devastated to find that I was no longer allowed to attend school. I just *loved* sitting in a room for seven hours, listening to lectures about the layers of the Earth.

In the absence of school, I spent six months outlining the novel, killing plenty of my favorite scenes and characters along the way. That part sucked. But I got it done! For the next six months, I rewrote the whole book to follow the new outline.

After doing so, I looked at the book as a whole and realized one simple fact:

It was still shit.

The story worked, sure, but much of the actual writing was immature and unrealistic. What do you think I did next? At fourteen, I rewrote it again!

After another six months, I had a 143,000-word monstrosity of adventure, death, and destruction. At that point, I began my freshman year of high school and started to do other things besides writing. I knew there was still a lot of work to be done on the book, such as copyediting it cover to cover, but I grew distracted.

I made new friends, got a girlfriend, and developed other hobbies. I was fourteen, after all. I was supposed to be having fun, right?

Wrong. I was supposed to be sitting in a dark corner of my room with a bag of Doritos, editing my book. So I did that too! With the help of my father, I got a nearly finished manuscript together in roughly... A YEAR AND A HALF. Yes, it took me just as long to edit the book as it took me to write it.

Still, I didn't give up.

After copyediting it—and rewriting way more scenes than I should have—I went through for the final proofread. Although I'm not proud of it, I rewrote even more scenes during that time. (It's a problem, okay?)

But there I was, nearly sixteen years old, with a polished manuscript of the novel I started when I was twelve. I'm not sure if it's truly better than all the books I claimed it would knock out of the water, but who cares?

I wrote a book!

At twelve years old, I said I would write a book, and I did.

That's all that matters.

It's up to the readers to decide if it's good, amazing, or worth using as toilet paper.

So, thank you for taking a chance on this book.

— J.B. Ryder

PROLOGUE

ZACH CROFT: 2053

ZACH'S LUNGS were on fire.

As he sprinted down the cracked cement sidewalk, the soles of his feet throbbed with each brutal impact. He looked over his shoulder, praying that his pursuer was no longer behind him.

But she was.

To make matters worse, the woman was gaining on him quickly. Her strides covered far more ground than his own, and her arms pumped with a precision that put Zach's movements to shame. Zach's body screamed at him to stop, to collapse on the ground and succumb to whatever came next, but his mind wouldn't let him give up. It was as if autopilot had kicked in and refused to relinquish control.

Zach veered suddenly as the sidewalk forked in three directions, hoping to lose his pursuer and give himself a fighting chance. He considered taking a shortcut through the grass but knew it wouldn't make a difference. She was too fast.

Zach glanced over his shoulder again. The woman's intense blue eyes locked onto him, and she began to run even faster.

Eight feet.

His legs lost all feeling. His hips swung like broken hinges, and his throat felt as though it was full of volcanic ash. He just wanted it to stop.

Six feet.

Four feet.

The woman reached for Zach, clawing for his shoulder. Dodging her hand, he swerved to the side and nearly tripped over his feet, barely remaining upright.

Then, just as the woman was about to grab Zach's shirt, he passed a sprawling oak tree and skidded to a stop. He slammed his palm down on his stopwatch.

5:46, ten seconds better than last week.

As Zach dropped to the bench of a nearby picnic table, the woman steadied herself against the tree. "Water," she said, making a claw with her hand. Zach tossed her his bottle and watched as she took a long sip. "I could have beaten you," she said, then tossed the container back. "You got lucky this time."

"Same excuse, different day," Zach said. She had said that every day for months, maybe even years. He did admire her unwillingness to admit defeat, though—it was one of the many things that made Cora Keaton special.

Zach untied his maroon Harvard sweater from around his waist and set it on the bench. Despite graduating from the astronomy program nearly nine years prior, he still carried the beat-up old thing everywhere he went. It was sort of a good luck charm for him.

Cora laid her hand flat, flipping through pages on an unseen notepad. "January 23rd, 2053. I beat you by twenty-six seconds."

"You threw a branch at me."

Cora waved his comment off. "Ah, it fell on you."

"From your hand."

Cora gave a breathy smile and turned away. "Yeah, yeah. How much longer do we have?"

Zach checked his watch. "An hour, but we better leave time." It was only eight in the morning, but the temperature had already soared into the eighties. Sweat streamed down their faces and soaked their clothes.

As much as Zach despised the sweltering Pasadena heat, coming to the park had been part of his routine for ages. Work at OSE started late, and Zach wasn't one to sleep in. Frankly, he had enough trouble sleeping at all. That left two options: he could kill time getting breakfast—coffee, bagel, whatever—or try to burn off the pent-up energy through running.

"You ready for your meeting with Carver?" Cora asked with her hands on her hips.

Zach shrugged and glanced at the ground. "Honestly? I don't know why he even keeps me around anymore."

"Just make sure you get your point across."

"It's not even my meeting. It's the MagRes team. He won't be listening to me."

"Then make him listen."

Zach gave a frustrated smile. "It won't be enough. It doesn't matter what I tell him. His mind is made up."

"*Make* him listen," Cora repeated firmly.

"Fine, sure." Zach grabbed his sweater and headed for his truck. "The meeting's at the MagRes center. Don't wait for me. It might be a while."

YOU'RE WRONG. You're all wrong. And we're gonna fucking die because of it.

Zach couldn't believe what he was hearing. The team was just telling Carver what he wanted to hear! Why couldn't he see that? Zach loved Carver—the man had taught Zach everything he knew—but damn, did confirmation bias do a job on him.

"Despite the recent setbacks, MagRes is still the best chance we have to beat this thing," one of the short, balding men at the front of the conference room said. Mumbles of agreement rippled through the room.

But Zach stayed silent.

They weren't just "setbacks." The program was a complete failure. OSE was wasting their time—anyone with a basic grasp of reality could see that. But reality didn't fit the narrative OSE had bought into, so instead, they were pinning the planet's future on faulty assumptions and convenient half-truths.

"We've revised our projections to account for the recent anomalies in the data," the greasy man continued. "After eliminating the outliers, we can see that the magnetosphere's strength is still trending upward, but not at the rate we'd like to see."

Holding his chin between his index finger and thumb, Carver nodded. "So, what do you propose?"

"Exactly what we've been doing. Just on a larger scale."

Carver tilted his head, not a single strand of his thick, black hair falling out of line. "This sounds... expensive."

"Somewhat," the man admitted. "If we can look at the next slide..." The man explained how they would need an additional fifteen percent funding over the next six months to achieve the levels of recovery in the magnetosphere they had originally predicted. Which was actually *lower* than their predictions from the previous year. They were going backward.

When the presentation was finished, Carver sat silently for a moment as he considered the proposal. Then he fanned his fingers out on the conference table. "Okay. You've got it. Anything you need. This is our home we're talking about."

Zach silently fumed. Yes, their home. A home that wouldn't be there in a year. A home that'd be no more than a burnt hunk of space rock if OSE continued to twiddle its thumbs. Clearly, Zach's title of Head Astronomer meant nothing to the Organization. He'd repeatedly told them that repairing the magnetosphere wasn't working, but his words seemed to carry no weight.

"I'll email you the details, Mr. Carver," the balding man said with a nod. He checked his watch. "It's about lunchtime. Anyone up for Chinese?"

A few men at the table grumbled in agreement as they stood, fixed their suits, and walked out. Carver stayed put, one arm resting against the side of his chair and the other on the table. Once everyone was gone, he gave a knowing look to Zach. "Lay it on me."

"What?"

"I'm not blind, Zach," Carver said. He rolled out from the table and wheeled his chair to Zach's side. "There wasn't exactly sunshine and rainbows in your eyes during that presentation."

Zach adjusted in his chair, gritting his teeth. "This isn't working, Nic. You know it."

Carver sighed. "The team says it is."

"That may have been true a few years ago. But the math has changed since then."

"*Your* math has changed since then. Theirs is the same."

"And they're wrong."

"Or maybe you made a mistake."

Zach looked Carver dead in his bright green eyes. "We're not too far gone, but we will be soon. If you allow me to allocate some funding to Exodus, I can—"

"There's no room in the budget for that."

"You just materialized an extra fifteen percent for them like that." Zach snapped his fingers. "Why can't you do it again for this?"

"MagRes needs the money more than ever."

"And we need to get the hell off this planet."

Carver scoffed and pushed himself up. "How do you suppose we do that, Zach? With no irogen. Are you suggesting we go back to Mars and mine some more?"

Zach got a sick feeling in his stomach at the mention of Mars. "If we have to."

"So, you want to set up another mining colony? Another *Prescott*?" Carver waved his hands through the air as if parting the sea. "A new colony would cost billions. And a new space station to get there?"

"We have the Gateway."

"A biohazard. We'd need a new one." Carver clicked his tongue. "That's a few dozen billion more down the drain. Then you'd need a facility to mine the fuel. A processing plant. Cargo runs back and forth. Supply ships. Oh, and a crew. After what happened in Prescott? Good luck finding a thousand people to sign up for that."

Zach clenched his jaw. "We can make it work this time."

"Oh! Right." Carver wagged his finger as if remembering one more thing. "Time. We'd need time. Years, probably. Which, according to your *excellent* calculations, we don't have. Am I right?" It wasn't an honest question. It was condescending.

Zach bristled. "Right."

"Great. So, we're on the same page, then. It's a non-starter." Carver patted Zach on the shoulder as he passed. "Good try, though. Good try."

———

"I TOLD you not to wait for me," Zach snapped as he stepped into the parking lot, blocking the sun from his eyes with his hand.

Cora pulled out a sun umbrella to cover both of them. Twenty years ago, it would have seemed stupid to be holding an open umbrella with no rain on the forecast that day. But with less and less protection from UV rays, sunburns did one hell of a job on people. "That good?" she asked.

"Yes, that good." Why was this parking lot so damn long? Why did they park on the opposite side of it? Why did Zach do anything anymore? "A lot of people are going to die, Cora."

"So, what are you going to do?"

"What do you think? I'm gonna keep trying until it kills me. Or the solar flares do."

"Sounds like a winning plan—"

A deafening boom silenced Cora, tearing through the hot morning air like a tank round through concrete. Zach and Cora threw their hands over their heads and ran beneath a nearby tree. A gust of wind blew through the parking lot, rustling the tree leaves and sending a crow perched in the branches into flight. Zach couldn't help but wonder if another country had finally nuked America.

Through the fluttering leaves, flickers of orange confirmed the worst of Zach's fears. The ball of fire torpedoed through the atmosphere, leaving behind trails of smoke and flame that made it look like some demonic jellyfish. Unable to move, Zach watched it burst through a cotton ball cloud. The fluffy white mass evaporated immediately.

As the flaming object drew closer to the ground, the fire began to peel away, revealing a metal shell in the orange haze. The back of the object coughed thick, black smog.

And at that moment, Zach realized it wasn't a nuke. Or a meteor. Or a ballistic missile.

It was a dropship.

ZACH'S TRUCK pulled up in front of the Organization of Space Exploration's complex and came to an abrupt stop. He threw open the door and jumped out, moving aside as several police cars rolled past him. A tower of thin smoke billowed skyward from the launch bay behind the building. Crowds poured out through the building's main entrance and huddled in the far corner of the courtyard. Security guards holding yellow lightsticks stood on stone ledges bordering the mob, guiding the waves of employees away from the building and into the parking lot.

Zach took his identification badge from his waist and pinned it to his chest, right in view. Then, he dissolved into the crowd, weaving his way upstream toward the main building. As he approached the front door, a guard stepped in his way.

"It's best if you follow the evac." The officer glanced at his board member name tag. "Sir."

"Can't I go in?"

"Not until we figure out what the hell is going on."

A figure traversing the lobby nearby caught Zach's eye. "Jason!" Zach called. He raised his hand to wave. "Jason, come here."

Jason maintained his purposeful stride. "I gotta go, Zach. Can't talk."

"Then I'll walk with you."

"Nope. Follow the evac."

Zach groaned, realizing that Jason wouldn't budge without good reason. "I'll call Carver down here. He'll give me the go-ahead."

With that, Jason stopped. "No. Don't bother him." Jason looked at the ceiling in exasperation, his hand on his security badge, then shot a slight nod to the guard restricting Zach. "Let him in."

The guard shrugged. "You're the boss," he said and allowed Zach in.

Jason placed a hand on Zach's back, gesturing across the lobby. "By all means... walk with me."

As they crossed the silver letters engraved in the lobby wall— spelling out *THE ORGANIZATION OF SPACE EXPLORATION* —Zach pressed Jason for answers. "What do we know so far?"

"Well..." Jason said earnestly. "There are no research flights scheduled for today. StarSet doesn't have any, either, so that's a dead-end. By the looks of it, the ship is from the Gateway."

The Gateway? That didn't make any sense. "How is that possible?"

"We don't know. Its dropships have autopilot, so it could have theoretically flown here on its own. But I have no clue how it might have launched. There's nobody on the station."

Zach nodded, but his mind was elsewhere. *Nobody?* he thought. *Yes, nobody... Nobody.*

As if reading his mind, Jason continued. "I mean, there *shouldn't* be anyone on the station. That doesn't mean there wasn't."

Zach's stomach turned over slowly as he considered the implications of what Jason said. "Who?"

"Another country, maybe? They could have docked to it and deployed their own crew, which would be a major problem for us. Or, maybe the Gateway just malfunctioned and launched the ship by itself. Either way, it's not good."

A minute later, they reached the doors to the launch bay. A

row of guards with assault rifles formed an impenetrable wall across the entrance, suggesting nobody was getting in.

Or out.

Jason took a left and headed up a staircase to the Observation Deck. Zach followed.

"What happens if there's someone on the ship?" Zach asked.

"If there is? They're going to jail." Jason's hand glided along the railing as he climbed the steps two at a time.

They reached the top of the stairs and entered the sprawling sun-lit Observation Deck. Against one wall, lines of monitors showed data feeds and security cameras. The other comprised a slanted window looking a hundred feet down into the launch bay. Through it, Zach saw the massive dropship on one of the eight landing pads.

It was the shape of a simple cylinder, with dark rectangular plates making up the outer layer. On the nose, the heat shield panels formed a honeycomb pattern. The fire of re-entry had completely blackened the surface.

"Unknown dropship, please identify yourself," one of the communications workers droned into a headset.

"Any response?" Jason asked.

"None yet, sir," the man responded. "The antenna looks damaged, so our messages might not be getting through."

"Keep trying." Jason hiked up the flaps of his jacket and hooked his thumbs on the edge of his pockets. "Can you find out when reinforcements are coming?"

"How about now?" another worker said, motioning out the window as she crossed to the printer. Down in the launch bay, a group of fully armored SWAT officers fanned out in formation, their assault rifles trained on the ship.

The SWAT captain's voice burst through the radio. "Tell them to come out with their hands up."

The comms technician relayed the message to the dropship, despite making it clear that whoever was inside was not listening. Along the edges of the launch bay, other guards secured any exits the passenger—or passengers—could use to escape, essentially turning the facility into one big containment unit.

After a few moments of tense silence, the front airlock of the ship let off a hiss of steam. The bottom edge separated, and a gap opened between the blast door and the ground.

"Identify yourself!" the SWAT captain called out.

The airlock drew open, and the steam settled. As it faded away, a backlit figure morphed into view. Zach could just make out the man's dazed expression, the way his jaw fell slack when he saw the barrels pointed at him.

With his eyes trained on the man, Zach's face went pale, as if he had seen a ghost.

Because he had.

PART ONE

LIES

ONE

ZACH CROFT: 2029

"I DON'T KNOW if this is a good idea," Ryker said as he peered over the edge of the jagged cliff.

Surrounded by tall pines on all sides, the glistening lake seemed to be cut right out of the middle of the forest.

Zach pushed his wet hair out of his eyes and scraped his foot across the loose sediment. "Come on, man. It'll be fine!"

They had gone to the waterpark for Ryker's ninth birthday only a few months ago. How was this any different? Did Ryker think his skinny frame would shatter when it hit the water? Zach was skinny too, and he was going to do it.

Still, Ryker trembled, brushing his shaggy blonde hair out of his eyes. "It's a really far drop."

"Maybe Ryker's right," said Cora, pushing her black hair over her shoulder. She squinted against the sunlight as she looked at Zach with concern. "I don't want anyone to get hurt."

"You really think we'll get hurt?" Zach motioned over the cliff. "It's water, not concrete." He picked up a pebble and tossed it over the edge. It plunked into the water, sending a series of perfect rings rippling across the sparkling surface.

"What if we get caught?" Jason Greene asked while looking down at the rest of the children. He was at least half a foot taller than any of them, so tall that his proportions seemed off. His joints were like the knobs in tree branches, and his legs looked like pool noodles. As his dark skin glistened with drops of water, he shivered.

"What they don't know won't hurt them!" With that, Zach turned and leaped off the stone ledge.

"Zach!" Ryker and Cora called after him.

As Zach fell, he swung his arms in circles and pulled his legs close to his chest. "Woooohhh!" He crashed into the water with a giant splash. A few seconds later, he popped back up and gasped for air. "I'm fine! You guys can come down now!" He didn't know why they were so afraid in the first place. It was just a little water.

Jason barreled off the cliff next, pinching his nostrils tight. He plummeted into the lake and swam over to Zach, who was crawling onto the sandy shore.

Cora jumped third. Although Zach applauded her for it, he could tell she just wanted to warm herself up. At this altitude, even the sunniest of days would be considered winter in Pasadena. Zach didn't mind. The pine trees. The clean air. The lack of towering skyscrapers. It was a nice change of scenery.

Once Cora climbed out of the water, Zach high-fived her and mentioned that he should have brought towels. Whatever. It was only a ten-minute walk back to camp. They would live.

"You coming, Ryker?" Zach shielded his eyes from the bright summer sun.

Ryker shivered as a gust of wind blew past him. "I— I think I'm okay."

"We all did it, man. It's fine!" Zach started toward the forest, where a path led up to the cliff. "Hang on. I'll come up there with you!"

"No, no. It's okay. I can do it."

"All right. Then you leave me no choice." Zach stopped and went back to the small shore, shooting a look at the others. He began to chant. "Ry-ker! Ry-ker!"

Jason joined in. "Ry-ker! Ry-ker!"

Cora followed soon after. "Ry-ker! Ry-ker!"

"Okay, I'm going!" Ryker bounced up and down a few times. Then, he shut his eyes and jumped.

NICOLAS CARVER: 2029

"Boom."

Carver thrust his pool cue into the white billiard ball and watched as it collided with the rest. He slicked back his uniform charcoal hair, ensuring not a single strand was out of line. Everything about him was like that: his hair, his pointed nose, his piercing emerald eyes. All were symmetrical and perfect in every way. Even though he was a few years into his thirties, he still got carded at bars.

"I see you've been practicing..." Victor Keaton took a sip of golden beer, then wiped the foam off his lip with the back of his hand. The light above him cast shadows beneath his prominent cheekbones and made his salt-and-pepper hair look even grayer

than it already was. He bowed his tall frame in Carver's direction, flashing a pearly white smile with one tooth that was sharper than the rest.

"Well, I've had a lot of free time," Carver replied. That wasn't really true. The game had always come easy to him. What could he say? He was a natural. As he circled around the table to get a vantage point for his next move, he glanced at Victor. "How's your kid doing?"

"Cora's good. I think she might be OSE material someday."

"Oh yeah?" Carver asked with a smile. Suddenly, the door opened, and light flooded in. Tightening his jaw and suppressing a groan, Carver turned to see Quinton Croft enter the lounge. He was probably there to give another lecture on why he was right and Carver was wrong. What a prick. Carver plastered on a smile. "Quinton! Glad you could make it."

"Hey, guys." Quinton sat down in a leather chair in the corner of the room. Compared to the other two men, he seemed much more excited, much more eager, bouncing his foot and pressing his thin lips tightly together. "Ready for your speech?" he asked Victor.

Quinton always had this nervous energy, as if he were analyzing every detail in his daily life and sorting it all by importance. His hair, his face, his posture, it all annoyed Carver. And his eyebrows—Carver could go on about them for hours—were permanently furrowed in concentration, making him look like a Neanderthal.

"Yeah. Big night," Victor replied. The comment hung heavy in the air.

Carver's eyes shot between Quinton and Victor. "If no one else is gonna say it, I will. It's not too late to call this off."

"The board has already voted." Quinton glanced at Victor, seeking confirmation. Victor nodded.

Yes. The board voted to ignore Carver's advice, despite him being the Director of Theoretical Physics. Apparently, they felt that theoretical physicists shouldn't get a say in anything that wasn't theoretical.

Carver pressed on. *"MagRes needs full funding. Half's not going to cut it."* Why was it even up for debate? It seemed so obvious to Carver that saving their home, the one planet they knew was survivable, was the rational thing to do. Anyone who thought otherwise was an idiot.

"We need a backup plan," Quinton replied. *"If restoring the magnetosphere goes as well as you think it will, then we won't need Exodus. But we've gotta have a Plan B."*

Carver didn't mind having a Plan B. But he had a problem with devoting half of the agency's money and manpower to it instead of doing everything possible to make Plan A work. *"And how many people will that Plan B save?"* Carver asked.

Quinton shot a glance in Victor's direction before replying. *"Enough."*

"A hundred thousand," Carver said, answering his own question. *"Out of seven billion."* Carver gripped his pool cue like a sword. The words felt unreal as they rolled off his tongue. OSE was spending hundreds of billions of dollars to save, what? A few thousandths of one percent of the population? What would happen to those who didn't make the cut? They'd be abandoned. Incinerated. Left to die. It made Carver sick.

"Like I said, it's a backup plan."

Carver could feel his frustration building. It didn't make sense. Why waste money fleeing Earth for an unknown planet *when they could put that money toward restoring the magnetosphere—the root of their environmental troubles? MagRes would mitigate the effects of the solar flares to the point where life on Earth could continue indefinitely. Spending money on anything else was suicide.*

"We don't even know if Alpha Cen is habitable," Carver reminded Quinton.

"We know enough to try," Quinton countered. "If your Plan A fails, Earth won't be habitable either."

"That's not—"

"Can we just finish this game in peace?" Victor interjected with an exhale.

"Fine." Carver waited for Victor to take his turn, then lined up for a shot. The cue rested between his thumb and forefinger.

Victor threw back the last gulp of his ale and wagged a finger at Quinton. "Are you sure you're up for this? You're gonna be gone a long time."

Quinton nodded thoughtfully. "As long as Zach is with me, I'll be okay."

Victor smiled. "That's why I picked you." He walked over and placed a hand on his friend's shoulder.

With Victor distracted with Quinton, Carver reached his hand down and discretely flicked one of his own pool balls into the corner pouch.

ZACH CROFT: 2029

The smoky aroma of the barbecue filled Zach's nostrils. The wood of the long picnic bench dug into the underside of his thighs.

But that didn't matter. All that mattered was the plate of perfectly roasted corn-on-the-cob and grilled vegetables that sat before him. He jabbed a plastic fork into a potato slice and brought it to his mouth.

"Apple juice?" Quinton asked from beside him, holding up a bottle to pour.

Zach nodded eagerly and watched his father pour the amber liquid into his cup. Before taking a sip, Zach peeled the back of his shirt off his damp skin and pushed his hair out of his eyes. Mosquitoes buzzed all around.

"How was the lake?" Quinton nudged Zach's arm.

Zach swallowed his food. "Fun. It was fun." He looked around. "So, what's going on?"

Quinton nodded toward the stage, where colossal speakers stood like pylons. "Just wait and see."

The possibilities sparked Zach's imagination. Could they be planning another trip to the moon? Were they de-orbiting some important satellite? Could they be building a new rocket? Or a space station, maybe?

Whatever the event was about, it was big. Really big. Zach couldn't remember ever going to something like it before. The whole trip was completely paid for by the agency; five-star cabins, unlimited food, video games, a gym, everything.

Carver approached the table from behind, accompanied by another man wearing an OSE t-shirt: Wilford Owen, whose bronze-brown skin contrasted with his shirt's light gray fabric. "Hey, Quinton. Have you met Wilford?" Carver said.

Quinton glanced back and recalled the man's face. "Oh, yeah. From Comms, right?"

"That's correct," said Wilford, hands in pockets.

Quinton slid along the bench closer to Zach, making room for Wilford. "Well, have a seat. Victor will start in a few."

"Thanks." Wilford smiled, sat, then reached for a handful of pretzels.

Zach's curiosity got the better of him, and he looked at Cora across the table. "Did your dad tell you anything about tonight?"

Cora turned away from Jason, who was laughing at a joke made by Ryker, and shrugged. "He said it's a surprise."

"I don't like surprises," Zach replied.

Nearby, a man strode toward their table with his hands planted on a little girl's shoulders. "See? Here are some kids." He lifted one hand to fix his dark, side-parted hair, which had a slight gloss, then itched his short beard. "Do you mind if I leave Sophia with you guys for a bit?" he asked Quinton. "I've got to handle something real quick."

Quinton wiped his mouth with a napkin. "Mm. No problem."

"Come on, Erik!" someone else called from several tables away.

The man patted his daughter's back. "Stay with them."

Sophia nodded shyly and took a seat beside Jason. From the looks of her, she was much younger than them, no more than six or seven years old.

Zach reached over and offered her an apple slice, giving her a friendly nod. "Want one?" Sophia nodded and smiled, then took a slice.

At the sound of a microphone, all eyes fell on the stage. Victor stood patiently as an assistant attached a lav mic to the collar of his cream-colored dress shirt. Then, he walked to the very front of the podium. A white screen hung behind him with a projected letter P surrounded by stars and planets.

"Hello, friends, family, and colleagues. For those who don't know me, my name is Victor Keaton, the head of the Organization of Space Exploration." He strode a bit to the right. *"We're here today to mark an important day in OSE's history."*

Nicolas Carver watched his boss with a stony expression.

"Thirty-two years ago, we saw the first traces of the solar flares. At first, they seemed insignificant. But it wasn't long before we realized they would get worse. Much worse. And they have." Victor changed the projection to a view of Earth from space. *"Earth has been a great home for millions of years, allowing our species to evolve to the point where we can venture out to find a new home, one that will continue to support us for the next chapter of human history. But where might we go?"*

The screen faded into an image of a blurry orb.

"This is Alpha Centauri, in the closest star system to our own. Of all the planets we have discovered, Alpha Cen is the most Earth-like. Our readings tell us it has water. Oxygen. And with Gateway station, we will get there."

Zach's eyes opened a little wider.

"Of course, it won't be a straight shot. We can't just pick up and go there now. After all, how do we get to a planet that's four light-years away? The answer, my friends, is irogen, a fuel one hundred times stronger than anything readily available in our neck of the woods."

An image of a massive desert crater popped up on the screen. In the corner was a small watermark reading, *"Saudi Arabia, 1996."*

"This meteorite impact led us to this conclusion," said Victor. *"Within it, we discovered small amounts of irogen, as well as minerals found in only one other place in the solar system:*

Mars." He made a knowing gesture. "It seemed we had our answer then. If we wanted irogen to get to our new world, Mars would be a necessary pitstop. And let me tell you: with the amount of irogen we've found on Mars, we'll have more than enough fuel for decades of travel to Alpha Cen and back."

Victor began to smile. He clicked a button on his controller, and a detailed rendering of a domed-in city dissolved into view. "So, with great pride, I introduce you to the Prescott Mining Colony."

The crowd erupted with applause as OSE employees rose from their seats to give Victor a standing ovation. Meanwhile, Zach glanced at Ryker with a confused expression. Ryker returned the look with a shrug.

"What's he talking about?" Zach asked Quinton.

Quinton leaned into Zach's ear. "You'll see."

"The Gateway will orbit Mars, acting as a relay station for the colonists to transport irogen back to Earth, where it will be refined and stored. After enough has been collected, the Prescott mission team will comprise the first generation of colonists to travel to Alpha Centauri. The first people in history to venture outside our star system. Pioneers. Revolutionaries. Heroes." Victor looked at the starry sky. "So... who should lead this mission? Someone who's been with OSE a long time. Someone brave, brilliant, and kind. A born leader." Victor looked directly at Zach's table. "That man is Quinton Croft."

The crowd exploded again as Quinton headed to the stage, waving and smiling. An OSE assistant passed him a handheld mic.

Zach's mind raced. What was Victor talking about? His dad

was leading the mission? He couldn't. Where would Zach live while Quinton was gone?

It took a moment before Zach realized the answer.

He was going to Mars too.

TWO

THE KEVLAR PLATES of the police captain's riot armor knocked together as he aimed his rifle and moved toward the man exiting the dropship. He shouted commands, ordering the stranger to get on the ground.

Outnumbered, the man on the ship dropped to his knees and held his hands above his head. Zach couldn't hear what the man was saying, but he seemed to be trying to explain, to reason with the officers. Before he could finish, two cops rushed up the ramp and knocked him to the ground. One officer drove his knee into the man's back while the other secured handcuffs around his wrists. The man cried out in pain and surprise, his face pleading for them to calm down.

As one of the officers yanked the man to his feet and escorted him out of the dropship, Zach got a good look at the stranger's face. It was all too familiar. His sharp brow. His pointy nose. The dirty-blonde hair parted down the middle and reaching to his cheeks on either side. Skin so pale he really could be a ghost. Zach recognized it all.

The guards stationed at the main entrance to the launch bay swung the doors open. The man and his captors stepped through, and the doors shut behind them.

Suddenly, Zach was on his feet. He ran for the watchtower's exit and barreled out the door. Jason called after him, but Zach was already gone. He rushed to the ground floor just in time to see the guards escorting the stranger down the deserted hall toward him.

Zach ducked back into the stairwell out of immediate view. His eyes found the man's torso, where he wore a loose bomber jacket with a patch on the left bicep: an embroidered *P* with stars and planets circling it.

Zach's heart raced in his chest. *No. He was dead. They confirmed it!* Zach thought, his breath shallow. *But what if they were wrong?*

Zach locked eyes with the man as the officers escorted the stranger past. The stranger's gaze lingered for a moment, then shifted to the badge on Zach's shirt. His expression changed from frustration to recognition as he spoke.

"Zach?"

ZACH CROFT: 2030

"We're going to be okay."

Quinton's warm hand wrapped around Zach's as their drop-ship prepared to detach from Gateway station. Zach nodded and forced a smile. No matter how often his father said it would be okay, Zach had trouble believing it. They had been preparing for this moment every day for the last year. Whenever doubts intruded into Zach's mind, Quinton would find some consoling words to wipe them out.

Zach looked around the dropship, studying the other colonists' faces. This was his life now. These were his people. He'd better get used to it.

At first, Zach had been upset about leaving Earth. About leaving his home. About abandoning ten years of his life and signing away the next fifteen. God, that seemed like so long. He'd be in his twenties by the time they finished, and then what? Onto to Alpha Centauri? Would he ever return to Earth?

Despite his worries, they still left their home planet, docked to the Gateway, and went into cryosleep for the voyage to Mars. During the month-long nap, images of his life on Earth danced through his thoughts, making him feel more homesick than ever.

"It's the right thing to do," his father would say. And Zach trusted his judgment. Although giving up everything was hard, it was for the greater good.

As the three dropships split from the Gateway and plummeted toward Mars, Zach thought about everything he would miss on Earth. He would never see another tree. Another blade of grass. Another skyscraper. This new world would be different, and not all in a good way.

Opening his eyes, Zach glanced across the ship's cabin. He saw Ryker, accompanied by both his parents: Cage and Kayla.

Zach felt a tug in his chest as a flood of images washed over him.

It was a sweltering summer night. The air conditioners strained to keep up. After spaghetti and meatballs, his mother walked him up the stairs and tucked him into his rocket-shaped *bed. With a warm smile, she read him a story—something magical and full of whimsy. He could never remember the details, just the sound of his mother's voice as she read. He fell asleep with her at the foot of the bed. By the time he woke up the next day, she was gone. His dad claimed she went for groceries and would return later that afternoon.*

But she never came back.

The book she had read to him was one of the few things he brought with him on the Gateway, although he hadn't the stomach to read it just yet. He never did. Even back home, it always sat in his drawer exactly where she left it, as if preserving the last thing his mother read to him would somehow bring her back.

"You all right?" Quinton asked from beside Zach, ruffling his hair. "Be strong. We're almost there."

And they were. Past the cabin and through the massive window that made up one of the dropship's walls, a small border of red appeared in the lower section. There were some bumps on the landscape, which Zach assumed were mountains. Above the line, the sky was bleak. It looked like somebody had mixed pale blue paint with gray and yellow.

"Gravity will be a little different down there. Try not to float off into space without letting me know first." Quinton winked.

"What's our current altitude, Carlo?" Zach heard the co-pilot ask. The navigator's eyes scanned the blue and green readouts before him.

"Twenty-five-thousand and dropping," Carlo said.

The other pilot leaned back. "Engage reverse thrusters at eighteen thousand feet."

Quinton seemed to sense Zach's dismay as the dropship

began to shake and thrash. "Don't worry. It's supposed to shake a little."

"We're at nineteen... eighteen fifty... eighteen. Mark!"

"Activate thrusters."

"Activating." Carlo pressed a pair of large blue buttons. "Both thrusters are active." The tops of Zach's shoulders snapped against his restraints as the dropship jolted upward. The shock felt much stronger and deeper than any training runs he had done in the last year. It felt violent.

Lights flickered off in succession. Computer screens and holo displays disintegrated into a collage of multi-colored squares. A few seconds later, they recovered.

"Relax," said Quinton. "Just some interference." He shut his eyes, inhaled through his nostrils, and mumbled something under his breath. Suddenly, the ship began to tilt sideways. All of Zach's weight shifted painfully to one shoulder.

"Hmm," Carlo grunted with a furrowed brow. He flipped a switch, and the ship seemed to level out. "Getting some pull."

"Does that happen often?" asked Quinton, leaning forward.

"Going to Mars doesn't happen often, so no."

The ship tilted again, this time with more force.

"Let's go manual," the co-pilot said.

They gripped their flight sticks, struggling for control of the ship as confusion buzzed between them. The slant got more extreme. What once was the right wall of the ship became the floor.

A boom rang out, and the dropship gave a violent shake. Zach's head smacked against the back of his seat. With the impact, dizziness overcame him. Transparent ghosts lagged behind his vision as he looked around the dropship, trying to focus.

Carlo did his best at the control panel, craning his neck to read a danger warning that appeared on the monitor. "Thruster One failed. We're spiraling!"

The centripetal force tore at Zach, pressing his spine against the seat. A supply crate dislodged from one wall and flew toward another, crashing into a set of pipes. The composite tubes snapped at the center, venting jets of fog-like gas into the cabin.

"Control it!"

"I'm trying!"

An umbrella of sparks rained from the ceiling, and the lights flickered again. Hot embers dripped down the walls like melted wax.

"We're too close!"

Then, with a flash and a roar, Zach's world went dark.

ZACH CROFT: 2053

"You lied to me!" Zach threw open the door to Carver's office with a crash. He stormed up to the head of OSE's desk and slammed his hands against it.

"Excuse me?" Carver leaned back in his comfy leather chair, running his fingers through the graying hair on his temple.

"You lied! About everything! You're a goddamn liar!" Zach threw his arm out to the side so fast and with so much force that his shoulder nearly dislocated. Everything. Everything was a lie. Nothing Carver had told him was true.

"What are you talking about? I haven't lied about anything."

"Then, explain to me how the fuck Ryker Gagarin came back today!"

"First of all, we don't know who came down on that ship, and second, you should watch your tone—"

"Who else could it possibly be?" Nobody. That was the answer. The only way someone could get onto the ship was from the Gateway. And who was the last person up there?

Carver's eyes narrowed. "I'll say it again: we have no idea who was on that ship. But we know one thing: it's not Ryker—"

"You abandoned him!"

Carver leaned forward in his chair. His jaw tightened. His voice was low and steady. "We did everything we could to find him." He counted off on his fingers. "We checked life support systems, cameras, motion sensors! Everything! There were no signs of life. Zero." He lowered his voice even more. "You think I'd leave a kid up there if I knew he was still alive? I'm telling you: Ryker is dead. Whoever was on that dropship is *not* Ryker Gagarin."

"Then how do you explain it?"

Carver sighed. "Honestly? I don't know. But we'll find out." He stood up and stepped out from behind his desk. "Zach, listen. I know you're upset. I am too. But stop and think about what you're saying. You know me. Would I do something like that?"

"I don't know..." Zach glanced at Carver, then back at the floor.

"When you got back, did I abandon you?"

Zach stared at his shoes and shook his head. "No."

"No. Of course not. I helped you build a new life. I watched out for you."

"And I appreciate that." Zach knew it was true.

Carver put a hand on Zach's shoulder. "Look at me." Zach reluctantly looked up at Carver. "You're like a son to me, Zach. I promise, if we could have saved Ryker, we would have."

Zach nodded. "You're right. I'm sorry. I was out of line. I'm just... I'm a little confused right now, you know?" He wanted to believe the man on the ship was Ryker, but the possibility now seemed absurd. Carver was right. It couldn't be him.

Carver squeezed Zach's shoulder and smiled warmly. "No harm done. Why don't you take a long lunch? Get your thoughts together. Then we'll figure out what's next."

"Okay. Thanks, Nicolas."

With that, Zach left Carver's office, quietly closing the door behind him. Through it, he could hear Carver fall back into his chair with a heaving sigh.

And a curse under his breath.

THREE

"YOU THINK he's telling the truth?" Cora asked as she and Zach climbed the steps into the small OSE museum.

"I'm not sure anymore." Zach held the door for her, looking side to side before he followed her in. As they wandered past a Prescott poster on the wall, Zach could almost hear the echoes of the past calling to him. "But if Carver says it's not Ryker, I have to trust him. I owe it to him."

And for so many reasons, too. When Zach graduated college, penniless and without options, Carver swooped in and recruited him to OSE. Later, while Zach was rebuying his childhood home, Carver financed the down payment with no strings attached. There was no logical reason why he would lie.

"Carver's not perfect, you know," Cora reminded him. "The way you describe the guy, he sure sounds like Ryker. And the jacket? With the Prescott emblem?" She leaned on the railing

34

of an exhibit, a miniature replica of a dropship. "I don't want to jump to conclusions, but something's not adding up."

The jacket meant nothing. There were hundreds of them on the station, each emblazoned with the colony's seal. And as for the stranger's appearance, plenty of people had blonde hair, so that wasn't solid evidence either.

"Let's say it's not him," Cora proposed. "Who else could it be?"

"Well, we thought we were alone when we woke up from cryo, but the Gateway is a big station. Someone could have been hiding somewhere, and we never found them."

"Were there any other kids at the time?" asked Cora.

"None that survived."

"That means this 'perfect hider' would have been an adult. They'd be elderly by now. You said the man on the dropship looked like he was our age. So he must have been a kid. And the only other kid left aside from you was Ryker."

Zach nodded, knowing she was right. By the time Zach returned to Earth, all the other kids had died or had been left behind on Mars. The only kid on the Gateway aside from Zach was Ryker Gagarin. "It doesn't make any sense."

"Sure, it does. You were separated. He was presumed dead. Now, someone who looks like him and is his age shows up. And you said he recognized you, right?"

"He said my name." Zach wiggled the badge on his shirt. "But it says it right here."

"There's a difference between saying someone's name and recognizing it."

Fine. Cora had a point. Something in the man's eyes had

suggested a recognition beyond what Zach was claiming, but still. Carver wouldn't lie. "So what do we do? How do we find out if it's really him?"

"Why don't you ask him something only Ryker would know?" Cora suggested.

Zach thought for a moment. There was one question he knew only Ryker could answer.

He just had to find a way to ask him.

CORA KEATON: 2030

The wind whispered through the schoolyard's swings as eleven-year-old Cora's feet dangled above the sandy ground. She swung silently, lost in thought.

Jason took a seat on the swing next to her. "What are you doing?" he asked.

Cora brushed back her long black hair and bit her cheek. "Slowly dying," she joked, then shook her head. "Just waiting. Same as you." There wasn't much else to do, honestly.

It was the third day in a row her father had left them waiting on the playground. Victor Keaton was too important to be on time, Cora guessed. She checked her watch and confirmed the school day had been over for nearly an hour. With a rumbling in her stomach and disappointment in her eyes, she pulled a pair of fruit bars from her bag and offered one to Jason. "It's going to be a while."

Jason seized the bar and tore open the wrapper. "Walking home would be faster." Although they lived almost ten miles away, Cora couldn't help but agree. Her father was a genius, but he couldn't manage a simple deadline like the end of school. "Yesterday, we were here until six," Jason continued. "Just saying." Jason took a bite of his snack bar and changed the subject. "I wonder what Zach is doing right now. And Ryker. You think they found any aliens yet?" His hands morphed into finger guns as he pretended to blast a swarm of unseen intruders.

Before Cora could answer, a black sedan sped into the parking lot and slowed to a stop in front of them. The window rolled down. "Hey, guys," Victor said while fiddling with his cuff-links. "Come on. Doors are open."

Cora and Jason hopped down from the swings and approached the car.

"How was school?" Victor asked Cora. "You had a test, right? Science?"

Pulling the door open, she shrugged. "I got a 98."

"That's my girl." Victor's freshly shaved face curled into a smile.

Cora crouched inside, sliding across the seat while Jason climbed in behind her. "You're late again."

Victor winced dramatically. "Sorry about that. I got caught up at work. Today's the day."

Of course. How could Cora forget? This morning, while Cora was trapped in English class, Zach was on a dropship headed to the surface of Mars. She was happy for him, though a part of her wished she could be there with him. It sounded like an amazing adventure. "Whatever. It's fine. Can we go?"

Victor pressed a button on the center screen, and the car zoomed forward. Cora leaned her cheek against the window. Her mind wandered to Mars, replaying what she had learned about

Zach's mission. First, the colonists had to settle into the habitation dome, a structure built over several years by a fleet of autonomous drones. Then, they had to get the mining plant up and running so they could start sending irogen back home. Cora smiled a bit at the thought of Zach as a miner, picturing him with a pickaxe and a helmet, covered in smears of red dust.

"Hey," Victor tried for her attention. "If you keep it up with those test scores, who knows? Maybe you'll take my place at OSE in a few years."

"A girl can dream," Cora answered with a sarcastic sigh.

Suddenly, an alert labeled OSE: URGENT appeared on the car's center screen. Victor glanced at the kids through the rearview mirror, then pulled an earpiece from the center console. He shoved it into his ear and pressed ANSWER on the screen. "Keaton," he answered. As he listened to whoever was talking, his expression turned confused, then grave.

Cora's stomach fluttered. "Dad?"

Victor waved her off, speaking to someone she could not hear. "How many? I see..." Cora sensed something terrible had happened. It was the way her father talked, the way his breathing hitched. "Okay. Get back to me as soon as you hear." He tossed the earpiece into the compartment and exhaled a deep breath.

"What happened?" Cora asked.

"It's work stuff. Nothing you have to worry about." Victor disengaged the car's autopilot and took control of the wheel.

"Something with Prescott?" Cora's thoughts traveled to the darkest places imaginable. Were they dead? Was Zach dead?

Victor hesitated, then relented, "It's just... the dropships didn't land as smoothly as we hoped."

"Is everyone okay?"

"If you'd let me finish—"

"Well, are they? Are they alive?"

Victor rubbed his eyes. "We don't know."

FOUR

ZACH CROFT: 2030

ZACH SWAM in and out of consciousness as his mind fought to regain control. He was only aware of a few things: sirens, flashing red lights, and screams. He reached up to touch his head and felt a patch of wetness under his hair. Blood?

The ringing in his ears was overpowering. Only the agonizing cries of those around him broke through the noise.

Two hands—not his own—found his restraints and yanked them free. "Zach! Hey, hey, can you hear me?" It sounded as if the words were spoken through a pillow: muffled, stretched, distorted. "Are you hurt?" Quinton asked, probing the nooks beneath Zach's jawline and then around the back of his neck. He briefly patted Zach's shoulders and chest before sitting back with a sigh. "Wake up. Wake up."

As Zach came to, the gravity of their situation became apparent. One of the dropship's walls had crumpled. Frayed wires dangled from above, raining hot sparks on the displaced floor panels. Dozens of seats were torn from their foundations.

And the people. Oh, the people.

The already-crowded cabin had succumbed to anarchy. Desperate screams and pleas for help echoed all around. Those who were able to stand frantically moved through the cabin. Some stopped to help injured loved ones or friends; others wailed over the bodies of the fallen; others pawed through whatever supplies weren't already crushed or destroyed.

However, the outer walls didn't appear to have been breached, so oxygen and pressurization seemed normal. That was one good thing.

Zach reached out to his father but found only empty air. He glanced around until he spotted Quinton ten feet away, tying a tourniquet around a badly damaged leg. His hands, slick with blood, pressed a square of torn cloth against the wound as he tightened the cord with his teeth.

Nearby, a man shouted for his wife repeatedly as he pushed through the aisles. A deep gash stretched from his cheekbone to his chin, and his eye was purple and swollen shut.

A small child clutched a torn teddy bear only a few seats away from Zach and spoke silent, tearful words into it. His mother slumped in the seat beside him, her body lifeless and unmoving, her head tilted at an awkward angle on her broken neck.

At the command module, one of the pilots lay dead with a broken back. The other, cradling a bruise on his forehead, called into a radio headset, "Dropships One and Three, do you read me?"

"Anything?" Quinton asked, rolling up his red-stained sleeves.

The man shook his head with a grimace. "One landed okay, but the other... I don't know."

Nobody knew anything. That was the problem. Zach found it hard to focus on anything but the pain in the back of his head and the blinding crimson lights.

As he studied the chaos, Zach cursed the decision to come to Prescott. Only a few moments before, he had accepted his new life. The change of scenery. The exciting possibilities. But all that was just a means to an end—starting over on Alpha Cen.

Would they even survive that long? They were just beginning their journey, and they'd already crash-landed. Countless people were dead; even more were injured. And they hadn't even made it into the actual colony yet. Would their oxygen work? Would the hydrofarm yield enough food? And what if it failed? What then?

"An extraction team is coming from Dropship Three!" the pilot announced.

Quinton frowned, assessing the damage to a young woman's ankle. "Extraction? What do you mean, extraction?"

"They're gonna get us out of here." The pilot glanced at the window, squinting at the reddish landscape beyond it. "One by one."

"No, that'll take too long," said Quinton. "There has to be another way."

"Half of these people can't walk."

Quinton thought it over while scratching his ear. "Okay. Get them over here." His fingers left behind a streak of red that ran down his neck. "Welcome to Mars, everybody," he said under his breath. "Welcome to Mars."

CORA KEATON: 2030

Cora anxiously walked the perimeter of her room.

She couldn't stop. She didn't want to stop. She would do anything to take her mind off the possibility of Zach being dead. She and Zach had been friends for so long, and she hadn't wanted him to go on the mission in the first place. But, of course, it wasn't her choice to make. And now, Zach could be dead.

It was all because of her father. He was the one who asked Quinton to lead the mission. God, why had he done that?

"Why don't you send Mr. Carver? He doesn't have kids!" Cora had argued.

Victor had been fastening his work tie in the mirror, not giving his full attention. "Quinton's the most qualified. And I'm not thrilled about him bringing his kid there either, but he can't leave Zach behind."

Cora stubbed her big toe on her wooden dresser, pulling her away from the memory. Pain pulsated through her foot, causing her to grab it with both hands. She hopped for a moment before settling down on her bed with a faint sigh.

She looked at the large fountain outside their house through the giant glass window that made up half her wall. The clear, burbling water. The vibrant green grass surrounding the property, always precisely level.

Most of the exterior was glass; a single rock could bring the whole thing down. She had a terrace with a blue-watered pool that overlooked the entire city. The liquid rippled in the warm sunlight, luminescence passing through the transparent walls of the pool and casting down on the beautiful driveway below. A half-dozen palm trees hung over the house, providing a spiky shade that cooled the property. Beyond it, a line of hedges assumed the job of a fence. Perfectly trimmed and tended to.

Her parents' room was on the other side of the home; she could see it through the window. The house had been constructed in a handlebar shape that allowed viewing of every room in the estate.

Cora felt the sudden urge to check the Prescott brochure, the pamphlet she had stolen from her father's drawer. She impulsively dug under her bed, fished the paper out, and read through it, scanning the words, taking in and analyzing them. It said just about everything she'd expect it to say—how many colonists were going, how families could communicate with their loved ones, how long they'll be gone, yada yada yada.

Her eyes lingered on the last sentence: **BE READY TO HEAR GREAT NEWS**. What did that mean? She didn't even know why she had the brochure. She only took it because she was curious. Creasing the tri-fold back to its cover, Cora spotted the infamous Prescott logo.

"Cora," Victor said as he entered the room. He noticed the pamphlet but seemed too tired to care. The tips of his fingers danced on her wooden desk anxiously.

"What is it?" Cora curled the brochure, wringing it tightly in her fists.

"We got news from Prescott."

Cora sat bolt upright. "Oh god. Is Zach okay?"

Victor nodded. "Yes, he made it through."

"Are you sure?"

"I am."

As Cora exhaled in relief, she noticed a brief flicker of something indecipherable crossing her father's eyes. Was it... doubt?

"What's wrong?"

"Nothing." Victor gave her a slight smile. He looked tired. "They're going to be okay."

Those were the words Cora wanted to hear. She just wished she could believe them.

FIVE

NICOLAS CARVER: 2053

CARVER SHOULD HAVE BEEN in the room.

He should have been at the table, asking the questions. It seemed only fitting. This man had been on *his* agency's space station, doing God-knows-what with *his* classified information. That, compounded with the fact that the man claimed the identity of a dead child, and Carver was cut out for one hell of an afternoon.

After all, the man couldn't be Ryker.

He couldn't be.

Ryker was dead.

Refusing his request to be in the room, the interrogators insisted that Carver watch from afar. So there Carver was, arms crossed against his broad chest as he peered at the disheveled man through a one-way mirror. To even look at the intruder made Carver's stomach churn. Still, he couldn't peel his eyes away.

"Something to drink?" the interrogator inside the room asked as he offered the man a can of soda. He adjusted his tortoiseshell glasses, scratched at a radiation burn on his neck, and gave an inviting smile to the man.

The intruder turned it down. "Why am I being questioned?"

"We're just trying to learn more about you. You understand, don't you?"

"I've told you everything there is to know. I survived the Prescott mission and have been stuck on the Gateway since. How many times do I have to explain it?"

"Hey," the questioner made a defensive gesture with his hands, "I believe you. But those guys out there," he subtly nodded to the one-way mirror, "won't have the same reaction. If you were to give us a sign of what your business is here, it would help clear this up."

The man shook his head with a frustrated smile. "You don't believe me. God, you can stop pretending. It's pissing me off already."

"Sir, with all due respect, the information you gave us about yourself doesn't add up in the way we would like. We have at least a couple dozen files that say otherwise."

"I understand how this may sound. But please, you have to trust me. I don't have a mental issue, and this isn't some sick prank," said the intruder as he twirled a silver ring on his index finger.

"Just see it from my perspective: a man shows up claiming to be someone who has been dead for twenty-three years. Now, I'm not completely ruling out the possibility that you're telling the truth, but—"

"I didn't just 'show up.' I flew on a goddamn dropship down from the Gateway! Name one way I could do that without already being up there with enough knowledge to launch one." He spoke through his teeth with forced restraint.

"Sir, I need you to remain calm."

Carver sensed that the interrogator needed help and moved for the door. He opened it, striding inside with the confidence of a man who hadn't been told to stay away. "How are things going in here?" Carver asked.

The interrogator stood. "I'm sorry, Mr. Carver. I seem to be having a little trouble." He dipped forward a little, hands folded behind his back. Then, he itched the burn on his neck again.

Carver clapped the interrogator on the shoulder. "No worries. If he's a spy, he's trained to stay quiet." Carver wasn't sure if the man was a spy, but the alternative was worse. Far worse. "You." He pointed at the man. "How many colonists were on the Prescott mission?"

"Before or after the crash? Or the meteor? Or the Red Plague—"

"The original crew," Carver said.

The man took a minute to think it over. "Nine-hundred-eighty-four, I think."

Carver nodded thoughtfully. "You studied. I'll give you that."

"I didn't *study*," the intruder said.

"Fine. Maybe you were a part of Prescott. Maybe I shit rainbows and have a pot of gold in my office. Regardless, we've gotta run some tests." Carver checked his watch. "First, we'll determine who you are, then—"

The man shook his head. "What kind of tests?"

"Second, if the outcome of the first test is in your favor, then we have to be sure that you're not infected."

"Infected? I lived up there for twenty-three years! Don't you think I'd be dead by now?"

"We can't take any chances."

"No? Then what are you doing here?" He pretended to cough. "Pretty risky, don't you think?" He coughed again. "If I'm infected."

Carver gave him a hard stare but said nothing.

"Well, I'm not doing it." The man sat back and crossed his arms. "Fuck your tests."

"If you've got nothing to hide, you've got nothing to worry about." Carver motioned at two guards in the hallway. They lumbered into the room and approached the man.

The intruder sat up straight, on alert. "Hang on. You can't—"

One of the guards grabbed his arm and hauled him to his feet. The other guard slapped restraints around his wrists as he pleaded, "No! No! I'm telling the truth!" The man looked at Carver as if he would find any help there.

The next thing he knew, he was being pulled toward the exit with kicking legs and thrashing shoulders. "Please! You have to believe me. I'm Ryker Gagarin. You don't need to use me as some fucking lab rat! I'm Ryker Ga—!" His voice cut off abruptly as the door shut.

Still in the room, Carver looked at the interrogator. He signaled for him to come closer, then lowered his voice. "About the tests..."

"We'll have them done right away."

"Right, yes... But if he is who he says he is," Carver paused. "I need to be the first to know."

ZACH CROFT: 2053

"Come on, Jason. You've got to let me see him," Zach said. He pulled out the cafeteria chair and sat down.

"I would if I could, but I can't. Nobody sees him. Carver's orders." Jason shrugged, then took a bite of his sandwich.

Zach looked to Cora for help. She chimed in. "Zach just wants to ask him a couple of questions."

"What's the point?" Jason said through a mouthful of food. "They're going to do DNA tests. That'll tell you if it's him."

Zach adjusted his approach. "Look, you know what we went through up there, what I've lived with since. This is important to me. Please."

"I know. I do. But I can't just—"

"Jason. Look at me." Cora said. Jason reluctantly turned his head in her direction. "This is important. Just do this, okay? For me?"

"It's not that easy."

"Just five minutes. Right, Zach?" Cora raised her eyebrows in Zach's direction.

"Or less."

Jason chewed this sandwich slowly, then nodded. "Fine. Five minutes. I'll radio in to get you clearance."

"Thank you," Zach said, then darted for the door.

Cora stepped forward and hugged Jason. "You're the best."

She gave him a peck on the cheek, then followed Zach out the door.

Jason took another bite of his sandwich, a small smile on his lips.

SIX

ZACH CROFT: 2053

THE DOOR OPENED into the empty office, and Zach's eyes immediately focused on the man curled up in the corner. Upon seeing Zach in the doorway, the man sat up and ran his fingers through his straight blonde hair. He still looked familiar, but Zach found himself seeking out features he didn't recognize, something to prove to himself that the man was not who Zach thought he might be.

Zach plucked at the collar of his sweater as he entered the room, permitting a nervous drop of sweat to fall down his chest.

"Harvard, huh?" the man said as he stared at Zach. "Must have been nice."

Zach glanced back at the guard who let him in, giving a nod that said *I'll be okay*. Then he stepped into the room, and the door shut. As he approached the man, Zach said nothing.

Lights flickered above them. The stale air in the old office smelled of dust and mildew.

In a raspy voice, the scruffy man prompted, "You need something?" He bit at a hangnail on his forefinger, keeping his shining brown eyes on Zach. His torso rested against his knees.

"Can I ask you a few questions?" Crouching in front of the man, Zach reached into his pocket and pulled out the sheet of questions he and Cora had prepared. He pondered it for a moment before crumpling it up and throwing it aside.

"I have one for you first," said the man, leaning forward in a borderline threatening way. "Why all this?" He gestured to the empty room.

"They aren't sure who you are. Or if you're a threat."

"Are *you* sure of who I am?" The man scratched his stubble, raising his eyebrows.

"Well, that's why I'm here." Zach cleared his throat, suddenly wishing for a bottle of water. "What's your name?"

"Ryker James Gagarin."

A lump formed in the back of Zach's throat. "How old are you?"

"Thirty-three."

"Okay." Zach's mind swam with all the possible questions he could ask. What would be appropriate? What would he do if the man really was Ryker? "What's my name?"

"I wouldn't have recognized you without your badge, but you're Zach Croft." The man cocked his head. "You know, I can see the resemblance. You look worse, but," he smiled, "you're still Zach."

Zach coughed at the insult. "If you know me, what did we do at the retreat before Prescott?"

"You forced me to jump in a lake." The man chuckled at the memory. "I was scared shitless."

Zach tried not to react to the man's answer. The lake was something only Ryker would know. He covered up his shock with another question. "Did all the colonists die *in* Prescott?"

"Oh, come on, Zach! It's me!"

"Just answer the question, please."

The man scowled with irritation. "No. The healthy ones went up to the Gateway."

"And the others?"

"Zach," the man said, fixing Zach with a hard glare, "you know what happened as well as I do."

Zach found himself speaking faster, the tension in the room building as the truth became clearer and clearer. "What was the last thing my father said to us?"

The man seemed to be taken aback by this. He looked at the ground. For a moment, he was quiet. Then, he said, "That he'd be there when we woke up."

The lump in Zach's throat grew bigger. His vision blurred. His chest tightened. His stomach did a somersault. Then, he looked down at the man's hands for the first time and noticed a glimmer of something.

A ring.

A silver ring.

With a G engraved on it.

Something burst inside Zach, and he threw himself at the man, wrapping his arms around his best friend. "Ryker."

Ryker laughed in surprise, then returned the hug. "Whoa there, Zach. Down, boy."

Zach couldn't believe it. He was hugging Ryker. He was

hugging his dead best friend. Zach laughed, let go of Ryker, and held him at arm's distance. "How are you alive? They told me you were dead."

"Oh yeah? And what made them think that?"

"Life support readings. They checked every system on the Gateway, and there were no signs of life. That's what they told me."

That's what they told me. It struck Zach that he had never seen any of the readings confirming Ryker's death. He had only been told.

Told by Carver.

Never mind that. It was something to worry about later. All that mattered now was that Ryker was sitting in the flesh, right in front of him. Zach wiped his nose and tried to regain his composure. "How did you make it this long up there? It's been—"

"A long time. I know. We can talk about that later. But I've gotta get outta here, Zach."

"You're not in any danger. These are good people."

"Oh yeah? Are they the same ones who told you I was dead?"

Zach hesitated for a moment, then shook his head. "I can't just break you out—"

"Please, Zach. You left me behind once," said Ryker. "Don't do it again."

"HELP! I NEED HELP!" Zach called out, his hands cradling his best friend's seizing form. Ryker's head bobbed up and down wildly, foaming spit pouring from his lips. His hands trembled against his chest, and his eyes rolled back into his head.

The guard appeared in the doorway. He stood over Zach in a confused panic. His eyes darted between Zach and the prisoner. "Should I call medical?"

"Get in here and help me!" He looked back down at Ryker and brushed a messy clump of hair off Ryker's forehead.

The guard did as he was told and knelt beside Ryker. "What do I have to do—?"

"Don't scream," said Ryker as his head flew up to collide with the guard's in a vicious head butt. The guard fell onto his back, stunned. Zach recoiled in shock. Ryker scrambled up and punched the guard in the jaw, knocking him out cold. Then he grabbed the guard's keycard and jumped to his feet. "Let's go."

Zach and Ryker left the office and set off down the hall. At the end of the hallway was a door. Upon reaching it, Ryker passed Zach the guard's ID, and Zach flashed it across the reader. The threshold opened into the building's main hallway. With his hand on Ryker's back, Zach led them both through it.

They couldn't go out through the front exit; there were too many guards. They had to use one of the back doors, one rarely guarded and generally ignored by employees. Two lefts and a right later, a service door came into view at the end of a narrow corridor. It led out into an alley decorated with dumpsters and trash bags. On an ordinary day, no one went near it if they could help it.

But today was not an ordinary day.

As he and Ryker turned into the hall, Zach caught a glimpse of a guard walking their way. And not just any guard

—it was Jason Greene. Zach made eye contact with Jason. The muscles in his face tightened. Jason's eyes flitted from Zach to Ryker. A small, almost imperceptible smile appeared on Jason's lips. His eyes traveled back to Zach. "Just five minutes, huh?"

"Or less," said Zach nervously.

They stood like that for what seemed like hours. Then, Jason nodded toward the service door, wordlessly giving Zach permission to leave.

Zach exhaled and nodded at Jason in silent thanks. Once in the service alley, Zach pulled Ryker to the side. "My house isn't far from here. Thirty-nine Hadfield Pass. I want you to go there—"

"No. You've already done enough."

"Ryker, you don't have any money. You've got nowhere to stay."

Ryker insisted, "I'll figure it out."

"At least take this." Zach removed his wallet and shoved a fistful of cash in Ryker's hand. "Find a cab, and take it as far away as possible."

"Won't the driver realize something's wrong?"

"There is no driver."

Ryker's brow furrowed. "What do you mean, there's no driver?"

"You've been gone a long time." Zach cocked his head. "Now, hit me."

"What?"

"Hit me, so they don't know I helped you."

Without another word, Ryker slammed his fist into Zach's face.

RYKER GAGARIN: 2030

"No, Ryker!" Cage yelled, holding a rough finger out in front of him. "That's the end of it."

"But Dad—!"

"No. You can't go." Cage pulled on a thick, insulated jacket and fitted himself with an oxygen mask. "Not everything's up and running, alright? It's not safe."

"Cage, you can always put a mask on him. He should see the plant," Kayla urged.

"He will. Soon. But we don't even have air running properly over there. God knows what else is wrong."

"Can I at least go and play with Zach and the other kids?" asked Ryker with a hopeful look.

"There's construction all over the place..." Cage paused for a moment, looking down at Ryker. "Maybe in a week or two, okay?" After zipping his jacket, Cage approached Ryker and caressed his cheek with one finger. "You'll understand when you're an adult."

"You can remind me again then." Ryker pulled away from his father. "We're all still gonna be here anyway!"

Cage and Kayla traded looks before Kayla crouched in front of Ryker and took his hands. "OSE worked hard to get us here."

"Worked hard? It's cold, we've got almost no food, and we're sleeping in tents!" Ryker walked to the other end of their quarters, where a cardboard box sat beside three pine-green cots. He reached down and swiped a few silver packets from its surface. "This is what we're supposed to eat?" He squeezed one, and a cream-colored sludge erupted from the top.

Cage closed his eyes and sighed. "It's only temporary. The engineers are building all the hab units, and the hydrofarm will be operational soon. We just have to deal with it until then. People are depending on us."

"But why us? Why'd we have to take one for the team while everyone else sits back on Earth?"

"We're not taking one for the team. This was our ticket out, honey," Kayla said. "You had no future there."

Of course, Ryker had a future there! It wasn't like they were about to get nuked. What did it matter if the sky lit up every few weeks? At least he'd be looking at the sky he knew. Not the foreign murk he was forced to look at on Mars.

Besides, the Prescott colonists weren't the only people going to Alpha Cen. Thousands of others were too! Were any of them eating what tasted like glue and sleeping on frigid cots? No! So why did Ryker have to be?

"And I have a future here?" Ryker raised his eyebrows. "Best case scenario, I'm in the mines at fifteen!"

"You have a future on Alpha Cen! Because we're here, we're guaranteed a place."

"And we just have to waste fifteen years of our lives to get it!" Fifteen years. Fifteen years. Ryker hadn't even been alive that long. And that was how long he had to live on that barren, disgusting planet? "Why didn't I get a say in any of this?"

Kayla cocked her head and smiled, her eyes glossy. "We're just doing what's best for you—"

"Why do you get to decide what's best for me?"

"Because we're your parents, Ryker," said Cage. "It's no different than back home."

"But it is. Back home, I could at least go and play!" Ryker bit his lip and vented a deep exhale. "Home. Home. Earth's not even home anymore," he said bitterly. "This is."

NICOLAS CARVER: 2053

"Explain it to me again," said Carver, swallowing the angry lump in his throat. "Go on. Tell me again how the only prisoner in this facility escaped."

Jason jumped into another explanation while Carver breathed in and out, in and out, and suppressed the urge to crush Jason's skull. He tried to summon a peaceful image to calm his fury. He was on a beach. The waves were crashing behind him—yes. He had his brushes and a canvas and was outlining the palm trees surrounding the bay. Like magic, he manifested a surfer frozen in a stride, with shaggy blonde hair, messy stubble, and a prominent brow—no, no, no! Carver choked.

"... faked a seizure ... punched Zach Croft ... knocked out the guard ... " Jason went on. "... Zach ran after him ... all he remembers ... "

Blah. Blah. Blah. The Carver from twenty years ago would have fired Jason and ensured he never wore a badge on his chest again. But today's Carver was trying to be more understanding, and for that, Jason could keep his job.

" ... not on the premises ... have people looking ... "

"Why did you let someone see him?"

"... doesn't know how—" Jason looked up. "Huh?"

"Why did you let someone see the prisoner when I told you not to?" Carver got closer, looking up at Jason. "The prisoner could be a biohazard."

"Sir?"

"He was on the Gateway, Jason, you can't be so stu—" Carver caught himself. "Naive."

"Should I call the police—?"

"No. Not yet."

The prisoner was, in fact, Ryker Gagarin. DNA tests confirmed it. How Ryker had survived for so long, Carver couldn't say. He racked his mind thinking of how his life could come crashing down if Ryker opened his mouth to the press. If he told anyone what happened to him, OSE could lose whatever meager funding it still retained. And Carver could lose his job.

"I'll talk to Zach," Carver continued. "Do whatever you can to track the prisoner down."

ZACH CROFT: 2053

Zach looked at the main building just in time to see Cora rush out. Running up to Zach, she grabbed him firmly by the arm and tugged him behind the propulsion lab. "What the hell happened in there?" Cora asked as she reached for Zach's black eye.

Zach winced away from Cora's prodding fingers. He debated telling her about Ryker's escape, about how they had knocked out the security guard, but he decided to leave that out. "You were right," he said. "It's Ryker."

Cora pulled back. "Oh, my god. Where is he? Can I see him?"

"I don't know."

"What? How can you not know?" Cora's face turned to stone, and Zach knew he was about to get the lecture of a lifetime.

"I gave him some money, and he ran away." Zach left out

the part where he told Ryker to punch him. Besides, the black eye was a nice touch for convincing anyone other than Cora that he'd had no role in Ryker's escape.

"He's been gone for twenty years, and you just let him go?"

"No, I just—I didn't have time to think of something else." That part was true. He just wanted to get Ryker as far away from the facility as possible, as fast as possible.

"He could get *hurt!*" Her eyes sharpened. "He doesn't know how bad the flares are now!"

"He's not a child, Cora. He knows where my house is; he'll go there when he's ready."

Cora's voice dropped two notches. "If it really is Ryker, that means Carver lied."

"Or he's just as in the dark as the rest of us."

"And how do we figure out which it is?"

"I don't know," Zach said, "but I'm going to find out."

SEVEN

ZACH CROFT: 2053

"Almost done," the doctor said.

Her hands were cold and sterile as she knitted the clear string through Zach's eyebrow, patted it with a stinging cotton ball, and wiped an antiseptic ointment over the stitches. Zach closed his eye tight and tried to ignore the pain.

After getting the all-clear, Zach prepared to leave the exam room. He pulled his sweater back on and fixed his hair in the mirror.

"Come back tomorrow so I can check on the swelling," the doctor said while peeling off her gloves.

"Will do." Zach hopped off the table, half-expecting his legs to have fallen asleep and gone numb, but they stayed strong.

As he exited the examination room, Zach noticed Jason striding down the hallway toward him. His footsteps punctuated the hustle and bustle of the corridor, where doctors in lab coats rushed by with leather briefcases and thick binders, the sound of their dress shoes echoing off the linoleum floor.

Zach approached Jason with a look of worry etched across his face. "What's going on?"

As he ducked around a low-hanging light fixture, Jason pulled Zach aside. "Carver's coming to talk to you," he said, glancing nervously over his shoulder.

Zach knew it was only a matter of time before someone came knocking, but he hadn't expected it so soon. What would he tell Carver? It felt like there was nothing he *could* say.

"What did you tell him?" A note of concern crept into Zach's voice.

Jason sent another look over his shoulder, then leaned in closer. "The truth. That Ryker faked a seizure, punched you in the face, and escaped."

Zach let out a sigh of relief. "Carver's not just gonna let this go. He'll try to find him."

"Actually, that's my job. And, considering Carver doesn't want to get the cops involved, it's gonna be pretty damn hard."

"Good. That's good. What about the news? Have they said anything about the ship?"

"They're too hung up with the flare down south. Now, where's Ryker?" Jason said in a low voice.

"I don't know. And what flare—?"

Jason ignored his question. "Ryker didn't tell you where he was going?"

"I said the same thing to Cora: he knows where I live. He'll find me when he's ready." Zach stepped aside, glancing behind him, as a nurse rushed past with a medkit in hand. "Listen, I've really got to go check out that flare."

"Looking at some numbers isn't gonna do anything for us now. You've got to get your story straight. If you mess up when Carver asks what happened with Ryker, we're both in hot water."

"I wasn't planning on messing up." Then again, Zach wasn't planning on his best friend rising from the grave either.

And that still happened.

NICOLAS CARVER: 2053

How long before Zach learned the truth?

It was only a matter of time. Days. Hours, even. What would happen if Zach already knew? Carver prayed Zach was still clueless, not only for his own sake but for the sake of their friendship.

As Carver entered the Medical building, he ran right into Zach on his way out. Noticing the black eye beneath Zach's ice pack, Carver gave him a pained wince. "That doesn't look good."

"It's nothing. Doc says it'll be gone in a few days."

"Great to hear." Carver walked with Zach out of the building. "Hey, come here for a sec." He took Zach by the elbow and led him around the corner into an alley. "I need to know what happened, Zach."

The words spilled out at once. "Okay, first let me say, you can't blame Jason. I pressured him into letting me see the guy. Don't take it out on him."

"I don't care about Jason. What happened with the prisoner?"

Zach allowed his head to rest against the wall, the frosty ice pack melting in the hot sun. "He kicked me in the stomach, beat up the guard, and ran out. When I tried to chase after him, he knocked me out cold. That's all I remember."

"I'm so sorry that happened."

"No, *I'm* sorry. I should have listened to you. That was not Ryker. He wouldn't have done that. Especially to me."

"No, of course not." Every muscle in Carver's body suddenly relaxed. He exhaled a deep breath.

"Do you have any idea who it was?" Zach asked.

"It's too early to know for sure, but the going theory is that a foreign power may have compromised the Gateway. Russia, most likely. They may have docked to it and tried to commandeer the station. But something went wrong, and they ended up launching the dropship."

"But..." Zach absorbed Carver's words, clearly not understanding them entirely. "Why would he have come here?"

"Autopilot. He might not have known how to override it." Fearing that Zach could see through his lie, Carver quickly changed the subject. "How are *you* doing? With everything going on." Carver knew Zach couldn't be taking this well. Getting beaten up by someone he thought was his dead best friend must have been heartbreaking. "I know how much you were hoping it was Ryker."

Zach shrugged. "Yeah, well... I'll get over it."

"I'm sure you will." Carver cracked a smile. "Anyway, just a heads up: someone'll probably come to your office and ask you some questions later. We have to cover all our bases. Just a formality."

"Sure, no problem. Whatever you need."

"Thanks, son." Carver patted Zach on the shoulder in

farewell, then walked to the main building, summited the concrete flight of stairs, and slipped into his office. As he melted into his cozy leather chair, he shut his mind off, forgetting the possibility of his career going to shit and allowing only one thought to slip through. A positive thought, one he was deeply grateful for.

Zach didn't know.

EIGHT

ZACH CROFT: 2053

CARVER HAD LIED right to his face.

As Zach shakily brought his coffee to his lips, he felt a tightness in his throat. Why would Carver do that?

Zach wanted to believe Carver knew just as little as he did. He *needed* to believe it. That Ryker Gagarin hadn't been intentionally abandoned.

Zach pulled out his phone and called Cora.

"Yep?" she said.

Zach sat down at his computer and leaned forward. "Found anything?" He tapped a pen against his desk.

Cora sighed on the other line. "Nope."

"Damn it." Zach returned a groan of his own. "Nothing from the Prescott Commission?"

"Nothing."

"How about the OSE Inspector General—"

"Zach, there's nothing. All the official sources say the same thing Carver told you: OSE checked the Gateway's systems and found no signs of life."

Zach ran his fingers through his hair, feeling defeated. Then, something occurred to him. "What about unofficial sources?"

"What do you mean?"

"People. Individual people. Who was around back then?" Zach asked. "Maybe someone else has a different story."

Cora huffed and suggested, "I can ask my mom if she still has contact with any of my dad's old colleagues."

"That's a good start." Zach paused for a moment, then said, "I wonder..." He opened the OSE website and began navigating through the menus.

"Wonder what?" Cora asked.

"Just hang on. I'm checking something."

He clicked on a History tab, then scrolled down to an image of the old Prescott logo and clicked that. After a few more clicks through a photo gallery, he found what he was looking for: photos from the Big Bear retreat where the Prescott mission was first announced.

In one of the pictures, Victor sat at a picnic table with a beer thrust in the air. To his left, a much younger-looking Carver leaned over his shoulder. His lips were slanted in something resembling a smile. *Get it over with!* Zach could imagine Carver thinking.

To Victor's right, there was Quinton. He, unlike Carver, smiled brightly. Bits of confetti stuck to his jacket, the remnants of an earlier party. Zach took a second to admire his father's cheerful grin. The moment the photo was taken—that retreat—was essentially the last normal day they had before things changed.

When Zach's eyes finally pulled away from Quinton, they landed on a man lurking in the background. His hands were thrust into his pockets, and his eyes seemed reddened by all the smoke. Zach couldn't tell whether the man hadn't known the photo was being taken or if he had simply not cared. Nonetheless, something about him registered with Zach.

Two out of the four people in the photo were dead. The third was Carver. That meant the fourth person could be one of his only chances. But who was he? A glance at the caption below the picture told Zach the man's name was Wilford Owen, Head of Communications. Splendid. If anyone knew what happened to Ryker, it would be the person who was supposed to *communicate* with him.

"Check this out." Zach sent the link to Cora. "What about that Wilford guy? You know him?"

"Wilford Owen?" Cora dismissed Zach with a laugh. "If you're worried about people lying to you, he's the wrong person to talk to."

"Why?"

"He stole tons of data from OSE, then started his own company on the back of my dad's hard work."

"Perfect."

"What?" Cora's voice pinched into something between confusion and disgust.

"Maybe he has something on Ryker."

"I doubt it. He stole, like, satellite data. Stuff about Mars."

Zach looked at the photo again. "It's worth a shot, though,

right?" He highlighted Wilford's name, copied it, then pasted it into the search bar.

"I guess..."

"It might be our only chance to figure out what's going on. And look, if Carver was lying, that means someone wanted Ryker dead. They may have wanted me dead too."

AFTER LOCATING Wilford's phone number, Zach dialed it, held the phone up to his ear, and prepared for Wilford Owen to ignore his call.

But surprisingly, he didn't.

There was a loud beep before someone on the other line cleared their throat and spoke groggily. "Hello?"

Running up to his home desk, Zach leaned forward. "Yeah, hello? Is this Wilford Owen?"

"That's right. And you are?"

Zach took a seat and attempted to steady his trembling hands. "My name is Zach Croft. I was a survivor of the Prescott mission."

"Yes, I know who you are." Wilford's tone was icy. Zach could hear a coffee maker beeping on the other side of the phone. Some liquid dripped into a cup.

Zach took a deep breath and continued. "I don't know if you remember, but there were originally two survivors of the mission: me and a boy named Ryker Gagarin." He listened for any acknowledgment from Wilford, but there was just silence. "I made it home, but Ryker was left on the Gateway. OSE thought he was dead, but he isn't."

"What makes you say that?" Wilford gulped his coffee and let out a satisfied *ahh*.

Zach clenched his jaw, rested his palms against the table, and looked at his feet. "Because he came back." He could hear Wilford pulling in a sharp breath. He added, "I don't understand it either. But I was hoping you knew something that could help."

The phone hissed with hollow static. Finally, Wilford said, "Why would I?"

"Well... you were the Head of Communications at the time—"

"Look, I left years ago, and I have no intention of ever dealing with that dysfunctional agency again. I can't help you."

"I know. I'm sorry. I understand that you left OSE under difficult circumstances, and you must hate them after what happened. But whatever bad blood exists between you and Carver—"

"Hate had nothing to do with my departure, Mr. Croft."

"Well, whatever happened, that's all in the past as far as I'm concerned. I don't care about any of that. But if there's anything in the files that might be from Prescott—"

"I didn't take any files."

Zach could sense the anger rising in Wilford's voice. He decided to back off. "I'm just going off what I was told."

"Well, you were told wrong," Wilford snapped.

"What matters is that Ryker is alive." Zach gripped the carpet between his toes, fidgeting to calm his pounding heart.

"I don't know what you want me to say. I wasn't involved."

Even if he wasn't involved, he still had to know *something*! Zach couldn't just accept that the Head of Communications hadn't done any communicating. It didn't sound right. "I understand, but... Mr. Owen, a child was left to fend for himself on a space station for over two decades. If there's any information at all that you might have..."

"Command told us he was dead. That's all I know."

Zach wished the bastard would stop cutting him off. "Alright. Well, if you think of anything else—"

"Goodbye, Mr. Croft."

And Wilford was gone.

RYKER GAGARIN: 2053

Two main thoughts occupied Ryker's head as he walked down the asphalt road: where to get some food and where to stay the night.

Ryker pulled out the wad of cash Zach had given him and thumbed through the newly minted bills. *Huh.* Even the money was different. Where there had previously been an image of a president or important figure, forms of printed artwork occupied the space instead. The bills added up to one-hundred-eighty-five dollars, which Ryker figured could get him through a few days. After that, well... he hadn't gotten that far.

Ryker fixed his bomber jacket and fell in step behind a group of college students. They turned at the next corner, and Ryker went the opposite way. Up the road, the number of people on the sidewalks began to thin out. Thank God. Having so many people around should have left Ryker elated, but it just put him on edge.

And it was hot. So hot. Too hot. Ryker took off his bomber

jacket and rolled it up in a ball, shoving it in the crook of his arm.

Then, at the sight of a sandwich shop across the street, Ryker began to salivate. The Gateway had supplies to make sandwiches, but it was all that disgusting dehydrated shit he had to soak in water to make edible. It was about time he had a decent sandwich. His first sandwich back on Earth. Yes! He'd remember this moment for the rest of his life.

With the money in his fist, Ryker stepped off the curb and walked straight into the street. A beetle-like car swerved around him, coming within inches of running him over. The driver spewed a string of obscenities as he passed.

"Sorry, sorry!" Ryker shouted. He quickly ran to the opposite side of the street, nearly colliding with a swarm of passing pedestrians.

"Watch it!"

"Sorry!" he said again.

As Ryker walked into the shop, the cashier crinkled her nose at his rough appearance. "What can I get started for you?"

Ryker raised his finger idly in the air, scanning the menu. There were so many things to choose from. So many things he didn't have on the Gateway. "Can I get a Number Three with cheese?" Cheese! Oh, cheese. That was something he hadn't had since he was a kid. He *loved* cheese.

The woman tapped a screen on the register. "Will that be all, sir?"

"Can I get a soda? A large soda?" Ryker planted his hands on the counter, glancing at the fountain machine on the other side of the room.

"Anything else?"

What else did Ryker want? Everything. He wanted everything. The works. "Do you have chips? Just plain potato chips? Or no— do you have tortilla chips?"

"We have both..."

"Great. I'll get both." He drummed his fingers on the edge of the counter. "That's it."

The cashier gave a faint sigh of relief, then added up the price. "It'll be—"

"Wait. Actually, can I get a Number Two with double turkey?"

The woman grunted, then gave him a frustrated smile. "Yes, you can. Should I void your previous order or just add it on?"

Ryker considered it for a moment, picking at his lip. "Ah, what the hell? Add it on."

The cashier raised her eyebrows with a judging tilt of her head. "Okay. That'll be one-hundred-nine dollars and thirty-nine cents."

Ryker choked on his spit. "A hundred dollars?"

"A hundred-and-nine. Will that be cash or card?"

"Cash. Cash." As Ryker unfolded Zach's money, he shook his head disapprovingly. When did things become so damn expensive? He couldn't imagine paying that kind of money just for some sandwiches! Still, he counted the necessary funds and handed them to the cashier. "You might as well rob me while you're at it." Ryker smiled awkwardly.

The woman didn't laugh. She took the money, placed it in the register, then wiped her hand on her apron. She handed Ryker his change, then shouted, "Next!"

Two minutes later, Ryker received his food and sat in the

corner of the restaurant, away from other people. There, he thought about the cashier's hand-wipe. Was he really that dirty? She could have at least had the decency to not do that in front of him, but apparently, Ryker didn't understand much about this new world. Maybe manners were different now. Maybe it was normal to be a steaming asshole.

Ryker carefully unwrapped his two sandwiches and looked at them like a prospector who had just found gold. He didn't know which to eat first, though he knew they'd both be gone in approximately three minutes. Ryker decided to start with the cheese.

Picking it up, he sank his teeth into the end of the sandwich, sending a buckshot of tomato juice to the back of his throat.

It didn't taste like metal! That was a development. He was eating a sandwich that didn't taste like the Tin Man took a shit in it!

He took another bite. And another. And another. The sauces clung to his lips. The juices ran down his fingers. Even though every set of eyes had shifted to Ryker, he took little notice of the other patrons.

As he started his second sandwich, he glanced at a TV above the front window. It was a broadcast of the news, with an emboldened headline reading: TRAGEDY IN GUATEMALA, FLARE KILLS THOUSANDS.

"Hey, what's the deal with that?" Ryker asked the closest person.

The man sipped his coffee and shrugged. "Another flare. Looks like a bad one." His eyes stayed glued to the screen on his table.

"Why didn't we feel it here?"

"Same as always. Hit at a different angle."

Ryker wiped his mouth, then took three quick bites of his sandwich, rendering the napkin's efforts futile. "And it just made things catch on fire?" he asked as he chewed.

The man glanced up from his tablet. "You been living under a rock, or what?"

"Something like that," Ryker mumbled. He scarfed down another bite. "While I have you, do you know where I can get a place to stay the night?"

"There are plenty of hotels in the area. What's your budget?"

Ryker reached into his pocket and shuffled through his remaining cash. "About seventy-six bucks."

The man adjusted his glasses and laughed. "A park bench will cost you more than that. Not to mention the medical bills."

"Medical bills?"

"For the skin grafts," the man explained. Ryker squinted in confusion. The man pointed at the TV. "The flares? You'll end up cooked like a chicken if one hits while you're out there."

"Ah. Right." So, homelessness wasn't an option either. Great. Ryker would have to figure something else out. He stood and got his trash together in a pile. "Do I just leave this here, or...?"

"What are you—six? Throw your garbage away."

"Right." Ryker disposed of his sandwich wrappers and headed for the exit, giving a curt nod to the cashier at the front. On his way out the door, the man with glasses whistled at him.

"Hey. You got any family you can stay with?"

Oh, sure. He could give his parents a call. Maybe their

phones would still work six feet beneath the Martian surface. "Nope."

"You've gotta have someone who's looking out for you, though."

Ryker snorted. He didn't need anyone looking out for him, nor did he need unsolicited advice from a stranger. He had survived for over twenty years by himself, with no help from anyone. Surely, he could make it on Earth, with its endless resources and opportunities. He just needed some time to adjust. To figure things out. To come up with a plan.

As lonely as life on the Gateway had been, there was one advantage that Ryker had never considered before: everything was free for the taking. He could eat what he wanted, sleep where he wanted, do whatever he wanted whenever he wanted. He didn't have any responsibilities to anyone but himself. But on Earth, none of that was true. He would need money. To get money, he would need a job. Doing what? He had a fourth-grade education. Sure, he had taught himself plenty on the Gateway, but nothing that exactly prepared him to enter the workforce for the first time. He was sure he could learn to do something that would make him employable, but that would take time. A few days, at least, if not weeks. Or months.

In the meantime, he was stuck.

Ryker suddenly felt ashamed. He had literally plummeted from the sky that morning, and yet this was the farthest he had ever fallen. He was sure of it. As much as he hated to admit it, he *did* need help. For a little while, at least.

The man persisted with his questions. "Do you have a friend? Anyone who'd be willing to lend a hand?"

Ryker hesitated, then nodded. "Yeah. I've got one."

NICOLAS CARVER: 2053

Carver's paintbrush glided across the canvas, manifesting a redwood beside a half-finished log cabin. He dabbed the spike of hair at the end of the brush into a glob of black paint, bringing it to the easternmost wall of the forest home. Precisely, he traced the stroke of paint downward in a perfectly straight line.

Then the phone rang. Carver's hand twitched, the line zagging to the side and smearing oily paint across the mountainous background.

"Goddamnit!" he mumbled. He took a deep breath and picked up the phone. "Yes?" Carver asked, suppressing his annoyance.

A scratchy voice sounded on the other side. "Carver?"

"Who's this?" Carver clutched the phone between his shoulder and cheek as he walked over to his bar and poured himself a glass of whiskey.

"It's Wilford."

"Wilford? What the hell—"

"Just shut up and listen." Carver opened his mouth to respond, but Wilford cut him off. "Zach Croft called me today."

Carver fell silent. He stopped pouring as he remembered what Zach had said that morning: that he didn't think the man on the dropship was Ryker. Clearly, the bastard was lying. "How does he even have your number?"

"I don't know, but he's asking questions about Ryker Gagarin. Says he came back. That he's alive. Is that true?"

"What did you tell him?"

"Nothing."

"Are you sure?" Carver's mind raced as he tried to process what was happening. What did Zach know? And how? Who else had he talked to?

"Carver, this is bad," Wilford said. "If he knew to call me, that means—"

"We don't know *what* he knows. He could just be fishing." The hint of optimism loosened Carver's muscles a bit.

"If he talks to anyone... the press..." Wilford's voice raised as he continued.

"I know." Carver dug his fingers into his forehead. He was developing the mother of all migraines.

"You need to go public," Wilford said. "Beat him to it."

"Are you crazy? I'm not going public!" Carver rubbed his temples and looked at the big front window, half expecting someone to be peering through it.

"It'll come out one way or another. It's better if it comes from you. You know this sort of thing better than anyone."

If Wilford meant good publicity, then yes. Carver could usually find some kind of angle to work. Except for now. "You want to go to jail? Because I don't," Carver said. He circled the marble island in his kitchen, stopping in front of the fridge.

"Listen," Wilford said. "If you're the one to announce Ryker's return, you control the narrative. You can make it into a celebration. A triumph of the human spirit. A miracle, even."

Carver gritted his teeth. "Do you know how bad that will make OSE look? Whatever the excuse, whatever the story. We left a kid in space, whether it was accidental or not. We'll look like fucking idiots. On my watch!"

"That's not my problem."

"Or maybe it is," Carver said, suddenly calm. "You don't have the best reputation here. Who's to say you wouldn't be blamed?"

"Is that a threat?" Wilford's voice started to rise.

"Of course not. I'm just saying... anything could happen."

"Don't think I won't go to the press myself if I have to. I've got plenty of stories! Why don't I tell them about how you—"

"You don't want to do that, Wilford." Carver's eyes narrowed.

"You're right. I don't," Wilford countered. "But if Zach goes to the press first, there will be an investigation. Congress. The FBI. Who knows who else? You don't want that. Neither do I."

"Why do you care? You're not OSE." Carver paced across his living room. Wilford was right. He knew it but wasn't willing to accept it. Not yet. He downed the whole glass of whiskey in one swig.

"Whether it's my problem or not, I get fucked over if you can't get this under control!"

"Tell you what," Carver said. "Give me twenty-four hours. If I don't figure out something else by then, we'll go public. Together."

"Just like old times," Wilford said with a bitter edge.

"Yeah," Carver smiled to himself. "Just like old times."

NINE

HE FUCKING TOLD THEM.

He *always* told them.

And they never believed him.

Even now, as Zach watched the catastrophe in Guatemala on the news, he was sure the MagRes team would brush it off as nothing. They always did. He turned up the TV's volume in an effort to drown out his thoughts.

The news broadcast showed a bird's eye view of a small rainforest village entirely ablaze. Black helicopters circled it, dropping thousands of gallons of water over the smoldering town.

Dark columns of smoke billowed into the air as flames surrounded the village like a border of molten lava. Trees were swallowed by the dozens. People were escorted out of their homes with only the clothes on their backs, herded onto evac helicopters, and flown to safety as their belongings were left to burn. The water hoses only seemed to aggravate the flames, suppressing them to embers before they exploded again, with their orange tendrils reaching higher than ever.

Suddenly, the camera zoomed out, revealing more fire as far as the eye could see.

"We are here at the village of *Corazón del Bosque* in southern Guatemala after a devastating solar flare hit earlier today." The reporter was in one of the helicopters, struggling to shout over the roar of the propellers. The wind whipped through his hair, and his eyes were puffy and red from the smoke. "Countries all along the equator have felt the effects of today's disaster." He explained the horrors on screen for a few minutes, then passed it over to a female reporter in Kenya. In the savannah behind her, flames consumed the tall grass faster than Zach could comprehend.

Zach took a sip of beer, shook his head, and let his neck go slack. He wondered if Carver was watching the same broadcast. Did it matter? Carver was probably looking at the flames and thinking, *Hm. They must be making smores.*

The doorbell rang, and Zach perked up. It was likely Cora coming over to check on him. Or maybe she had found some lead on Ryker. Not wanting to keep her waiting, Zach pulled his tired body up and walked to the door, wincing as the bell rang several more times.

"Alright, alright! I'm coming!" What was so urgent? As he opened the door, Zach knew in an instant what was so urgent.

Ryker Gagarin was on his porch.

ZACH CROFT: 2030

The stock of the rifle felt cold against Zach's shoulder. As he wound through the labyrinth of red boulders, his finger tensed against the trigger, ready to fire at the first sign of his target. But where to look? The Slabs, a secluded part of the dome densely populated with rocky overhangs, seemed deserted. But it wasn't.

Zach could sense that the creature was nearby. He kept the weapon pointed straight, ducking into the shadows behind one of the rocks. The war paint was beginning to dry on his face. It mixed with the sweat and sand from when he dove to safety earlier, along with a streak of blood from where he had scraped his chin on a jutting blade of rock. It didn't matter now, though. What mattered was survival.

After collecting himself for a moment, Zach pulled himself back up and returned to the hunt with renewed strength.

Suddenly, something hit him from above. A rock? He turned to see a cloaked figure jumping from one overhang to another.

Then it tripped, losing its footing and sliding ten feet down, where it landed curled up in the soil. Zach readied his gun, training the barrel on the beast. As he drew nearer, his legs were swept out from under him. The creature got on top of him, wrestling the weapon from his hand. Zach managed to knee it in the stomach, flip it onto its back, and pin it down.

"Okay, okay! You've got me!" Ryker conceded.

With a laugh, Zach released him and seized the toy dart gun from a few feet away, aiming it at the wall of orange rock beside them. "You work for me now. Tell me where your allies are!" Zach swiveled around and pointed it at Ryker's head.

"Please don't shoot me! I'll tell you anything." Ryker peeled off

the green cloak meant to resemble alien flesh and tossed it aside. "Look! I'm human again. It's a miracle! Now, we're on the same team, right?"

Zach allowed it. "Fine. But don't get in my way." He pulled out a smaller weapon, a blue pistol, from his back pocket and tossed it to Ryker. It traveled slowly in the low-gravity environment but eventually made its way into Ryker's hands.

Ryker carefully loaded a foam dart into the barrel and held it at the ready position. "The Zorbotrons are camped out at the schoolhouse. I'll escort us there if you allow it."

"Permission granted," Zach said hesitantly. "Go. Get a move on, alien scum."

"I already told you I'm human again!"

"I know what your species can do. Changing from this to that and back again. I don't trust you for a second. But for now, you're my best shot at taking down the emperor." With Ryker out in front, they twisted through the maze of stone and reached the far side, leading out into an empty stretch of sand.

"We have to be careful," Ryker warned. "They usually have sentinels posted."

Zach scoffed, patting the body of his gun. "A couple of guards isn't anything to worry about." They continued silently. After crossing the long expanse of sand, Ryker led the way back into the settlement, where stone roads had been paved during the past few weeks. Rows of hab units, arranged similarly to neighborhoods, lined the paths and provided cover as they slithered to the schoolhouse.

The newly operating mines and processing plant ensured that most workers were gone during the day, either a hundred feet underground or sweating in the nearby processing facility. Of course, stragglers still roamed the regolith streets, mostly the children and spouses of the miners.

When they reached the school, Ryker ducked into the alley behind it, signaling for Zach to follow. "The coast is clear, Commander."

But it wasn't. When Zach popped around the corner, a boy hidden behind a trash can shot a dart at him. Zach lunged out of the way and landed on his stomach, looking down the scope to see three others emerge from where the trash can was, armed to the teeth, ready for battle. Damn Zorbotrons.

Ryker proved to be a traitor, claiming a rifle from one of the assailants and firing on Zach. "For Zorbia!" he called out, foam darts whizzing through the air.

Zach managed to get in a few shots but was forced out of his position. How could he pull this one off? He was outnumbered five to one! He ran through the school's back door, nearly tripping over one of the desks, and made his way to the front entrance. Crashing through it, Zach made for the residential district. Retreating was probably the best option he had, however cowardly it was. But one of the Zorbotrons, a girl named Sophia, cut him off on the other side of the street and landed a shot to his head.

He recoiled, fell to the ground, and plucked the suction cup dart from his forehead. The other aliens surrounded him. There was no way out. No path for escape. This was the end. Zach nudged his weapon to the side, spreading fingers across his thighs. "Okay. You win." He rose to his feet and accepted a pat on the back from Ryker, and a playful punch from Sophia.

They all started laughing. Doubling over in the sand. Pointing finger guns at one another. They were so excited they *neglected to notice the object streaking across the sky or the ground beginning to shake beneath them.*

Then, the blast threw them off their feet.

RYKER GAGARIN: 2053

Zach finished pouring Ryker a cup of coffee, then the two men entered the living room and sat down.

Ryker clutched his mug as if his life depended on it, not caring if it was burning his hands. Zach studied him from across the zoom. "I just don't get it," Zach said.

"Get what?"

"How you're alive right now. I keep running it over in my head, and I still can't understand it."

Ryker's life was simple up on the Gateway. Wake up at the same time every day. Eat produce from the hydrofarm. Glance through the windows every so often for signs of rescue. Space-walk, if he had no other choice. Rinse, and repeat. Then, something would go into catastrophic failure every few months, and he would figure out how to fix it. He could feel Zach's eyes on him, awaiting a response.

"Things weren't that bad," he lied. "After a while, the days blended together, and I accepted that—" Ryker hesitated, unsure whether he should continue.

"Accepted what?"

Silent, Ryker stared into the ripples of his black coffee, remembering the vast blue oceans visible from orbit. "That nobody was coming back for me," he finished with a glance at the sky outside.

An awkward silence swept over them.

"They told me you were dead," Zach said. He seemed unable to meet Ryker's eye.

Ryker offered a flat smile. "And what made them think that?"

"I already told you. They said there were no signs of life. No motion, no heat, no vitals." Zach paused. "Why didn't you radio to the ground? The Comms system was—"

"I tried... God knows I tried." Ryker looked at the TV, wanting to change the subject. He could only answer so many questions before the ones he didn't want to answer came up. "So, what's the deal with all this? The world's just on fire?"

For a moment, Zach seemed hung up on continuing his interrogation. But he soon relented and gestured at the TV. "Yeah, that..."

"It's gonna be okay, right?"

"Do you want the 'welcome back' answer? Or the 'we're all fucked' one?" Zach winced a little.

"The... welcome home one?"

"Basically, we're all fucked." Zach took a sip of beer.

Ryker awkwardly chuckled. "I see I came at a weird time." He picked at the arm of the couch. "So... what, exactly? Why are we fucked?"

"See that?" Zach pointed to the TV with his beer hand. "Take everything you see and multiply it by fifty. Then, add enough radiation to make Chernobyl look like a grape juice spill. Add a dash of charged particles from the sun, a sprinkle of mass extinction, and you've got yourself a party."

Ryker crossed his hands over his thighs. He'd seen forest fires from space, but never anything like Zach described. Part of Ryker didn't want to believe him. It was simply too unreal to consider. "How long do we have?"

Zach checked his phone. "It's October, so..." He looked at the ceiling, a sigh sinking through his chest. "About eleven months. A little more with some luck."

Eleven months until the world ended? Suddenly, Ryker wished he could go back a day and stop himself from leaving the Gateway. "Well, you're doing something about it, right?"

Zach smiled, a vacant look taking hold of his eyes. "God knows I tried." He stood up and turned the TV off. "And I'm going to keep trying. But right now, I can't do anything about anything except for you. So I'm gonna figure out why you were left behind."

"The airlock closed, Nancy Drew. What more is there?"

"Yeah, but why did it close? We were about to go home. Why then?"

"You think someone did it on purpose?"

"I don't know what I think." Zach tossed the remote on the couch. "I'm going to sleep. We can talk about this more once we're both well-rested."

Zach headed for his room, but Ryker stopped him at the last moment. "Hold on."

"What's the matter?"

Ryker hated what he was about to ask. He hated himself for it. For years, he had done everything himself. Looked after himself. Cared for only himself. It had been so long since he'd had anyone that the idea of asking for help seemed unfathomable.

He knew he could fend for himself, so why was he there

instead of figuring out how to rebuild his life? "Do you mind if I crash here for the night?"

Zach nodded. "Of course. Stay as long as you need. Blanket's in there." Zach pointed to a nearby closet. "Top shelf." Then, he walked into his room and shut the door.

As nervous pins and needles danced across his skin, Ryker pulled out the blanket and settled on the couch.

THE NEXT MORNING, silence filled the house like the wind had lost its voice. Orange-red sunlight streamed in through the window beside Ryker. He opened his eyes, lifted his hand, and looked at the G-engraved ring. Good. It was still there.

The silence made the hair on Ryker's arms stand up straight. If there was one thing he didn't miss about the Gateway, it was the constant machine hum. He had gotten so used to it that the quiet almost hurt his ears. But the silence didn't last long.

Ryker sat up as a disheveled Zach walked into the living room. His eyes were sunken and purple. He grabbed a loaf of bread from the kitchen and peeled off the plastic. "Sorry if I woke you."

Ryker pinched the bridge of his nose. "I've been woken by worse." Memories of blaring sirens, mysteriously closing airlocks, and sudden shifts in the Gateway's trajectory jabbed at the back of Ryker's head. Once, he'd been choked awake when the station's oxygen generators had failed. "Do you have any apple juice?"

"In the fridge. Bottom shelf."

As Ryker stood, a ringing phone echoed from another room. With a grumble, Zach went and answered it. "Hello?"

From the kitchen, all Ryker could hear was a murmur on the other line. He pulled out the bottle of apple juice and took a swig straight from it. Then, he heard a hiss behind him and turned around.

Zach leaned against the doorframe of his bedroom, the phone sandwiched between his cheek and shoulder, and waved Ryker over.

Ryker sauntered into the bedroom and mouthed, "What's the matter?"

"Wilford Owen," Zach whispered.

"Who's Wilford Owen?"

"He's—" Zach stopped, listening to the voice on the phone. "Yes, I'm with him right now. I'll put you on speaker." Zach tapped a button on the screen.

"No—don't!" Wilford said, then sighed. "Fine. Just listen. I have information for you."

Zach crossed to the drawer beside his desk. "Hang on. Let me grab a pen."

"No. I can't tell you over the phone. I need to give it to you in person."

"Okay." Zach sat down on his bed. "Where?"

"My cabin. It's on Morton Road in Big Bear. Last house on the right. Just keep driving until you see my mailbox."

"Okay—"

"Don't tell anyone you're coming. And make sure you're not being followed."

Zach and Ryker exchanged worried looks. Why all the secrecy? "Yes, okay," Zach said. "I can do that. Thank you."

There was a knock at Wilford's door. "Ah, jeez. I gotta get that." Wilford groaned as he stood and walked across creaking floorboards. "I'll see you in an hour, Zach."

"An hour—?"

The line went dead.

TEN

ZACH CROFT: 2053

WHERE IS IT? Zach thought, white-knuckling the wheel of his sky-colored truck.

He looked from window to window, his eyes scanning the dense forest that lined the narrow road. Finally, he spotted a small mailbox nailed to a tree, carved with one word: OWEN.

Zach swung his truck into a cutout on the side of the road and parked. He got out and took in a breath of clean forest air. Ryker climbed out of the passenger side. He anchored a hand on his hip. "You really think this guy knows anything about what happened?"

"He said he didn't at first. But then, why would he have called?"

"It just seems a little sketchy to me. Why didn't he want people to know we were coming? What if it's a trap?"

"He's an old man, Ryker. What's he going to do?"

Zach stepped off the road and ducked under an arching

branch. His feet shuffled through leafy detritus as he listened to the rustle of animals rooting in the underbrush and the scrabbling of lizards on tree bark.

"And you're sure you know where we're going?" Ryker asked while dragging his fingers across a patch of syrup-like sap.

"Think so," Zach replied. He saw a stone-lined pathway that led deep into the woods. The gravel crunched as they stepped onto the path.

Zach looked up at the trees looming overhead. They waved back and forth like slow-dancing giants, and he couldn't help but notice how beautiful his surroundings were. There weren't many trees in Pasadena anymore. Just a few sad, drooping palms. But the mountains were lush with towering pines and ancient redwoods.

"This certainly beats the Slabs," Ryker commented, taking in the forest. He cautiously stepped over a fallen branch, then swiped at a hanging cobweb.

Zach thought back to playing Alien Hunter in Prescott, realizing it was the last moment they spent truly happy in the colony. Beyond that point, all Zach could remember was the blood. The boils. The bruises. The egg-yoke eyes. He and Ryker taking turns watching their parents die. All of the suffering.

"Is that all we have in common anymore?" Zach flashed an awkward smile. "Mars?"

"Well, look at you, and look at me. How much does it look like we have in common?"

"We *were* friends once. We've gotta have something."

"We don't, okay?"

"Come on. It's been a long time, but you're still the same old Ryker."

Ryker puffed in exasperation, stopping in the middle of the path. "We're both alive, Zach. Who gives a shit if we both like the color blue?" Ryker continued down the trail and caressed his scarred wrist and forearm. A scoff escaped him. "Same old Ryker, my ass. What about the flares? According to you, we're both gonna be fried in a year. We have that in common!"

"I know it's not what you were expecting—"

"You're damn right it's not."

"If you're so disappointed, why'd you come back? After this long?"

"Took me a long time to override the system." Ryker eyed Zach.

"And how did you manage that?" Zach passed under a stone overhang. Dew drops dribbled down the walls, creating small, reflective puddles in the paste-like sludge. A drop splashed on his forehead. He wiped it away.

"Can you stop asking questions, Zach?"

"Yeah... sure." As he approached a bend in the path, Zach wrinkled his nose. An acrid smell filled the air, dense and smoky, like ash. He started walking faster.

Ryker spoke from behind him. "Hey, do you smell—"

"Yeah," Zach said as he rounded the bend. He stopped. His eyes went wide.

"What is it?" Ryker asked. He came around the bend and saw what Zach was seeing.

Wilford's house was ablaze.

ZACH RAN toward the cabin with Ryker just behind him.

As they got closer, they saw that, despite the thick smoke, the fire had mostly burnt itself out, except for a few small spots of lingering flame and glowing embers. The house's walls were stone, so only the wooden parts had burned. It was a miracle the blaze hadn't sparked a forest fire, but thankfully, the house was in a wide clearing lined with fire-proof hardscape that seemed to have kept the damage contained.

Zach leaped over the collapsed porch and rushed to the front door. It was locked. He hammered his fist against the paneling. "Wilford! Wilford, can you hear me?"

There was no response. Zach threw his shoulder against the charred wooden door until it split. He pressed his face to the opening. Smoke burned his eyes, but he refused to pull away.

"I can't see anything!" he said to Ryker, then shouted through the opening, "Wilford!"

"Zach, move!" Ryker pulled him out of the way, stuck his arm through the gap, unlatched the door, and threw it open. Zach pushed past him and into the house.

"Wilford! Are you here? Wilford!" he called. Black ash fell in noxious clouds from above and settled on the uneven floor. Scraps of papers that had escaped the feathers of flame drifted through the air. The entire structure creaked and groaned.

Zach moved across the remains of the sprawling living room. Ryker went in the opposite direction, then announced, "Zach! In here!"

Zach followed the sound of Ryker's voice and found him peering through a hole punched in the drywall. Inside the room, a pair of boots stuck out from behind a large desk. "Is that him?"

A fallen bookshelf blocked off the door to the room.

"Come on, help me!" Zach said.

Together, they took the two sides of the heavy shelf and heaved it aside. Zach grasped the doorknob, then drew his hand away with a hiss. It was still hot to the touch. He banged on the door, shouting, "Wilford! Are you okay?"

A series of pops echoed behind them, and a massive portion of the ceiling collapsed in a swirl of smoke and ash.

"We've gotta get out of here," Ryker said.

"Not yet." Zach drove his shoulder into the door, refusing to leave Wilford to the flames. The wood splintered on impact, but the door held strong.

Ryker begrudgingly did the same, charging at the door with his face pressed inside his jacket. After a few hits, the frame finally cracked, and the door collapsed inward. Ryker tumbled into the room with Zach at his rear.

As they entered the office, Zach nearly slipped on a carpet of torn book pages and letters, all singed and jagged at the corners, some still shrinking from flames. A fallen cabinet stood between him and the desk, its contents spilled out over the crumbling ground. Vaulting it, Zach circled the table and prepared to help Wilford. But upon seeing the old man, he recoiled in disgust. The back of his hand found his lips. "God-damn it!"

Zach let Ryker pass, then looked at the crumpled body behind the desk. Its skin was blackened, burnt to the bone. Its skeletal fingers still clutched the melted remains of a phone.

"What happened?" Ryker asked.

Zach shook his head. "I don't fucking know!"

Ryker walked over to the large stone fireplace. The remains of several logs were still glowing orange. "Maybe the fireplace?" He scooped up a metal poker and jabbed at logs. A swarm of embers swirled up the chimney like fireflies. "Maybe a spark flew out and started a fire?"

"How would it get so out of control? He's right there! He could have just stomped it out! Or thrown a glass of water on it."

"Unless he was already dead," Ryker interjected. "Before the fire started."

"We don't have time for this." Zach pulled his phone out of his pocket and typed in his passcode.

"What're you doing?" Ryker asked.

"Calling the cops, what do you think?"

Ryker snatched the phone out of his hand. "You can't call the cops."

"Why not?"

"You really think the police will believe we just *happened* to find a burning cabin in the forest? They'll think we did it."

"So, what do we do?"

Ryker handed Zach's phone back to him. "Get as far away as possible."

"We can't just leave him!"

"Why not? He's not gonna know the difference." Ryker started walking out of the room. "Come on."

"Hang on a second," Zach said, but Ryker didn't stop. "Okay, fine. Wait up!"

"We shouldn't have come here," Ryker said as he headed for the front door. "I told you—" Suddenly, there was a loud crack.

Ryker stopped, wobbled, then froze. Before he could react, the floor under him caved in. Ryker yelled in surprise as he disappeared into a pitch-black chasm.

"Ryker!" Zach sprinted to the edge of the hole and peered in. A choking cloud of dust, smoke, and ash billowed out. From somewhere far below, Zach could hear coughing and groaning. He got down on his stomach and leaned into the hole, waving the smoke out of his face. "Can you hear me?"

"Yeah, yeah. I'm okay," grunted Ryker from the darkness.

Zach swiped at his phone screen and turned on the flashlight. He shined the beam down into the hole until he spotted Ryker lying on his back in a pile of rubble, his face smeared with soot. A thin trickle of blood leaked from his hairline, which Ryker caressed with his finger as he sat up. He looked up at Zach. "Where am I?"

"I'm not sure." A wave of embers rolled across the ground behind Zach, and he jumped away in surprise. Pretty soon, he wouldn't be able to stand anywhere without igniting his pants. They needed to get out of there fast.

Ryker looked around at his surroundings and squinted into the darkness. "Toss me your phone."

Zach dropped it through the hole. "What is it?"

Ryker caught the phone and shined it around him. "Looks like the fire never made it to the cellar." He struggled to his feet and limped out of Zach's view.

Zach leaned further over the hole, trying to see where Ryker went. He heard Ryker curse under his breath. "What do you see?" Zach asked.

Ryker appeared back under the hole and looked up at Zach. "You better get down here."

RYKER GAGARIN: 2030

Once the ground stopped shaking, the rumble of crumbling buildings was replaced with screams, sharp and blood-curdling, slicing through the air like serrated knives. Ryker could barely contain his wails as the schoolhouse wall, which had snapped at the center, pinned him to the ground. A bent shard of it dug into his thigh.

The pain radiated from his knee up to his hip, but he was unsure how much blood he had lost or how deep the jagged metal burrowed. It tore at his nerves and made suppressing a whimper that much harder.

What happened? A pulsing sensation on his brow suggested a blow to the head, but he couldn't remember.

He did his best to search the landscape, but all he could see were corpses, wreckage, and smoke spilling from the ruins. As far as the eye could see, nearly every hab unit had crumpled to the ground. All that remained were the steel frames that used to hold them up, along with tangles of torn fabric and cabling scattered across open sand.

No, wait, there was Zach. And Sophia. A few others, too. They were lying face down in a messy half-circle where the schoolhouse used to be. All around them, desks were turned over and bent, and a fire had started near the entrance. Zach started to regain consciousness, holding one of the desks for leverage and standing up.

"Help," Ryker croaked. Before he could repeat his plea, Zach stumbled over and fell down next to him.

"Ryker!" He wrapped his arms around the free parts of Ryker's shoulders. "I'm going to get you out of here." Then, he

looked over his shoulder and called, "Sophia, we need help! Wake up!"

Sophia raised her sand-covered face. At first, she seemed confused. Then she realized what Zach was referring to and swooped in to help.

Fingers poked at Ryker's damaged skin. Someone pulled a cloth under the stabbing metal to soften its edge. The pain weakened a bit. Ryker was vaguely aware of Zach and Sophia pulling up on the debris, then rolling him out of the way as it crashed back down.

With the metal no longer covering Ryker's wound, Zach could tear away some of his pants and wrap the strip around the deep gash. "Does it hurt?" He found a bottle of water and poured it over Ryker's leg. "We'll get you to the medbay, okay, Ryker?"

The water felt like acid against the cut. "Where?" One look around could tell you there was nowhere safe, sturdy, or even in one piece. "You know what..." He couldn't even finish, his mind too foggy to form anything intelligible. But he just had to know one thing. "What happened?"

"I don't know. It doesn't matter right now. We'll deal with it later." By this point, Zach had managed to get Ryker standing, testing his damaged leg's strength. "Sophia, go get my dad."

"What about you?" she asked.

"I'll get Ryker to the medbay, but have my dad meet us. Go."

With her orders, Sophia ran in the direction of the medbay. Zach supported Ryker as they limped through the sand. Ryker wondered where his parents were. He hadn't seen his mom since breakfast when she dropped her dehydrated egg plate. And his father... When was the last time he saw him? Last night?

As Ryker limped through the lines of crumbled buildings, he

began to notice the number of people who were dead or injured. Bodies were strewn around the street, broken and crumpled, trapped under collapsed hab units. Ryker noticed a pile of sheet metal and pipes beside the crumbled maintenance bay. Legs jutted out from beneath it. He recognized the boots. "No..." Ignoring the pain in his leg, Ryker limped toward the boots and crashed down next to the pile.

He pulled back handfuls of rock and metal, his fingers turning bloody from the rubble's jagged edges. He kept shoveling, throwing the debris aside to uncover the body underneath. By the time the pile was reduced to only larger beams, Ryker's fists had turned the color of the sand beneath him. He picked at shreds of fabric, eventually uncovering a face.

The flesh was pale as paper, with cuts drawn across the cheeks and forehead. "Dad!" Ryker yelped. "Dad, can you hear me? Wake up!" He tapped Cage's face several times, but his father didn't stir.

"Step back." Ryker turned to see Quinton jogging up behind him. He rolled up his sleeves, and checked Cage's pulse. A flicker of hope crossed his face. "His heart's beating."

Ryker smoothed out his father's hair as he spoke to Quinton. "Please, do something."

Ryker tuned out the world as memories of his father filled his thoughts. He wasn't as close with Cage as with his mother, but Cage was a good dad. Ryker could remember one time in particular when they went on a trip to the Bahamas for the summer. There was good food. Great weather. It was awesome. But on the third day, Ryker ventured too far out in the clear-as-day ocean, and with his swimming skills not dialed in yet, he found himself in a precarious situation. He clawed to stay above the surface as water filled his lungs. Miraculously, Cage had seen him from the dock and dove in to get him. Just as Ryker lost consciousness, his father's powerful arms closed around his body and pulled him to shore. He had saved Ryker's life.

So now, as Ryker watched Quinton fail to do the same for his father, something tore within him. Tears welled in his eyes, but he told himself to get rid of them and wiped them away with the back of his sleeve. His father would wake up. There was nothing to worry about! Cage would open his eyes and be carried off to the medbay. Ryker looked around in search of the medical building but realized that it, too, had been destroyed. Whatever. That was only a minor setback. Some of the supplies must have survived. The colony hadn't had an explosion; it was just an earthquake, right? Or a meteor? Something like that. Okay, yeah. Once Cage was awake, Quinton could get the necessary supplies, remove the shrapnel in his torso, and patch him up! They'd be eating dinner together before they even knew it.

The first part of Ryker's plan seemed to fall in place as Cage's eyes opened. He gave a painful cough, blood—wait, what?—splattering on his chin. His mouth hung open, flooded with red. It didn't look good.

Quinton said things to him like, "Can you hear me?" and "You're going to be okay." Cage's eyes, wide with terror, moved from Quinton's face to his son's. He extended his damaged hand to caress Ryker's face. Ryker pressed it against his cheek.

"H-Hey, there," Cage sputtered with something resembling a smile. His teeth were stained with blood. "I'm okay. Don't you g-go worrying about me."

Ryker nodded. "Quinton's going to make you all better. You hear?" Quinton looked at him with a solemn expression, clearly *hesitant to make the obvious known. Cage's eyes traveled to his son's thigh. "Your l-leg."*

"I know, Dad. I know. It's fine," Ryker lied.

"You were always the s-strong one," Cage started but was interrupted by Quinton.

"I'll go to medbay to see if anything survived. Just sit tight; try not to move. We'll get you through this." Quinton took off.

Cage nodded and managed a look at the lower half of his body. One chunk of steel was embedded deep in his abdomen. Another smaller one bulged from his side. "I guess I'm p-pretty m-messed up, aren't I?" The life slowly drained from his face.

"It could be worse," Ryker said with optimism, swallowing hard. "Really. I mean it."

Cage tried to laugh, but a trickle of blood from the corner of his mouth set him back. "Mhm. I'm right as rain." As his eyes began to close, Ryker pushed them back open. "I'm just r-resting, son. Don't worry."

How could Ryker not? He'd seen this before in movies. The moment they closed their eyes, it was a done deal. There wasn't any bringing them back. How long was Quinton going to take, anyway? "I know you are, Dad. But you just have to stay awake a little longer. We're having mashed potatoes tonight."

"Oh, r-right. I'll be there. Save me a spot at the end of the table." He looked up at the sky. "It sure is nice out. What do you s-say we go to the beach?" Was he forgetting where he was?

"That sounds nice," Ryker commented, giving his hand a firm squeeze.

"H-Hold on." Cage slid a silver ring engraved with a G off his finger. "Take this. Don't lose it, okay?" His words suddenly became clear.

"You're going to be okay." Ryker creased his brow.

"Sure, I am. But I still want you to have it." He nudged the piece of jewelry through the sand. "Please take it. For me." Proper speech began to take its toll on him, and his face contorted in pain. He coughed again, sending a volley of red a few inches into the air.

He couldn't just give up. That wasn't like him. Ryker had once been told a story where Cage had gotten kicked out of a college class but stayed four hours after the day's end to convince his professor otherwise. Safe to say, he wasn't a quitter. But then, why was he giving up now?

"Take it, Ryker," he spat. "P-Please."

Hesitantly, Ryker moved to claim the ring, sliding it over his finger. "Okay. I promise. I'll never take it off." Before he could pull away, Cage took hold of his wrist and held it for a moment, dragging his fingers delicately across Ryker's skin.

Then, his breathing hitched, and he went still.

ELEVEN

ZACH CROFT: 2053

ZACH LOWERED himself through the hole in the floor where Ryker had fallen. The darkness enveloped him, broken only by the thin beam of light emanating from the phone in Ryker's hand.

Zach strained to take in his surroundings. His eyes drifted past a dusty concrete staircase leading up to a metal hatch, then settled on a series of rust-scarred metal shelves. Zach approached one of the shelves and picked up a dusty ID badge. Emblazoned with the OSE logo, the card sported a small photo of Wilford from decades before. He looked so young; his dark skin appeared smooth and without blemishes, his eyes a piercing amber. Zach thought of the dead man upstairs and had trouble associating the two.

Beside the ID card was a box that shared the OSE emblem. Zach pulled it to the ground and began sifting through it. His hands dashed across the various papers and keepsakes, eventually landing on a thin black laptop with the OSE logo embossed on the lid. Zach opened the laptop, but the screen remained dark. Flipping the computer over, he examined the serial number sticker on the bottom. It was a 2028 model. "Perfect." He smiled and began digging through the box for a power cord.

"What is it?" Ryker asked.

"An OSE computer. There could be something on here that we can use." Zach found the cord. "Take the box, and let's go."

———

WHEN ZACH and Ryker got home, Zach immediately plugged in Wilford's laptop. It took a few minutes before it had enough charge to power on. In the back of his mind, Zach couldn't stop seeing images of Wilford's burnt corpse. And he couldn't forget the smell either. Whenever he thought of it, he had to suppress a gag.

When the laptop finally powered on, the screen lit up with a brilliant blue OSE emblem. After a few more seconds, Wilford's desktop appeared. Dozens of folders were scattered across it. Below each one was a title.

SATELLITE 37-b
BALLISTIC H-6
EDEN

Zach located one labeled *PRESCOTT* and clicked on it. The file explorer overtook the screen and prompted Zach to choose a sub-folder.

"Where do we start?" asked Ryker, swinging his legs over the edge of the bed and leaning over Zach's shoulder.

"Right here." Zach clicked on the Communications Logs folder and scrolled through a long list of files. "I just need to find the date..." Zach trailed off.

"September 26th, 2030. The day we came back, right?"

"No, the days after that." Zach filtered the logs by date to find those for the week following his return, then furrowed his brow in concentration. If there was proof of foul play, he would find it. He had to. For Ryker, for Prescott, and for himself.

Once the filter was applied, fourteen entries remained, two corresponding to each day. As Zach opened each log and scrolled through it, his heart sank. His breathing went shallow. He wasn't sure whether to feel relief or disappointment.

There was no evidence of any wrongdoing on the part of OSE. Each log detailed an attempt made by the agency to contact Ryker, including biometric readers, motion detectors, cameras... everything. It seemed like they had used every possible means of determining whether Ryker was still alive. It was exactly as Carver had said. Did that mean he hadn't lied? But then why would he make up that bullshit story about foreign spies landing the dropship? Why would he want to cover up the fact that it was Ryker?

"What're you seeing?" asked Ryker.

"Nothing," Zach said simply. His eyes were empty as he stared at the screen.

"Nothing?"

"Nothing. They weren't lying. They looked for you."

"Then why didn't they find me?" Ryker stood up. "I'm alive! I was up there, and you're telling me they didn't know?"

"The logs say that they found nothing. No signs of life."

"How is that possible?" Ryker angrily flung his arm, then balled up his fists and rubbed his eyes. "No. That's bullshit. They knew I was alive. Keep looking."

"Where were you on the station? After I left, where did you go?" Zach glanced at Ryker in the reflection on the screen.

"Why does that matter?"

"It just does. Where were you?" Zach kept his voice low, not wanting to enrage Ryker more than he already had.

"The dropship bay. I didn't want to miss them if they came back for me."

"Maybe there are no life support readers in there. Or maybe the system isn't sensitive enough to detect one person."

"So we're speculating now?"

"The station was abandoned for a month before we woke up. Who knows what equipment fell into disrepair? Maybe the sensors were damaged somehow."

"They would have found something! Heat signatures, motion, airlock open requests. Something!" Ryker looked at the ceiling and blinked half a dozen times.

Zach sighed. "Maybe you're right. But there's nothing in the logs. They're useless."

RYKER GAGARIN: 2053

Ryker watched soot spiral down the drain, then lifted his face to the water. The cool shower soothed his heat-damaged flesh, washing away the pain of the day and the uneasiness of what was to come. He had no idea what he was going to do now. As far as society was concerned, he was still dead, and the agency that left him behind had done everything under the sun to save him.

Ryker took a big gulp of water and then shampooed his hair. A faint cry from the other room caused his ears to perk up. It sounded like Zach was shouting.

"What?" Ryker called. He listened for a response, but the steady drum of the water hitting the tile floor made it hard to hear. There was another muffled shout. Ryker turned off the water to better hear what Zach was saying. "What?" he called again.

Suddenly, Zach burst into the bathroom. "I got it!"

"The fuck!" Ryker yelled. He reached for a towel to cover himself.

"You're not gonna believe this! Come on!" Zach hooked his hand on the door frame and bolted back into the hallway. Groaning, Ryker quickly dried himself off, pulled his pants on, then followed Zach across the hall.

Zach's bedroom was a disaster. Papers were scattered around the laptop. More were strewn about the bed and littered on the floor. On the far side of the room, a printer pumped out more sheets into a messy pile on the carpet.

"You found something?"

"Yes! Yes, I know how to save the fucking world!" Zach swiveled in his chair. He brushed some papers off the bed to clear a spot for Ryker. "Here. Sit."

"I was gone for fifteen minutes." Ryker leaned against the edge of the bed.

"A lot can happen. Check this out." Zach started handing

Ryker pages full of graphs, data tables, and calculations. "I started going through the other folders on Wilford's laptop. It's a goldmine." He passed Ryker a satellite photo. It appeared to show a view of Prescott from orbit. Zach tapped the logo embossed in the corner of the photo. "That's from Owen Industries. Wilford's company."

"What does it have to do with me?"

"Nothing. Look. Here." Zach tapped the area of the photo showing the meteor crater where the Prescott processing plant used to be. It was partially covered in blue and purple dots. "You see those?"

"Yeah..."

"Now, look at this." Zach handed Ryker a printout entitled *Irogen Multiplication*. "Irogen. Multiplication," Zach said, emphasizing each word. He picked up another printout from the desk. On it was an exponential equation next to an emboldened graph. "You get it?"

"Get what?"

Zach ran his fingers through his hair. "Irogen has been multiplying. And it's on the surface. Not underground. *On the surface.* That's what Wilford's company was working on. Or at least researching. I don't know."

Ryker put his hand on Zach's shoulder. "Zach, I understand you're excited. But I have no idea what you're talking about right now."

"Listen. Prescott was a mining colony, right?"

"Right..."

"Why? Because irogen had to be *mined.* It was only found deep under Mars' surface. After Prescott failed, OSE would have needed to set up a whole new colony if they wanted to continue mining irogen because the first was a biohazard. But Carver said that was too risky, too expensive. So, the Board canceled the Exodus program and poured all of OSE's money into Carver's magnetosphere restoration project instead." Zach picked up a pile of printouts. "MagRes, of course, isn't working, and we're all gonna die because OSE doesn't want to 'waste' funding. But if irogen is on the surface, the whole game changes. There's no need for an expensive mining colony, no risk of long-term exposure to the Red Plague. All OSE has to do is send a small crew to pick up the irogen and load it onto a dropship. It'll cost pennies compared to Prescott."

"If it's so easy, why didn't Wilford's company do it?"

Zach turned to Wilford's laptop and began scrolling through a long document. "It looks like they tried, but their funding dried up too. At that point, everyone had given up on leaving Earth for Alpha Cen."

"Except you."

Zach nodded. "Except me."

"What makes irogen so special? I never got all the details."

"Warps spacetime," Zach said bluntly.

"And that's... a good thing?"

"You could say that." Zach reached across his desk for a blank paper and a pen. "Say this is Earth," he drew a dot on the left side, "and this is Alpha Centauri." He scribbled another dot on the right side. "Even traveling at near light speed, it would take decades to get from here," he started drawing a line from the Earth dot to the Alpha Cen dot, "to here." Next, he pushed the edges of the paper together so that an arch formed in the center. "By warping spacetime, we can effectively shorten the distance between here and Alpha Cen, allowing us to get there in a fraction of the time. But there's only one element in the universe with enough raw energy to power a continuum drive." Zach picked up Wilford's satellite photo again. "Irogen." He indicated the cluster of blue and purple dots. "You're looking at humanity's second chance. If we can get this irogen, we can restart the Exodus program and get the hell off this planet before it turns to ash."

Suddenly, Ryker's problems seemed a little less important. "All right. So, let's say OSE wants to send a crew on the Gateway to retrieve the irogen," Ryker proposed. "How would they get to the Gateway from Earth? That's not free, right? OSE would still need to build a shuttle of some sort."

Zach deflated a bit. "True." He raised his eyebrows. "Unless..." A broad smile formed on his face. "Unless one showed up at our door." Ryker gave Zach a puzzled look. "The dropship, Ryker! *Your* dropship."

Zach grabbed his Harvard sweater off the hook on the wall, then rushed out of the room, leaving Ryker alone and mystified.

"Zach?" Ryker called. "Where are you going?"

But Zach was already out the door.

TWELVE

ZACH CROFT: 2053

THIS IS GOING to be harder than I thought.

The more Zach considered how to ask Carver to send a mission back to Mars, the harder it seemed to be. From Carver's perspective, there was no reason to leave Earth. No reason to get the irogen sitting in Prescott. He was perfectly content overseeing MagRes and providing space cruises for the StarSet Corporation.

It gave Zach a headache piecing together how they'd reached this point. Had there ever been a time—before Carver, before Victor—when things had worked? Dysfunction ran deep in the agency. Zach knew that. For instance, the decay of the magnetosphere had first been detected more than fifty years ago, in the late 90s. OSE could have done something about it right away, could have solved the problem before it grew too severe. But that would have taken money, and a lot of it. So OSE ignored it, like everything else that required additional funding.

With the magnetosphere slowly disintegrating, the effects of solar flares—which usually wouldn't have been much cause for concern—grew exponentially worse. Satellites began to work less and less. Entire towns would burst into flames without any warning. Cancer rates grew exponentially higher as people were exposed to ever-increasing radiation levels. Decreasing plant life due to massive wildfires caused oxygen levels to drop, and droughts were more severe than ever. Earth's defenses against solar radiation grew weaker and weaker until the mid-2020s when the board finally decided that something had to be done. Earth was dying.

What would remedy the situation? Some OSE scientists suggested the obvious: they had to repair the magnetosphere. After all, that was their initial plan, wasn't it? That way, the planet would bounce back from the crisis stronger and more equipped than ever.

But others in OSE, including Zach's father, knew restoring the magnetosphere was a lost cause. It was simply decaying too fast. They foresaw that even if OSE poured every dime it had into the program, it would never be enough. Earth would die regardless of what they did, so the best option was to leave, to set up an outpost on some distant planet where humans could have a second chance, so that some minuscule number of people, however tiny, would survive.

Through countless studies, Alpha Centauri was chosen as the primary candidate for human habitation. It had water, a survivable climate, breathable air. In theory, it was a second Earth.

With both proposed projects in mind, it was left up to a vote. Countless votes, actually, over the span of a year. And every time, it was split right down the middle. Half pro-MagRes, half pro-Exodus. Eventually, a compromise was made that divided OSE's money evenly between the two programs.

Prescott was built, with plans for a colony on Alpha Cen once enough irogen had been mined. Back on Earth, OSE commenced efforts to rebuild the magnetosphere.

Soon after, Prescott died out, and the Exodus program was deemed a failure. All the money shifted to the magnetosphere restoration under Carver's leadership. And for a time, it was working. The magnetosphere grew stronger until the decay suddenly increased, and OSE couldn't keep up. Using far more funding than initially intended, the agency fought against the decay, and everyone but Zach accepted that it was getting better. Another twenty years of that, and here Zach was.

Given how much Carver had pushed for the program in the first place, Zach would surely have difficulty convincing him it wasn't working. He only hoped that Carver would see it from his perspective, from someone who spent his life studying solar flares and the magnetosphere they sought to rebuild.

Zach navigated his way through the launch site of one of StarSet's acclaimed space cruises. OSE did most of the construction for the company—a suitable way to generate money after the government had cut their budget so much—and they did a damn good job of it.

Even the body of the rocket seemed luxurious. Pastel hibiscus flowers surrounded a milky Pina Colada glass about mid-way up the ship, giving the craft a sort of tropical feel, despite its destination having nothing to do with warm weather or sandy beaches.

All Zach knew about the StarSet cruises was that you had to be filthy rich to get a seat on one. All-inclusive dining and drinks, viewing platforms to look out over the stars; it had everything you'd need on a cruise ship through the cosmos, except for a reasonable price tag.

Zach would have never set foot in one if Carver hadn't been there for an inspection today, and Zach needed to talk to him as soon as possible. He summited the red-carpeted staircase and neared the airlock. When he stepped inside, his sense of belonging fizzled away. The ship looked like a five-star hotel.

The first floor of the rocket consisted of a circular bar ten feet from the entrance. The counter was solid granite, perfectly polished to where Zach could almost see his reflection. Behind it, a shelf was packed full of bronze and clear liquors, jars of lime slices, and cups of almonds. The bartender, clearly masking sleep deprivation with excessive concealer below the eyes, nodded to Zach as he passed. Why she was there when the cruise was not active, Zach didn't know. Maybe she was new and learning the ropes before her first voyage.

A winding set of stairs brought him through the library, dining area, computer room, and finally, the lounge. Only one person was in the lavender-smelling room: Carver, sitting in the corner with a book propped open on his knee, and his right hand hooked to his collar.

Zach took a minute to examine Carver. His hair was slicked back, with a few strands dangling over his forehead. Green and black oil paint stained his fingertips. "Shouldn't you be inspecting?" Zach asked while posted at the top step, his elbow resting against the silver railing.

Carver pushed his book aside, addressing Zach with a wink. "Loosen up." He peeked out the window and at the agency below. "We're all looking for ways out of there."

Zach put on a show-you-agree-without-getting-yourself-fired smile as his bullshit meter climbed into the red zone. He knew Carver loved OSE, how he'd remade it into something new, expanding the agency in the days of struggle after Prescott.

"How've you been doing?" Carver asked. "How's the eye?"

Zach touched the faint purple smudge above his cheek-bone. He winced. "It's fine... Listen, I need to talk to you about something. Do you have a minute?"

"Of course." Carver gestured for Zach to sit. "What's on your mind?"

Zach sat in the recliner opposite Carver but kept his back straight as an arrow. Taking a breath, he started, "You've always been one to do the right thing."

Carver nodded. "I like to think so."

"And you're reasonable when it comes to doing what must be done."

Carver began to catch on. He deflated a bit in his chair, rubbing his tired eyes. "What'd you come here to tell me, Zach?"

This was it. Zach's one chance. If he messed it up, bye-bye humanity. The stakes sharpened his voice. "We need to reopen the Exodus Program."

Carver smiled while shaking his head and kept reading his book. "This again."

"Rebuilding the magnetosphere isn't working." Carver's eyes narrowed, but he said nothing. Zach continued. "I know I've said it before, but the solar flares are still getting worse. People are dying. And we're still pouring money into a failing program—"

"Once again, three-fourths of your department says it's working."

"How can you say that after Guatemala? An entire rain-forest gone, like that!" Zach snapped his fingers.

"We have to accept that it's going to get worse before it gets better." Carver stood, and, for a second, Zach thought he would leave. Instead, he strode to the counter, picked up two glasses, and poured some scotch. "But the latest report says there's been a four-percent increase in its strength in the past six months alone."

Zach shook his head. "No way. They must have flipped the numbers. It's *dropped* that much. And if it goes down another ten, the planet will burn with all of us still on it."

"You always were an optimist," Carver smiled sarcastically. "Let's say, for a moment, that you're right, and everyone else is wrong—"

"A year," Zach said. "A year until we're wiped out, and we're here arguing about it."

Carver offered him the glass of amber liquid, which he swiftly declined. "Zach, I've got things to do. If you're gonna waste my time..."

"We *need* to reopen the Exodus program," Zach said again firmly. "Just let me explain. I know how to do it right this time."

Carver studied Zach with a squint. "You're so much like your father." The words hung in the air.

"How so?"

"I had this exact discussion with him twenty years ago. He wanted to leave. I didn't." Carver's eyes were drawn to a maintenance worker climbing the spiral staircase to the living quarters. Carver waited for the man to leave, drumming his fingers on the arm of the chair. Then he continued. "It's crazy how much you take after him. It's like you're an extension of him. That's what worries me, Zach. I know you have the best intentions, but the last time OSE went out on a limb listening to a Croft, Prescott happened. The agency fell into shambles. We lost funding. I can't take the risk that Victor Keaton did."

"And yet, my father was right. We couldn't just *magically* rebuild the magnetosphere!" Zach stood and walked across the room as he tried to place his anger. "And if they'd just..." He closed and opened his fists. "And if they'd followed through and not given up at the first fucking chance, we'd have already sent *thousands* to Alpha Cen!"

Carver leaned back in his chair.

"Want to know how many we can save now?" Zach ranted. "A thousand. One trip. One trip before *everyone else* dies! So, I'm begging you to hear me out. I know you and my father didn't see eye to eye, but just out of respect for him, give me a chance."

"Okay." Carver opened his hands in a welcoming gesture. "Go ahead."

Zach calmed down, pushed back his hair, and took a breath. "I have a plan. You won't like it, but let me get it out."

"Enlighten me."

"We're going to finish what Prescott started." Zach sensed Carver about to object, so he spoke quicker. "I, of all people, know how that sounds. But I know how we can do this right."

"Go on."

Zach dragged a folded paper from his pocket: the photo of the crater he found in Wilford's files. The one displaying hundreds of irogen crystals. He carefully unfolded it, wiped off some dust, and showed it to Carver.

"The last few days, I've been thinking of Prescott. Yesterday, I logged onto one of the old satellites and took this image," he lied. "Look at all this. I don't know how, but irogen has spread to the surface of Mars. It's not just in the mines. And there's a *lot* more of it. If we could just get there, all that irogen is waiting to be picked up. No drilling operation required."

"And how do you suppose we get there?"

"The dropship. The one that just came back. We can take it up to the Gateway. If the station still has its residual fuel reserves, it should be enough to get to Mars and back."

"Should be?"

"Yes, it should be," Zach repeated. "We wouldn't even need a full crew. We can go with half a dozen, tops."

"Have you considered that Prescott is a biohazard? Have you considered what would happen if you brought the Red Plague back to Earth?"

"We won't. Even if someone got infected, the cryo would kill it before we returned."

"Well, I still don't know about that. And what about the irogen itself? What if some of the Red Plague gets in the fuel? You're going to have to store the fuel somewhere. You might not bring it back to the ground, but what about the thousand people you want to send up there? What about their lives?"

"We could quarantine the fuel while we figure out a way to kill any bacteria in it. It'll be challenging, but—"

"If you want to help, figure out what you did wrong. Find the error in your numbers."

"My numbers are right."

"Your word against your entire staff."

"My numbers are *right*," Zach repeated, firmer this time. "This is our only chance. We have to try."

"The answer's no." Carver got to his feet and strode over to the staircase. Before descending them, he gave one more look in Zach's direction, then left.

Zach had hoped it wouldn't come to this, but Carver had made up his mind.

And so had Zach.

───

"WHAT ARE YOU GONNA DO?" Ryker asked.

Zach drew in a deep breath, confirming his thoughts were his own and not whispers in the stale air of the house. Was he really about to suggest *it*? *It* was just about the most insane thing he'd ever considered. But strangely, it was also the sanest thing that had ever crossed his mind. The most logical option, considering the circumstances. With that in mind, he gulped and said, "We do it ourselves."

"What does that mean?" Ryker retorted.

"We take your ship, go to the Gateway, and fly it to Mars.

The plan stays the same, except OSE doesn't provide the crew... we *are* the crew."

Ryker melted in his chair. His mouth hung ajar for a few seconds. "Are you crazy?"

"Ryker, we need to. It's the only way—"

"Look at me!" Ryker shot out of his chair and pointed at his face. "Me getting left on the Gateway, fine. Maybe that was a mistake. But it wouldn't have happened if we had just stayed the fuck away from Prescott in the first place."

"We were kids! We didn't have a choice."

"Exactly. And now we do." Ryker's hands formed fists, pressed against the table. "I don't expect you to understand. You weren't the one who was left behind. I was. You didn't—" He cut himself off. "You know what, never mind."

"Ryker..."

"No, Zach. I lost *everything* because of Prescott! My mom. My dad. My friends, my life! Everything. Now I finally have a chance to live a normal life, and you want me to go back there?"

"I get it. But if we don't do this, you won't have a normal life. Or *any* life. Nobody will."

Ryker scoffed. "Don't try to guilt trip me." He walked out of the kitchen and collapsed onto the couch.

Zach knew that Ryker had a point. His anger was justified. Restrained even, considering. What if Zach had gotten left behind instead of Ryker? What if he had been abandoned? Survived twenty years. Somehow found a way back. Would he have wanted to turn around and run back to Prescott so soon? Of course, he wouldn't. It would be insane.

"I think about it every day, too, you know." Zach turned off the stove, then followed Ryker into the living room. "But this isn't just about us. It's about everyone. The whole human race." Zach sat down across from Ryker. "I need a pilot. Someone who's flown a dropship before. I'm begging you. Come with me."

"You think you know more than a fucking space agency," Ryker said scornfully. "They must have a reason to not go back there."

"OSE doesn't know anything—"

"And you do? What if you're wrong? What if more people get hurt? It wouldn't be the first time."

"You have to trust me when I say this is our only option."

Ryker faced the ceiling and shook his head, recalling some distant memory. "The last time I followed you somewhere we weren't supposed to go, people *died*. I'm not making that mistake twice."

Before Zach could give a reply, Ryker got up, grabbed his jacket, and stormed out of the house.

THIRTEEN

ZACH CROFT: 2053

IT WAS ALL TOO REAL.

The hovercraft releasing bombs over desert terrain. Paratroopers dropping in, barrels lit up with bullets. Planes whizzing by on all sides. Zach knew it was a simulation. Still, his heart thudded in his throat, just waiting for one of the bombs to detonate at his feet.

Of all places, why did Rhea have to be in a military simulator practicing for a war that would never come? She was a cruise ship pilot, not a soldier. Not anymore.

Zach approached the training rig—a hollowed-out F-32 equipped with a VR headset and fully immersive controls—but didn't startle her. He felt like he was tiptoeing around a bear guarding her cubs: one false step, and Rhea would pounce, mostly likely with a punch to Zach's jaw. So he opted to stay quiet, to wait for her to finish.

A massive screen covered one of the walls. It housed a

real-time feed of Rhea's simulation. Zach had to admit, she was good. He watched as her plane dashed toward the rival citadel, a tall metal tower with massive cannons and flamethrowers. She flew directly above it, shut off her engines, and allowed the ship to free fall. The guns tried to align themselves with the newfound intruder, but the shots kept falling short.

It wasn't until a second before the ship crashed into the roof that Rhea engaged reverse thrusters. A moment later, she slammed her hand onto the EJECT button and glided through the air. Why would she do that? What was the point of ditching her craft when she was already safe?

Her decision became clear when her plane exploded, taking down the upper half of the citadel. The rest crumbled into a pile shortly after. Her parachute engaged, and she touched down safely on the sandy ground.

The words "MISSION SUCCESS" faded onto the screen, and Rhea peeled off the VR headset. Her raven hair stuck to her sweat-dampened forehead in clumps she swept to the side. She breathed heavily, fixed her black tank top, then heaved a sigh. She clawed for a water bottle near her feet. But as her fingers wrapped around it, she noticed Zach staring. "Admiring the view?"

There was no point in keeping his distance now. Zach strode up to the rig and looked around with an impressed nod. "What are you doing in the simulator?"

Rhea took a sip of water. "It's the only place I still get to blow shit up."

"I noticed." He imagined her in a real dogfight, swerving enemy fighters while blasting those in front of her to bits.

Perfect accuracy. Perfect control. "Do you have a second before you start shooting again?"

Rhea shrugged, stood up, and dropped a few feet to the floor. "My time's up anyway. Those council bastards only give me thirty minutes a day."

Zach was on the council.

"No offense," Rhea finished with a wry smile.

"None taken." Zach glanced at the screen, which still showed the SUCCESS message. "Impressive work."

"That's what four years in hell gets you."

"Thank you for your service," Zach said awkwardly, not knowing how to respond.

"So," Rhea clapped her hands. "I know you didn't come here to tell me how awesome I am. What do you need? A hitman?"

"A pilot."

"For what?"

After swearing her to secrecy, Zach told her about the mission. The solar flares. Taking the Gateway to Mars. Loading up on fuel. Alpha Cen. He expressed his dire need for not only a pilot but a *great* pilot. "You're the only person I can go to, Rhea. I need you," he told her. It wasn't a lie, but it wasn't the whole truth. OSE had plenty of pilots on par with Rhea Vasquez, but one thing set her apart from the others: she had a reason to go with him.

"I'm flattered, Zach. I really am." She spoke flatly, as if bored by his crazy, possibly-suicidal mission. "What I don't get is why I'm the *only* person you can ask. It's not like we're best buds."

Zach took a deep breath. "Your father."

"What's my dad got to do with anything?"

"Carlo Vasquez, thirty-four years old, lead pilot for the Prescott mission." Zach paused for a moment. "Deceased."

"That's why you need me?"

"I need you because you're the best pilot I've ever met." And also, because Ryker said no. But he wasn't going to tell her that. "Look." He took a seat on the edge of the rig. "I may be wrong, but don't you think finishing what Prescott started would do some kind of *justice* for our parents' deaths? Like their work amounted to something?"

"Does Carver know about this? Your little odyssey?"

"No, and you can't tell him." Carver finding out that Zach was going ahead with the mission—after Carver definitively rejected it—would be catastrophic. Zach would be fired. Maybe jailed. Hell, *probably* jailed. Any hope of humanity's survival would be erased.

"How do I know you're right? About any of it?" Rhea asked as she started for the exit. Zach followed.

They walked a few meters, then stepped out into the hall. "It's all in the numbers," Zach replied. "If you can't believe that, just step outside when a flare is happening. I assure you, it won't end well."

Rhea pondered Zach's offer, strolling down the corridor. Her gray eyes moved to the floor. "I get paid a shitload of money to fly cruise ships full of rich people. It's kind of a stretch to assume I'd go to Mars."

"If anyone can do it, it's you—"

"I never said I couldn't. The question is whether I want to." Want? That was her reason. He just told her that the world would end, and she was pretending that she had better things to do? As if her *exciting* life as a StarSet pilot was too important to let go. "Why should I risk my career? Or ruining my reputation? Or worse, *dying.*"

Zach and Rhea turned a corner and descended a flight of stairs. "Because you'd be a hero. Well, more of a hero than you already are." A few seconds later, they exited the facility and crossed to the StarSet building.

"If I agree to do this, I'll never see Earth again, right? Next stop, Alpha Cen?"

"We wouldn't see the ground again, but we'd return to orbit. To pick everyone up. That's the plan."

"I don't want a plan. I want a promise. I do this, I get a seat on that ship to Alpha Cen."

Zach took a moment to collect his thoughts, glancing around the courtyard. "I promise."

Rhea stopped him once they reached the plaza's center, a large oak surrounded by short brick walls. She sat down, listening to the leaves rustle. "Okay..." After a moment of silence, she nodded to herself. "You've got yourself a pilot."

RYKER GAGARIN: 2053

He didn't know where he was going, but he knew where he ended up.

As Ryker planted himself in the driveway of his old house, he watched the yellow sun dip behind the roof. Gazing into his old room, he could see that the walls were still blue, and the ceiling fan was still as shiny as the day he moved in. Being there made him feel weird. But how else was he supposed to orient himself in this strange world he'd left so long ago?

Ryker stuffed his hands into the pockets of his worn bomber jacket. Memories of his parents flickered before his eyes.

Why'd he come here, of all places? He knew there was nothing for him here. Nobody waiting for him. "What am I gonna do?" he whispered to the house. For a moment, he listened as singed palm fronds crackled in the wind.

"Sir? Can I help you?" a woman's voice asked.

Ryker's mind was blank. The voice wasn't in his head. Not this time. "What?"

As Ryker turned to face the woman, she gestured toward the house. "You were just staring up at that house. Thought you might be lost."

Ryker exhaled and gave a light smile. "No, I— uh... I used to live here."

The woman faltered. She stared at him for a moment, lip twitching. "Ryker?" The woman searched Ryker's eyes for some sign of recognition. The color in her skin drained paper white. "It's me... Cora."

Cora? Now Ryker could see the resemblance. She didn't look much different than she did as a child. "Holy shit. Cora!"

Cora laughed and ran over to hug Ryker. After a smiling embrace, she pulled away and glanced back up the road. "What are you doing here without Zach?"

Ryker frowned. Why wasn't she surprised that he was back? It had been decades since they'd seen each other, and upon reuniting, all she cared to ask was, what are you doing here without Zach? Ugh. Zach must have talked to her. What else had Zach told her? Did he involve her in his kamikaze Mars mission? Instead of exploring these questions deeper,

Ryker answered, "I don't know. This was the first place I thought of."

"I get it... Well, you need to tell me everything. I need to know how you've made it all these years." Cora looked at him with a hybrid look of amazement and sorrow.

"I—"

"You know what? Just come back to my house, and let's talk about it over a cup of tea."

"TWENTY-THREE-YEARS..." Cora said, soaking in what Ryker said. "How, after twenty-three years, did you come back safe and sound? What changed?"

"I was on the Gateway the whole time. Every dropship was locked when I got stuck there."

"Then how'd you finally get onto one?"

Ryker took a sip of his hot drink. "Twenty years of trial and error."

"What did you eat?"

"Produce, if you could call it that. The hydrofarm was built to support a lot of people, so there was more than enough for just me. Until half the beds died out." Ryker drove his tongue against the roof of his mouth a few times. He could still taste the bitter protein paste he'd been forced to eat after the beans died. *The fucking beans.*

The doorbell rang, and Cora looked at Ryker. "Shit. I forgot about lunch..."

"Lunch with who?"

Cora did not have time to answer before the sound of the

front door opening exploded through the house, and a tall blonde woman walked into the kitchen. As her thick, worn shoes clacked against the floor, she exclaimed, "Oh, Cora, the new kitchen looks fabulous!" Her eyes wandered across the walls and appliances. Meanwhile, Cora's eyes were set on Ryker.

The woman stopped in front of the counter with a leather bag dangling from her forearm. Files and papers stuck out from the hastily clasped opening, and Ryker caught a glimpse of one that read OSE.

"Who's this?" the woman asked, motioning to Ryker. But before Cora could introduce them, the woman offered her hand in greeting. "I'm Mabel."

Her eyes had a slightly manic look, as if a billion thoughts were tumbling through her brain at once. The side of her hand was stained with graphite. Little marker doodles covered her wrist.

Ryker hesitantly offered his own scarred hand. "Ryker."

"It's good to meet you, Ryker." Mabel took off her purple and blue flannel and set it aside on the counter, then touched the surface of Ryker's bomber jacket and smiled. "My brother has one like this. Vintage."

Cora stood up and ushered Mabel down the hall. "I finished my research paper if you want to see it." She opened the door to her home office. "It's on the desk. Give it a read while I finish with Ryker, then we can discuss it."

Mabel scratched ·her frizzy blonde hair, ducked into the room, and closed the door. Cora returned to Ryker's side. "We have to make this quick. Where's Zach?"

"Trying to go back to Prescott," Ryker said bitterly, his

imagination taking the wheel. He felt the red soil of Mars between his toes, the dropship crashing into the ground, watching as his dad died under a pile of rubble. And after all that, Zach wanted to go back there? More memories flashed through Ryker's head. The first few days on the Gateway. The never-ending machine hum that penetrated the depths of his skull. Endless days of hunger as crops died out. How he wanted so badly to turn back the clock to before they left for Mars.

"Go back to Prescott? What does that mean?"

"He has a ridiculous plan to go back to find some irogen that magically appeared. He asked his boss—"

"Carver."

"Right, but Carver said no. So, Zach wants to do it himself."

"He didn't tell me about any of this." Cora's face showed a twinge of betrayal. "How does he even know all that's true?"

"We went to see some guy. Wilford something."

"Wilford Owen?" Cora's eyebrows shot up in surprise. She propped her elbow up on the marble countertop. "What did he say?"

An image of Wilford's charred and curling flesh flashed through Ryker's mind. He decided to skip over the details. "We got Wilford's old laptop, and Zach found something that made him think going back to Prescott is the solution to all his problems."

Cora digested his words. "Okay, but Carver said no, right? So, that's it. He can't do it without OSE. He's just one person."

"That's the thing. He doesn't think he needs them. Not based on what he told me." Ryker still had a hard time wrapping his head around it.

"Prescott's on Mars," Cora said, pointing out the obvious. "What's he gonna do, teleport there?"

"He doesn't need to. He has my dropship, and he has the Gateway. I'm sorry, Cora, but he thinks the world is ending. He's doing it."

Cora rested her forehead against the counter, swearing under her breath. "This is crazy." She looked up at Ryker. "You've gotta talk him out of it."

"You think I didn't try? He doesn't care what I have to say. He only asked me to come because he needs a pilot."

"No, you mean more to him than that. "

"Apparently not."

"Ryker, you were *dead* two days ago! Now, you're not." Cora got up, walked to the nearest window, and pointed outside. "Zach stood out there every night for years, hoping you would come home. He never gave up on you. And you're just gonna give up on him?"

"What do you expect me to do?" Ryker asked, frustrated. Zach was going to get himself killed. The very thought angered Ryker. Not because one of the only friends he had left was going to die, but because Zach didn't appreciate the second chance he has been given after Prescott. Ryker would kill to be in Zach's shoes.

"Talk him out of it," Cora repeated, pacing around the living room. "Keep trying. I can tell my mom too. She might be able to convince him."

"Why would he listen to her?"

"We were raised together after Prescott. It'll be like it's coming from his own mother." Cora nodded to herself. "We have to stop him. Will you help me?"

Ryker had already done his part. He had tried to talk Zach down, and it didn't work. They could only hope Zach's plan would fail before he got into too much trouble. But deep down, Ryker knew it wouldn't fail. Zach wouldn't let it. Not with so much at stake.

Ryker pushed his mug of tea away. A bit sloshed over the edge and pooled on the counter. "There's no saving him, Cora." Ryker stood, wiping his nose on his sleeve. "He thinks he's saving us. And you know damn well there's nothing we could say to stop him."

ZACH CROFT: 2053

"Mr. Croft, how inevitable of a threat to life on Earth do you think the solar flares will be in the long run?" the tall, lanky student with tortoiseshell glasses asked, gripping the mic with his skeletal hands.

How do I answer this without Carver flaming me tomorrow? Zach thought. "They're concerning. I'm not going to lie," Zach said from the Caltech podium. "But we still have time to get them under control."

The student returned to his seat, and another took his place.

"Have you heard anything from NASA or the other federation agencies about ways to mitigate the impact of the flares?" the petite girl asked.

Zach looked at the high vaulted ceiling, studying the wooden cross beams as he leaned into the mic. "OSE's been working on rebuilding the magnetosphere, but other agencies haven't made headway, no." Every word out of his mouth was sticky and smelling of death. He wished he could be doing something to save these people instead of just lecturing them.

But no, not tonight. While Zach could be out recruiting more people or working out a plan to steal the dropship, he was instead answering questions he'd fielded a million times before. It wasn't lecturing that was the problem—he loved educating people about the cosmos. It was the fact that he couldn't speak his mind truthfully. He couldn't admit that OSE was lying to the public about conditions getting better. He couldn't reveal that only a thousand people out of six billion would survive. He couldn't rally troops to come with him to Mars. The most he could do was allow Carver to speak through him, contradicting everything he stood for. At least he'd been able to recruit Rhea the previous day.

The next woman to take the spotlight drew Zach's attention. She was tall, with frizzy blonde hair and pale blue eyes that locked on his as she adjusted the mic to the proper height.

Mabel.

Mabel Liora was an OSE bacteriologist who worked closely with Cora. Zach didn't work directly with her, but he was familiar with her accomplishments. Why was she here, at an astronomy lecture? Zach furrowed his brow.

"Mr. Croft, given the neglect of the Exodus program on OSE's part, do you think we should consider leaving Earth rather than saving it?" A few murmurs of agreement rippled through the crowd.

"Leave Earth?" Zach tensed up. "We don't have the resources to leave Earth. We'd need a ship and fuel—the latter of which is only on Mars. And... OSE isn't going back there anytime soon." Maybe that was a good enough cover, but he still was unsure. Could her question just be a coincidence?

"Of course. Why would anyone *ever* want to go back to that desolate place?"

It might have been an innocent question, but it made Zach uncomfortable. The way she asked it, it was almost like she knew what he was planning. Zach coughed and checked his watch. "I think our time is about up, but I'll be back for the solar energy lecture in a month. Have a good night, everyone." He left the podium to massive applause and retreated backstage.

His fingers found his hair, and he shut his eyes tight.

She knew. She had to know; her question was too specific. But how could she? Who told her? Cora? No, Cora had no idea what Zach was doing. And anyway, it didn't matter who had told Mabel—just that she knew. What troubled him was what she could do with that information if he was right about her.

After cooling down, Zach exited the lecture hall and entered the chilly night. Crossing his arms over his Harvard sweater, he walked to the courtyard fountain and sat down. He pulled out his phone and debated texting Cora for advice but managed to suppress the urge.

He heard the footsteps before he saw her face, but he instantly knew who was approaching him. Mabel stopped just in front of him and gave him a calculated look. "Everything okay?"

Zach shook his head, not wanting to give himself away until he had all the information. "I've got a migraine. Used to get them all the time, and they're starting to come back."

Mabel sat beside him and pulled a little bottle of aspirin

out of her bag. "I got the drugs. Now, where's my money?" she said jokingly.

"I'll set up a payment plan." Zach smiled, then accepted the painkillers and downed four. He melted a bit, allowing his shoulders to stoop. "What are you doing here, Mabel?"

A cold breeze swept through the college courtyard, and as if blending in with the wind, Mabel whispered, "I heard about your plan."

"I don't have a plan."

"Sure you do. Cora and a friend of yours were talking about it." She made eye contact with Zach, sending an uneasy chill down Zach's spine.

Zach fell silent as he tried to keep calm. It had to be Ryker. What the hell was Ryker doing talking to Cora? "Did he at least look well? My... friend?"

"A little ticked off, but he seemed okay." Mabel crossed her legs, resting one hand on her thick black boot and the other just above the fountain's surface. Her fingers skimmed back and forth through the water. "If you're worried about me ratting on you, don't be."

"What *are* you going to do then?"

A silent interval passed.

"Come with you, of course," Mabel said. "I've wanted to study the Red Plague for years. It's why I became a bacteriologist." Mabel kept her eyes stuck on Zach's to hold his attention. "The scientific benefits will be incredible."

"Why does that matter if Earth is going to be destroyed? You'd be wasting your time." Zach hated being so negative, but he had to make sure she backed down.

"Sure, but what we learn will be very important on Alpha

Cen. If we could bring some samples from Mars back up to the Gateway—"

"No. We're not going to purposely bring the Plague onto the station. It's too dangerous."

"I know how to safely handle bacteria, Zach. That's kind of my thing."

"That ship will hold the last thousand members of the human race. I'm not going to chance it more than I already am."

"And once you get to Alpha Cen, what then? Think of the viruses, the bacteria we'd be exposed to. When the Europeans came to America, infection nearly wiped out the Natives, and that was just smallpox—not a xenobacteria." Mabel got closer. "Do you understand my point? I need to get some kind of understanding of xenobacteria, so we have a head start when we get to Alpha Cen. Maybe we could have the basics of a vaccine worked out before we even land."

"Look, OSE didn't choose Alpha Cen for no reason. They had to have thought of the risks."

"Is this the same OSE letting our planet die in the first place?" Mabel cocked her head. Then, she blurted out, "what if someone from your crew gets hurt?" as if it had just struck her. "I'm a doctor. I went to medical school. I can be there to help. And I'm an extra pair of hands. I may not look the part, but I used to rebuild classic cars with my dad back in Michigan, so I can make myself useful."

"I don't know, Mabel." Zach got up to leave.

Mabel stood and took Zach's hand. "I can help you, Zach. Why won't you let me?"

"Are you going to tell Carver if I say no?"

"I already said I'm not a rat." She raised her manicured eyebrows. "But do you have any clue how dangerous your mission is? As much as you want to deny it, someone could get hurt. Or killed. I don't want that. *Cora* doesn't want that."

Zach looked to the stars for advice as he had done for so many years. He sighed and nodded. "Don't speak a word of this to Cora. She doesn't need to know any more than she already does."

"So, can I come?"

"It's your funeral," Zach said, then rethought his words. "*Our* funeral."

FOURTEEN

ZACH CROFT: 2053

"WE'RE GONNA GET FUCKING SHOT," Rhea said, knuckles scooping at her purplish eyes. She forced a bite of microwaved mashed potatoes into her mouth and signaled Mabel to give her the laptop. "They're not just going to let us sneak onto the dropship. We'd be lucky to get anywhere near the launch bay."

"Don't you have an ID badge?" Zach asked, his throat filled with barbed wire. He had picked Rhea not only because she was a pilot but because she was someone OSE trusted. Trust meant clearance. Clearance meant access.

Rhea nonchalantly flashed the card pinned to her shirt. "It doesn't matter if I have a badge. You guys wouldn't be able to get in with me."

"My ID can get me in, but only if a guard checks it," Zach said.

"How many guards are there?" Mabel sat on a stool in the kitchen, elbows resting on the marble countertop.

"Ten. Fifteen. I don't know," answered Rhea.

Zach would figure out their shifts that night.

"Are they armed?" Mabel asked. "Are *we* armed?"

"We're not trying to start an insurrection," said Zach.

"It might be good to have something to protect ourselves," Rhea replied.

"Even if we were armed, we wouldn't risk shooting near a ship full of rocket fuel." Zach cocked his head. "But that also means they probably won't either. So, it doesn't matter if they're armed."

Mabel shook her head. "There's no guarantee."

"Then we have to take our chances."

"How do we even get to the ship?" asked Mabel.

Zach explained his plan and watched Mabel's head clunk against the countertop. "Rhea's right. We're gonna get shot."

"I already said—" Zach cut himself off and shut his fists tight. "They won't shoot near a ship full of rocket fuel. Rhea, how long will it take to get us off the ground?"

"Five minutes for preflight checks and safety protocols, but that's just an estimation. I'm going off what I know about the cruise ship. I've never been inside a dropship, let alone flown one."

Great, just great, Zach thought. "So, how can you fly it?"

"I can fly anything." Rhea shrugged, then continued, "A simulator would be nice, though."

"Is there one?" Zach asked.

"Not sure. There's probably some old software for it that the Prescott pilots used." She paused as something hit her. Rhea's shoulders stooped. "That my father used."

Zach considered the possibility. It seemed to make sense.

How else would the colony's pilots have learned? Not in the real thing. Not after the prototype was blown to bits.

"That was a long time ago. Think it's still around?"

"If it is, I'll find it."

"Are you sure it'll—" A knock at the door shut Zach up. He sat in confusion for a second, trying to piece together who could be outside. Zach gestured for silence and quietly stood, walking into the front room. At the door, he glanced back at Mabel and Rhea and mouthed, *Hide.*

Zach opened the door, and there was Carver, holding what looked like a bottle of whiskey in the crook of his arm. Zach leaned against the door frame and pulled the door mostly closed behind him, subtly blocking Carver's view into the house.

"Hey, Carver... what are you doing here?" Zach peeked around Carver's shoulders to see if any security vans or armed guards were poised around his house, ready to bust in on his operation.

Carver tilted his head and extended the bottle of whiskey toward Zach. "I feel bad about how we left things the other day."

"Oh... Don't worry about it."

"Really. I know things got a little personal, and I came to apologize." Carver shrugged. "I said some things I regret, and I just don't want you to think I shut you down over personal reasons. It wasn't because I thought your idea was bad, per se —in theory, it could work. But it's just too dangerous, Zach. For everyone here, for... you. I can't risk anything bad happening."

"Hey, I understand—"

"The whiskey's single malt, by the way. Can I come in?"

"Oh, I actually have company right now. I'm really sorry."

Carver squinted and looked around Zach's shoulder. A sound of confusion escaped his lips. "Mabel?"

Zach turned to find Mabel peeking around the kitchen corner. Spotted, she stepped into the open and waved before returning somewhere out of sight.

Carver leaned into Zach and whispered, "I didn't know you guys had a thing," with a fatherly smile.

"We don't. Cora's here too. She's just... She's in the bathroom right now."

Carver's face twisted with confusion. "How'd she get here so fast? I just saw her at the office fifteen minutes ago."

Zach's mouth was dry and sandpapery. He choked, "Well, you know how Cora gets when lasagna's involved."

"God, I remember when you guys were just kids." Carver smiled at the memory. "Have you heard from Sarina at all? We haven't spoken in a while."

"Yeah, she comes by every so often. Listen, I've really got to get back to—"

"Right. I just wanted to apologize. I hope we can start fresh." Carver outstretched his hand to Zach.

Zach took it, his hand like leather compared to Carver's soft, uncalloused skin. Seriously, what deal had the man made with the gods to make him immune from aging? "See you tomorrow."

The door closed, and Zach returned to his guests. "I told you to stay hidden!" he hissed in frustration. "That could have been it, Mabel. It."

"I'm sorry."

"You almost blew it," Rhea chimed in.

Zach took his seat. "It doesn't matter anymore. We're okay, so let's get back to what we were doing." He opened the bottle of whiskey and took a swig straight from it. "We've got a long week ahead of us."

RYKER GAGARIN: 2053

I'm dead, Ryker thought as the rain battered him from above, soaking his overgrown blonde hair and turning it the color of mud. The locks clung to his damp face as he looked at the tall marble monument that stood before him.

His thoughts were punctuated by the water hitting the dirty, algae-filled fountain ten paces back. He could hear the two bronze orbs representing Earth and Mars creak on their pikes, suspended above the swampy pool of water. *I'm dead,* he thought again. *Dead.*

And there it was, written in stone. His name. Ryker Gagarin. Etched into the slick marble wall adorned with the names of a thousand people. A thousand dead people. People he knew, lived with, and cared for.

Quinton Croft.

Kayla Gagarin.

Cage Gagarin.

Him.

As he ran his finger over the engraving of his name, he imagined a man twenty years ago carving it into the rock by hand, beating a hammer against a chisel, signing Ryker's death certificate in stone.

Ryker looked at the title at the top of the wall and shook

his head at the words. *THOSE WE HAVE LOST.* Was this all his parents had gotten for their sacrifice? A chipped, faded wall in an empty courtyard? A fountain that looked like it hadn't been cleaned in years and bronze sculptures discolored with age?

The sound of footsteps splashing through puddles behind him caused Ryker to turn around. A man was approaching. He wore a thick, black overcoat and had hair the color of platinum. He stopped next to Ryker and stared at the wall with narrowed eyes.

After a respectful interval, the man asked, "Did you know anyone who passed?"

Ryker looked at his name on the wall and nodded. "Did you?"

"My daughter." A car flew down the road behind them, cutting through a large puddle in a spray of muddy water. "It seems like so long ago, doesn't it?" He glanced at Ryker. "You must have been only a kid."

Ryker zipped up his bomber jacket and scratched his stubble. He wondered if he had ever met this man's daughter. Could she have been an engineer, or a cook, or perhaps one of the doctors that cared for Ryker's mother when she got sick? Ryker didn't know. He wasn't sure he wanted to.

"Where'd you get the jacket?" the man asked, nudging a pocketed hand toward Ryker. "That's standard issue, right?"

Ryker was about to give a generic answer, but then he remembered the Prescott patch on his sleeve and quickly thought up a lie. "It was my dad's. From the training program." Yeah, that made sense.

"Huh. I thought they didn't issue those until launch day. I remember seeing my daughter in one as I sent her off."

"They gave it to him early. Do you have any other questions?" Ryker's response was a little sharper than he intended. "Sorry. It's been a weird day." He looked back at his name on the wall. He couldn't stop thinking about it.

"I understand," the man said. "Believe me." He looked over his shoulder toward the road, then back at Ryker. "I'm gonna go grab a coffee. Care to join? I'm buying."

"No, it's okay. I'd hate to be a burden."

"You're not. I'm headed there anyway."

Ryker paused a second, then smiled. "Sure. That would be great."

"You ever been to StellarCaffiene?"

Ryker nodded. "My parents used to take me there when I was little."

The man rubbed his hands together and blew into them for warmth. "My name's Mike, by the way. Mike Ike."

Ryker snorted. "Like the candy?"

"Just like the candy," Mike said. They walked away from the memorial wall and wandered down the street in the blowing rain toward StellarCaffiene.

As they approached the coffee shop's entrance, Ryker got a good look at his reflection. God, he never knew how pale he was. His skin was paper-white, almost sickly. The fluorescent lights of the Gateway did a poor job of replicating natural sunlight. Bright, stinging sunlight.

He studied himself, glancing at others occasionally, trying to discern whether he stood out too much. His bomber jacket was ill-fitting, his hair was overgrown, and his hands were covered with scars. At best, he looked like a drug addict.

Inside the shop, Ryker and Mike got coffee and chose a table at the back of the room. The smell of coffee beans lingered in the air, commingling with a damp scent that rushed in from the street every time the door opened. Ryker tried to ignore it.

Carefully, Mike took off his jacket and placed it on the back of his chair. He again rubbed his hands together for warmth. "If you don't mind me asking... who did you know from Prescott?"

"I, uh..." Ryker pressed his lips together, looking down at the glossy wood table. "Sorry, it's hard for me to... to—"

"Don't worry about it." Mike took a sip of his coffee, furrowing his wiry silver brows. "It took me years to get over my daughter." He frowned, rumpling one of his cheeks. "Though I don't think I ever really did. If that makes sense."

"More than you know."

Mike leaned back in his chair. "I think I'd feel better if her death meant something, you know? It feels like she died for nothing."

Ryker sipped his latte, ruining the alien face the barista had drawn with milk on the surface. "I think about that every day."

"I mean, they didn't even finish the mission. We're just as bad off as we were before. Worse, actually." Mike leaned over and pulled a small box of candy cigarettes from his jacket pocket. Addressing Ryker's look of confusion, he elaborated, "I've been trying to quit smoking for years. Having something between my fingers, even if it's just gum, makes it easier."

Ryker hadn't eaten candy in years, not since he polished off the last of the Gateway's reserves nearly a decade back. Once Mike returned to a normal, seated position, Ryker went out on a limb and asked something he probably shouldn't have. "Do you think they should go back?"

Mike raised his eyebrows. "Go back to Mars? Depends on if they'd succeed or not. If it were up to me, I'd go back in time and redo the whole thing. I'd get the irogen, get my daughter, and get the hell off this dying planet."

Ryker smiled. "Living in space isn't as great as people think."

"And who told you that?"

"People."

Mike laughed, lifting his hands as if saying a prayer. "Well, there you go. Don't believe everything people say, I guess. That's the lesson here." Mike looked through the window at the front of the store, grinning at the beams of golden light streaming through the clouds. "Hey, look. The rain cleared up. That's my cue." He grabbed his jacket and started to get up.

"Wait, where are you going?"

"I told my wife I was going out for milk... I don't want her to think I was serious." Mike winked. "You take care." As the man put on his overcoat, Ryker wished him good luck.

Mike left, and Ryker slouched in his chair. The man was right: all the colonists' deaths were for nothing. Ryker closed his eyes and pictured the faces of his parents. The Gateway. Prescott.

But his thoughts were interrupted by a cacophony of vibrations and alert tones filling the shop. As people pulled out their buzzing phones to identify the problem, their faces sank with dread. The barista rushed out from behind the counter and ordered everyone into the back room.

"What's going on?" Ryker asked hurriedly.

"Solar flare," the barista responded.

A dozen people rushed for the small storage unit. Workers rolled shelves of coffee grounds, creamers, and cups out of the chamber in a desperate attempt to make room for the scrambling customers. But for some reason, Ryker couldn't move. All he could do was turn to the window and gaze out into the street as the sky shifted from cloudy and gray to searing white. As the brightness spread, Ryker watched trees and shrubs being reduced to their bone-like frames. Branches and twigs were stripped of their colorful leaves in a split second.

Ryker's eyelids fluttered in disbelief. He could sense one of the baristas running up behind him. Still, he stayed put. Part of him swore it was all an illusion, that none of this was truly happening. Maybe he was still asleep at Cora's. Or even Zach's. Perhaps he'd dozed off when Zach went to tell Carver about Mars. He'd dreamt of being asked to go back to Prescott, an attempt his mind made to scare him, to keep him from doing anything crazy that would get him killed.

A hand clamped around his arm and nearly yanked it out of its socket. With the jolt, he fell backward, then grabbed onto the table for support.

"What are you doing? Come on!" The server fought against the brightness as she gave Ryker a firm push toward the back room. The door was still ajar, with one worker preparing to close it once everyone was inside. It seemed Ryker was the last of them.

Swiftly, he ran for the back of the shop. Though he was

indoors, patches of red were already popping up on his skin. As soon as he and the barista were inside, the heavy door shut, and labored breathing resumed. One server went around making sure everyone was okay, a small first-aid kit in hand. Nobody appeared to be injured or burned except Ryker.

"Your skin," the worker said. "Let me help you." While she walked over to get the first aid kit from her colleague, Ryker turned his hands over to survey the damage. It wasn't too bad, just a couple of blotches of inflammation. The numerous scars already covering his arms seemed to be brighter. Maybe she mistook the years-old marks for burns.

Over the next few minutes, everyone stayed relatively quiet. The barista slapped a couple of gauze patches over Ryker's arms and handed him a water bottle. "Drink up."

Eventually, the light began to fade, and everyone's phone buzzed. An alert informed them that the flare was subsiding. Single file, they left the storeroom in a dazed state and spread out around the store. Someone near the front window gasped. Ryker jogged over to see what was wrong. He stared through the window, trying to discern what was lying still in the street. Then, he realized: the deformed shape was a body. *Mike's* body. The man's face was covered in bright red boils that reminded Ryker of the Red Plague.

"We have to go out there!" Ryker said and made for the door.

One of the workers stopped him. "It might not be entirely safe yet."

"Safe? Who cares about safe? A man is dying out there!"

"He's already dead, man," the worker proclaimed.

Ryker moved to the corner of the room. He dropped to the

ground, rested his head in his hands, and scratched his scalp. As he recalled his conversation with Mike—the colonists' deaths meaning nothing, irogen never making it back to Earth, wishing to do it all over again—he realized what he needed to do.

ZACH CROFT: 2053

"Zach."

Zach recognized Ryker's voice immediately. He approached his front door and found Ryker sitting beside it, his back against the plaster. Ryker stood up unprompted and gave Zach a defeated look.

"What are you doing back here?" Zach asked. His tone was sharper than he wanted.

Ryker forced a weak smile. "We need to talk. Preferably inside, before another one of those *things* lights us all on fire." He turned his head, revealing light burns all along his neck.

Zach extended an arm to the front door. "Please. Come in." He quickly unlocked it and pushed it with a firm hand. The lights inside were off, causing Zach to stub his toe as he searched for the switch. "I wasn't sure I'd see you again," he said. The lights turned on.

"Me neither. I was going to hitch a ride up north, but that didn't pan out." Ryker stood awkwardly in the front room, arms crossed against his bomber jacket.

Zach walked into the kitchen and grabbed a few sand-wiches he had left over from the previous night. "Why'd you come back?" He handed a sandwich to Ryker, along with a few napkins. "Here. Eat."

"I've been thinking..." Ryker started. "About Mars. About you. About everything." He laid the sandwich down on the table.

"What about it?"

Ryker smiled uneasily, shifting his weight from foot to foot. "I..." His voice seemed trapped in his throat, unable to break free. "I want to help. If you'll let me."

His face contorted like the words were poison. Studying him, Zach could practically see the images of Mars, blowing sandstorms, and the colony in Ryker's dazed eyes.

"Why?" Zach urged. "I mean, what changed? A few days ago, you were about ready to snap my neck. Now, we're... what? Buddy-buddy again?"

Ryker exhaled. "You know what, maybe I should go." He got up to leave, but Zach stopped him.

"I didn't mean it like that. Just sit down." After Ryker hesitantly sat back at the counter, Zach shrugged. "I understand why you said no. It was stupid of me to ask after everything you went through."

"In the last week, I've been locked up, homeless, and caught in a solar flare. The world is a fucking mess." Ryker laughed a bit. "I want to go with you. Just tell me where I need to be."

"Don't worry about it. We've got it covered." Zach got up from his seat, went to the sink, and filled a glass of water. "We figured out a way to do it without you."

"What do you mean 'we?'"

"I got a pilot to help." Zach went back to the counter and set the cup down on it. "So, you don't have to do it. I've got it under control."

Ryker raised an eyebrow. "Have they ever flown a drop-ship? Even stepped inside one?"

Zach pictured Rhea strapped into the simulator, hands dashing across a screen as she guided the ship through reentry. "Yes, she has," Zach lied, giving a confident nod.

"You're saying she knows more than me?"

"She knows enough," Zach said, then sunk into his chair. For a few seconds, he looked Ryker up and down, remembering the little boy with sandy blonde hair that Ryker used to be. That Ryker was gone now.

"Why would you go back to the Gateway?" asked Zach. "You spent decades trying to escape."

Ryker smiled just barely, slouching his shoulders as he planted his hands against the table and locked his elbows. "I'm not cut out for this world, Zach. Look at me." A few strands of hair fell over his forehead. "I should have died with my parents in the colony—after everything that's happened, I wish I did—but I'm here for a reason." He looked to the ceiling. "Besides... I want to say a few words to my ma."

Zach rubbed his eyes in exhaustion. "Okay. I'll put some coffee on. We're gonna be up for a while."

CORA. Cora. Something of Cora's.

Zach rushed across his room and grabbed a silver frame from his shelf. In it was a drawing Cora had done for Zach's fifteenth birthday. It depicted the two of them standing side-by-side, Cora pressing her pointer finger into her cheek and

Zach suppressing a smile. The drawing was so detailed. It was a shame Cora had stopped making art.

Zach carefully placed the frame into his bag, covering it with a few white T-shirts. Then he took Wilford's laptop from the same shelf.

Ryker appeared in the doorway behind him, gesturing at the laptop as Zach slipped it into his bag... "Why are you bringing that?"

Zach threw a glance over his shoulder and shrugged. "Doesn't hurt, right? It has all that information about Prescott."

"True." Ryker drummed his fingers on the doorway and walked away.

"Hey, wait. You're not bringing any clothes?" Zach asked. "I can lend you some."

Ryker stopped and pivoted with a smirk. "You think I just ran around naked on the Gateway for twenty years?"

"God, I hope not."

Ryker moved into the kitchen. Zach got the rest of his things together, then grabbed his Harvard sweater off the hook on the door and slipped it over his shirt. He followed Ryker through the kitchen and out the front door.

Zach turned and looked back at his house as they walked down the driveway. The big wooden door. The green-tinted shingles. The grapefruit tree in the yard. Zach wished he could bring it all with him, somehow ripping the whole house from its foundation and strapping it to the side of the dropship. But he couldn't. As hard as it was to believe, this was the last time he'd ever see his home.

Zach joined Ryker in the car, backed out of the driveway, and drove up the road. As they passed Cora's house, Zach spotted her exiting through the front door, her eyes glued to her phone. He wanted so badly to tell her goodbye. No, not goodbye.

So long.

He *would* see her again. The second they had the irogen, the second it was time to leave Earth for good, he'd make sure she got a seat on the trip to Alpha Cen. Cora Keaton. The OSE biologist at the top of her field. The daughter of Victor Keaton. And Zach's best friend.

Cora disappeared from view as Zach's car zoomed ahead and left the neighborhood. For a brief moment, Zach thought about the possibility that he might never see her again. He never told her where he was going—though Ryker had done that much— or how long he'd be away. Of course, the second she heard about the stolen dropship, she'd know it was him. But by then, it would be too late.

He would already be gone.

THE DOOR to Zach's office opened a crack, revealing a glimpse of blonde hair. Mabel's eye appeared. It went wide as she saw Zach standing outside. The door swung open.

"Zach! Get in, get in." Mabel ushered him inside. "I got everything you told me to. And some other stuff, I think..." She trailed off as her eyes found Ryker standing behind Zach. Her jaw went slack. "What's he doing here?"

"Don't worry. He's with us." Zach glanced back at Ryker. "Come on." Zach stepped past Mabel and into the office. Ryker followed him in.

"With us?" Rhea echoed.

Zach's lips formed a straight line. "There have been some developments."

"No shit.'" Rhea said. "I'm putting my ass on the line, and you're not even taking your own rules seriously? Whatever happened to 'don't tell anyone?'"

"Trust me, he's legit. I actually went to him first, before either of you."

Mabel flicked a strand of hair off her forehead. "Yeah. I know." She glanced at Ryker. "I thought you wanted out."

"I did," Ryker answered. "But not anymore."

Rhea looked between Mabel and Ryker. "You guys know each other?"

"We've spoken," said Mabel.

Rhea nodded warily, then turned to Zach. "And what exactly do we need him for?"

"Well, he's a pilot." Zach winced at the baffled expression that crossed Rhea's face. "I know how it sounds. Believe me."

"Can I talk to you for a second? Outside?" Rhea grabbed Zach's arm and yanked him into the hall. The second the door shut, she lowered her voice to a whisper and snapped at him... "What the hell is going on?"

"Listen—"

"You're replacing me?" she huffed, trying to keep her cool.

"Relax. Nobody's getting replaced."

"Who is he?"

Zach glanced at Ryker as he tried to decide whether he should put it all out there: where Ryker came from and why he was here. Honestly, Zach could barely believe it. One minute, Ryker was a dead ten-year-old on a space station, and the next, he was eating sandwiches in Zach's kitchen. He found it hard to reconcile the dopey kid that Ryker used to be with this man who taught himself to pilot a dropship through countless hours in the Gateway's simulator. He barely had a fourth-grade education—formally, at least—and yet he understood the dropship better than probably anybody on Earth.

At that realization, Zach's mind was brought back to Rhea. Her eyes were surrounded by dark, raccoon-like rings, bearing the weight of her exhaustion. By the looks of it, she'd been in the simulator all night. He realized it must seem to her like she was being fired after all the hard work she had put in. And not because some other world-class pilot had strolled into the lab and offered his services. No, it was because a scruffy-looking stranger had somehow won Zach's favor. If Rhea truly knew who Ryker was, would she understand? Would she accept him as a co-pilot?

Zach settled on just telling her the truth. He could at least give Rhea the courtesy Carver never gave him. "He's from Prescott, alright? That ship we're about to steal? He flew it down here. It's *his*."

Rhea took a step back and gave a baffled shake of her head. "If you picked up a random pilot off the street, just tell me. You don't have to lie."

"I'm not lying," was all Zach could say. After all, why would he lie? What did he have to gain from deceiving Rhea? Nothing. She was willing to help him, to risk her entire career in favor of this mission, so the least Zach could do was be honest.

"Okay, fine. Let's say you're telling the truth," Rhea proposed. "Why do you still need me? You have someone who's flown the ship. For real, not just a simulation. Knowing that, what's the point in settling for me?"

Zach considered how to answer. What could he say to her? As callous as it was, he didn't *need* Rhea anymore. Not when he had Ryker to fly the ship.

"You know what, I don't care," Rhea continued. "Just tell me what I'm supposed to do now. Be second in command to some liar from Prescott? That's crazy."

"It's Ryker! Don't you remember him from Bring Your Kid To Work Day? The barbecues? The Big Bear retreat?"

"I barely knew Ryker, and he's dead."

"*No,* he's not. He's in my office right now while we're arguing like kids! Now, I'm not replacing you. I need you both."

"Am I even flying the ship anymore? Or am I just a back-up?" Rhea posed the question like she already knew the answer and despised it.

Zach looked over his shoulder, wishing he could escape his problems. "Look. He's flown it before. He knows it like the back of his hand." At least, Zach assumed he did. "He can get us into orbit, then you can—"

"And the truth comes out!" Rhea flung her hands out in that proud-parent sort of way. "Congratulations, Zach. You actually have the stones to kick me out. Good for you."

"That's not what I'm saying."

"Then what are you saying?" Rhea raised her eyebrows. "Because it sure seems like that to me!"

"Lower your voice." Zach led Rhea a few feet down the hall and entered a small storage unit where nobody could hear them. "If you come with me, you're guaranteed a spot going to Alpha Cen. That's not changing."

Rhea chuckled. "Being in the simulator all night got me thinking. Does it really matter if I come with you? I still get a seat on the ship." Rhea read the confusion on Zach's face, then cocked her head. "Don't act like you haven't thought about it. You said it yourself: I'm the best pilot OSE has," she insisted. "They'd never leave me behind."

The nerve.

"You wanna go to Mars, fine," Rhea continued. "But you got someone to fill my position. I don't need to go anymore." Rhea shrugged, starting down the hall.

Zach went after her and grabbed Rhea by the arm. "So that's it? You're out?"

Rhea stopped and glanced back at him. "I hope you survive, Zach. I do." She sighed, then cracked a small smile. "But yeah. I'm out."

Zach waited until Rhea disappeared down the corridor, then placed his hand in his pocket and fingered a small card. Once he was sure Rhea was far away, he returned to his office.

Now, she was just another person who knew his plan. A liability.

When he got back, Mabel was sitting behind his desk, with Ryker a few feet from her. They were in the middle of what Zach perceived as small talk. They stopped when he entered.

"Where's Rhea?" Mabel asked, straightening her spine.

"Gone."

Mabel looked around as if expecting her to appear out of thin air. "What do you mean 'gone?'"

"She's out." With a sodden look, he plopped down in the corner chair. "It's fine. We don't need her. We've got Ryker."

"What about getting into the launch bay?" Mabel remarked. "We need her ID."

Zach pulled the small card from his pocket and held it up. "This one?"

ZACH COULDN'T THINK of anything more noticeable than the reflective orange vests they were wearing. Most OSE employees wore civilian clothes, pale-colored jumpsuits, or lab coats. And there Zach and his crew stood, covered in neon. It was impossible for them to go undetected. But in that way—in that strange and clever way—they were hidden. Hidden in plain sight. Hidden because no security guard could think a wrongdoer would wear something so attention-grabbing. They could evade the guards by walking right past them.

Poking out from the armholes of the vest was Zach's Harvard sweater, clashing with bright orange and even brighter yellow stripes. He slipped on his hard hat and looked in the mirror, satisfied with his appearance.

Ryker situated himself next to Zach, fixing his collar. "Look at me, a functioning member of society."

Zach took a moment to observe Ryker, considering what could have been. "It suits you. Now, let's go."

"Once we're on the ship, what's to stop the guards from keeping us grounded?" asked Mabel. "Rhea said it would take her at least a few minutes—"

"I can do it in one," responded Ryker.

"What about the pre-flight checks?"

"I can bypass them once we're on board. Most of them are

bullshit." Ryker clapped Zach on the back and walked to the door, rubbing his hands together. Zach and Mabel followed, turning a corner into a wide hallway. The entrance to the launch bay was at the end of the hall. A security guard at a small kiosk next to the door scrolled idly on his phone while waiting for his shift to end.

Zach pulled his own phone from his pocket. He punched in a number and held it to his ear. A few seconds passed before the sound of someone on the other end brought Ryker and Mabel to attention.

"Mr. White?" asked Zach. "This is the Oakburn Academy office. I'm sorry to bother you at work, but your son hit his head on the playground during recess, and we're concerned he might have a concussion. He needs to see a doctor for evaluation as soon as possible. How quickly can you get here?" A panicked, muffled voice replied. "Okay, we'll see you in a few. Thank you, sir." Zach hung up.

The guard rushed down the corridor ten seconds later, leaving the launch bay door unprotected.

Ryker nodded at Zach approvingly. "Impressive."

"I feel bad, but... Let's go." Zach ushered the group into the hall and sped to the launch bay door. The terminal beside it demanded a keycard. Equipped with Rhea's badge, Zach waved his hand over the sensor and stepped back as the door separated from the ground and retracted into the ceiling.

The launch bay was mostly clear; most workers had dispersed late last night and wouldn't return for at least another twenty minutes. But that didn't include the overnight engineers, such as those tinkering with the StarSet space cruiser stationed on the farthest launch pad. Zach didn't see them as much of a threat. The only real danger was the cameras—which couldn't do much to harm them once the ship was launched—and the guards who patrolled the bay in intervals.

Tipping his hard hat over his face, Zach crossed the threshold into the launch bay, leaving the comfort of the empty hall. He walked with his eyes on the ground, glancing up for only a second to confirm the location of the dropship. It was maybe a hundred feet away and was mostly unprotected.

The trio passed by a security guard, at which point Zach tipped his face in the other direction. The guard didn't seem to notice him. They continued—

"Hey, Mr. Croft," the guard said. "What's going on?"

Zach turned around slowly, making eye contact with the guard. He felt sweat run down his back. "I was told to survey radiation damage to the ship's computers." *Radiation damage?* Was that the best he could come up with? "The ship was likely exposed to solar flares in orbit and might help us to answer some questions."

The guard raised an eyebrow, turning his head a bit. "Huh... Carver sent you?" He looked past Zach and into the distance.

Zach turned around, following the guard's gaze. Carver was standing near the dropship, talking to a small crew of engineers. Zach's stomach dropped. "Oh," he said with a casual chuckle. "He's right there. I can go get him if you want." *Please, for the love of God, don't call my bluff. I'm begging you.*

"No reason. Carry on, Mr. Croft." The guard stepped aside to let Zach pass.

Zach continued striding toward the dropship. After a few

paces, he glanced over his shoulder. The guard had his eyes fixed on Zach, with a radio to his mouth. When Zach made eye contact, the guard looked away and paced out of sight.

"We have to go," Zach said, reaching around and placing one hand on Ryker's back and the other on Mabel's. He guided them to the back of the dropship.

A guard to their right said something into the small radio pinned to his shirt, then followed behind Zach. "Sir? Can I have a word with you?"

"No. Sorry. We have a deadline we have to meet."

By this point, they were speed-walking nearly to the point of running. Another guard closed in behind them, hand placed on a baton. Zach shot a quick look to his partners that said, "Now," before sprinting for the secondary airlock at the back of the dropship.

"Hey!" one of the guards yelled.

Boots pounded behind Zach.

When his group reached the airlock, Zach slammed his hand into the airlock's release. The two guards were maybe twenty feet back. One was yelling into his radio, and the other had his eyes set on Zach as he sprinted full speed for the ship.

An ear-wrenching siren blasted for a moment, then the airlock began to open. "Let's go!" Zach slipped inside, shooting straight for the blast door's internal controls. Ryker and Mabel rushed in after him.

One of the guards ran up the ramp, but Ryker drove his thick boot into the man's chest before he could get on board. Ryker ran down the aisle, crashed into the pilot's chair, and clicked his restraints on. "Get those doors shut, Zach!"

More guards were gathering nearby. Their hands hovered

over their pistols, but they didn't draw them. Zach was right—
they wouldn't shoot near the ship.

Then, Carver appeared. He was much closer, practically at
the foot of the ramp.

Zach grabbed the thick lever beside the airlock and forced
it down abruptly.

Carver stared at Zach with his chest rising and falling
rapidly. "What are you doing?" The door started to shut, but
Carver stayed put. His eyes were glassy. Perhaps he knew it
was too late to stop Zach with anything other than words.
"No... No, no. Don't do this! You're gonna get yourself killed!
Do you hear me?!"

The airlock slammed shut before any of the guards got to
it. Zach took his seat beside Ryker. "Get me a radio. One that
can broadcast to the outside."

"Alright," Ryker said in a raspy voice. He reached over,
pressed a blue button, then handed him a microphone hand-
set. "You have ten seconds. Say what you have to, then I'm
getting us the fuck out of here."

Zach clenched his fists and spoke into it. "Everyone. Get
out of the launch bay if you want to live." If anyone was still
around the dropship when it launched, they'd be reduced to
ashes. And that was the last thing Zach wanted.

He could only pray that those outside had heard the
message, that the speakers hadn't been fried when Ryker flew
back to Earth. There was no way to tell from inside, and he
wasn't about to open the doors to check.

"We're ready," Ryker declared. His hands swiped across the
screen and opened the authorization commands. A digital
button showed up with the word *LAUNCH* displayed across it.

"Please tell me you still got some juice in you," he said to no one in particular.

Zach's eyes went blurry as he struggled to breathe. "Do it." He clutched the sides of his seat, just like he'd done as a child. For a moment, he could sense his father sitting beside him. Zach wondered—would Quinton be proud of him now?

As Ryker gave the final command, the floor under them began to rumble. Zach could feel his bones vibrating, his teeth chattering. A countdown appeared on the screen.

Ten. Nine. Eight.

Zach glanced at Mabel, giving her a confident smile. It did nothing to calm the petrified look on her face as the clock ticked down.

Seven. Six. Five.

His thoughts brought him back to Cora. He should have told her he was leaving. He should have said goodbye.

Four. Three. Two.

They would finish what Prescott started. They would do what they were never able to do before. And he would do everything in his power to make Quinton proud.

One.

Zach shut his eyes as flames erupted from beneath him.

PART TWO

DEMONS

FIFTEEN

CORA KEATON: 2030

"CORA," her mother called. "Come to the table, please."

Cora sighed. *Why couldn't she ever eat in front of the TV?* She was so comfortable, with her legs crossed against the leather couch, eyes trained on the colorful images on the screen. Cora reluctantly pulled herself up and walked around the sofa. "Okay, I'm coming." The tile felt cold against her bare feet as she padded through the kitchen and propped her elbows on the marble island.

"Chair. Now," Sarina approached the table and set two plates of ravioli across from each other. She filled up a few glasses of water and arranged them nicely.

With a roll of her eyes, Cora sauntered over and plopped down in the fine wooden chair, slouching in defiance. "Can't we wait for Dad?" *He was late. Again.* Cora wrapped her fingers around the fork and swirled it lazily through the pasta.

Sarina sat down across the table from Cora. "He," she looked at Cora a second before continuing, "is probably getting held up at work right now."

"What else is new?" Cora gazed outside as if the answer was in her pool.

"You know he loves you," Sarina assured. "He just..." She took a bite of her food, smearing a speck of sauce on her chin. "He has a lot of weight on his shoulders. People depend on him." She patted her face with a napkin.

"What about us? We're his family."

"We have food on the table. A beautiful home. Sometimes he has to work overtime." Sarina considered something. "Or he's off with his secret family in Sweden."

"I'm sure he is," Cora said flatly. Her mind wandered to Zach. She wished they could communicate. He would tell her about his exciting life on Mars while she unloaded gossip about her boring Earthbound elementary school existence.

The phone rang, and Sarina got up to answer it. She grabbed the metallic slab and held it to her ear. "Keatons."

Cora strained to hear what the other line was saying but couldn't piece together anything significant. A full minute of silence passed before Sarina's eyes found the floor. Her jaw went slack. "Okay... Okay, we'll be there." She returned the phone to its dock and quickly scooped up their dinner. "Get your shoes on."

"Why?"

"No questions. Get on a jacket and flip-flops. Meet me in the car."

Cora did as instructed, grabbing her dark green sweatshirt and the pair of sandals she used at the pool. They hurried out of the house. The car door popped open with a beep, and Cora slid inside. Did something happen to her father? Was he dead? A heart attack? A stroke? As they raced onto the road, Cora probed Sarina for answers, but her mother brushed her off. Cora watched the streets glide past, not taking her eyes off the window until they pulled into the OSE parking lot.

A large crowd blocked the area, so Sarina retreated and drove to the back entrance by the loading docks. At the gate, the security guard recognized her and radioed to the higher-ups. After a beat, he gave a firm nod that permitted her to continue. "Go ahead."

They found a parking spot and jumped out of the car. With one hand pressed against Cora's back and the other clutching her purse, Sarina ran into the building. A worker directed her to the launch bay. So this had to do with space? With Prescott?

Cora squeezed her mother's hand tight as they entered the launch site. The room was so packed that the back doors had been propped open to allow viewing for the dozens of people outside. Cora located a makeshift stage on one of the launch pads, where her father stood before a mic. "We cannot confirm nor deny anything yet," he said calmly.

Confirm or deny what?

"All we can say is that we lost contact with the colony." Victor visibly braced for the uproar. "But that's not necessarily a cause for concern! Sandstorms are frequent on Mars; one easily could have blocked their transmissions." Someone called out for OSE's plans, so he added, "We're doing everything we can. I assure you we will figure this out. Your loved ones are in good hands."

Cora thought back to the pamphlet and the confident

message printed across its bottom: **BE READY TO HEAR GREAT NEWS.** *So this was the dazzling great news? Eek. What did they consider bad news?*

By now, the official monitoring station was supposed to have been activated in the colony. It was one of Prescott's most heavily protected locations—it controlled the supply caravans they received from Earth. That meant outside food, equipment, people, and everything else the colony needed to survive. With communication so highly valued, it should have been kept crystal clear. The fact that they had lost contact could only mean one thing: the monitoring station was damaged. Or, worse than that, destroyed. And if the most protected part of Prescott has been destroyed, everything else could be too.

Was Zach suffocating under an airless dome as Cora stood there, hyperventilating? She wondered how long it would take for him to die.

Or if he already had.

NICOLAS CARVER: 2053

The whiskey wasn't doing its job.

Two glasses in, and Carver's mind was still flying faster than a bullet, trying its hardest to comprehend what Zach had done. How could he be so reckless? So insubordinate?

Carver poured himself another drink, not caring whether anyone saw him drunk at his desk. What were they going to do —fire him? They would, but not for that. Someone stealing a dropship under his watch was a much more serious offense.

Carver groaned and glanced at the mirror beside him. The disheveled face of an exhausted man stared back at him. After everything Carver had done for Zach, how could Zach go behind his back and betray him like that? And how dare Zach undermine his authority and question his judgment? It felt like being kicked in the stomach.

Carver thought of his own father—wasting their money on booze, drunk most of the day, barely conscious enough to tell which way was up—and wondered if he'd failed just as badly. He took another sip of his drink, fully aware of the irony.

A sigh escaped Carver. Something was gnawing at his brain. Who was flying the ship? Zach was brilliant, but he wasn't a pilot. Flying a dropship was the type of thing you learned over the span of years, not just a few days. Zach needed someone with experience. Someone who'd flown a dropship. Someone he trusted.

And who, just who, came back *on* that dropship?

Carver gave a joyless laugh as he replayed what Zach had told him hours after Ryker escaped from containment. *"I should have listened to you. That was not Ryker."*

Great. There was the answer. There was Zach's pilot. Zach knew it was Ryker from the start. He probably helped the guy escape. Carver cursed himself for being gullible enough to believe Zach had nothing to do with it.

Carver groaned. Swallowing another sip of liquor, he thought about all those years he wasted trying to mold Zach into the perfect person, a shining example of OSE at its finest. He wanted Zach to do good, to be protected, and to follow in his footsteps.

Whatever. The only thing Carver could do now was to find out who had helped Zach hijack a dropship. It couldn't have been just him and Ryker alone. Carver closed up the bottle of whiskey and placed it in a filing cabinet. Then he grabbed the phone and called for Jason Greene, the head of security. He ordered that Jason bring him security recordings from the past few days. With any luck, Zach hadn't covered his tracks. Jason agreed, claiming they would find out who helped him in no time.

As Carver awaited Jason's arrival, he ran through the risks of Zach's endeavor. An outbreak of the Red Plague on Earth would be the worst-case scenario. Zach could go to Mars, get infected, and return to Earth. Not only would *he* die, but millions of others would join him. Even if he didn't come to the ground, dragging a thousand people to the Gateway for them to get sick and die wasn't much better. They'd be a pile of corpses by the time they got to Alpha Cen.

Say for a moment that Zach was extremely careful. He didn't get sick, and he didn't bring the Red Plague back to Earth. It was still likely he would get himself killed. Mars was an unforgiving planet: violent sandstorms, unbreathable air, unbearable cold; the list went on and on. What was left of the Prescott colony would serve little protection against the elements. It was in ruins, after all. Zach was a scientist—he knew nothing about how to survive under such harsh conditions.

Carver wished there was a way to stop Zach before he got to Mars, to turn him around and bring him back safely. He dismissed a fleeting hope that Zach would wise up and return on his own. No, Zach was gone, probably never to return. So was Ryker, although Carver had a much more positive feeling about that. It saved Carver the trouble of figuring out how to get rid of him without raising any red flags. Zach had done that job for him.

The moment Jason walked in, Carver shot up. "You've got the footage?"

Jason nodded. "Got it."

"Show me."

Jason walked over and assumed a position beside Carver. "I found this, sir. From yesterday morning." He produced a tablet, tapped the screen alive, and then navigated to the security video. At first, it showed a still frame of an empty room. There was nothing special about it. No indicators that anything out of the ordinary was happening. Then Zach stepped into the frame. He quickly scanned the room to confirm it was empty, then motioned back the way he entered. A woman walked in behind him, wearing a lab coat customary to the biology department. In an instant, Carver recognized her as Mabel Liora. A moment later, another woman stepped inside. She was short, with dark hair.

"That's Rhea Vasquez," Jason said. "She's a StarSet pilot."

"Yeah, I know her," Carver replied. How could he not? He'd seen her less than a week ago when he visited one of their cruise ships. Did that mean Zach had asked her to pilot instead of Ryker? Carver felt a momentary wave of hope. Maybe Zach really didn't have anything to do with Ryker's escape. Perhaps he didn't know it was Ryker at all. Yes, that was it. Rhea was the pilot. Rhea, not Ryker. Carver shook his head with disappointment. "I never would've thought she'd be involved with this."

"She didn't go with them."

"What?" Carver felt the blood drain from his face.

"I saw her in the lounge twenty minutes ago."

Carver was vaguely aware of Jason asking him a question, but he wasn't listening. Instead, he croaked out an order. "Bring her here."

"On it, sir," Jason said, then walked out.

Carver dropped his chin against his chest. He didn't know if he should be relieved or furious. Someone who had helped Zach get away with all this was still in the building, pretending nothing was wrong. *Furious.* On the flip side, that meant he could get some answers. *Relieved.* Answers wouldn't do anything to bring Zach back, but they would at least help Carver understand what had happened. And confronting Rhea would give him some sense of control over the situation. Her career was over. He would see to that.

Carver's train of thought was derailed at the sight of Rhea strolling into the room at Jason's side. Her attitude was nonchalant. "What can I do for you?"

"Sit down," Carver said firmly.

Rhea pulled out the chair and sat. "Something wrong?"

"You have some nerve."

Rhea raised her eyebrows. "I do?"

Carver glanced at Jason and wordlessly instructed him to leave. Jason exited, closing the door behind him. Once he was gone, Carver continued. "I know you helped Zach."

"Helped him with what?"

Carver let out a long exhale, trying to maintain his patience. He grabbed the tablet and brought up the security cam footage. The video of Rhea entering replayed. This time, he didn't pause at her arrival. Instead, he fast-forwarded a few minutes, stopping on a frame of Zach, Rhea, and Mabel talking at a table. No, not just talking. *Planning.*

Rhea waved her hand at the video dismissively. "Yeah, he *asked* me to help. But I didn't. I bailed the second I heard what he had in mind."

Carver tapped the video, then scrubbed it along the time-line. "You were there for hours. *Hours.*"

"So what? It was just talk. There's no law against that."

"No law, no." Carver acknowledged as he placed the tablet on the desk. "But I can still fire you."

"Fire me?" Rhea glared at Carver in disbelief. "Over this?"

"You're an accomplice to a crime. A serious crime—"

"I never knew he was going to steal that ship," Rhea snapped.

Carver gritted his teeth, trying his hardest not to show his anger. "Give me your clearance card."

"I can't believe it. You're seriously going to fire StarSet's best pilot? I don't think they'll be fond of that decision." Rhea reached into her back pocket, then froze. Her jaw dropped a little. "That son of a bitch," she mumbled. "He stole my card."

"Stole it," Carver scoffed. "Right."

"I swear—"

Carver stood and walked to the door. He opened it, then motioned to Jason to re-enter. "Jason, if you could show Ms. Vasquez out..."

"Hang on, Jason," Rhea said. She glared at Carver. "Close the door." Her tone was cold. Commanding.

Carver was taken aback. How dare she order him around like that? Who did she think she was? However, despite his dismay, he couldn't help but admire the balls it took for her to challenge him like that. He nodded to Jason, then closed the door. "Yes?"

"You're not firing me."

"Is that so?" Carver arched an eyebrow.

"In fact, you're giving me a raise."

Carver laughed at her audacity. "And why would I do that?"

"Because I can bring them back."

SIXTEEN

ZACH CROFT: 2053

THROWING up in zero-g was probably the worst thing he could do.

Zach clutched his stomach and tried to suppress the bass-boosted speaker system in his abdomen. Despite his best efforts, his stomach continued to gurgle and vibrate. Through the wall-sized window, Earth danced in and out of view while the dropship blasted away on a rounded trajectory. It only made the dizziness worse.

From six seats over, Mabel looked down at her drifting hands. After a few moments, she ran her fingers through her hair to find every strand was pointing straight up. She brushed her blonde locks away from her forehead and smiled.

At the command module, Ryker floated with his toes pointing perfectly forward, his feet levitating an inch or two above the floor. Then, he wedged his toes in the gap beneath the control module to steady himself.

Ryker took a deep breath and stared intently at the screen. "We should be approaching the Gateway any minute now." Ryker turned his attention to the window. As he predicted, the Gateway—small at first but gradually growing larger—materialized from the darkness.

A shiver shot down Zach's spine. They were really doing this; they were really going back to the Gateway. After twenty years, it was finally time.

What if I'm wrong? What if we can't get the fuel?

Carver didn't want to reopen the Exodus program, but the man wasn't an idiot. He'd abandon Earth and evacuate whoever he could to the Gateway if it came down to it. But to do that, the Gateway needed to be in orbit. Earth orbit. And Zach was taking it to Mars. If they made it safely to Mars, got the irogen, and made it back to Earth, no problem. But what if they died trying to get the irogen? The Gateway would be stuck orbiting Mars, far outside OSE's reach. Humanity's last hope would be eliminated.

Zach made a promise to himself that they weren't going to die on Mars. They would make it back with the irogen in one piece.

"Holy shit," Mabel said in awe.

Zach broke from his thoughts to focus on the window. The Gateway was just outside now. It was massive, over a mile long, and half a dozen stories tall. The station was a marvel of engineering, one Zach still had a hard time believing OSE had been able to build. It was a different time back then, with a vastly bigger budget and unimaginable resources at OSE's disposal.

The cylindrical station was divided into three sections: the Spark, the Homestead, and the Works.

The closest section—the Spark—was relatively short and covered in solar arrays that laid flat against the metal armor. To pack in as many panels as possible, the plates had mere inches between each other. Together, they generated enough energy to power an entire city.

Beneath the arrays, inside the Spark, was the continuum drive that allowed the Gateway to warp spacetime. Originally developed using the irogen deposits found in the Saudi Arabian desert, the engine was intended to run on the irogen that would be freely available once Prescott was operational.

But that, of course, was a mistake.

The entire reason for Zach's journey to Mars was to secure enough irogen to power the continuum drive. With the drive operating at full power, the Gateway could make it to Alpha Cen, ferrying a thousand people to the new world. They wouldn't be able to save as many people as they would have if the Exodus program hadn't been canceled, but it would be enough to ensure humanity's continued existence.

Past the Spark was the Homestead. It was the largest sector, designed to house the colonists while they weren't in cryo. A thousand people used to call it home. Now, it was a ghost town. Gigantic metal discs bordered the Homestead on both sides, radiating a subtle green light. Zach had never learned what they did, but they made the station look like something out of a movie.

"So are we going to be tumbling around up there, or...?" Mabel asked.

Ryker gave her question little notice. "No. There's gravity."

"How?"

Ryker snorted. "Shit if I know. Ask OSE."

The Works was toward the front of the ship. It contained some of the Gateway's most essential systems—the hydrofarm, waste treatment, and water filtration—plus the cockpit, which jutted like a bird's beak from the front.

Ryker had a solemn look on his face as the Gateway drew near. His shoulders rolled forward. His eyes were full of dread, although he tried to hide it. Being back there so soon after he escaped must have been weird for him. It was strange for Zach, and he *hadn't* been trapped there for decades.

A burning sensation on Zach's skin made him realize how hot he was. Sweat rolled down his face and dripped into his lap. He pulled his burgundy Harvard sweater off, taking one last look at the big embroidered H before stowing the sweater beneath his seat. He made a mental note to come back for it later.

With the sweater off, he wore nothing but a plain white undershirt. A ring of wetness stained the neckline and the middle of his back. He hated the way sweat felt.

"We're going to enter through Z-Deck." Ryker manipulated the control stick. The dropship veered skyward. "Just a heads up."

The ship shot up, rising maybe a hundred feet before it leveled out just above the Gateway. Then, after a moment, the multi-directional thrusters sent the ship flying down at a sloped angle until it was barely thirty meters from the station. The dropship tilted farther until it pointed straight down at the cosmos below.

Zach could almost feel the vibrating station beneath his

feet. The ship sputtered downward—following the curve of the Gateway—then began to back up against the station. Zach blinked at the starry darkness outside the main window, then glanced over his shoulder at the main blast door. The porthole window provided just a glimpse of the outside of the ship. A flicker of gray here. A glint of light there.

Zach looked back at Ryker's control module. Hazy footage appeared on the screen. The grainy live stream settled until the image was crystal clear. It showed their target airlock—octagonal in shape, the cylindrical decon shower jutting ten feet out like a sore thumb, the letter Z molded into the metal just above the fixture—along with big rectangular spotlights on either side that shone on the dropship.

"Ryker, you seem like a smart guy..." Mabel said, her eyes squeezed tightly closed. "How many times have you flown one of these things?"

Ryker pressed his lips together and craned his neck to read something on the screen. "Thousands of times in a simulator. Once for real."

"Hm," Mabel replied, clearly dissatisfied with his answer. Her bony fingers closed tighter around her restraints. "Are you sure you—"

"Yes, I know what I'm doing," Ryker answered calmly. "But I need to focus, so—"

"I'll shut up," Mabel said.

Just then, a series of thick gray tethers shot from unseen compartments on the sides of the dropship and latched onto the rim of the airlock. Once in place, they began drawing the dropship toward the Gateway.

Zach's sweat turned cold against his neck. To calm his

nerves, Zach imagined he was in a cabin high up in the mountains. So high up, in fact, that the sky was pitch black and full of stars. He pictured himself looking out a window at the snowy landscape, the trees, the rocks. And then, at... *what's that? Yes, that there.* The tumbling white. The shaking of the ground. His eyes widened at the avalanche barreling toward him, getting closer every instant he sat idle. But he couldn't go outside. No, he could never do that. Where he was, so incredibly high up in the mountains, the air was far too thin for him to breathe. There was nothing he could do but sit and watch his end come to him. That's how Zach felt watching the Gateway get closer and closer—first sixty feet away, then forty, then twenty.

A moment later, there was a loud thud, and the dropship went still. For a few seconds, everyone remained rigid. Not a single muscle in Zach's body dared to move.

Then, Zach kneaded his stomach with his knuckles and realized it was no longer gurgling. Gravity—that was it. It had to be. Cautiously, Zach undid his restraints and pushed on the arms of his seat until he reached a standing position. Sure enough, he didn't float toward the ceiling—he stayed upright against the plated floor. The dropship was attached to the Gateway. They had made it.

Ryker looked between Zach and Mabel, nodding to unheard words in his head. "I'll go in first... I should make sure everything's online before you guys board."

Zach knew Ryker wanted to go first so he could have a minute to himself, so he replied, "Go ahead. I need a moment to catch my breath anyway. Mabel?" Zach glanced at her with raised eyebrows. She nodded.

"I'll let you know when it's all clear." Ryker cut through the center aisle between two rows of smooth leather seats. He reached the blast door, pulled the steel handlebar release, and stepped back as the airlock parted in the middle. He stepped through and shivered as jets in the decontamination shower drenched him in icy gas.

Eventually, the plumes of chemical-laced air fizzled out. The door on the other side opened, giving way to a small deck —maybe thirty by thirty feet—with white-colored walls and bluish overhead lights. With the blast door open, a flood of antiseptic-smelling air crept into the dropship and burned Zach's nostrils.

The odor reminded him of the infirmary back at OSE. The last time he'd been there, Ryker had just punched him in the face. Then, Carver showed up and spewed some bullshit about the man on the dropship—Ryker—being a spy from another country.

Zach cleared his throat and wiped Carver from his mind. He took a minute to look around, then walked over to Mabel and extended his hand to her. She took it and stood up with a wobble.

"Should we wait for Ryker's all clear?" she asked.

"The lights wouldn't be on if life support was down. I think it's fine."

"If you say so," Mabel said as they started for the airlock.

The decon shower looked as if someone had halved a school bus and welded it to the side of the station. The room was empty. The grated ceiling hummed overhead. On one wall was a glass case embedded in the paneling. Zach could see spacesuits, flashlights, radios, and oxygen tanks stowed neatly on racks or in small, translucent bins.

Once inside the decon shower, a cold, unwelcoming gas blasted from the ceiling and completely engulfed them. Zach tensed up. It felt like being in one of those money-grabber games from the arcades of his childhood, with hair and flaps of clothing flying every which way. He could picture the bacteria and other contaminants dying on his skin as the disinfectants blew from above.

Once the shower ended, Zach waited patiently alongside Mabel for the airlock leading into the station to open.

Two seconds. Nothing.

Ten seconds. Still nothing.

Zach shot a glance at Mabel, then up at the ceiling. He wondered whether the sensors had found something on them, some sort of biohazard. He considered retreating into the dropship, but before he could step back, the blast door closed behind him. With the entrance to the Gateway still sealed, they were trapped.

The lights went red. A siren began to blare, filling the decon shower with an ear-splitting wail.

"*LAUNCH INITIATED,*" said the intercom.

"What does that mean?" Mabel yelled through the racket.

Zach knew what it meant.

He ran to the Gateway airlock and pressed his face against the glass. The deck inside was flooded with the same bloody light, along with the illumination of a few flashing yellow bulbs against the walls. Ryker stood in the center of the room, looking around with confusion. Zach pounded on the porthole. The motion seemed to catch Ryker's attention. He made eye contact with Zach, then bolted for the far corner of the dock. He consulted the readout on a terminal embedded in the wall, then turned around and shouted something at Zach. His words were inaudible between the shrieking siren and the thick airlock door.

Zach signaled that he couldn't hear. Ryker sprinted to the airlock, tapped his finger on the glass, and pointed at something behind Zach.

Zach glanced at the glass case of spacesuits and realized what Ryker was trying to tell him. "Get a suit on!" Zach roared to Mabel and ran over to the case. He yanked the doors open and pulled out a pair of suits.

"Why?" Mabel asked.

"Just do it!"

He and Mabel pulled on their suits and connected their oxygen tanks. Zach's helmet clicked on and, with a hiss, the suit pressurized.

Ryker's voice crackled in the helmet's intercom. "Zach, Zach, can you hear me? Mabel?" His voice sounded strained, distant, and grainy.

Zach went back to the window and looked into the deck. At the terminal, Ryker was standing with a headset on. He continued, "Am I patched through to the suits? Hello?"

"Yes, I'm here," said Zach. "What's happening?"

"I don't fucking know!" Ryker breathed out in exasperation. "The dropship's decoupling."

"Why?" Mabel asked, then looked back at the dropship. Steam wafted up from the tiny crack in the floor between the docked ship and the Gateway.

"Can you stop it?" Zach asked.

"I'm trying," Ryker's fingers clacked loudly against the terminal's keyboard, "but nothing's going through. I'm locked out."

"You've got to get us out of here!" Mabel shouted.

"I said I'm trying!" Ryker yelled in frustration.

In the dim red light, Zach scanned for anything to grab onto. The glass case would shatter under stress, so that was a no-go. A few pipes ran along the wall but were too thin to bear much weight.

"Here!" Mabel said. Her gloved fingers worked their way into the groove between two sections of the vented ceiling. She pushed up, slid the panel to the side, and hooked her hands into the newly revealed space.

Zach was about to do the same when another thought crossed his mind. If Mabel was so easily able to move the plate, what in the world would the vacuum of space do? It would tear the ceiling to pieces, turning it into a barrage of shrapnel and taking Mabel along with it. "Wait!" Zach shouted.

Before the warning had escaped his lips, the dropship separated from the Gateway, and all the air in the decon shower was sucked out into space. Zach managed to get hold of one of the sturdier pipes on the wall. Mabel was not so lucky. Her feet were swept out from under her as the ceiling tile she had grasped tore away from its rivets.

Zach had always thought that in moments like this, time would slow down. But no. Time didn't slow, falter, or change in any way as Mabel bent into a flying L, shot ten feet back, and was thrown against the airlock of the now-separated dropship. Her hands shot out in front of her, pawing desperately for something to grab onto as her legs kicked at the abyss below.

Since all the air in the decon shower had been vented out to space, Zach could safely let go of the pipes without fear of being sucked into the void—the Gateway's artificial gravity was still holding his feet to the floor. He swiveled around to look at Mabel. Taking hold of the pipes again, he ran to the edge of the decon shower and extended his hand.

Mabel reached for him, her fingertips brushing his.

But she was just out of reach.

Zach stretched further away from the wall, barely hanging onto the pipe. Mabel clawed at him desperately until she finally managed to get hold of his hand. Zach pulled her back into the module. Once inside the gravity field, she dropped to the floor, gasping for air inside her helmet.

Zach kept his eyes on the dropship as it drifted into space. Once it was a safe distance from the Gateway, its engines ignited, and it made a purposeful turn back toward Earth. Zach realized then that it wasn't just some random malfunction—someone at OSE was controlling it, piloting it remotely.

The dropship would inevitably return to Earth, and OSE would open it up, expecting Zach and Ryker to be inside. But all they'd find would be air and empty seats. And the Harvard sweater he left behind.

Damn it, Zach thought. *I loved that sweater.*

Once their breathing had returned to normal, Zach and Mabel came to the inner airlock.

"Ryker! Open the door!" Zach yelled.

A moment passed before a response came. "I can't."

"Why not?"

"Open it!" Mabel added.

"It won't let me."

Zach groaned as he realized: opening the airlock without a vessel docked on the other side of the decon shower would suck Ryker and everything inside the deck into the vacuum of space. It would probably vent a lot of the station's air too.

"What's he talking about?" Mabel asked.

"We need to find another way in," Zach mumbled. Then, to Ryker, he said, "How do we do that?"

Though Zach could only see the back of Ryker's head through the window, he could almost picture Ryker's expression as he said, "I don't know."

RYKER GAGARIN: 2053

"What do you mean, 'I don't know?'" Zach stared at Ryker through the porthole window.

"Just give me a minute," Ryker rasped. His throat felt like sandpaper. His hands shook. Sweat filled the creases of his palms. He looked around the deck for answers, studying the dim screens on the walls while trying to think of an alternative.

"Open the fucking door!" Mabel shouted into the intercom.

"There's no way! The station won't allow it." Ryker clenched his fists and pressed his knuckles against his temples, teeth grinding together as he wracked his brain for an idea. "Is there anything on the outside of the ship? Another airlock or a service duct, maybe?"

"I'll check," Zach said and took off toward the wide opening of the decon shower.

"Tell me what you see," Ryker approached his side of the

airlock and leaned his hands against the edges of the window, "and I'll try to get you in through there."

"I'll do my best." Zach reached the edge of the tunnel. Then, holding onto the wall, he maneuvered his body out of the decon shower and against the outer shell of the Gateway, where Ryker could no longer see him. Zach clicked his tongue, searching, then said, "There are a few windows, but I can't see an airlock or..." He paused for a moment before cursing under his breath. "Shit. Yeah, nothing." He carefully returned to Mabel's side. "No other doors or hatches that I can see."

"So?" Mabel asked. She tugged on the arms of her spacesuit and tilted her head downward. A piece of sweat-slicked hair fell over her narrowed eye.

"I'm thinking," Ryker said. He paced back to the center of the deck, trying to remember Z-Deck's layout. There had to be vents out there somewhere. Or were there?

Frustrated, Ryker's mind returned to opening the door. *How can I do that?* He wasn't lying when he said the station wouldn't let him.

With his brow tensed so hard that the muscles in his face hurt, Ryker thought of an idea. It was bad. Really bad. But it could work. He would have to go down to the data center where the Gateway's primary control systems were housed. From there, he could manually override the door. The proper entrance to the data center was clear across the station—it would take him at least thirty minutes just to get there, plus who knew how long to figure out how to override the door. Zach and Mabel could be dead before he finished.

The only way to get down there faster was via the maintenance ducts, but they were risky. First, they were a labyrinth of poorly marked tunnels barely wide enough for a man to pass through. They were designed for quick access to make essential repairs, not for traversing the whole ship. Second, the heat inside could be unbearable. If Ryker got lost, he'd cook in there before he found his way out.

Time was slipping away. The oxygen tanks keeping Zach and Mabel alive would only last so long before they were empty. Ryker realized he had to accept the inevitable: there was no other way to open the airlock. He had to get to the data center as fast as possible, which meant passing through the service ducts and hoping not to melt in the process.

"Where are you going?" Zach asked as Ryker headed for the exit.

"Just stay on the line with me!" Ryker tightened his headset, opened the ship-side blast door, and entered the hall. It was cold. Freezing. The air was thinner than he remembered.

As he looked down the wide corridor, his exhales lingering in the frigid air, he suddenly felt dizzy at the thought of being back on the Gateway.

After everything he did to escape.

Ryker closed his eyes and tried to push the thoughts out of his head. He couldn't allow himself to go there, not with Zach and Mabel breathing on borrowed time. After taking a moment to center himself, he opened his eyes and sprinted down the hall. At the first intersection, he turned right, then left, then left again, then right. As he ran, he caught a fleeting glimpse of Earth through one of the wide-framed windows that lined the corridors.

He stopped at a small computer lab and grabbed a laptop, patch cords, and a thumb drive. Then he continued running until he reached the entrance to a stairwell—the biggest stair-well in the entire ship. It went down six levels, winding and winding, each step painted with a neat stripe of blue, ulti-mately leading into an expansive warehouse-like room with a low roof. The flickering lights above him buzzed and whined.

"You still with me?" Ryker asked.

"For now," Mabel replied. "But hurry."

"I'm trying."

Ryker ran into the service bay, expecting the motion-trig-gered lights to go on as he moved. They didn't. He didn't have time to wonder why. Instead, he continued through the shadows and into the dark. It was the type of dark that made Ryker feel watched, as if he might turn around and see a pair of yellow eyes staring at him from the shadows. Fighting his fear, he made his way to a thick-handled hatch adjacent to the wall and lifted the lid with a creak.

A light turned on in the duct, and Ryker stared into the cavity for a moment. He listened to the station's deep rumble, to the air whistle through winding vents. Then, he climbed in and shut the hatch above him. A series of LED bulbs lit up in rapid succession down the narrow duct. Ryker extended his arms into the main portion of the tunnel, which was about chest level, and pulled himself into it. He immediately remem-bered how much he hated tight spaces.

"Keep talking, alright?" Ryker said to Zach. "You're being too quiet... I need to know you're okay." A beep sounded over the intercom, prompting Ryker to ask, "What was that?"

"It's my damn oxygen," replied Zach. "I grabbed a half-empty tank."

"How much do you have left?"

He heard Zach shift a bit. "It says twenty-seven percent."

Ryker cursed and pressed his lips shut. Dust had accumulated in the ducts over the years, and Ryker fought to avoid inhaling it. He wheezed and coughed, each convulsion causing his back to arch and hit the aluminum ceiling. Another few meters down the duct and the air began to heat up.

The stifling air seemed to press in all around Ryker, nearly confining him in place and rendering his lungs inoperable. The metal was hot to the touch, and every second his arms rested against it, he felt like the skin was melting. He thought of how eggs cook in a pan, the bubbling flaps around the edges of the egg whites rippling in the heat. He could almost hear the sizzling, the crackling. He could practically smell it.

"What are you going to do?" Zach asked.

"I'm gonna try to override the door commands."

"Try?"

"I've never done this, but the system's controls are pretty similar. Worst comes to worst, I can open up the airlock controller and manually bypass the failsafes."

"You know how to do that?"

"Don't worry. I had to do something similar to the artificial gravity controller when it broke."

"And how'd that go?"

Ryker paused. "For six months, I slept on the ceiling."

"Great," Zach said, his voice dripping with sarcasm. "I feel so much better."

Ryker continued down the air duct. The weight of his elbows caused indents in the thin metal that quickly flattened out after a second or two. The toes of his shoes screeched along the duct as they dragged behind him.

Another beep came through the grainy radio. "Twenty-five," Zach reported.

Thankfully, the closer Ryker got to the data center, the more the heat faded—the data center was kept at an icy temperature to prevent the computers inside from overheating.

Soon, Ryker could see the exit. Mustering his remaining strength, he crawled toward it until his fingers grasped the grate. He pushed it until it came off and landed with a crash on the tiled floor.

After slipping from the grate and into the data center, Ryker looked up to survey his surroundings. It was an expansive space with dozens of rows of towering server racks. Terminals with glowing screens lined one wall. The light burned his eyes.

"Twenty," Zach said. Ryker could hear the tension creeping into his voice. "Almost done?"

"Almost."

ZACH CROFT: 2053

"Get hold of something," said Ryker through the radio. "When the door opens, all the air will rush out—probably whatever's not strapped down too. Stay close to the walls."

"Okay." Zach and Mabel took hold of a pipe. Zach's suit beeped again.

"Ready?"

"Ready."

"Okay, here we go. One ... two ... three."

The airlock slid open, and Zach's and Mabel's feet were swept off the ground.

Two boxes from the deck flew through the open cavity and ejected out to space. Zach hugged the wall as tightly as he could, resting the glass forehead of his helmet against the surface, his hands clasping over one another around the pipe.

A third box tipped over before exiting the deck, and its contents—power tools, spare parts, and handfuls of loose screws—spilled out. Like a barrage of shrapnel, the items tore through the decon shower. A giant power drill spun directly at Zach's face. Reflexively, he let go of the pipe with one hand, using it to block the tool from shattering his helmet's face mask. Although he managed to deflect the worst of the impact, his arm redirected the drill's diamond-tipped bit into the side of his oxygen tube, puncturing it.

"Shit!"

A beep emitted from Zach's suit.

Then another.

And another.

The beeps sped up, one succeeding the other until they blended with Zach's increasing gasps for air. It was pulling the air out of his suit. It wasn't just stopping the flow of new oxygen. It was practically sucking the air straight from Zach's lungs.

"Zach's suit is breached!" Mabel declared. "Ryker!"

"Just hold on a little longer!" Ryker answered.

Zach's voice came next, scratchy and pleading. "Air. I—I..."

"I know!" cried Ryker.

Zach's movements grew slower. Weaker. He could feel himself slipping away, his grip on the wall becoming increasingly difficult to maintain.

"Screw this!" Mabel yelled, then placed a hand on Zach's back. "Pull yourself in! I'll help you!"

"Okay," Zach gasped. Freeing a hand, he reached forward, grabbing at a pipe that was closer to the airlock. The first time, it slid off. But the second, he felt a push on his back, lurched forward, and took hold of the pipe.

The pull on their feet lessened as the last bits of air in the deck rushed out. Mabel took the opportunity to shove Zach through the airlock. She tugged herself after him. "We're in!" she shouted. "Close it!"

Behind Mabel, the airlock slid shut and sealed with a hiss. As Mabel began taking off Zach's helmet, Ryker suddenly yelled, "Stop! It'll take a minute before the oxygen system repressurizes."

"He's suffocating, and we're inside the station! I'm taking it off!" Mabel replied.

"You'll kill him!"

Ignoring Ryker, Mabel pulled off her own helmet to test if the air was breathable. Then, after pulling in a deep breath and confirming that conditions were okay, she relieved Zach of his too. He gasped, turned over onto all fours, and lurched as he gasped for air.

After a few seconds, he fell onto his back and drifted into an exhausted sleep.

SEVENTEEN

CORA KEATON: 2053

THE BENCH FELT empty without him.

Cora ran her hand over the rough metal surface, feeling the bumpiness between her thin fingers. Pollen loaded the air, but that wasn't why her eyes were red and watery.

Cora got up, walked a few feet, sat on the ground, and propped herself against one of the only oaks left in the park. The grass tickled the underside of her legs. And, for a moment, she was eight again.

The hose was hooked up to a massive water slide, climbing twenty feet into the sky. The air was simmering with heat, but the water made it better. Cora scaled the inflatable ladder with Zach at her side as they raced each other.

Upon reaching the top, Cora leaped over the rainbow divider and crashed onto the slide. She slid down fast as a bullet, barely avoiding friction burns all along her back.

When she reached the bottom, she overshot the small pool

meant to catch her and shot into the grass. One of her water shoes went flying.

Once she got her composure, she wiped off the mud clinging to her sunburnt skin, stood up, and realized she was missing one of the bright pink slippers. Zach reached the bottom of the slide a moment later, his wet hair falling over his eyes.

"Where's my shoe?" Cora had said, her hand running over her bare foot. Her face shifted to concern as she realized it had flown deep into a rose bush. Thorns jutted from every stem within the foliage—she couldn't retrieve it without her arm being sliced to bits.

Zach didn't care, though. As soon as he saw her shoe, he sloshed through the flooded grass and drove his arm right into the rose bush. His fingers wriggled as he attempted to grip the slippery mesh. He winced, scratches on his skin dripping the color of the roses around it. Eventually, he got hold of the shoe and pulled it free.

Cora expressed worry about the cuts running up Zach's arm, but every time she tried to wipe off some of the blood, he swatted her away, claiming he was fine.

Naturally, Zach neglected to tell Cora about his suicide mission to Mars. If she'd freaked over a few cuts, he must have known she'd stop at nothing to talk him out of his foolish plan. Instead, he had avoided her entirely in the last week: not returning her calls, ignoring her texts, dodging her attempts to speak to him at work.

She never would have found out about his plan if it wasn't for Ryker, who seemed just as disgruntled. Over a cup of tea, she implored Ryker to talk Zach out of going through with it.

Funny how that worked. Not only had Ryker *not* talked Zach out of going to Mars—he'd gone *with* him.

There was nothing Cora could do about it now. All she could do was pray that Zach was right about everything. That he could really do it—and do it right—saving lives in the process.

Cora rested her head against the tree trunk and closed her eyes. Suddenly, a large boom echoed through the park. She opened her eyes, scanning the sky until she spotted a fiery object plummeting through the clouds. She reeled with *deja vu*, recalling the morning when she and Zach had first spotted Ryker's dropship.

Was *that* a dropship? *Zach's* dropship?

Cora's heart soared. He was coming back. He had to be. He had changed his mind about the mission and had set a course for home. Cora could barely contain her excitement. She smiled and leaped to her feet, then jogged out from under the tree to get a better view of the sky. Her eyes traced the object as the flames began to peel back, revealing a dropship. *It's him!*

Her lips were just forming Zach's name when the dropship exploded.

RYKER GAGARIN: 2053

How goddamn ironic.

He lasted one week on Earth. One scary, dangerous, eye-opening week, and now he was back on the Gateway. A sigh escaped his lips as he, Zach, and Mabel walked past his old bedroom. The door was still ajar, so he could see everything was exactly how he had left it. The stack of old books he always read was still leaning on his nightstand, a bookmark jutting out from one. The bed was messy, with sheets balled up at the end and the pillow wrinkled. His clothing was piled in the corner, a tangled mass of jackets and jumpsuits.

"I missed laundry day," Ryker commented. So, this was his life again. He pictured himself only a few days earlier, giving the middle finger to the Gateway as his dropship flew away. The joy he felt as he vowed to never return. With what he went through, it would have been surprising if he ever looked at the sky again.

After all that, he was right back where he started. It felt like going back to an abusive ex.

When they reached the cafeteria, Ryker shot straight for the pantry. He'd been working through the pre-packaged food for the past few years and still hadn't gotten to the good stuff. If there was any in the first place, that is.

"Did I ever tell you about the time I got blasted out of an airlock?" Ryker asked as he sat down at the metal table.

Zach shook his head, preparing for whatever nonsense Ryker had in store. "I don't believe I've had the pleasure."

Ryker swallowed a bite of vacuum-sealed bread and leaned in. "So, one morning—I think I was 15 or so—all the intercoms went crazy. I almost shit myself. One of the outer radars had been hit with debris and got super fucked up. Me being the only person here meant I had to fix it."

Mabel walked around the table wearing a loose gray hoodie she found in a supply closet. Dark circles surrounded her eyes. "Then what?"

"I was getting on a spacesuit that barely fit, and I stepped into the airlock. Then boom, the outer door opened just as I got the helmet on and blew me out into space. No tethers. No connection to the station. Luckily, I slammed into a solar array and was able to climb back in."

The room fell silent for a moment.

"So it's true, then? You really lived here?" Mabel asked.

Ryker slowed a bit, setting down a can of fruit punch. "Yeah."

"I never left Pasadena," Zach said. "After I got back... there wasn't much I wanted to do, you know." Ryker didn't know. "For years, I just hung around with Cora. A lot of years." His face suddenly looked sadder than it had been a moment ago.

"You'll see her again," assured Mabel, flicking a speck of dust off Zach's shoulder. She turned to Ryker. "I was in Michigan. Ann Arbor. Hated the place."

What could possibly be so bad about a city? On Earth, with the world in her backyard? "Why's that?"

"Imagine standing in a meat locker, then aim a few degrees lower."

Zach frowned and took a bite out of his apple. "You should have moved."

"My parents didn't want to. They were studying electro-magnetism, going back and forth between Michigan and some island in the South Pacific. I don't know." Mabel scratched her cheek. "So, cryosleep. What's it like?"

"It's just like Michigan," Zach said. "Freezing cold, but tolerable when you're asleep."

Mabel crossed her arms. "Why are we using cryo at all if Mars is so close? It'd take a few minutes going at lightspeed, no?"

"Yes, but we're not going at lightspeed. There's likely only a little irogen left in the ship's reserves, and it's not nearly enough to activate the continuum drive. It's enough to travel the long way, though."

"Aren't we trying to get this done as soon as possible?" Ryker asked.

"Obviously, but there's not much we can do without the drive. It's the long way or no way," Zach answered.

"Then what are we waiting for?" Mabel moved for the exit, then realized she had no clue where to go. "Finish your food, and come on."

Ryker and Zach gobbled down what was left and walked into the hallway.

"This way," Ryker said. After a few steps, he angled his face toward the ceiling. "Gateway, set course for Mars."

A few minutes later, they came to the massive steel door labeled *Cryobay*. Surprisingly, Ryker hadn't stepped foot in it since Prescott. There was no reason to. Ryker placed his palm on the identification scanner and waited for the door to open. Nothing happened. The light didn't turn green.

"What's wrong?" Zach furrowed his brow.

"It's not taking my print. Gateway, open the cryobay."

"*NEGATIVE, GAGARIN. POWER TO THE DOOR IS OFFLINE. CONTACT MISSION CONTROL FOR HELP.*"

"Goddamnit!" Zach growled.

"The power is offline?" Mabel looked at Zach, then Ryker. "What's that mean?"

"It means we're fucked." Zach paced away from the cryobay door.

Ryker slumped against the wall. "It doesn't make sense. It

can't be because of the Emergency Protocol. I overrode it last week. That's how I was able to launch the dropship."

"Can you do the same for this?" Mabel asked.

"I don't know," Ryker replied. "Maybe? It only took me twenty years to do it last time."

"Well, then, you better get started."

ZACH CROFT: 2030

The plant was obliterated.

From the colony, it was hard to tell how much damage it had sustained. But standing where Zach was, on the edge of a steep dropoff into the crater, the destruction was self-evident.

Twisted metal. Piles of rubble. Mines blown wide open. The cavity spanned about a hundred meters across, ending in a portion of the plant that had remained standing. Its gnarled beams extended over the crater like a skeletal hand.

Ryker had hesitated to come here, but Zach convinced him otherwise. They were due for a fun day, especially after the havoc unleashed on their lives over the past few weeks. The crash. The meteor. The death of Ryker's father, which had taken a considerable toll on him. Zach and Ryker's hab units were beside one another, and Zach could hear the stifled sobs through the thin composite walls every night. After several days of this, Zach decided it was time he got Ryker's mind off the bloodshed. So he suggested going into the crater and exploring the mines.

The objections had come immediately.

"We're not allowed to."

"What if we get caught?"

"What if the mines collapse?"

But Zach had come equipped with all the answers Ryker would ever need, typically using a simple "what they know won't hurt them." An hour of convincing later, they were trekking through the tunnels leading to the dome erected over the meteor impact zone. The dome had originally been intended to house a second colony once Prescott was up and running, but the council had decided to use it to cover the meteor crater instead, so crews could work on repairing the mines and irogen processing facility without needing to work in bulky spacesuits. It was a smart decision—there wouldn't be a second colony if the first one failed.

When they arrived at the edge of the crater, Ryker hesitated. He looked uneasy. Zach patted him on the back. "Come on. It'll be fun."

Of course, they had to take precautions when entering the crater. It was massive and was covered in debris, but it wasn't anything they couldn't work around. A steep, rocky ramp, likely formed by the blast's shockwaves, provided access to the surface below. Once they got down into the cavity, the search for something interesting began. At various points along the crater's walls, the mouths of the mineshafts gaped open, just waiting for brave explorers to venture inside them.

"How about that one?" Zach proposed, pointing to a nearby mineshaft. They'd have to pass through a labyrinth of half-standing walls and ledges to get to it, but the dark tunnels beyond the entrance seemed promising.

"Really? Don't you think it looks a bit... menacing?" Ryker shoved his hands in his pockets.

Fun couldn't exist without a bit of risk-taking. Zach went to work convincing Ryker to at least check it out, claiming they could back away whenever it got too scary. After a few minutes, Ryker caved.

Zach carefully led the way to the blown-open maw in the side of the crater. It was terrifying—pitch black—but this might be their only chance to explore the mines before operations were up and running again. They had to seize the opportunity. Besides, no one would find them; it was forbidden to go into the crater. Zach faltered a bit as he considered the possibility.

No one would find them if they got lost.

Zach dismissed his concerns. There had to be ways out of the mines, right? Even the workers would need some way to escape in case of emergency? Zach accepted it as truth and ducked inside. Ryker followed. The darkness quickly engulfed them. Thankfully, Zach had the foresight to bring flashlights and promptly handed one to Ryker.

The light revealed metal walls, floors, and pipes. There were several points where the alloy had melted from the explosion. But after another few meters, their surroundings appeared reasonably intact. Zach supposed that was a perk of having the mines deep underground; it was almost like a fallout shelter.

They didn't seem like mines on these upper levels, per se. More like... hallways. Perhaps these levels had already been plucked of whatever irogen crystals they held and had been transformed into metallic passageways. There were doors here and there, small storage rooms by the looks of them. Zach briefly entered one but got bored after finding it was empty. They continued walking.

An elevator with a fence-like door was at the end of the long mineshaft. Zach rattled the handle. It pulled open. He stood for a second while staring into the steel box. "That looks like something..."

Ryker seemed uncomfortable. "I—I don't know. Can we go back?"

"Why? The miners wouldn't use it if it wasn't safe." Zach entered the elevator, dragging his hand over a set of buttons painted with numbers 1-13.

"I know, I know. It just gives me the creeps."

Zach threw his hands up. "This is a once-in-a-lifetime opportunity, Ryker!"

Ryker sighed. "If you think so." He silently took his place in the box. Zach pressed the button for level 13, the lowest one, and held onto the railing as the elevator began descending, level by level. As it dropped, glimpses of other floors passed by the grated door. The lower the elevator went, the less developed the structures—the ceilings, walls, and floors—seemed to be.

The box stopped halfway between levels nine and ten. It sputtered, tilting a bit to the side... Then, it plummeted. The elevator dropped down two floors, as if the cables holding it upright had snapped. Zach and Ryker screamed as the grimy air whipped all around them. The elevator shuddered briefly, slamming the two kids against the floor, then continued its drop. Zach looked at Ryker, seeing the fear in his eyes. Were they about to die? The elevator fell another floor, then crashed to a complete stop. Level 13.

Ryker skittered back against the wall, hyperventilating. "I don't want to be here anymore." He coughed as a thick cloud of dust wafted in from the shaft outside.

Zach didn't have the heart to confess he had no idea how they'd get out. Surely, there was another elevator. Or ladder. Or staircase. *Something to carry them back to the surface. "Let's see if we can find an exit." Zach got Ryker to his feet and stepped out into the tunnel.*

This level had no metal walls, only rock. Red emergency lights along the floor provided the only illumination, shrouding the passageway in a deep, bloody glow. Ryker clutched Zach's arm for safety as they stepped forward.

The first level had been scary, but this was way worse. Even Zach, who took pride in his ability to hide his fear, felt his stomach churn. They were hundreds of feet underground, alone in a silent tunnel. Or were they? Could someone else be down there, lurking in the shadows?

Nope. No way. Zach wasn't going to indulge in that line of thinking. It was already petrifying enough to be alone; he wasn't about to add even more. About thirty feet ahead, the rocky mineshaft split off in two directions. To the right, a gargantuan machine sat with claw-like appendages grasping the wall. It looked like it was frozen in time. To the left, there was only more empty space. It was obvious which direction they should go.

The center of the floor was lined with steel tracks. Something that looked like a pickaxe leaned against the wall. Zach took it in his hands, holding it up in a ready position. It was stupid. What did he expect to find down there that warranted having a weapon?

The air was definitely thinner underground. Zach had heard about how they pumped oxygen into the mines but couldn't help wondering if they'd stopped doing that after the meteor. Zach tried to breathe easy and told Ryker to do the same. "We'll find a way out. We will," he said. Zach was about to repeat it when something caused them both to freeze. A sound. A roar. Something.

Zach could hear it maybe a hundred feet up, grinding away. Was it a person? A monster? Whatever it was, it took away his ability to breathe altogether. He exchanged a look with Ryker and wordlessly suggested, "Let's get out of here."

But where was the way out? The presumed other elevator? Back the other way, the tunnel was blocked off by that big machine, and here, well... there very well might have been a monster waiting for them to draw near. This was the only way. The only chance they had. As scary as it might be, they had to keep moving forward in the direction of the crunching sound.

"No. No, we can't," Ryker said shakily.

"We have to." Towing Ryker behind him, Zach pressed forward. With his other hand, he clutched the pickaxe tight, ready to use it to defend himself if he had to. Slowly but surely, they inched down the tunnel. The deeper they went, the fewer emergency lights there were. Darkness surrounded them. They turned the flashlights back on.

Wait. Was that a good idea? Or did the creature now know of their presence? Warily, Zach shined the light down the tunnel and...

Another machine. That's all it was. A massive blue mechanism carving out more tunnel space from the Martian rock. Was it doing that automatically? Zach couldn't see a driver, so it must have been. He started to laugh. "Oh, thank god." With the indicator lights on the machinery, he could see another shaft that split off from this one. Zach started down it.

"What are we going to tell our parents?" Ryker asked. "We're covered head to toe in dirt."

"That we were playing in the Slabs?"

"My mom might believe that, but your dad won't."

As they continued down the tunnels, they discussed other possible alibis. Maybe they were playing hide and seek or pretend war? He didn't have much time to dwell on it before things got strange. This deep in the mines, any real sign of humanity was nonexistent, other than the tracks. No lights. No structures. But there was something else: up ahead, Zach could make out a faint, murky glow around the next bend. It was bluish-purple, twinkling as if there was a portal to another world just ahead. As they turned the corner, they entered a vast cavern. Zach's jaw went slack.

Hundreds of blue and purple crystals clung to the walls and ceiling. They jutted out in every direction, their centers glowing vibrantly with ethereal light that streamed through the sides of their hexagonal structures.

Irogen.

A single track ran through the cavern from the tunnel. On it, a mine cart was piled high with loose crystals. As Zach shone the light at the translucent spikes, they reflected it in all directions. Zach grabbed one of the crystals, rolling it around in his hand. Without thinking it through, he blurted out, "Let's take some."

"What?"

"They're cool looking, don't you think? Maybe we can make something with them."

"Like what?"

"I don't know. Lamps or something. Here. Hand me your backpack."

"Are you sure?" Ryker handed the backpack to Zach, who began filling it with crystals.

"Sure about what? There's nothing to be sure about." Once the bag was full, Zach tossed it back to Ryker, turned around, and resumed his search for the exit.

Right. Left. Left. Right.

Emergency lights reappeared. Then, miraculously, they found another elevator. This one was nicer, probably newer than the other. And while Zach wasn't prepared to put all his trust in it, there didn't seem to be another way out. So they entered it. He punched the button for the first floor and held on tight as it ascended.

By the time they reached the light, it was as if they had never been there.

EIGHTEEN

ZACH CROFT: 2053

HOURS.

It had been hours since they tried to open the cryobay, and they were still locked out.

Zach leaned over Ryker's shoulder, studying the lines of complex computer code scrolling on the screen. It looked like complete gibberish to him.

"Do you mind?" Ryker said without taking his eyes from the terminal.

"Sorry." Zach stood up and backed away a few steps. "What are you looking for?"

"If I knew, I would have already found it."

"Why don't you check the code you patched to launch the dropship?"

Ryker pivoted in his chair and looked up at Zach, dumbfounded. "Gee, thanks, Zach. I hadn't thought of that."

"This is ridiculous," Mabel said. She looked at her watch and sighed. "What happens if we can't figure this out?"

Zach dropped into the seat next to Mabel. "Worst case? We put up with each other for a few weeks until we get to Mars."

Mabel brightened. "Okay. That doesn't sound so bad."

"Speak for yourself," Ryker said dryly as he opened another file on the terminal.

"Are you sure every cryobay on the station is locked?" Mabel asked.

Zach shook his head. "There are no other—" He stopped mid-sentence. At the same time, Ryker spun his chair around to face Zach. It seemed they both realized the same thing at the same time. Their eyes met, and a wave of mutual memories flowed between them. "Have you checked them since we were last here?" Zach asked.

"Nope."

"Let's pray they still work then."

"What are you guys talking about?" Mabel slowed behind them, blowing a curl out of her face.

"There are more pods. Not many. But more than zero," Zach said, smiled, and clapped the side of her shoulder. "Come on."

On their way to the storage room, Mabel hounded Zach for information.

"Why are they there?" Mabel asked.

"I have no idea. All I know is that Ryker and I were the first —and last—people to use them."

"But they work just as well as the ones in the cryobay?"

If they didn't work properly, he and Ryker would have been turned into ice cubes as kids. "Well, we're alive."

"And Plague free," Ryker added.

They had Zach's father to thank for that. They had his father to thank for knowing the pods existed in the first place.

"And the other colonists—did they know about these pods?" Mabel brought up.

"Not that I know of," Zach answered.

They descended several flights to C Deck, then entered a large storage room. Zach walked to the center of the room, knelt beside a floor panel, yanked on the plate, and slid it aside. As expected, a set of controls were hidden beneath it. Zach tapped on the touchscreen, navigating through options until he found the one he wanted. A few seconds later, the floor on the far side of the room completely retracted into the wall.

Ten cryopods arose in its place, and for a brief instant, Zach could see himself climbing into one. Not now, of course, but as a child. Zach glanced back at Ryker, who had a similar look about him, caught up in his own memories.

Something occurred to Zach, and he couldn't help but ask, "Ryker, you knew these pods were here. Why didn't you use them? Instead of living alone all those years?"

Ryker gave a small, sad smile. "I wanted my rescuers to be able to find me."

Not knowing what else to say, Zach walked up to the pods. "Let's just get this over with."

He crouched beside one and tapped the disengage switch. As the pod slid open, he squinted through a cloud of gas.

"You're sure this is safe?" Mabel asked.

"Definitely."

With a final worried look, Mabel climbed into her pod and

closed the lid. Zach sat beside her as ice crystals produced a frame around her face.

"The bodies are still there, Zach. In Prescott," Ryker suddenly said. "The colony's gonna be a graveyard."

Zach considered it. "We're standing in a graveyard. Prescott's not gonna be any worse than being here." He knew that was a lie, but what else was he supposed to say?

"Very reassuring." With a shake of his head, Ryker approached his pod and got in. "Thaw me out when we get there?"

"You got it."

Zach waited for Ryker to freeze over, then climbed into the third pod. The hood clicked into place, and an ice-cold gas began pumping in from all sides. He used his last few seconds of consciousness to look at his friends through the pod's glass wall.

They both seemed so peaceful. Zach drummed his fingers against his leg, swearing to do Prescott justice. He'd make sure the colonists hadn't died in vain.

Zach turned his head to the other side to gaze into the empty chambers beside him. But as he squinted through the glass, his heart stopped. Not because of cryo. Not because of his fear of returning to Prescott.

Because there was someone in the next pod.

It was a young man with his arms crossed over his chest. He had a short beard. Sunken cheeks. A yellowed jumpsuit.

Zach gasped as panic seized him. He pressed up on the lid of his cryopod, but it was already locked. He tried commanding the Gateway to let him out, but cryogenic gas filled his lungs and froze his vocal cords.

As his consciousness slipped away, he looked at the man in the pod next to him one last time. Embroidered on the man's sleeve was a series of simple block letters.

PRESCOTT COLONY // PRISONER

NICOLAS CARVER: 2053

He's dead. And I killed him.

It seemed unbelievable, yet there Carver was, standing amidst the wreckage of Zach's dropship. No bodies had been found yet, but no one could have survived such a catastrophic explosion. Every inch of the dropship had been engulfed in flames. Every piece of shrapnel was charred and melted, forged by the blast into twisted shapes that jutted from the loose earth.

Smoke poured from the debris, blanketing the sky and blocking out the orange light of the sinking sun. Through the smog, Carver could see blue and red flashing lights. Fire trucks slammed their brakes at the entrance to the park. Cops strung yellow tape between trees as onlookers watched in horror.

All Carver wanted was to bring Zach home. But in so doing, he had gotten Zach killed.

Zach was like a son to him. A stubborn, arrogant, disobedient son, but still a son. Carver had watched him graduate elementary school, had coached his sports teams, had helped fund school field trips when Sarina Keaton was too tight on money, had paid Zach's way through college, and had landed him a job at OSE. Initially, Carver's support was a way for him to keep a close eye on Zach, but eventually, he began to genuinely care about the kid.

Carver didn't have any children, but he felt like he could be a better father than his own dad had ever been. The past few weeks had proven to Carver that he had failed. Despite his efforts, Zach had turned out more like Quinton: strong-willed, refusing to back down, always doing what he thought was right no matter the cost.

In a way, Carver understood why Zach did what he did— he honestly thought going to Mars was the only way to save lives. He never considered that he could be wrong.

Carver's head pounded as he stepped over a patch of smoldering grass. Waves of guilt washed over him. Not for his hand in Zach's death—not entirely—but rather for the fact that he saw the *light* in it.

With Zach gone, his problems were solved.

The entire Prescott chapter—the colony, Exodus, the Red Plague, Victor, Quinton, Ryker—was closed. It was over. Every loose end was tied up. There was nobody left to challenge him. To question him. To stop him.

Carver hated himself for seeing the bright side in Zach's demise, but he couldn't deny that the positives could outweigh the negatives in the long run. He'd feel terrible for a time, but eventually, things would return to normal. MagRes would continue. The solar flares would be stopped. Billions of lives would be saved. All of Carver's struggle, all of his sacrifice, all the tough choices he had to make... it would all be worth it in the end.

Carver's eyes drifted to an ambulance stationed by the playground. It sat still, back doors wide open, with a woman wrapped up in a blanket sitting on the tailgate: Cora. Her eyes were glazed over and vacant. An EMT wiped her forehead with a wet rag, consoling her.

Carver headed in Cora's direction. When he reached the ambulance, he sat down beside Cora. She didn't acknowledge him. She tightened the gray blanket around her shoulders and watched blades of grass lean in the breeze. Soot covered her face, only thinning in the spots where the EMT had wiped her brow.

"Were you here when it happened?" Carver asked.

Cora answered with a nod. She was silent for a minute, then asked, "Why were they coming back?" Her voice was raw and scratchy.

"What do you mean?"

Cora swallowed, adjusting her hair. "They were headed for the Gateway. Why'd they come back?"

Carver couldn't tell her that they hadn't chosen to come home. That he'd allowed Rhea to hack their autopilot and change their course back to OSE. "Maybe they realized going to Mars wouldn't help anything."

Cora shook her head. "There was no changing his mind." She slowly peeled off one side of the blanket and revealed a scrap of burgundy fabric. The letters *HARV* were written across it in white. "I found it in the wreckage."

Carver felt a knot forming in his throat. He struggled to find the necessary words. Ultimately, he could only muster, "What do we do now?"

Cora stared at the smoldering grass in the distance. "We pray that he was wrong."

NINETEEN

ZACH CROFT: 2053

THERE WAS a sudden burst of light, a wave of warmth. Thick steam blurred Zach's vision, making him feel like he was waking up in slow motion. It was as though he was in a meat locker, his skin taut and slightly sticky with condensation. A moment passed, and his heart rate began to regulate after so long in stasis.

Thump. Thump. Thump.

Once the fog cleared, Zach sat up, unhurried, and rubbed his eyes. He ruffled his hair and took a deep breath. He felt like he had a hangover.

"ENTERING MARS ORBIT," the intercom blared, making Zach wince. A *month, overnight. Crazy.*

Still drowsy, he turned his head to the left, where Mabel was shivering. Apparently, his warm waking experience was an *acquired* feeling. He tried to remember the first time he had gone on ice, clawing at a layer of fog that separated his memories. He knew he was ten at the time, on his way to Prescott. And if someone had told him then that he would be going back, he would have laughed in their faces. Coming to terms with it all was hard enough.

Suddenly, he remembered something. Something bad. Something that stole his breath away from him. Balling his hands into fists nervously, he turned to the other side and looked down into the pod beside him.

Ryker walked over from his own cryopod. "What is it?" he asked, shifting to see what Zach was gazing at. Zach jumped out of his chamber, standing rigid before the seam separating the storage room floor from the cryopod beside his. The way he stood resembled one of those bony, gray-skinned horror movie girls from classic films. "What are you looking at?" Ryker said.

"There's someone in there," Zach said shakily. He scratched his neck, scared, sick to his stomach, and most of all, confused. Confused by everything. Confused by how someone could be asleep under the floor for god-knows how long without them even realizing it.

"There can't be." Ryker stepped closer to the occupied cryopod and bent down toward the glass. Sure enough, there was a person inside. "What the fuck?" he said with a strangled gasp.

Woozy from cold sleep, Mabel made her way over and planted herself next to Ryker. "What's going on?"

Zach studied the man in the pod with caution. Ignoring Mabel, he asked Ryker, "Who is it?"

"How the fuck do I know?" Ryker replied. He pointed at the patch on the man's torso. "It says Prescott."

"I know, I know." It was the most obvious thing about him. "But how?"

"Someone better tell me what's happening right now," Mabel demanded.

The man began to stir, shifting on the rubber bed.

"There's no way he's been here all this time," Ryker said. He clasped his hands behind his head, suggesting he had a massive headache.

"You said you wanted your rescuers to find you," Zach reminded him. "You never checked the pods." As much as he wanted to pretend he never found the man, Zach's need for answers kept him in check. How long had the man been here? What did the patch on his chest mean? Prisoner? What crime would a colonist have committed? Everyone in Prescott was like family.

Zach wondered how long until the prisoner woke up and saw them staring down into his pod. It wouldn't be much of a warm welcome. But for all they knew, he didn't deserve one. Again, prisoner? Zach knew there were things his father didn't tell him, but this was among the biggest.

Another colonist. Alive.

No, no, they didn't know that yet. They didn't know anything about the guy. Where he came from, where he was going, and why he was on the Gateway. He could have been a stowaway that hopped onto their dropship before they left OSE. But then, he would have had to get onto the station, avoid being seen, and jump into the pods before they closed. The idea was preposterous, and Zach knew it. Somehow, someway, the man was already here. Asleep. Under the floor. For decades.

"Has he been here since..." The words caught in Ryker's throat. "Since *we* were?"

Zach thought about it, his father putting them in the pods while a criminal—possibly a murderer—slept beside them. "I don't know. Let's just take a step back and work this out. When he wakes up, we'll question him."

"We're not interrogators," Mabel pointed out.

"We can be." Zach ran his fingers through his hair. "We have to be."

The prisoner opened his eyes. He squinted against the bright light, then fixed his gaze on Zach. "Is my time up?"

Zach ignored the question. "Your name?"

"Erik Trivett." He itched his hair and propped himself up on his elbows.

"Are you from Prescott?"

"Of course. Where else would I be from?"

"What was your assignment?"

"I'm a geologist."

"Why were you in cryo?"

Erik hesitated, then sighed. "I stole rations."

Cryo-prison for stealing rations? That seemed a bit harsh. "When?"

"After the meteor." He sat up and swung his legs out of the pod. "Why all the questions? It's all in my file." With a yawn, he stretched his arms high and wide. "When can I see my daughter?" Zach tensed, unsure of how to answer. Before he could speak, Erik looked him up and down warily. "Wait. You're not a guard." His eyes darted to Ryker and Mabel, who were standing a few feet away. "None of you are."

"I'm Zach." Zach paused, then extended a hand. "Zach Croft."

Erik tentatively shook Zach's hand. "Croft? Like, Quinton Croft?"

"He was my father."

"Was?" Considering Zach's words, Erik glanced to the side. "Zach, you say?" His eyes found their way back. "That can't be. Zach is a kid."

Recognizing Erik's confused expression, Zach nodded. "We need to talk."

ZACH STARTED with the meteor and the destruction of the processing plant. Erik had been there then, so not much had to be said about it. Then came the part Zach was dreading: what happened after. He explained the Red Plague, how people started getting sick, and how they abandoned the colony. Recalling everything was painful for Zach, and detailing it all to Erik was even worse. But nothing compared to what he had to do next: breaking the news that twenty-three years had passed since.

Zach kept his voice steady, all the while feeling horrible for Erik. A few days ago, the guy was with his family. Happy, or as close as one could get to it in Prescott. The next moment, some random person was telling him that everyone he loved was dead. His daughter, his friends, everyone.

"Why did you wake me?" Erik asked, his voice trembling.

"We didn't know you were here."

"Oh? You didn't? Nice to know the council was gonna leave

me forever." Erik leaned his hands against the cryopod, letting his head hang low. "Are we home?"

"Not yet." Zach clenched his jaw. He couldn't yet break the news that Earth was basically doomed. It was too much for one person to handle all at once. "We're orbiting Mars."

"So, what? You guys never left? After all these years?"

"No, we left. And now we're back."

"Why?"

"For the irogen." The lights flickered as if tuning in to Zach's announcement.

"The irogen." Erik gaped at Zach in disbelief. "Not the people. The irogen." His voice began to get louder. "Nobody went back to see if anyone survived? They just left my daughter? And my brother?"

"I'm sorry," Zach whispered. "I really am."

Erik took a deep breath to calm down. "You were just a kid. It's not your fault." He squeezed his eyes shut as if trying to return to the darkness of cryo. "Twenty-three years." Then he opened his eyes and looked at Zach again. "Why are you here?"

"I told you—"

"No, *you*. Why are *you* here? Why come back after so long?"

Zach thought for a moment before responding. Everything had happened so quickly that he hadn't even really thought about why. Finally, he gave the best answer he could. "I'm trying to do better."

Zach explained the series of incidents that had led him back to the Gateway, in orbit around Mars, twenty-three years after he left Prescott. Still groggy with the sedative from cryo, Erik strained to understand. Zach mentioned Wilford and the files showing how much irogen was in the crater; it turned out that Erik knew the guy from before the mission. Zach told Erik about the solar flares and everything happening on Earth. Then he moved on to Alpha Cen, emphasizing the absolute urgency to get there before Earth went up in flames.

"I think I got it," said Erik. He waited a moment before elaborating. "You woke me up just in time for the end of the fucking world."

ZACH CROFT: 2030

Zach saw the crater in his dreams.

He saw the reddish sand beneath his feet, the rocky walls surrounding him on all sides, the pale orange sky towering above. These did not seem out of the ordinary. But other things seemed peculiar and out of place, as if they didn't belong in this memory. The impact site was covered in thick grass up to his knees. The mines were fully illuminated and broke off into dozens of rooms filled with scientists.

Oddly, no one noticed the ten-year-old boy roaming in their midst. He descended the elevator, the same as in real life, but level 13 was not a mineshaft at all. It was a cavern with no discernible floor, walls, or ceiling. Only crystals. Bright blues and purples, beautiful to the eye. But when he walked out over them, it felt like he was running over kitchen knives.

He awoke in a sweat, immediately clawing for his feet to confirm they were intact, then laid back against his pillow in exhaustion. What time was it again? Zach glanced at the clock on the wall and noted it was past noon. Why had nobody come to wake him up?

Never mind that. He had more important things to worry

about than breakfast. The dream reminded him of the backpack of crystals he and Ryker had stashed under the hab unit when they returned from the mine.

Zach scampered out of bed, cleaned his teeth, and went to move the floor panel. But when he looked into the space under the floor, it was empty. No bag in sight.

That wasn't good. Where was the bag? Zach strained to remember if this was where they put it, yanking up a few other floor panels to check. Had his father found it? He began to sweat at the thought but realized Quinton would have woken him up, furious. So his father hadn't found it, and Zach hadn't misplaced it. Who else would have gotten hold of the crystals?

Ryker.

He was the only other person Zach could think of, and frankly, he was the most likely suspect anyway. After all, Ryker didn't want to go into the crater because he didn't want to get caught. Was he trying to destroy the evidence as Zach sat there, doing nothing? He had to be.

Zach swiftly threw on some clothes, barreled out the door, then headed for the tunnels that lead to the crater. Any attempt to return to the mines would be risky, but it was the most likely place for Ryker to go. Dumping the crystals there, where everyone would expect them to be found, meant no connection would be made back to either of them.

As Zach neared the tunnels, he slowed his pace. Three guards carrying semi-automatic rifles stood around the mouth of the tubes, not threatening anyone but not being inviting either. Oh god, it had to be because of him and Ryker. Someone had discovered their foray into the mines and had ordered guards to stand watch. Zach only hoped it was for a different reason.

Zach veered away from the tunnels and tried to guess where else Ryker might be. He recalled their conversation a few nights ago about the upcoming week. Zach claimed he had to study for their upcoming science test, while Ryker said something about learning to drive a rover.

With that in mind, Zach set course for the rover garage. He crossed into the mecha district, passing a workshop with an engineer building a prosthetic leg. A side street brought him to the back of the rover garage, a giant building too mighty to be toppled by the meteor, and he entered through a smaller door. The smell of fuel and exhaust burned his nostrils, and although the giant roller doors were wide open, the interior of the garage was boiling.

A mechanic stopped Zach as he entered between two rovers. "Can I help you?" the man said in a gravelly voice. A cough rumbled through his chest, sounding like an unoiled engine. He wiped a dirty rag across his grimy forehead and leaned against the rover.

"Oh, yeah. I'm looking for my friend."

"Short kid, blonde hair?" the mechanic confirmed, fanning his torso with the collar of his shirt.

"That's the one."

"You just missed him, actually. Left five minutes ago." Then, he added, "Almost ran me over."

"Sorry about that. Thank you." Zach turned to leave when he noticed something weird about the mechanic. "What happened to your arm?" Zach pointed to a cluster of red bumps swelling from the man's forearm.

"Good question," the man said. "I just noticed them myself." He ran his finger over the bumps.

The same bumps that would kill him three days later.

RYKER GAGARIN: 2053

Erik was right there all those years, and Ryker never knew.

Would things have been different if he did? Would the days have gone by easier, hours passing more quickly? Would he have spent less time wandering aimlessly around the ship and more time caring for his sanity? Would he have been able to have real conversations with real voices instead of the ones in his head?

As Zach and Mabel discussed what to do with Erik, Ryker focused on everything he *could* have done. It seemed so pathetic. He knew that. Friendships were the last thing that mattered to him, but would one have been so terrible? Someone to chat with over breakfast, other than the monotonous Gateway AI.

On the other hand, something was eerie about Erik being there the whole time, asleep. It was like finding a corpse in your childhood home. Something just felt off about it, and Ryker wasn't sure how to feel.

"So, what do you suggest we do?" Zach asked, bringing Ryker back to the real world. The three of them were standing in the hall outside the storage room containing the cryopods. They had locked Erik inside so they could have a frank conversation without him listening in. It wasn't ideal to leave him unattended, but at least he was contained until they figured out what to do with him.

"We should bring him with us," Ryker suggested. Zach

looked at him like he was crazy. Before Zach could protest, Ryker continued. "I get it. You don't trust him."

"And you do?" Mabel asked, her eyebrows raised in surprise.

"I don't know, but I think we should give him a chance."

"Oh, hell no," Mabel said. "I barely trust you guys, and now him?" She gazed through the hall window into the vast blackness of space. "I say we leave him here."

"So he can take the ship and ditch us?" Zach said.

"Of course not. We'll put him back in cryo."

Ryker may have just met Erik, but he knew the guy wouldn't go for that. How could he, after his entire world was just upended? "Look, we can't treat him like a stray dog, okay? He's a person who's been through the same fucked up shit that I have."

Being asleep all that time didn't change it. They both lost people in Prescott, got trapped on the Gateway for decades, and emerged into a world so different from the one they remembered that none of it seemed real. In a lot of ways, Ryker saw himself in Erik. A warped, miserable version of himself, but still him nonetheless.

"We have a launch window that we can't risk missing. Especially not with this," Ryker continued, shooting a look in Mabel's direction. "Whether you realize it or not, he's in the same boat as us."

Mabel crossed her arms over her chest. "Do we even know if he's telling the truth? About what he was arrested for?"

"Why would he lie?" Ryker asked. "He's in shock."

"Either we get some answers, or he stays here," Mabel finished.

"I can't stay," Erik's voice called out from the other side of the door.

Zach cursed under his breath. "Shit. He heard us."

"Now, what do we do?" Mabel whispered.

Zach punched the access code into the control panel on the wall. The door to the storage room slid open. Erik stood there with pleading eyes. "Please. I have to find my daughter. Dead or alive."

Zach exchanged uncertain looks with Ryker and Mabel. Mabel shook her head.

"I don't want in on whatever you're doing," Erik continued. "I just want to find out what happened to her. I won't be a bother. Trust me."

Ryker spoke before Zach could decide for himself. "What was her name?"

Erik's eyes went glassy. "Sophia." He smiled, lost in a memory of the girl.

The room was quiet for a moment.

"Fine. You can come," Zach said, breaking the silence. "But you might not like what you find."

———

RYKER'S STOMACH turned to stone as the dome appeared in the dusty haze. His blood congealed. His muscles tightened. The closer the dropship got to the ground, the faster his heart beat.

Leaning against the control module, Ryker couldn't really see inside the dome. Every inch of the glass bubble was covered in dust and grime, making the whole thing look like a mole or pimple on Mars' sandy surface.

The dome itself was massive, maybe a mile or two in diameter. Ryker couldn't remember exactly how big it was. But it was big. The secondary dome, which covered the crater a few hundred meters away from the colony, was not nearly as big. It honestly shocked Ryker that it was still intact. After all, it wasn't made of the same meter-thick glass as the primary dome. Instead, it was built from a type of plastic that would retain its shape after being blown up like a balloon. It was efficient when the colonists needed a temporary air bubble, but Ryker couldn't have imagined it would survive this long.

At the front of the main dome, a long tube extended to a trio of stone landing pads. Ryker vaguely remembered that the pads had once been emblazoned with the Prescott emblem, though he could see no signs of lettering now. Worse, the pads were in complete disrepair, with deep fissures spanning their widths and jagged chunks reaching into the air.

"Shit," Ryker mumbled, drawing the attention of Zach and Mabel.

Zach straightened his back to look out the window. "What's wrong?"

"The landing pads are fucked," Ryker said. He switched to manual flight controls.

"Shit."

Ryker flicked a few switches and took hold of the flight sticks. The ship veered to the right, forcing Prescott out of view. Ryker scanned the landscape for a suitable place to land.

"What're you doing?" Zach asked.

"There's a sand flat." Ryker pointed at a wide clearing a few hundred meters from the dome. "We'll land there."

"So we have to walk?" Mabel complained.

"Yep. I hope you packed some sneakers." Ryker maneuvered the controls as the dropship quickly approached the ground. "Brace for landing."

Zach and Mabel tightened their restraints and pinched their eyes shut. Ryker could read the fear and anxiety on Zach's face. Sweat trickled down his forehead and dripped from his nose.

The dropship landed with a thud.

Ryker smiled at Zach as he opened his eyes. "Better than the last time?"

Zach breathed a shaky sigh of relief and swiped the sweat from his eyes. "Much."

TWENTY

ZACH'S BOOTS crashed down in the Martian soil, his gelatin legs struggling to keep him upright. His joints felt as though they had disappeared entirely, and as he inhaled, the suit forced decades-old air into his mouth like a balled-up T-shirt.

"Have you considered that Prescott is a biohazard, and we'd bring the Red Plague back to Earth?"

"The bodies are still there, Zach. In Prescott."

"Going back isn't going to solve anything."

It seemed like everything was trying to keep him away from Prescott, from Carver denying his request to return to Mars to the dropship outright disobeying them when they docked on the Gateway.

He stepped forward, sat beside the ramp, and waited for the others to join him. "Days are shorter here. Get a move on." Through the haze, Zach could just make out the shape of the colony, and he reminded himself of why they were there.

233

"How do we get the fuel onto the ship?" Ryker asked.

"Here's what I was thinking..." Zach started with the rover. They'd find one in the motor pool, load it with empty fuel drums, and drive it to the crater. There, they'd carefully pick as many irogen crystals as possible until they had filled all the drums. Half the crew would shuttle the drums back to the dropship while the others continued harvesting. They'd repeat the process until they had enough.

"Why would you go harvesting crystals when there's a tank?" asked Erik.

Zach hadn't a clue what Erik was talking about. "What tank?"

"The tank of irogen we filled up last wee—" Erik paused. "Sorry. The tank from back in the day. The one we managed to fill up before the meteor. It was last week for me."

"There's no way that wasn't destroyed," Ryker said.

Erik stomped his boot a few times. "Maybe. It was underground, though, so there's a chance it's still in one piece." His eyes found Zach. "The crystals take up a lot of space—it's the liquid inside the crystals that we need. If the tank's there, we should use it."

Zach considered Erik's suggestion. "Fair point. We'll start with the tank. If that doesn't work, we'll take the crystals. Agreed?"

"Agreed," everyone said.

Together, they left the comfort of the ramp and began the arduous trek through a rocky gorge. Zach studied the cliffs surrounding them. The dunes and rock formations created a landscape that reminded him of Utah or Arizona.

After a few minutes, the group had topped one of the

formations. The stale air in their suits provided little support, and they all found themselves gasping in exhaustion. Zach recognized the feeling from when he visited Big Bear as a child. It was always so damn hard to breathe, likely from the elevation.

Fearful of repeating history, Zach checked his wrist reader for O2 levels. Thankfully, they were stable and would be for a long time. One foot over the other, Zach watched his footprints disappear with the oncoming breeze and tried to remember the layout of Prescott.

He didn't have to search his memory for long—once he pictured the town hall, everything else fell into place. The ration dispensary. The residential district. Zach could remember them all. He wondered what the buildings would look like now. Would they be in ruins? He pictured his old hab unit, no more than a pile of scrap.

By the time they reached the colony, Zach's muscles had gone stiff. He didn't know whether it was fatigue or despair, but it left him almost unable to move.

Leading into the colony was a long, glass tunnel that extended out from the dome. At the end of it, the main airlock sat wide open. Zach didn't know why it was open or how long it'd been like that, but he wasn't sure he wanted to know.

A large sign, bent and corroded, greeted them as they entered. On it, Zach could just make out the words 'WELCOME TO PRESCOTT,' but he had trouble reading the smaller text below.

"What's all this?" Mabel asked, gesturing at the half-circle of barricades that surrounded the entrance. Most of the waist-high blocks were tipped over in the sand, though some remained upright, stained with what looked like dried blood. Straight ahead, the barricades met at a long line of railings extending into the sandy expanse.

It was the same story there. Many were half-buried in the Martian soil, while others stood tall in the orange haze. Zach shot a nervous glance at Ryker and continued walking. "It's just a security checkpoint... for when people came back from EVAs," he lied and averted his gaze. "The town's not far."

The group passed the barricades and carefully navigated the line of railings. In the distance, a stretch of buildings in no better shape than the checkpoint cluttered the horizon.

Those last few weeks in Prescott trickled into Zach's mind. He remembered the disrepair after the meteor, all the damaged homes. Even so, that paled in comparison to what he saw now.

Empty metal frames jutted from the dirt. Torn pieces of canvas flapped like flags against the foundations of decimated tents. The paved regolith streets were cracked and crumbling.

Looking out over the village, Erik glanced at him. "So, you just picked up and left?" His words had a bitter edge.

Zach barely shook his head. "It was more complicated than that."

The group traipsed through the colony silently, allowing a few well-deserved moments to collect their thoughts. Zach paced himself to not use his oxygen too quickly, doing his best to push away the haunting question that kept popping into his mind: where were all the bodies?

"Zach..." Ryker flagged him down.

Zach followed Ryker's eyes to the wall of a still-standing structure. He looked at the red and faded text splattered across the bumpy surface, his jaw dropping ever so slightly.

WE'RE ALL DEAD ANYWAY.

Then he realized why there were no bodies, no trace of the colonists' demise. He'd always avoided thinking of what happened after leaving the colony—to the settlement itself or the people left behind. With the Red Plague tearing through the population, it seemed like a given that they would have died quickly. But as Zach stared into the writing on the wall, he knew that wasn't true.

How long did they wait for rescue?

More and more people would have died every day, dozens becoming hundreds, graves getting harder to dig. Kids losing their parents. Wives losing their husbands. Day after day, the number of survivors would slowly diminish. Eventually, only one would remain. He'd look out over the colony with teary eyes, knowing his time would soon come.

Zach's legs shook as he kept walking, reading the messages scrawled on the walls as he passed.

WHY?

DAY 48.

NEVER COMING BACK.

The last message shook him the most. Initially, it read FORGIVE THEM, but another word had been added later, in a different color: NEVER.

NEVER FORGIVE THEM.

Eventually, Zach passed the graffitied buildings. Even though the words were out of sight, they stayed with him—they would be burned into his memory forever.

What had they done?

He wondered what the paint was made out of. Dirt, maybe?

That was red. Then, there was the darker possibility: it was blood. And lots of it.

Zach's boots crunched on something metal. He lifted his boot to look, then froze. He was standing on a pile of bullet shells. The type used in assault rifles. "What happened here?"

"Whatever it was, it wasn't good," Mabel commented, nodding toward a few automatic weapons piled in the dirt a few meters away. "This place gives me the chills. Can we get this over with?" Mabel took a shaky breath and passed the stack of rifles. The others followed, and the storage center came into view soon after. Half was entirely collapsed, lying in a heap beside the upright portion.

Upon their arrival, they discovered even more text on the wall. Only this one didn't have a cryptic message.

It was a list of names.

JOSE CURTIS

CRO JORDAN

LANCE FREMONT

It spanned the entire thirty-foot wall, each name carefully engraved. Zach noticed the similarities to Earth's Prescott Memorial. The remembrance wall. A shrine to all those who passed away. There was something sick and twisted about this version, though. No, maybe not sick, but so, so different. The monument back home was refined. Dignified. Made from expensive marble.

Then, there was this. A steel wall with jagged carvings, the pocket knife used to make them still plunged carelessly in the sand. Zach kicked it aside and dragged his hand over the etchings.

He scanned the names and recognized a few. John Stouts, a

doctor Quinton had worked with. Emma Heymont. Edgar Ferrano. Seraphine Reiner. Many were in their twenties and thirties. Now, they were gone, destroyed. Buried somewhere under the irradiated soil.

Zach noticed Erik scanning the names, likely looking for his daughter. What was her name again—Sophia something? Sophia Trivett. That was it. Erik's eyes opened wide behind his visor, and he whispered something inaudibly. "Not here," he said louder. "She's not here." A smile crossed his face.

That doesn't mean she's alive, Zach thought. But he just smiled too. "That's good, Erik. That's good." Sometimes false hope is better than no hope. Zach stopped and motioned to the group to huddle up. "Okay, let's get this sorted. We need some kind of containers to transport the irogen in. Mabel and I will find something for that." He pointed at Ryker. "You and Erik head to the rover garage. Find one that works and bring it back here. Got it?"

RYKER GAGARIN: 2053

"I'll help you get the rover, but nothing else," Erik said to Ryker as they crossed through the mecha district. "I don't want to get tied up in whatever y'all are doing here."

"Fine by me," Ryker answered. The sky had gotten lighter, a grayish color quickly filling with orange.

Erik angled his chin to the heavens. "You know, it was night the first time I saw this place."

Ryker wrinkled his brow. "Didn't we land during the day?"

"I spent the first week in the infirmary, so I didn't have a chance to see it."

"That's a shame."

"When I was discharged, my daughter ran up and hugged me. The first thing I said to her was," he cracked a slight smile, "'aren't you up past your bedtime?'"

Ryker breathed a laugh. "Then what?"

"Then, she showed me our living quarters. She made me a Welcome Home sign out of whatever junk she could salvage from the crash. Only she didn't have enough to make the last 'E,' so it just said 'Welcome Hom.'" He laughed at the memory.

Ryker chuckled too. "She sounds like a great kid." His words lapsed into silence.

Up ahead, there were more signs of a firefight. A dozen bullet holes were punched through a hab unit wall and what looked like a barricade nearby. A helmet was tipped over beside it.

"She'd be my age now," Erik said. "Or is... I don't know." His voice broke, and he shrugged. "I'm sorry. It's just..."

"I get it," Ryker assured. "Everything you're going through, I have too." He didn't mean to make it a competition but was worried it would come off like that.

"How?"

"I watched both my parents die." Ryker went to itch his forehead but hit the spacesuit's helmet instead. He changed the subject. "Also, you and I were neighbors."

Erik looked around. "Here?"

"No, not here. Well, I don't know. Maybe," Ryker said. "I'm talking about the Gateway."

"Let me guess: Cryo slumber party?"

Ryker laughed. "Not that, no. I was there just as long as you were, only... awake. The whole time."

"For twenty-three years?"

"For twenty-three years," Ryker repeated. "I was just a kid."

"Holy shit, man. How did you do it?"

Ryker shrugged. "I figured shit out. Didn't have much choice."

They walked another few minutes before Erik realized they were going in the wrong direction. He pointed to where the rover garage was.

"I know," Ryker said. "We're making a pit stop first. It won't take long."

"Where?"

"My father's grave. I want to see if they buried my mother there too." With everything she sacrificed for her family, a proper burial was the least they could do. She deserved it. When Cage had volunteered for Prescott, Kayla initially opposed it. *"Ryker should have a normal childhood,"* she had said. But when Cage explained the flares, about how bad they'd get, Kayla reluctantly agreed.

As Ryker felt Cage's ring through his glove, he wished his mother *hadn't* been so nice. Maybe she would have stood her ground and rejected the idea of leaving Earth. Things would have turned out so differently. "I don't know what happened to her after she died."

"How did you get over it?" asked Erik.

"Honestly? I didn't."

Erik gave it some thought. "That wasn't the answer I was looking for."

"But it's the truth." Ryker could have sugar-coated it. He could have told Erik everything gets easier. That one morning, he'd wake up and think, *Sophia? I've never heard of her!* But he wasn't a liar. Things wouldn't get better unless he built up his defenses. Grew numb to the pain. It was the only way to move past it. "It was our fault. Me and Zach," Ryker said bitterly.

"What was?"

"This." He motioned to the ruined colony. "The Red Plague. Everything. We snuck into the crater and brought some irogen crystals back to the colony. And right after that, people started getting sick. It wasn't a coincidence. It wasn't just bad luck. It was us."

"It was *you*?" asked Erik. "It was... it was... it..." He trailed off, looked at the ground, and thought something over. "You brought back crystals..." His mouth fell slightly open as he was consumed by thought. He took a deep breath, then glanced back up at Ryker. "You didn't know. You couldn't have known."

"We didn't. But that doesn't make it okay."

"No. But we can't go back and undo it. So, let it go." He stepped over a pile of rubble and continued walking. "Let's find your mom."

Ryker caught up with Erik. Together, they wove through the metal labyrinth before reaching a stretch of empty sand. It went on for a few hundred meters, leading into a slope about halfway in. "It should be just up..." Ryker stopped. "Here."

Where he expected to see five, possibly ten graves, there were hundreds. Mounds of dirt, most with markers made of debris jutting from them, spanned as far as the eye could see. Was everyone buried here? Ryker could recall there only being a few; the council wasn't big on taking up colony space for 'non-essentials.' They only allowed Cage to be buried there because of his ties to Quinton.

Ryker walked between the mounds, searching for his

father's grave. He identified Cage's headstone about thirty feet in and knelt beside it. What was he supposed to say? Could he say things were going well? That would be a lie. The world was falling apart more and more every day, and it'd be silly to say something to the contrary. What, then? *Hey, dad. No matter how often life fucks me, I'll always live to see another day!* Finally, he mumbled, "I'm sorry this happened to you."

Next, he searched for his mother's grave. Part of him was unsure it would even exist given the circumstances of her death, but he couldn't believe that the others would have left her to rot. Finally, he found it. He gave a tired smile. "Hey, mom."

The grave was nicer than the others. Not by much, but noticeably so. The mound was a little neater, the metal used for her marker flat and rectangular, resembling a headstone. "I'm happy to see they took care of you." The thought of her lying dead in that hab unit for who-knows-how-long found its way back into Ryker's thoughts.

God, he missed her so much. Everyday. He hadn't been that close to his father, but his mother... She was something special. And the fact that she was gone still seemed unbelievable.

Ryker glanced over his shoulder, scanning for Erik. He spotted him crouched over one of the graves, the face of his helmet cupped in one palm. Carefully, Ryker approached without startling him. The tombstone came into view.

"Do you think she was alone?" Erik asked. "When she..." The last word stuck in his throat.

Ryker got down on his knees beside Sophia's grave. "Hey," was all he could manage before Erik abruptly stood up. "At least you know for sure."

"She was just a girl." Erik's resolve crumbled. He began to quietly weep.

Ryker placed a steady hand on Erik's shoulder. Seeing Erik like this made the man's losses feel like Ryker's own. As if their shared trauma somehow bound them together. He had been in Erik's shoes more than once. More times than he could count, in fact.

After a minute or two, Erik regained his composure. He stood and faced Ryker. His expression was grim but determined. "I'll help," he said.

"What?"

"With the irogen." He pulled in a sharp breath. "Sophia's dead. I don't want her to have died for nothing."

ZACH CROFT: 2053

The rover pulled up in a whirl of dust. Zach loaded the drums inside, then climbed up after them. He turned to help Mabel before shifting his attention to Ryker in the driver's seat. "What took so long?"

Ryker waved his hand as if swatting away a fly. "It was a long walk." The rover rolled forward, sputtering and jerking as it picked up speed. Zach was unsure whether to blame Ryker's shabby driving skills or the machine's twenty-year neglect. It was probably both.

"Is it safe to take off our helmets?" Mabel asked.

Ryker turned down an alley between the schoolhouse and the canteen. "I barely got this thing to start. So, probably not."

Mabel dropped her hands. "What's the point of it being sealed off if it doesn't have air?" Annoyed, she stared through the foggy window, squinting to make out the surrounding structures.

A relative calm occupied the next few minutes as decimated buildings rolled past. Zach pressed his eyes shut, willing his thoughts to cease.

"What the fuck...?" Ryker suddenly muttered with his mouth ajar.

Zach opened his eyes, looked out the window, and immediately wished he hadn't. Hanging from the crossbeam of a partially collapsed building were five desiccated bodies in blue and black fatigues. Nooses of metal wire suspended them high into the air. Across the chest of each one, white paint spelled out *TRAITOR*.

Zach felt his stomach turning. His mind went blank. He had expected to see bodies in the colony, but not this. Not corpses strung up for public display.

"I think I'm gonna be sick," Mabel groaned.

"Is there anything else you want to tell me about what went on here?" Erik asked firmly.

"I have no idea. Really." Zach searched his mind for answers but came up dry. "I— I don't know—"

"He's telling the truth," Ryker said, glancing at Erik. "This must have happened after we left."

When they reached the tunnels leading to the crater, Ryker slowed the rover to a stop so they could get out and inspect the landscape. Zach stepped out of the vehicle and tried to make sense of his surroundings.

This was it. This was where it all started. His foray into the mines with Ryker had brought the Red Plague back to the colony, resulting in hundreds of deaths and leading to the failure of the entire Prescott mission, along with humanity's best chance of escaping the solar flares.

And now he was back.

While Zach lingered beside the rover, Ryker jumped out and ambled to a steep drop-off into the crater. As he drew near, he froze, then turned and motioned frantically for Zach to join him. "Zach!"

"What's the matter?" Zach called out through the intercom.

"Check this out!"

Zach went to Ryker and stopped at the edge of the dropoff. He grabbed Ryker's arm to steady himself.

As he scanned the crater, he didn't know whether to smile or scream.

CORA KEATON: 2053

"This is a day of mourning," Carver said, adjusting the lapel of his fine black suit as his eyes dragged across a sheet of paper on the podium. He held back tears. "We have lost not one but *two* of our dearest friends."

Friends, Cora thought. Zach was so much more than that. He was a brother, someone to rely on when things got tough, a good person with a good heart. The list of Zach's merits was so long that Cora couldn't finish it in one go. Instead, she stared straight ahead with a stony glare.

She knew she should be crying. People expected it of her. But how would that help Zach now? Breaking down in a sobbing fit would only make things harder. Instead, Cora ran her fingers over the coarse fabric of her dress, tracing them in circles to take her mind off the ceremony.

Carver's voice boomed from the stage. "I knew Zach better than anyone. He was my apprentice and the closest I'll ever get to a son. I'll never forget all he did for me. For this agency."

Cora didn't know why Carver was leading the proceedings. It felt like the memorial should have been led by a priest or someone like that. Then again, Zach hadn't been particularly religious, and Carver was closer to him than almost anyone.

Almost.

Cora and Zach had spent decades together. She didn't have a single memory that he wasn't a part of, from her fifth birthday, to graduating college, to the countless hours they spent jogging through the park. *This* park.

The wreckage had been cleared, and the city had filled the large craters it left behind with fresh soil. But it didn't matter. Nothing grew in the new patches of land, as if the plants could sense it was hallowed ground.

I really failed this time, Cora thought. She had been unable to protect Zach. The promise she made to him twenty-three years ago—that nothing bad would ever happen to him again—had been broken. How could she have let him do this? How had she not tried harder to talk him out of it? It was her one job! And she couldn't even do that.

She watched Carver lean against the podium. "In many ways, I saw myself in him," he continued, making Cora wince.

Zach was nothing like him, not in a single way. Carver was selfish, controlling, and, most recently, a liar. Suggesting they were at all alike was an insult to everything Zach stood for.

If her job wasn't on the line, Cora would have punched Carver across the jaw right then and there, smiling as he hit the ground in a crumpled heap. The nerve he had, standing up there while he pretended to give a shit. If he cared about Zach, he would have trusted him when Zach said the solar flares were getting worse. He would have funded Exodus. He would have authorized Zach's request to return to Mars to harvest the newly-discovered irogen. And Zach would still be alive.

It had been a month since Cora saw Zach's ship descending from the sky. The hope she had felt, thinking he was coming home, had been overwhelming. Then, the dropship exploded. She dodged falling bits of debris, barely able to catch her breath before the world erupted into flames. Chunks of metal burrowed into the ground as soot rained on her face. Trees were set ablaze. Fire trucks filled the streets. EMTs arrived and took her into their care, wiping her face clean. In those moments, she remembered thinking—was it Zach's ashes they were wiping off? Mixed with burnt wood, vaporized composite, and god-knows-what else? Cora hadn't gotten a good night's rest since, tossing and turning for a few hours before giving up and watching reality TV until the sun came up. At this point, she practically survived off coffee and stale bagels. But who could blame her? She had just lost her best friend.

A few days ago, her mother had come by with a large basket of wine and chocolate, claiming the sweet stuff helped her through Victor's death. Unwrapping it, Cora assured Sarina she was doing fine, though her voice showed little confidence. They reminisced about the past for a while, then clocked out on the couch. Sarina had wanted to come to the funeral today, but Cora informed her that only OSE personnel were in attendance; they could honor him once she got home. With a saddened look, Sarina nodded. *"Go along, then. Don't want to be late."*

Cora looked away from Carver, her eyes settling on a table beside the main stage. It boasted framed pictures of Mabel and Zach. The shrine had been set up in their honor, compensating for the fact that their bodies had never been recovered. It seemed dumb to bury two empty coffins. But that's what OSE was doing.

Jason sat next to Cora, nodding at Carver's words of sorrow with one hand clutching a handkerchief and the other closed into a fist. Cora patted him on the back, whispering, "It's okay."

"Today, we join their spirits with the Earth, as their lives were so swiftly taken from them," continued Carver, looking from person to person, face to face. His eyes settled on Cora. "Ms. Keaton? Would you like to say a few words?"

Hearing her name, Cora nodded and mumbled a soft "Yes." She reached down under her seat. Her fingers closed around what was left of Zach's sweater, and she stood, holding it tight in her arms.

Cora cut through the lines of chairs and people, approaching the podium. When she reached it, Carver bowed his head and stepped aside, allowing her to take his place. For a few seconds, Cora surveyed the crowd and studied each member.

"Zach," she started, "was a brother to me as he was a son to Nicolas." Good. Getting a few Carver mentions would dilute the hatred she felt for him right now. "There was a time... We were thirteen or fourteen, and I broke my leg while mountain biking. The closest hospital was a few miles away, but neither of our phones had reception. While I was lying there, half-conscious, with my ankle shattered, Zach had to make a tough decision: leave me there and get help, or pray that someone found us." She went quiet for a moment, reaching up to wipe her eyes. "Then, there was a third choice: pick me up and trek four miles to the clinic, not stopping until I was on a stretcher. Which do you think he did?"

There were murmurs of assent from the audience.

"It took three hours. By the time we got there, he was too weak to stand and had to be admitted alongside me. I don't know what would have happened if he didn't do what he did. Would help have eventually come? How long would we have been stuck there? I'm just grateful I never had to know."

Carver took back the stage and celebrated Zach's good nature with some experiences of his own, then handed the charred piece of his sweater to someone just off the platform. The shred of fabric was carried to the empty coffin and placed inside. Was that truly all they had left of him?

At the reception, Cora stared helplessly into the void with a glass of champagne in hand. She reluctantly ate a serving of pasta, thinking of Zach until every ounce was gone.

On occasion, someone would offer their condolences. Cora would explain that he'd live on through them all and through his work. *The work Carver ignored.*

There Carver was, nursing a glass of whiskey as he accepted apologies from all around.

"He was a great boy. You did a good job, Nicolas."

"The smartest guy I've ever met!"

"You guys were two peas in a pod. I'm sorry."

If it wasn't for Carver, Zach might have still been alive.

He was to blame.

TWENTY-ONE

ZACH CROFT: 2053

ZACH WONDERED if he was dreaming. He walked a few feet forward and sat on the crater's edge. Mabel approached him from behind. She breathed heavily into the intercom as she asked, "Is that...?" before trailing off.

After a moment, Zach finished her sentence for her. "Irogen."

Light refracted off thousands of blue and purple crystals, sending rays in all directions. The crystals covered every last inch of the crater, growing at all angles and in more sizes than Zach could count. Some were long and narrow, reaching up the walls of the crater. Others were crowded in small, crystalline clusters that reminded Zach of giant sea urchins. The light streaming through them was so brilliant that Zach could barely look at them.

Erik's voice crackled through the intercom. "Shit."

Ryker turned to look at him. "What's wrong?"

"The irogen tank is on the other side, in the mine."

"So, fuck the tank," Ryker said. "We'll just take the crystals."

Zach joined Ryker and nodded in agreement. "I agree. Let's do this the easy way and get the hell out."

"We could," Erik admitted, "but it might not be enough."

"Why not?" Mabel asked.

Erik gestured to the jagged remains of the mining operation. "The whole point of this place—of Prescott—was twofold: irogen mining *and processing*. The mining is just the first part. The processing is what extracts the fuel from the crystals. The crystals themselves are useless, and they take up a ton of space. One tank of liquid irogen has probably a hundred times more fuel than a tank full of crystals. It's like the difference between a barrel of firewood and a barrel of jet fuel."

"We should get as much as we can while we're here, right?" Mabel asked Zach rhetorically. "Unless we're planning on coming back for more."

"No, you're right. That makes sense." He motioned to the field of glittering crystals. "Let's just drive over the crystals. The rover can handle it. We'll get the tank, load it up, and go."

"That's a great plan if you don't mind exploding into a billion tiny pieces." Off of Zach's confused look, Erik continued. "Irogen is UV reactive. Enough solar radiation and it goes boom."

Zach looked at the dim, orange sun through the murky sky. Ryker did, too, then said what Zach was thinking. "So, why haven't they exploded? The sun's right there, Erik."

Erik breathed a smile. "The crystals absorb the UV. But if you crush them by, for example, driving over them with a rover..." Erik looked up at the dust-streaked dome overhead. "They'll be scraping chunks of us off the dome for a month."

"So, what do we do?" Zach asked.

"Hang on," Mabel burst out, her eyes turning angry and shifting to Zach. "You're asking *him* for a plan?"

"Do you have one?"

"What would we have done if we hadn't found Mr. Convict over here? Just blown ourselves up?"

"I'm not a convict," Erik remarked bitterly. "I'm a scientist. I only stole food to feed my kid. And you would have done the same."

Ryker put his hand on Erik's chest to calm him down. "Hey, relax. Let's just wait until the sun goes down. Would that work?"

Before Erik could answer, Zach tapped the oxygen readout on his sleeve. "We can't wait that long. We don't have enough oxygen."

Mabel threw up her hands in disbelief. "This is nuts! So what, do we just leave?"

"We'll clear a path," Zach replied, trying to sound more confident than he felt. "For the rover."

"Will that work?" Mabel asked Erik doubtfully.

"It—" Erik's voice snagged. "It's a bad idea. If one of those crystals breaks, we're going up in flames."

"We're going up in flames no matter what," concluded Ryker. He bent down and carefully wiggled an irogen crystal free from the crater's edge. "Might as well get started now."

"We'll be careful," Zach assured Erik.

"Oh, you'll be *careful*? Why didn't you just say so?" Erik

declared, fiddling with the belt of his suit. "I was all worried for nothing."

Zach watched Erik in the corner of his eye. "Are you going to help or not?"

"I..." Erik opened his mouth to speak, then quickly shut it and scanned the crater. He squinted at the crystals, likely searching for a path through them. His eyes shifted to the sky. "I guess I'm not getting home if you blow yourselves up."

Zach located a slope leading into the crater and led the way. The group spent the next hour carefully clearing a path to the mines. They plucked crystals from the ground one at a time, inspecting each for cracks before setting them in a neat pile next to the ramp.

After clearing a route through the forest of glowing spikes, they returned to the rover and drove it down the slope until they faced the path head-on. It was crooked in places, pock-marked with footprints and divots from the plucked crystals. Ahead of them, the dark and unwelcoming mouth of the mines threatened to devour them. At various points around the crater, other mouths opened into other parts of the mines. But according to Erik, the one just ahead housed the tank.

Craning his neck, Ryker inspected the path immediately in front of the rover. Then, he slowly pressed on the gas, remaining hunched over the wheel as the vehicle crept forward. Zach and Mabel kept their eyes on the sides, warning Ryker when he veered too far to the left or right.

Through the slit windows, it looked like they were driving through a crystalline forest. The spikes of irogen rose six, seven, even eight feet into the sky, with thick, translucent undergrowth filling in the gaps between the larger crystals.

Zach could imagine a crystal bunny or squirrel curving between the pikes, burrowing into the soil underneath, or skittering into the road.

After a few tense minutes, the rover halted before the hollow socket at the end of the crater. The darkness inside was flat, textureless, and all-consuming. It seemed to absorb the light outside and cast a shadow on the blood-colored sand, turning it a demonic crimson. Broken rails extended a few feet from the opening, an iron tongue flanked by teeth of warped metal. Swirls of dust rose as the darkness exhaled red powder on the rover. Zach swore the mine snarled at them.

"This thing got headlights?" asked Erik, leaning between the front seats with his hands clamped around both.

"Yep." Ryker reached under the steering wheel and flicked a switch.

In succession, two bright beams shot from either side of the rover and punctured the dark opening of the mines. Inside, the metal walls were twisted and broken, with jagged rock protruding from underneath. A few feet in, a pair of lightbulbs swung from a corroded wire, taunting a third that had fallen to the ground and shattered years ago. All over the floor, bits of litter and scrap metal jutted from the sand. Farther down, Zach could see intact steel floors and cross beams that weren't sagging and pocked with holes.

Only fifty feet of the long corridor were visible with the light. Further down, the tunnel grew dimmer and dimmer until Zach was once again left peering into the darkness.

"Let's get this over with," Zach said, then opened the rover door. Dust whooshed around his boots as they landed in the sand, forming a cloudy haze that spiraled up his frame before dispersing into the surrounding air.

With the help of Erik, Zach unloaded the oil drums from the back of the rover and carried them carefully to the mouth of the mines. Then, Ryker shut off the rover's headlights to save energy. When the blackness reemerged, so did Zach's dread.

"How far in do we have to go before we reach the tank?" inquired Ryker.

"Not sure," Erik answered and flicked on his helmet light.

The others quickly followed suit, and before long, they had picked the drums back up and plunged into the wicked tunnel before any of them could think twice.

Columns of light streaming from their helmets illuminated the dusty air. As they looked around, the columns clashed and crossed one another, haphazardly flitting from the floor to the walls to the ceiling. From the sound beneath their boots, there were still partial metal floor panels in this part of the mine; a thin layer of sand had simply blown in from the crater. Before long, the sand seemed to thin out, revealing the solid floor underneath.

Patches of crystals sprung up along the edges of the walls in irregular intervals. In the tunnel's darkness, the spikes faintly glowed, vibrated, sang. Zach didn't know what made the crystals glow or why they grew like weeds in the cracks of a sidewalk, but boy were they beautiful.

"Where is this damn tank?" Impatiently, Ryker walked a few meters ahead of the group.

"Slow down," said Zach in a firm tone.

"We're moving too slow, all right?" Soon, all that remained

of Ryker was his voice on the radio. His footsteps grew more distant and faint before they seemed to cease altogether.

Mabel dragged her hand along the steel wall, slowing down a bit. "See anything...?"

Ryker didn't respond. It was as if the darkness had eaten him alive.

"Ryker?" Mabel asked shakily. "Do you see anything?"

"You all right?" Erik called out over the radio.

"I'm not going anywhere, okay? I'll tell you what I see." Ryker coughed. "A fucking disappointment."

The others caught up to him a hundred feet up and looked upon a sudden gap in the floor. It spanned maybe ten feet across, jagged and wiry around the edges and opening into a lower floor of the mines. A pool of broken glass and red sludge completely coated the ground below.

"That's it," Erik said in a deflated voice. He strode away as if too disappointed to look. "Floor must've given way."

"And no explosion?" questioned Ryker.

"There's no sunlight."

Zach groaned. "Okay. New plan. We'll harvest crystals here —where it's safe—then Ryker and Mabel, you can shuttle the drums to the dropship. By the time you get back, Erik and I will be ready with more."

With their joints aching and their lungs heaving, the quartet did their best to pluck crystals from the ground and deposit them into the drums they had lugged down the tunnel. The crystals here seemed to have deeper roots than the ones outside and required massive force to rip each out.

As Zach dropped an armful of crystals into one of the drums, they rattled like gumballs before settling in a glowing pile. Sighing, he turned his head to the ceiling, where he spotted a crooked air vent. He could barely make out a subtle purple hue behind the grate.

It took half an hour to fill up the first drum. Then, they worked together to carry the loaded canister back to the rover. Luckily, Mars' low-gravity environment, combined with the low density of the irogen crystals, made it relatively easy to move.

Once the rover was loaded, Zach clapped Ryker on the shoulder and sent him and Mabel off to the dropship. As they drove away, Zach bent over his knees and tried to catch his breath. His eyes found Erik, who was dusting sand off his gloves. Zach felt a strange pit in his stomach. Erik had spent the longest time in cryo of any human in history. He was a man out of time. Zach could hardly comprehend the fact that he was real. He was a living, breathing man, probably born around the same time as Zach's father. And there he was, the same age as Zach. Zach felt torn between treating Erik as an elder or as an equal. Where was the manual for this sort of thing?

"You gonna stare at me, or are you gonna help me pull more crystals?"

Feeling called out, Zach sniffled and returned to work. After a bit, he broke the awkward silence. "Did you ever see me as a kid?"

Erik paused with his hands fixed around a particularly stubborn crystal. "Once, I think." His brow tightened. "That retreat... back in Big Bear. You were with your blonde friend too." Erik nodded toward the opening of the tunnel.

Zach tried to recall seeing Erik but couldn't quite remember. He nodded silently to himself, then turned and said, "I'll have to take your word for it."

Erik dislodged the crystal. "What's your stake in this whole thing anyway? I'm sure you've got things to lose. And taking one look at this place," Erik scanned the tunnel, "it doesn't seem like there's much to gain." Zach started to answer, but Erik stopped him. "I mean you personally. I get the whole world ending thing, but why you?"

"Having things to lose isn't an excuse to do nothing." Zach rolled a crystal in his hand, feeling its heft, then placed it in the single drum that remained behind. "If I had nothing to lose, I'd have nothing to fight for." Zach thought of Cora. He thought of his work. His colleagues. Hell, he even thought of Carver.

The tunnel fell silent, and they spent the next half hour harvesting crystals without another word.

"We're on our way back," Ryker said over the intercom. "Maybe ten minutes out."

"Sounds good—" The ground under Zach wobbled. Dust rained from the ceiling in a single, fluttering burst, coating his visor in a thick haze.

"What the hell...?" started Erik. A second rumble knocked them both off their feet. Then, a third shook the walls. Erik made eye contact with Zach, jaw clenched, and swallowed. "Explosions."

They looked at the tunnel entrance a few hundred feet back, then hastily got up. Sweat poured down Zach's back, making his skin sticky against the rubber interior of the suit. "Ryker, did you run over a damn crystal?" Zach tried to keep his calm.

"Huh? Of course not."

Erik breathed an angry smile. "You sure about that?"

"I— I—I don't think so, but..."

"We don't have time for buts!" Erik yelled. He looked firmly at Zach. "We've gotta get out of here."

A boom sounded above them. A few rocks fell from the ceiling. "Look, if the crater's exploding, we can't go through there!" Zach shouted.

"This tunnel's exploding, too, and I don't see another way out! Come on!" Erik pushed Zach toward the exit.

"What about the crystals?" Zach pointed back at the nearly-full drum next to the hole in the floor.

"Screw the crystals! We have enough!"

"I'm not leaving without them."

Erik looked at Zach with burning eyes, then bit his lip, cursed under his breath, and shoved Zach in its direction. "Get it, and let's go!"

An explosion in the wall sounded, and a pair of panels flew free. The rock behind the plates disintegrated, revealing a crawlspace full of crystals.

Zach hurried to the barrel and wrapped his arms around it. Dropping to a squat, he channeled as much force through his legs as gravity would allow and attempted to lift it. After hoisting it a few inches into the air, he dropped it with a thud. "It's too heavy!"

Erik grunted in frustration and ran to Zach's aid. Angry veins bulged in his forehead, looking as though they, too, would explode any second. Together, the two men lifted the drum and started for the exit. Then, another explosion in the wall threw them both to the side. The drum toppled over, and all the crystals spilled out. Several cracked, dripping red ooze into the sand. Zach looked at them with wide eyes, breathing heavily, then got to his feet and pulled Erik up. "Screw the drum."

They ran for the exit with the ground rumbling beneath them.

Boom.

Boom.

Boom.

A large chunk of the ceiling came loose and crashed down behind them. Sunlight poured in, chasing them as they ran in the opposite direction.

Boom.

Boom.

Boom, by Zach's ankles.

Up ahead, Zach could see a series of explosions in the crater bordering the path they had paved. It seemed comical that they were running toward the detonations, but what else could they do? As if the planet had a beating heart, the ground, walls, and ceiling thumped, releasing a constant mist of blood-colored sand.

"What's going on in there?" Ryker's voice suddenly penetrated Zach's intense concentration. "We're coming now!"

"Are those explosions?" Mabel yelled. "Are you guys out of the tunnel?"

"No, no, we're not. Get as close as possible, and we'll come to you!" Zach shouted.

Boom.

Boom.

BOOOOOM!

A truck-sized boulder fell from the ceiling and crashed

down onto the ground. A cloud of dust erupted in the tunnel as Zach stumbled forward. He landed on his palms, the world blending into flat shapes and colors around him. He slowly rose to his elbows and looked back, uttering Erik's name.

Zach crawled to where the boulder landed and grabbed hold of something rubber. A glove. No, no, there was a hand inside of it too. In an instant, Zach registered he was holding Erik. The dust cleared around him, and Erik's unconscious form appeared, lying still in the sand. The boulder leaned against the wall, with Erik's leg pinned beneath it.

Zach located Erik's helmet and tapped it a few times. "Hey, hey, buddy. Can you hear me?" Nothing. "Come on! Can you hear me?"

"What happened?" called Ryker.

"Erik's pinned! We need your help! Get down here!" Zach slapped Erik's helmet a few more times. "Please, come on, wake up. Wake up, come on."

Erik gasped awake, choking on air. He clutched at his chest, attempting to regulate his breathing, before he leaned back and exhaled. His eyes rolled in his head.

"Just stay put!" Zach said. "They're coming to help."

Boom.

Two booms overhead.

A muffled blast deep in the mines behind them.

A roar from beneath the crater itself.

At that moment, Zach saw a grim future laid out before them. That last explosion came from a lower level of the mines —the same mines that ran under Prescott. In order for irogen to have spread to the surface, it must have filled up the mines and run out of room to expand. That meant there were probably crystals underneath the entire colony—and the colony was about to explode.

Erik looked down at his crushed leg and began to wail in agony. His cries filled the intercoms, sickening Zach. Not knowing what else to do, Zach took Erik's wrist—where his suit's control board was—and disabled his intercom. Even then, his voice was still audible through the visor, through the dust, and through Zach's labored breathing.

The rover sped through the crater, caring little for the crystals it ran over, and continued straight into the mines. It stopped just in front of Zach and Erik. Ryker and Mabel emerged from it, ran over, and crashed down beside Erik's squirming body.

"Is his suit breached?" asked Mabel.

"I don't know," Zach answered.

"He'd be dead if it was." Ryker eyed Erik.

Mabel gave Zach a pained, sympathetic look, then jumped back to her feet. "We have to move the boulder."

Erik swung his hand and slapped his opposing wrist. Gurgling, he said, "Leave me," and gritted his teeth in pain. "Get— get out of here!"

"We're not leaving you," said Zach.

"Come on, let's do this," barked Ryker from beside the boulder.

Zach got his footing and joined them next to the boulder. They all dropped to a squat, burrowing their fingers beneath the rock, and drove up with their legs.

The boulder didn't move.

"We have to push it, tip it, something!" Ryker yelled.

Boom.

Boom.

Boom, at the mouth of the mines.

"If we push it, it might rupture his suit and kill him," said Mabel, as calm as she could.

"We're all dead if we don't!" Ryker retorted.

Mabel looked at Erik, then back at Ryker. "Fine."

As a particularly heavy explosion rumbled the ground, all three of them assumed pushing positions around Erik. They dug their heels into the ground, pressed their palms against the rock, and pushed as hard as they could. At first, it didn't move in the slightest. But then, it wobbled a bit, teetered, then rolled backward and released Erik.

As the rock tumbled away, Zach thanked low gravity and turned his attention back to Erik. With the boulder dislodged, Erik's leg was entirely in view. The rubber exterior of the suit seemed intact, but the leg itself appeared flattened and twisted. It was as if every bone in Erik's leg had been broken, melted in a three-thousand-degree oven, and reformed like Play-Doh.

Working together, Zach, Ryker, and Mabel lifted Erik and transported him to the rover. Taking his seat, Zach stared off vacantly through the front window. The engine started, and the rover rolled forward.

It wasn't until they were nearly free of the tunnels that Zach realized their path was now covered in sharp, dripping, bubbling crystals.

ZACH CROFT: 2030

"We've got to get a handle on this," Quinton said, cupping his face in his palms. "We've already lost six people."

Through a crack in the medbay wall, Zach could see a doctor sitting beside his father, fidgeting with a pen. "The symptoms all seem to be related. Bumps under the skin, bruises, sores."

"Plus, internal bleeding," Quinton added grimly. "Coughing up blood. Crying blood." Quinton got up and seized a file on top of a cabinet, flipping through it. "It's got to be some type of hemorrhagic fever."

"You think it's a virus? Like Ebola? Or Marburg?"

"Maybe, but here? On Mars? How?"

Zach leaned back against the outer wall of the newly rebuilt medbay. If his father didn't know what was causing the illness, nobody did. Which meant more people were going to die. A lot more.

"Think it's airborne?" the other doctor asked.

"Seems unlikely, or more people would have gotten sick. All of us, for that matter." Right. They were literally under a dome. "It could be transmitted by touch. Or food, maybe? Is there something the sick have in common that they ate?"

"Possibly. But that'd end the same way. We're all eating the same diet." The doctor stood and paced across the room. "Let's just look at the facts. We're on Mars. There isn't much in terms of life other than us. That means we must have brought whatever it is with us from Earth."

"Then, why weren't people getting sick right from the beginning? Or even before, on the Gateway." Quinton washed his hands at the faucet. "No, this had to have been here."

"What about the meteor?"

Quinton furrowed his brow. "What about it?"

The doctor continued. "The outbreak didn't start until after the meteor hit. Maybe it brought something with it. Some kind of, I don't know, xenobacteria."

"Right, right." Quinton paused for a minute as he considered the possibility. "But even if it was that, how would this xenobacteria have gotten into the colony? Nobody's been out to the crater."

Zach gulped. He'd been in the crater and had brought back those crystals. When he had tracked down Ryker and pressed him for the backpack, Ryker claimed he had tried to dispose of them in the crater first—as Zach had assumed he would—but when he saw the guards, he kept the bag on him until he figured out something else. He went to the rover garage, drove around a bit, then went home.

Zach nearly had to wrestle the bag from Ryker's hands when he said it was time they turned them in.

"Are you crazy?" Ryker had said, bear-hugging the pack. "We'll get in trouble!"

"Trouble, no trouble. Why does it matter? It's better that it happens sooner than later."

He'd wanted to come clean because the repercussions would surely be less severe. But with this new information from Quinton, it seemed like Zach's fun day trip could be the cause of the outbreak. He couldn't sit idly by while colonists were dying, and the doctors didn't know why. He looked at the glowing pack beside him, wondering if it was the root of all this.

"Let's check the security footage," Quinton suggested. "See if anyone has been in the crater."

This was it; the time to reveal the truth. Zach psyched himself up, taking a deep breath and wrapping his hand around the bag's strap. He didn't know what good showing the crystals *would do—they were just* irogen—*but they could prove that Zach had gone into the crater. At the door, Zach considered walking away. After all, how could he have brought this 'sickness' back with him? Wouldn't he be ill too? Zach was suddenly unsure of whether this was his fault.*

He sighed. Turning himself in was the best thing he could do. Even if this wasn't his doing, he could get it off his chest once and for all. Looking down at the spikes of blue and purple one last time, he pushed the entrance open and fielded a confused look from Quinton.

"Zach? What are you doing here?" His father's eyes narrowed with concern. "Is something wrong?"

"No, I'm okay. But can I talk to you in private? It's important."

Quinton glanced at the other doctor and said, "We'll finish this later." Then, he got down on a knee and beckoned Zach over. "What's on your mind?"

"Um, I..." Zach hesitated. "Can we sit down?"

"Sure." Quinton brought him to one of the hospital beds and hoisted him onto it. Quinton sat next to him. "Continue."

"I don't know how to say this right, so I'll just say it." Zach conjured up his last bit of will, his gaze flitting around the medbay. "I went into the mines. Me and Ryker. A few days ago."

Quinton studied him briefly as if to tell whether he was joking, then slowly rubbed his brow with two fingers. "Oh, Zach..."

"I know. You told us not to, and..."

"You could have gotten seriously hurt."

"I made a mistake. Really." And Zach truly meant it. Going

into the crater was wrong, but he had the right intentions. To cheer Ryker up. To be a good friend. "I'm really sorry."

"You shouldn't have done that." Quinton sighed. "I'm disappointed in you." He looked like he wanted to say more but fell silent instead. Then, his eyes found the backpack. "What's that?"

Reluctantly, Zach peeled it off his shoulders and handed it to his father. "We—we brought this back with us."

Quinton pulled the zipper and froze. "How deep were you? In the mines."

"I don't know. It said level 13."

Quinton quickly sealed the bag and placed it behind the bed. "Christ. This stuff is explosive. Not to mention that those mineshafts could have collapsed at any—!" He stopped himself before getting too heated. "Look, that was a dangerous thing you did. You could have gotten not only yourself, but a lot of other people hurt too. If these exploded..."

"I'm sorry. I had to tell you," Zach confided in him. "You said people are getting sick, and... and... I'm worried it's my fault. Because it only started happening after we went there. Is it my fault?"

Quinton pulled Zach in. "We don't even know why people are getting sick. Until we do, nobody's at fault." Zach relaxed a bit. "But I'm keeping my eye on you. And Ryker. I mean, going into the crater? I wasn't lying when I said it was dangerous."

"I understand."

Quinton swallowed. "We're going to fix all this. In the meantime, let me know if you're not feeling well, okay?"

Zach thought about the symptoms he had just heard his father and the other doctor discussing. Coughing up blood? Crying blood? That sounded a lot worse than "not feeling well."

That sounded like dying.

ZACH CROFT: 2053

"Don't stop! Don't stop!" Mabel yelled, clutching the shoulder of Ryker's seat as the world exploded around them. The ground spat sand and dislodged rocks like the planet was a pod of whales breathing through blowholes.

The rover crashed through a fluttering tent, taking a piece of canvas with them before skittering onto the main road. The street rumbled as more and more tunnels below Prescott exploded.

So, this was how Prescott would fall. A chain of unstoppable explosions would destroy every hab unit, every tarp, every piece of equipment, before leaving the colony in a cloud of dust. For years, Zach had believed Prescott fell in 2030, with the Red Plague. But looking around him—at the skeletal buildings collapsing, at the sinkholes opening in the ground, at the webs of cracks forming in the regolith streets—Zach knew he was watching the actual downfall of Prescott.

Propping Erik's head up in the back of the rover, Zach stared out the foggy window and wondered how it had gone wrong so quickly. They were collecting crystals in the mines, and then—BOOM!

Zach dared to look at Erik's crumpled leg, which was shielded only by the rubber EVA suit. He felt his throat close up. Erik was dying because Zach wanted to return for the second drum of irogen. It was Zach's fault.

"Is he breathing?" Ryker called back in a raspy, weathered voice.

The flower of condensation that periodically appeared on Erik's visor confirmed that he was. But what would Zach do if he stopped? It's not like Zach could pull off Erik's suit and give him CPR.

BOOOOM!

The rover swerved, barely avoiding an explosion a few feet in front of them. Sand rained down on the glass. Ryker craned to see through the few clean parts left, cursing wildly. "I can't see anything... I can't fucking see anything!" he yelled.

They continued on regardless, speeding down Prescott's abandoned streets, armed only with their will to live.

Boom.

Boom.

Boom.

As a child, Zach had often heard munitions testing from the nearby military base. He remembered the hollow thud in the air, as though god was knocking on a mountain-sized door. He remembered hiding under the covers as his dad promised the blasts were no danger to them.

What would his dad say now, as they drove blind through a minefield?

Zach shook away the thought and focused on the danger at hand.

"I think that's the exit!" Mabel yelled, her visor pressed against the small window in the door. "Turn right!"

The rover veered, sending anything not strapped down slamming against the left wall. As Zach collided with it, he extended his arms to ensure Erik wouldn't meet the same fate. Gasping, Zach stared at Erik's closed eyes. The man looked worse than he had a minute ago. His skin was pale, dark rings had appeared around his eyes, and he shuddered periodically. Still, he remained asleep, his back rigid and his arms straight at his sides like poles.

Boom.

Boom.

Boom.

The dust on the front window thinned a bit, revealing the gaping airlock to the colony a few hundred feet ahead. The road here was less defined, covered mostly by sand, yet it was the most beautiful thing Zach had seen in a long time. They just had to follow it, staying perfectly straight, and they'd be okay.

The buildings were also more intact, at least when compared to the piles of molten scrap in their rearview mirror. That was a good sign. Clearly, fewer crystals were detonating beneath them. Not zero, but fewer. They were almost out of the woods.

But how far did the mines under Prescott extend? Could the tunnels have reached all the way to the dropship? Had their only means of escape already been blown up?

Boom. A tower of dust jumped up to their left. As it fell, a hole expanded in the ground, drawing surrounding rocks and sand inside. A narrow watchtower tipped over and fell onto it, the weight of its center causing it to snap in two. The dual halves then disappeared into the ground.

Boom. The ground cracked behind them. Several fissures appeared, forming a crumbling web that seemed to chase the rover as it fled. A few faults connected with the hole that had consumed the watchtower, and more of the ground sank in the tunnels.

BOOM. The rover shuddered, creaked, and whined for help. It began to slow as a mechanical chug vibrated the floor beneath Zach.

"What happened?" Mabel yelled.

"One of the wheels blew out!" Ryker yelled.

No, no, no, no, Zach thought. They were too far from the dropship to walk with Erik. The rover was their only way out.

"Is there a spare?" Mabel asked.

"Do you want to get out and change it?" retorted Ryker, slamming his foot on the gas. The rover sputtered forward, rocking from side to side. "We're still moving!"

They passed through the airlock of the colony, officially leaving it behind. As they chugged along, Zach resisted the urge to blink for fear that in the split second it would take to do so, a hole would open up in the ground and swallow the rover. In the distance, he spotted a ridge line. The one that reminded him of Arizona. Yes, that was the one. Just beyond it was the dropship.

"We're slowing," Mabel said frantically. "We're slowing. Are we slowing?"

The chug in the floor got louder and shakier, causing the rover to bounce slightly in one corner.

"We're fine!" Ryker yelled with enough conviction that Mabel closed her mouth.

She did not, however, appear to stop worrying. She leaned forward in her seat, eyes scanning the red landscape for explosions, as she white-knuckled the handle beside her.

Boom. One to their left.

Boom. One behind them.

This continued for the next minute, each explosion getting

gradually closer to the rover. In response, Ryker swerved the vehicle wildly, creating a zigzag in the sand. Soon, they reached the ridge line. Sluggishly, they crawled up the rocky incline.

"No, no, no," Ryker bashed his foot on the gas, but the rover slowed to a crawl. "We're gonna have to walk the rest of the way!"

"What? No!" yelled Mabel.

"Shit! Get us to the top, and we'll go on foot." Zach looked at Erik, wondering if he and Ryker could support the injured man. But as he stared at him, Zach registered that the flower of condensation in Erik's visor, the telltale sign of his vitals, had disappeared. "He— he's not breathing!"

"We have to get out now, then," declared Ryker.

"No, it'll take too long! We have to drive."

"With no fuel?"

Zach fell silent. Then, an idea struck him. "It's downhill after this, right?"

Ryker shot a look back. "Yeah, why?"

"Then we don't need fuel."

Clearly conflicted but proposing no alternative, Ryker banged his head against his seat in frustration and kept his foot on the gas until they reached the top.

As he glared at the steep incline of the ridge, Zach gulped. The dropship seemed like it was still at least a half-mile away. Ryker tapped the fuel meter, alerting Zach that it was nearly zero. This was their only option.

"Do the brakes work?" Zach asked. He looked at Erik, who was becoming more discolored by the second.

"Haven't tried them," answered Ryker cynically.

"Now's a good time to start."

Ryker sighed, shaking his head. Then he used the last of their fuel to send them barreling down the ridge.

They descended quickly, wheels turning so fast Zach was sure it would be impossible to stop. The rover shook wildly. It rocked back and forth, going airborne every few seconds, before crashing down on the sharp and misshapen surface. When they reached the bottom, the rover quickly leveled out and flew toward the dropship.

They were going so fast. Too fast. What if they drove right into the spacecraft and blew up?

Five hundred feet.

Two hundred feet.

Ryker slammed on the brakes, prompting the vehicle's ancient gears to creak and whine. The rover began to turn slightly to the left, likely because of its impaired wheel. Or was it *wheels* after their journey down the ridge? Zach couldn't tell, nor could he think clearly enough to figure it out.

A hundred feet.

Fifty feet.

Thirty.

Twenty.

Ten.

The rover came to a stop a mere five feet from the dropship. Immediately, they all flung their doors open and jumped out. Zach and Ryker pulled Erik from the rover and divided his weight between them. Together, they ran up the ramp. Mabel pulled the airlock release, they all scurried inside the ship, and the blast door closed behind them.

Right away, Zach yanked off Erik's helmet and moved aside

as Mabel prepared to do CPR. Ryker assumed his place in the pilot's chair, flipping switches and pressing buttons. Zach sat down next to him. He growled with anger as he wiped his sweaty hair off his forehead. Anger at himself. Anger at Prescott. Anger at the universe.

Behind him, Erik gasped awake. He sat up briefly, then recoiled back as the pain in his leg subdued him. Mabel reassured him that he would be okay, then glanced up at Zach with a pleading look. She shifted to Ryker. "Get us out of here."

Ryker took the control stick and jammed it forward. With a jolt, the thrusters kicked on and lifted the dropship a dozen feet into the air. Ryker turned a dial, flicked several more switches, then pressed the single blue button in the center of the control panel.

As they shot into the sky, Zach watched the Prescott Mining Colony sink into the ground.

TWENTY-TWO

ZACH CROFT: 2053

ZACH AND RYKER carried Erik out of the dropship and into the docking bay. Mabel lagged behind, trying her hair in a tight knot, before joining the others in their walk. While it had only been a few hours since they left for Mars, the station seemed to have aged a decade. The lights above them were dim, making navigating the halls much more arduous. The air was thin and cold.

"Does the medbay have operating equipment? Surgical tools? Cauterization?" Mabel asked.

Ryker nudged a chair out of the way as they passed through the cafeteria. "I'm not a doctor, but I think so. Yeah."

When they reached the medbay, the door opened into a chamber smelling of antiseptic. The main room splintered into three others, each with an operating table and an assortment of complicated medical equipment. Zach and Ryker placed Erik on a gurney in one of the rooms, then obeyed when

Mabel demanded that they leave. Things were about to get messy.

Ryker sat against the wall in the hallway while Zach looked through the porthole window into the medbay. Plastic tubes ran from machine to machine, pumping drops of liquid between one another. Massive, circular lights hung from the infirmary ceiling. The brightness reached into the hall and projected aurora-like images on the wall beside Zach. It almost felt like a dream. Not a good one, of course. More like the semi-lucid ones where Zach was aware of himself, yet he was powerless against the whims of the world around him.

Zach pressed a button on the wall intercom connected to the medbay. "How does it look?" He tried his best not to reveal the rawness in his throat.

Mabel continued working as she spoke. "How do you want it to look, Zach?" She walked around a metal stand holding a pouch of liquid, the small tube connecting to an IV port inserted into Erik's forearm. An oxygen mask clung to Erik's face like an alien. His eyes were closed but twitching wildly. The loud beep of his vitals rang through Zach's head, sounding like an unstoppable countdown to the moment of Erik's death.

Zach dared to look at Erik's leg. It was a mess of exposed bone and muscle. A pile of blood-soaked gauze leaned against it. Zach suppressed a rising wave of bile, then sat down beside Ryker.

For a few minutes, they said nothing. Trapped in his thoughts, Zach focused on the wall, scanning its intricate paneling and the caution signs left over from the Prescott era.

"It's going to be a while. We should try to get some sleep," Ryker advised, getting to his feet. Exhausted, Zach agreed and

To accept

allowed him to lead the way to nearby living quarters. They each chose a bed close to the exit so that they could hear if Mabel was calling, then climbed under the covers. The mattress was hard, but Zach permitted himself to doze off. He sank into the warmth of the blanket.

ASSESSING FUEL USAGE.

The message flashed across the screen as Zach battled his fatigue with a cup of coffee. The assumption that a cozy bed and a few hours of quiet would solve all his problems proved incorrect. After an aborted attempt at sleep, Zach and Ryker found themselves in the Works with a drum of irogen at Zach's side. They dragged in a scale, connected it to a diagnostic computer, and placed the drum on top. It was way more difficult to lift than on Mars, with the Gateway's Earth-like level of gravity, but they managed.

Zach went to the computer and pulled up the fuel consumption data. He discovered that most of the emergency fuel supply that had gotten them to Mars had been depleted. It worried him. He had expected it to take them round-trip. But now, there wasn't much to do but figure out if they had gotten enough irogen from the mines.

Once the computer finished synchronizing, two orbs—Earth and Mars—appeared on either side of the screen with dotted lines between them.

"How much of this fuel is required for Earth waypoint?" Ryker asked the computer. Then, he quickly added, "Without the continuum drive?"

"One moment, Gagarin," the computer replied in a shockingly human voice. The system factored out the weight of the metal drum and the crystals inside, measuring only the amount of pure irogen within the spikes. "THREE PERCENT OF AVAILABLE IROGEN REQUIRED FOR EARTH WAYPOINT."

"Three percent? That's it?" Mabel entered, nursing a mug full of tea.

Zach and Ryker turned, surprised to hear Mabel's voice.

"How is he?" Zach asked.

Mabel sipped her tea. She looked exhausted. "Resting," she said.

"And his leg?"

"I did the best I could, but..." She looked down at the steaming mug in her hands. "I couldn't save it."

Zach's stomach dropped. Ryker put a consoling hand on Zach's shoulder. Zach shrugged it off. "Can I see him?"

"Not for a few hours. He's heavily sedated." Eager to change the subject, Mabel walked over to the drum of irogen. "So, we have enough, yeah?"

Zach placed his hand on the drum. "I told you. It's powerful stuff."

"Hang on. We're not done." Ryker mulled something over, picking at his lip. "Using the continuum drive, how much do we need for Alpha Cen?"

"NINETY-FOUR PERCENT OF AVAILABLE IROGEN REQUIRED FOR ALPHA CENTAURI WAYPOINT."

Reality hit Zach, and he was unsure whether to be relieved or disappointed. "That gives us one trip."

"That's all we needed... right?" Mabel asked.

"Doesn't leave much room for failure," Zach replied. And there were plenty of failures to go around. "If we're wrong about Alpha Cen, there won't be anywhere else to go. We'll be stranded."

Mabel sipped her tea one more time. "So, let's not be wrong about it, okay?"

"HEY," Zach said, slowly approaching the recovery bed in the corner of the medbay. Propped up by a few pillows, Erik sat with his hands folded in his lap and his eyes trained on his bedside window. A sterile white blanket covered the lower half of his body. Even with his legs concealed, however, Zach couldn't help but notice only one foot poking up through the sheet.

He bit back his guilt and sat on a stool next to Erik's bed. "We're going into cryo soon." Erik said nothing, so Zach prompted him, "You wanna talk about it?"

What exactly would he have to say? How it was all Zach's fault that he lost his leg and that he'd never forgive him? Maybe approaching Erik so soon was a mistake. They were all so, so tired. Erik, most of all.

But instead of attacking Zach, Erik simply adjusted and quickly glanced at him. "Mars is kind of beautiful, you know. Even with all that's happened."

Zach glanced out at the Red Planet and its eggshell-white ice caps. Happy for a distraction, he noted, "It will probably end up being habitable at some point."

"How?"

"Well, when the sun expands in five billion years, it'll melt the ice caps. Water will flood the surface, and slowly, it'll become habitable."

"Then, a species will emerge and destroy itself. Just like we have."

"That's something to drink to," Zach joked. "To beginnings and endings." He raised an invisible glass.

"To beginnings and endings." Erik mimed a sipping motion.

As Zach sighed, the room turned quiet. Even the beeping machines that cluttered the medbay seemed to pause in anticipation. There was no escaping the elephant in the room anymore. Zach had to come out and say it. "I'm so sorry, Erik."

Erik waved him off but didn't meet his eye. "Not your fault. You tried to make me stay."

"I could have tried harder."

"I still would have gone."

"But—"

"How about we blame OSE for not doing its damn job?"

Erik had a point there. They wouldn't have even been on Mars if OSE hadn't rejected Zach's proposal. Still, Zach had allowed Erik to put himself in danger. Even worse, Zach had insisted on taking the irogen with them as the tunnel exploded. That same decision had cost Erik his leg. But none of it would have been necessary if OSE had done its job. "Okay. Sure."

Erik bit his top lip. "What were you saying about cryo?"

"Everything's ready to go," Zach answered. He nodded at the red planet outside the window. "I'm done with this place."

"That, we can agree on."

Zach stood up and extended a hand. "Here, come on."

As Erik took hold of his forearm, Zach helped him into the wheelchair beside the bed. Then, they traveled to the storage room, where the others were waiting to go into cryo.

Mabel rushed over to Erik as Zach wheeled him in. "Erik. How are you feeling?"

"I'm okay. I keep feeling like I forgot something, though..." He patted his pockets, then his empty pant leg. Mabel laughed awkwardly. Erik took her hand and squeezed it. "Seriously, though. Thank you. You saved my life."

Erik's words of gratitude seemed to calm Mabel a bit. "No problem." She ran her fingers through her hair. "You would have done the same for me."

"All right. Let's head home," Zach said. He proceeded to the corner of the room and activated four chambers. After the others climbed into their pods, he closed the lids and slipped into his own.

As the sedative gas pumped in from all directions, he thought of the irogen. Despite everything that had gone wrong, they had enough. They had prevailed.

Zach thought about Carver, smiling while relishing one final thought.

I proved him wrong.

RYKER GAGARIN: 2030

Thump!

The sound of a body hitting the floor jolted Ryker to attention. "Mom!" He ran to his mother's side of the tent and knelt beside her, feeling her sweat-covered forehead. She was burning up.

In a panicked frenzy, Ryker ran into the open and called for help. He didn't stop until his mother was carried away on a stretcher, and even then, he pressed the doctors for answers. On the way to the medbay, they shooed him left and right, telling him to calm down.

But he couldn't manage to contain his worry. What was wrong with his mother? Was she getting sick like those other people? She didn't have any of the symptoms other than the fever. That could mean anything, right? A cold? The flu? It didn't have to be the Red Plague... right?

At the door to the medbay, Ryker was handed a blanket and was instructed to wait outside. He propped himself against the wall, curled up, and tried to doze off.

Sleep eluded him. Instead, he attempted to quiet his panicked thoughts with happy memories and optimism. That always seemed to work for his mother. Unfortunately, she hadn't passed that gene down.

He didn't know what time it was when a doctor came to collect him, but the sky was somewhere between black and dull orange. "You can go in," the physician told him. "But you have to wear this." He revealed a long hazmat suit and handed it to Ryker. So his mother was sick? And not just 'lay in bed watching television' sick. Really sick.

Once the uncomfortable suit was against Ryker's clammy skin, he pulled open the door and stepped inside. A subdued light radiated from the ceiling, making the patients look pale as ghosts. He approached the bed in the middle, smiling at his sleeping mother.

But the relief quickly faded at the sight of several tubes protruding from her arm. A cocktail of drugs dripped through them. Quinton stood by her side. He hid his shaking hands, thrusting them into his pockets as Ryker appeared beside him. "She's going to be fine, kid."

Was she? It didn't look like it. The sunken eyes, the twitch of her lip, the feverish sheen of perspiration. "Is she...?"

"We gave her a light sedative to help her sleep through the night. It should help with the fever, too," Quinton claimed, looking at a monitor that displayed her vitals.

"What happened?" asked Ryker.

Quinton hesitated momentarily, then glanced at the other people asleep in beds. "We don't have a name for it yet. But we'll get it under control."

"So there's a cure?" A bit of hope rose in Ryker's chest.

"No. Not yet," confided Quinton. "I'd suggest you get some rest and come back in the morning."

"Is it okay if I stay here?" Ryker put on his best pleading face.

"I don't know if that's a good idea."

"I won't be a bother. I'll just pull up a chair and wait for her to wake up. Besides, I wouldn't get any sleep knowing she's like this anyway."

Quinton sighed. "Yeah, okay. I'll grab you a seat." He wheeled over a small stool.

It wasn't pleasant, especially with the hazmat suit, but it would have to do. Ryker burrowed his head into the blanket and placed his arms under his temple.

A few hours later, his mother's voice cut through the air. It was weak, almost too quiet to be heard. Ryker shot up, grabbing onto Kayla's hand. "Are you okay?"

She seemed confused. Probably a side effect of the drugs. "What's going on?" She examined the tubes taped to her arms and gave up on trying to sit up. She looked at Ryker. "You're yellow."

Yellow? Why was he yellow? Ryker looked down at himself, then laughed a little. "Oh. It's a hazmat suit. They made me wear it."

"That's not good," she said. "Am I that sick?"

"You don't look that bad, actually," Ryker declared.

During the night, two more beds had filled up. A few doctors stood around one of them, discussing the patient's condition. When Quinton saw that Ryker was awake, he came over. "I'm sorry to do this to you, kid. But you've got to go. Right now isn't the best time for you to be here."

"Why?" asked Ryker. He peeked between two doctors' shoulders and saw a woman beside the bed, sobbing.

"What's going..." Kayla started but trailed off before finishing.

"You need to go. Now, Ryker." Quinton's tone hardened.

It didn't take long to figure out why. As two doctors stepped aside, the man in the bed came into view. He looked far worse than Kayla, with boils sprouting across his brownish skin. Ryker would have thought it was a corpse if not for the beeping vital signs above his head that informed him he was still clinging for life.

"Get out. Please." Quinton tried to nudge Ryker in the direction of the door.

The man's heart rate quickly increased. 140. 150. 160.

"Guard," said Quinton. "Get him out of here."

But Ryker couldn't take his eyes off the monitor, the green line bouncing up and down in jagged lines.

The last thing he saw before he was dragged outside the tent was the line spiking one last time before it went flat.

ZACH CROFT: 2053

We're back.

Zach sat up with a start, pulling himself through the layers of cryogenic gas. His heart hammered in his head as the light at the end of the tunnel became clear. They were going home! To see trees again and breathe fresh air! Not for long, of course. They were off to Alpha Cen not long after. But seeing Pasadena one last time, albeit for only a few days, still dominated Zach's thoughts.

The rest of the group awoke and helped Erik out of his pod. Mabel did a quick examination, peeling back his bandages and whispering under her breath as she dragged her finger along deep scars. "The cuts have almost entirely healed."

Erik touched his stump. A pained look crossed his face. "When can I walk again?" The question would have seemed impossible to answer if not for Mabel's comment on the morning of his surgery.

"Oh! And I found a prosthetic. A really good one. I can't fit it to his leg yet, because of the swelling, but it'll work great once he heals."

Zach mentioned it, and Mabel confirmed that Erik could be ready. "You want to go see? I'll get your crutches." She handed them to Erik. "Hopefully, you won't need them after we finish."

Erik rubbed the sleep from his eyes and nodded. "Yeah... okay."

While Mabel escorted him out of the room, Ryker pulled on his bomber jacket and waited until they were gone to speak. "You think what's-his-face is going to let us off easy?"

"Carver? I wouldn't be worried about it. Once he sees the irogen, he'll realize we were right."

"Is he getting a seat on the ship?" Ryker asked. "To Alpha Cen."

"It's not my choice, so I have no clue," Zach admitted. He was conflicted. On one hand, Carver had filled the role of Zach's father in those terrible years following Quinton's death. He wasn't obligated to; he could have just written Zach off as someone else's responsibility. And yet he looked over Zach anyway—guiding him through life, ensuring he stayed positive after such a tragedy—all while Quinton's corpse was floating in space. Part of Zach would always appreciate that. But on the other hand, he had lied about Ryker. And who knew what else?

Zach stopped himself before saying any more. Who lived and died wasn't up to him. But if not him, who *would* make the tough choices? It then occurred to Zach that deciding who got a seat went far beyond Nicolas Carver. Of six billion people, he could only take a thousand. He had known it since the beginning but always brushed it off as an issue for tomorrow.

Well, tomorrow had finally come.

If Carver hadn't been so stubborn all those years, maybe they could have taken more people. But the past was in the past, and there was nothing he could do. "Look, we have at least a few months until the flare hits. We'll pick from OSE personnel, qualified parties."

"And that includes...?"

"I haven't gotten that far yet." Though Zach knew Cora

would be included. It was a given. Which of his colleagues would also get a spot, he didn't know.

Unsatisfied with the answer but too tired to care, Ryker shrugged. "Let's go to the medbay and check on the others."

Zach thought more about the Carver situation as they marched down the corridor. Would things between them return to normal? Or better yet, did he *want* things to go back to the way they were? Yes, was the simple answer. He would welcome returning to a simpler time when solar flares weren't killing thousands every week. A time when Zach's most significant worries were how long it would take to cook dinner and review calculations at the same time. A time when he could depend on Carver. Sure, he would love that more than anything in the world. But to return with all the knowledge he had now? That was a different story.

He knew things now. He was less naive. And he didn't think it was possible to return to bliss when he was no longer so ignorant.

As they approached the medbay, a cheer echoed through the door. They entered to find Mabel with both arms raised above her head and an enormous smile on her face. Zach was about to ask what was so exciting when he noticed Erik taking a few shaky steps on the far side of the room. A bafflingly futuristic prosthetic leg was strapped to his stump.

Mabel noticed them standing in the doorway and pointed at Erik. "Look, look! He's controlling it with his brain!" Was he? A short inspection suggested there were no pulleys or wires. "It interfaced with his nerves. Thank God they weren't too damaged!"

"Are you sure he should be walking on two feet?" Zach asked. "Doesn't it hurt?"

"A little, but it's okay," said Erik. He took several steps back, then forward, testing his new leg's ability to bear weight. "I can feel the floor."

"Can you?" Mabel said excitedly.

"Through the toes." He wiggled his metallic foot, then reached down to feel it.

"Incredible." Mabel looked at Zach. "Just incredible. I don't even know how this is possible... were things this advanced in 2030?"

"Apparently," said Zach. "Now come on. Let's go to the ground."

Their way to the ground was simple. On board the station, seven or eight vacant dropships were still waiting to be used. It was a shame they couldn't use the one they came up on, seeing as it had flown back to Earth by itself, but the others were identical, so it didn't particularly matter. When they reached the docking bay, the massive blast door slid open and gave way into the deck. All along the walls were airlocks leading into the dropships. Seven had green indicator lights above them, while the other three shone red.

"It's going to be a surprise when they see us," Mabel commented, touching the glass of one airlock. "They probably think we're dead."

Ryker frowned. "Wouldn't be the first time."

"Come on. Let's get ourselves set up," said Zach.

"Wait. I... don't know if I want to go back yet," Erik said slowly.

Zach squinted. "Why? What's the matter? Don't you want to go home?"

"Home, no home, Earth, Mars. It doesn't matter. It's been a long time, and I can't imagine going back."

"I thought the same thing," assured Ryker. "It'll get better."

Erik cocked his head. "That's not what you said on Mars."

"Well, maybe I was wrong."

"If not the ground, where will you go?" Zach asked Erik.

"If you'll allow me to, I'll stay here. I promise I won't mess with anything. And besides, I've lived up here before. With the colonists. There shouldn't be much difference."

Ryker shot Zach a look of disapproval. "We're not leaving him here alone."

"It could be good, having an eye in the sky while we're gone."

"No way."

"Why? You were here for years and fared okay," Zach said, not realizing how distasteful his words must have seemed. He didn't mean for them to be malicious or spiteful, but Ryker appeared to see them that way.

"Alright. You're the captain; you decide what we do. It's not like I've done anything to get us here—"

"I just meant you were able to survive on your—"

"Oh, I know what you meant. You're just *so* ready to leave another person up here."

"*I* didn't leave you here."

"Then who did?"

"*DOCKING PROCEDURE ACTIVATED,*" the intercom blared. The lights above them turned yellow.

"What was that?" Mabel backstepped toward the exit, feeling for the door. "What does that mean?"

Zach didn't know what to say. He watched as one of the indicator lights went from red to a pale blue before it went dark altogether. "Something's docking."

Yes, that's what it meant. A ship was latching onto the station. But who could it be? As Zach's eyes scanned the room, he barely had time to register what was happening. "Everybody move!"

The floor rattled as the mystery ship locked in. The lights shifted to a blood red. Zach stepped back, putting as much distance between himself and the airlocks as possible.

Then, all went silent. Even the machine hum seemed to tune in. After an excruciating wait, one of the blast doors inched open with a gust of steam. Shapes manifested in the gas.

People.

As the smoke began to clear, a man stepped in. He wore dark clothing and walked with a confidence Zach had only seen in one person.

Carver.

He considered the dock for a moment, then noticed Zach. His eyes went wide. "Zach?"

Zach was too shocked to form words. A dozen questions raced through his mind. *How did they get here? Why are they here? Who did they bring?* But then it struck him.

He knew why they were there.

Zach collected himself and solemnly asked, "Who survived?"

PART THREE

TRUTH

TWENTY-THREE

ZACH CROFT: 2053

"THERE'S room for everyone on board," Zach said as he ushered the hordes of survivors out of the docking bay and into the Gateway. The flood of people seemed endless. Their clothes were wrinkled and torn. Soot covered their faces.

At first, Zach wondered how they had gotten off the ground, considering they had no working transport. Then, it hit him. The cruise ship. The one in the launch bay meant to shuttle wealthy businesspeople to orbit for a week-long stay amongst the stars. The vessel was overflowing, with far more people crammed into it than intended, eight or nine hundred at least.

Zach scanned the crowd for people he knew. It appeared that most of them were from OSE—Zach could tell by the assortment of lab coats, ID badges, and uniforms. He recognized a few: an astronomer here and there, Rhea Vasquez with her midnight black hair, a biologist he often saw when visiting

Cora in her office. Cora, *Cora*, where was she? Had she made it? He wouldn't know what to do if she hadn't. He wouldn't be able to go on. But as the crowd thinned, the chances of seeing her again dwindled.

Would Jason have made it? He was tough as nails, so if anyone could survive the end of the world, it was him. At least, Zach hoped.

Zach's mind was blank. The sheer magnitude of the situation overcame any thoughts that tried to intrude. Earth was gone. Gone forever. The solar flare had happened. Billions of people were dead. The few hundred who had escaped were the last of the human race.

He was too late. He was *wrong*. Right about the severity of the solar flares, but wrong about how much time was left. How could he have known for sure? He was so confident they had a year, yet he was gravely mistaken.

Zach flagged Carver down. "Did Cora make it? Jason?"

"Not sure, son. I'm praying they did." Carver smiled at an older woman and helped her toward the exit. He gave a look back at Zach in confirmation.

Son? Was Carver pretending as if nothing had happened between them? He was about to respond when he noticed a woman cutting toward the front of the crowd. For some reason, his eyes focused on her. She nudged people aside, repeating, "Excuse me, excuse me." The woman reached the front of the pack, gazed at Zach with crystal blue eyes, and called out his name.

Before Zach could even register what was happening, Cora had wrapped her arms around him so tightly that he nearly buckled to the ground. "Oh, my god!" she exclaimed. Laughing, she slapped his chest several times and exclaimed, "You're real! You're really here!"

"I'm here, I'm here!" he answered with a smile. Zach hugged her for what seemed like an hour, then pulled her to her feet. "I'm home."

"Yeah." Cora's laughter tapered off. "Home..."

———

"THERE'S NOTHING LEFT, IS THERE?" Zach asked as he gazed through the octagonal window and down at his old home. The world was an orb of fire, bright and painful to look at. Thunderous waves of orange circled the surface, not an inch of land visible past the blaze and smoke in the atmosphere. The tendrils of fire twisted demonically, forming ribbon-like curls in the hot smog.

Zach took a long swig of bourbon he'd found in a supply closet. The bottle was labeled *FOR A SPECIAL EVENT*. Intricate carvings of roses decorated the glass. As the burning liquid trickled down his throat, he rolled the red cap in his palm. He looked at Earth longingly. His hair stuck to his forehead in sweat-coated vines, hanging over his eyes. Through the slick strands, he blinked disbelievingly as the tumbling flames rolled over the continents, molten clouds swirling and roiling. The bourbon did little to quiet his thoughts.

Slowly, Cora walked up behind him, hands in her pockets, and stood at his side. Her sleeveless red shirt hung loosely on her figure. Eventually, she said in a low voice, "You saved us."

"No," was all Zach could muster. "I— I always knew it

would end like this, but..." His eyes went glassy, and he felt a stinging in his nostrils. "It's all gone, Cora. It's gone."

Pasadena. America. Earth. Everything.

What had become of their world? And how had he let it get to this point? For a split second, Zach understood why Carver had backed the magnetosphere restoration so heavily. But he quickly snapped back to reality after remembering how many more people could have survived if Carver had held an ounce of common sense and realized the restoration was a lost cause.

"You did," Cora said but kept her voice low.

"I thought we had a year!" Zach's vision went blurry, and he gritted his teeth so hard they felt like they might crack. He glanced at Cora, registering how emaciated she was. Her cheeks were hollow, and her eyes were sunken and dark. Even her olive skin was paler than it used to be. How had he not noticed his best friend's condition before?

Cora exhaled through pursed lips. "But we're alive. If you hadn't returned with the Gateway when you did, we'd still be stranded out there."

Zach nodded a little and drew his eyes back to the ravaged Earth.

"I thought I'd lost you... again." The word caught in Cora's throat as she stared straight ahead. The volcanic light illuminated her grime-covered face. She swallowed. The tears in her eyes threatened to spill over.

"I didn't see Jason in the crowd," said Zach. Cora didn't respond. She nudged a strand of hair from her face. "Did he make it?"

Cora shook her head. "He didn't get to the ship fast enough. I saw him... He was almost there, but we... we had to launch."

Zach let his head hang low. "He always had a soft spot for you, know that?" He drank another burning sip of liquor.

Cora's tears finally fell, and she closed her eyes tight to contain them. She nodded. "I know."

They stayed a little longer, passing the bottle back and forth before they split up and went their separate ways. For the next few hours, Zach helped people get settled into their bunks, showing them where they could find supplies, changes of clothes, or whatever else they needed. Many recognized him, claiming they had been to his funeral. "Must have been one hell of a party," Zach joked, trying to break the utter despair filling the room. One woman even proposed that they were all dead and trapped in Purgatory. Zach moved quickly on to the next person.

Later, he met back up with the others in an observation room to discuss what to do next. Carver's fingers hovered just above the steel table. "I'm glad to see you, son. We thought we'd lost you."

"Is it just us now?" Zach asked. His voice was raw and raspy. "None of the other agencies got off the ground?"

"I don't think so."

"How about other countries? Allies? Enemies, even?"

"It's not impossible, but..." He trailed off.

They all stood around the observation window, staring at the planet like Zach had earlier that day. Cora hovered in the background, her arms clasped closely to her sides.

"There's still the possibility of the current orbital stations. NASA had a few still operating," Carver suggested.

"They weren't built to survive something like this. And even if they made it, you're looking at, what, a dozen people?"

Zach motioned to the window. "Close it up, Ryker." He didn't want to look at his ravaged world any longer. A mechanical buzzing sound began as Ryker closed the window shade from his place at the command module. "That means less than a thousand people are left in the human race."

"Is that enough?" Ryker asked. "To... to keep it going?"

"It should be." A look of dismay crossed Zach's face. "But barely."

Suddenly, Erik appeared in the doorway. "Sorry I'm late."

Zach motioned Erik over. Erik limped in his direction. "Nicolas, this is Erik. We wouldn't have gotten the irogen without him."

Carver looked confused, perhaps searching for some distant memory but coming up dry. "You're not OSE."

"I am. Just not your OSE."

Zach sensed the tension between them and decided to step in. "Erik's a Prescott survivor. We found him in one of the pods when we got up here."

"What?" Carver turned to Zach with wide eyes.

"We found him in one of the secondary pod clusters. He's been helping us—"

"You do mean the prison chambers, right?"

"I only stole some food," Erik began.

"And he was on ice for twenty years for it," Zach finished. "He did his time. And then some."

"Hey," Cora interrupted. "I had a chance to look at the farm. Half the plant beds are dead. The others are wilting. It would take a miracle for that thing to sustain us."

"It doesn't have to. Cryo will. We'll go to sleep and wake up when we need to, not a day older," Zach said. First-gen stasis pods could only preserve a person for a month or two. The next gen used a system of holding back cell deterioration so that the passenger would age ten times slower, but they still couldn't stay indefinitely. Gen Three brought a permanent solution. True immortality, though only while asleep.

"If I may," Ryker prompted, one of his legs outstretched and his back pushed against a chair. "The cryobay is shut down. The system said the only way to override it is with ground control access."

"Well, that's a problem," said Carver dryly.

"I can help with that," Cora volunteered.

"How?"

"I'll put together a team to get it open. We'll figure it out."

Carver reluctantly agreed, then turned to Zach. "Can I speak with you for a moment?"

"Okay."

Carver beckoned Zach to step away with him. They exited into the hall, shooing away a few stragglers camped outside. Once they were on their own, Zach started in. "Is there a problem?"

Carver scratched the beginnings of a stubble beard. "I know you're upset with me."

"For what? Lying about my entire life?"

Hurt flashed across Carver's face, but Zach couldn't discern whether it was real. "I care about you, Zach. You're like a son—"

"Don't even start with that shit."

"Zach, please." Carver held out his hands in a peacemaking gesture. "We have to let bygones be bygones. The survivors look up to us, you and me. We got them here."

Oh, so there was a *we,* now? Carver had done nothing but obstruct Zach at every turn, and suddenly they were on the same team? The thought made Zach livid. Regardless of Zach's feelings, Carver was right about one thing: they were responsible for a thousand people.

The *last* thousand people.

And for that reason, Zach would have to accept a truce, for everyone's sake. After all, he never found solid proof that Carver had anything to do with Ryker's abandonment, only suspicion. There was something strange going on. Zach knew it. But for the time being, it would have to wait. "Fine. But I don't want to hear from you unless the ship is about to explode. Understand?"

"You got it." Carver tried to pat Zach on the shoulder, but Zach stepped away.

They rejoined the others and devised a plan to integrate all the new survivors. Ryker explained where the last packaged food stores were. There wasn't enough for everyone—they would have to ration until another solution was discovered. The idea was met with nods of agreement. Cora mentioned that the influx of people could strain the life support systems. Oxygen levels might drop.

"True," Ryker admitted. "It's broken down multiple times, but as long as we figure out cryo soon, it won't be a problem for us."

"I've got to go help get people situated," Carver announced, gathering his things. "In the meantime, Zach, you can look into those other stations you were talking about. Good?"

"Yeah, okay. We'll regroup later and figure out what to do next." Zach walked out of the room and turned the corner.

Carver was about to do the same when Ryker planted a hand on his chest. "I'm watching you."

ZACH CROFT: 2030

Guilt. That's what he felt.

As more and more bodies were carried off to the growing cemetery, Zach's level of unease—which was already through the roof—grew even more. Some mornings, he could barely pull himself out of bed.

This day, though, he got up. He put in earbuds while he got ready, trying to tune out the pained wails and gurgling coughs from outside. At the door, he hesitated.

It wasn't the fear of getting sick himself that stopped him. No, it was something beyond that. Whenever he walked out into the open, it felt as though everyone was staring at him. Like they knew everything happening was because of him.

Zach remembered his father's words of comfort: that nobody was at fault until they figured out what was causing the sickness. But that was obviously a lie. Everything had gone downhill since Zach entered that crater, and no one could deny it. Well, no one would deny it if they knew what he had done. That made it all the more difficult for him to bear.

Forty-seven had died so far. Five times as many had contracted the illness. More were sure to follow. A dim mood had swept over the colony as the grim reality of the situation settled in.

People called it the Red Plague, named after the Red Planet they were on, as well as the red bumps and boils that were a tell-tale sign of the affliction. To contain the epidemic, those who weren't showing symptoms—maybe two hundred or so— remained confined to their quarters whenever possible. Quinton had ordered that Zach only leave when strictly necessary and, even then, with great caution. He was allowed to go out for rations. That was all.

Zach was about to break that rule.

People who were too weak to walk home lay strewn about along the roads, the healthy unwilling to help them up, for fear of infection. Sometimes, the sickly huddled in groups, but they rarely spoke to one another.

Nobody looked up at Zach as he walked out of his hab unit. They kept their bloody, egg-yolk-colored eyes glued to the ground, jaws slightly ajar to accommodate the blisters surrounding their lips. And despite the muted sun rays on Mars, their skin was red as ever, making even the worst of sunburns look minor.

Zach ran his hand over his olive skin, thankful to be healthy but secretly wishing to have been amongst the forty-seven who died. That way, he wouldn't have to deal with the knowledge that the disaster was his fault.

With sixty percent of the population barely holding on, upkeep on Prescott had come to a near standstill. Any efforts to rebuild after the meteor were suspended, leaving only the shabby tents, shacks, and the few hab units intact. The remaining work- force was enlisted to operate the oxygen scrubbers, hydrofarm, and all the systems they needed to survive. Ironically, the job got easier every day, with fewer and fewer people draining resources. It was a dark thought, but it was true.

Zach headed for the town hall, having overheard his father mention a council meeting later that day. He didn't know what it was about, but something told Zach it was important. If he could slip in, maybe he could get some information. It was a long shot, but he needed to understand what was happening.

The town hall—a wide, rectangular building with red-tinted windows made from Martian sand—was one of the larger structures, such as the rover garage, that had stayed intact after the meteor hit. Zach summited the steps and slipped inside. He went straight for the staircase in the lobby, passing a small viewing room, library, and personal cafeteria. At the top, it led into a vast space.

At the sound of a voice, he ducked behind a piece of furniture and peeked around it. The seven surviving council members sat at a table in the middle of the room.

"Let's begin," Quinton said. "Councilman Faren, here, has called for this meeting."

Councilman Faren was a skinny man. His nose was long and narrow, and his eyes bore a striking resemblance to that of a corpse. With the screeching of chair legs across the floor, he stood, fixed his jacket, and nodded to the other councilors. "I apologize for calling an assembly with such short notice, but I feel that something must be done to address what's happening here."

Quinton gestured for him to sit back down. "You have the floor."

"Thank you, sir." Faren reclaimed his seat and leaned over the table, rubbing his hands together. "I'm sure you've all seen the numbers. Even without scouring the medbay logs, take one look outside, and you can see the urgency of the situation."

"We're very much aware of the urgency, Faren, so why are we here instead of out there treating the sick?" a blonde councilwoman said.

"*Treat them with what, Lindsey?*" another councilman retorted. "*Let the man speak.*"

Faren nodded thanks. He exhaled through his nose, then continued. "*Fifteen years we're supposed to spend here?*" He shook his head. "*Let's face it: we're not making it a month at this rate, let alone fifteen years.*"

From the other councilors' looks, it appeared Faren had said what many of them were secretly thinking. Sensing this, Faren continued, "*We need to do something, and it's not treating the sick. We've got—what—a few weeks' worth of basic medicine left? I don't suppose we have an alien cure somewhere in there.*"

"*What about the resupply ship?*" Lindsey interjected. "*One's supposed to come in a few weeks, right? That'll have more medicine.*"

"*And how do you know that medicine will do anything?*" Faren retorted. "*Or better yet, how do you even know the ship is coming? We haven't had contact with OSE in weeks. They probably think we're dead.*"

"*Suppose that's true. Suppose the ship isn't coming.*" Quinton leaned back in his seat. "*Are you saying we should let all those sick people die?*"

"*No, that's not what I'm saying.*" Faren turned his gaze to Quinton. "*But what's the point in waiting around while more and more people get infected? We're trapped under a fucking dome with no way to quarantine and nowhere to hide.*"

"*So what do you suppose we do?*"

"*We need to leave! We need to take the healthy back to Earth, develop some kind of cure, then return to help the rest.*"

Quinton squinted at him. "*You said it yourself: they won't survive a month. They'll be dead by the time we send a team back. No."*

"Would you rather have all of us die? Because that's what's going to happen if we stay. At the very least, we can ensure those who aren't infected stay that way. Think about your people, sir."

"How do you know the healthy would even want to leave?" another councilor asked. "Almost everyone has sick family members. Nobody will want to leave their family behind, even if staying spells their own deaths."

"Then we make them leave," said Faren.

"We're not actually entertaining this idea, right?" Lindsey exclaimed. "Quinton?"

Quinton took a breath. "It's not our choice to make. We can't force people to leave."

"A good leader would save as many of his people as he could," Faren insisted.

"Even if you're right, how would we ensure no sick people get onto the ship?" Quinton asked, keeping his head.

"The yellow eyes," Faren said. He looked around at the other councilors, searching for validation. Several nodded in agreement. He continued, "It's the first symptom they show. We can check for that."

"Person by person, that'll take hours," Quinton pointed out.

"It's either that or risk bringing it back to the Gateway."

Lindsey shook her head in disapproval. "There's no way people are gonna go for this."

"Can we just vote and be done with it?" one of the councilors asked. "We're not doing any good stalling. All in favor?"

"Aye," said Faren immediately.

"Aye."

"Aye."

"...All opposed?"

Lindsey crossed her arms over her chest. "Nay."

"Nay."

"Nay."

Faren breathed a frustrated sigh, then turned to Quinton. "It seems you're the tiebreaker... sir. The decision is yours.

TWENTY-FOUR

CORA KEATON: 2053

CORA COULDN'T GET the image out of her head.

Light exploding through the sky. Fire erupting on the horizon. The confusion and panic that followed. Boarding the cruise ship. The wave of flames growing closer and closer. Jason appearing at the entrance to the launch bay with a second swarm of employees. Carver giving the order to shut the doors, claiming they would all die if they waited any longer. Launching. Fire consuming the launch bay. The growing darkness. Open space, stars every way she looked, no gravity.

The two days they spent drifting in orbit, with nowhere to dock or land. The careful rationing of food and water. The hunger. The exhaustion. The Gateway manifesting out of thin air, prompting weak cheers from everyone onboard the cruise ship. Docking to the station. And finally, seeing Zach.

At first, it had seemed like a desperate hallucination, a

vision created to suppress the rumbling of her stomach. But the moment Zach spoke, she knew he was there. Alive and well.

Seeing him just made her so happy. Confused, too, but that was a separate issue. She hadn't failed after all. He was still breathing and well-fed, which she couldn't even say for herself. Her cheeks had gone hollow in those two days of near-starvation—she could feel her ribs through her shirt. But she was alive, and so was Zach. That was all that mattered.

Then, her thoughts returned to Jason, and she suddenly felt guilty. He was so close to the ship, so close to safety, but not close enough. She didn't want to leave him behind, but she had no choice. It was Carver. He made the call. And yet, she still felt responsible. Was that how Zach felt about Ryker, always thinking it was his fault? Cora had tried to assure him that it was purely a mistake for which no one was to blame, but he could never accept it. *This is what it was like for him. I understand now.*

Jason had always wanted to see outer space. On those summer nights when he, Cora, and Zach would sprawl out a blanket on the grass and stare up at the stars, he'd speak of venturing to Saturn. The remarks were usually met with wild suggestions of surfing on its rings, ending with them all laughing. But instead of seeing outer space or working to study it, Jason became a security officer. He hated that job. Though he never said it, Cora could always tell that going home was the only good part of the day for him.

Now he was dead, after working a job he despised all his life. It was truly sad. Cora wished she could turn back the clock, but she couldn't. Time only moved forward. She would have to accept that.

Cora sighed, then focused on the immediate problem before her: opening the cryobay. Over the past few days, a team led by Cora had attempted to find a way to get the cryobay's doors open. It seemed like such an easy task. But it wasn't.

On the first day, the priority was to get into the system. That was simple and something small enough to get their heads around after the traumatizing events of the prior week. But after five hours of failure, Cora retreated to her bunk and let the coders do their job.

The second day, she awoke to some amount of success. During the night, they had cracked the firewall and had gotten into the logs. But where to look? The entries seemed to extend for miles, and they decided to take shifts scanning through them. For obvious reasons, Cora didn't stay within her time-frame. What if they found something while she was getting food or asleep? She didn't even know what they were looking for, exactly; just something that would explain the door's shutdown. A hint.

As she paced back and forth across the dimly lit room, she bit her nails and kept her eyes open for fear of missing some great discovery. She feigned confidence, nodding to unheard words in her head, thinking of Zach. They would figure out a way to open the cryobay. With so many talented coders and engineers, there had to be a solution.

"Anything?" she asked, leaning her hands on the programmer's shoulders as he sat slumped in the chair, eyes red with exhaustion.

He wiped his nose and gave a deep shake of his head. "I'm not even sure what to look for. So no, nothing."

The logs were endless. Unlike those that Mission Control kept, the entries on the Gateway detailed *everything* that happened on the station, as well as external commands sent from Earth or Prescott.

"Keep looking. We're not going anywhere if those doors don't open." Cora hooked her hands on her hips, sauntered a few paces to the side, and leaned against a dusty shelf. "If we don't do it, no one else will."

"Yep. If you want something done right, do it yourself," the programmer took a sip from his twenty-year-old soda, "as they say."

"As my mom says." Cora laughed, remembering the wisdom her mother bestowed upon her as a child. Then her shoulders slumped. "Said, I mean. As she used to say."

It pained Cora that she couldn't say goodbye to her mother. With no knowledge of what was coming, Sarina most likely died sitting in her home with the TV droning in the background. Maybe she passed in her sleep. Hopefully.

"Just check the logs from the last ten years. If something happened, it probably happened within the decade," Cora said, although she had no way to back up her hunch. She figured the cryobay being locked may have had something to do with Ryker going home. She wasn't sure why, but the station worked in weird ways, and Ryker claimed he couldn't remember the cryobay being locked while he was on the Gateway. He had also confessed that he'd never actually gone inside it, but without any other concrete clues, Ryker was their most promising lead.

The programmer reduced the logs to the last ten years. As Cora looked through them, none seemed to jump out as significant.

"Go another five years back," Cora instructed.

The programmer set the new starting date as 2038, slightly broader. But the logs they found were minor, most not even regarding the cryobay. Many of the entries were most likely from Ryker and his time there. The ones about cryo possessed an emboldened CB beside the entry title.

"Look, I'm not finding anything. We should tell Carver and start figuring out a way to break the blast door open..." said the programmer in frustration.

Cora pushed him aside, his rolling chair scraping across the perforated metal floor. "I'm setting it to the past fifty years." A little overkill, but it would get the job done.

"The Gateway hasn't been around for fifty years."

"Exactly. That means it'll give us the full history. See?" Cora leaned over his shoulder and took the mouse. She clicked the filter setting, then set it to a complete timeline. When it showed up, she filtered it further to only entries labeled CB.

The list shrunk to a few lines, and several stood out. The first was from 2029, likely from the ship's early testing. Another from early 2030, when they departed for Prescott. One labeled a month after, the moment they reached Mars. It was the last one that confused her.

August 26th, 2030.

Exactly a month before Zach returned from Prescott.

The entry claimed Mission Control had sent the command to shut down the cryobay. Cora didn't know why or how, but that was their answer. The ground disabled it. But why?

"It's been locked for decades," Cora thought out loud, piecing together the details in her head.

"Well, there we go," the programmer said.

Cora cleared her throat and furrowed her eyebrows. "How do we see who sent the command?"

"We can't. The Gateway's computer can only see a command was received from Mission Control, but not who sent it."

"There's no way to find out?"

"Not unless you've got access to Mission Control. Which..." The programmer trailed off, his point already understood. Mission Control was gone.

Cora frowned. "All right. Well, let's tell Zach what we found."

WHEN ZACH GOT to the computer room, Cora brought him up to speed on the situation.

"Mission Control shut it down? Are you sure?" Zach asked.

Cora glanced at the programmer, who nodded in confirmation. "Yeah," Cora replied. "We're sure."

"But why would somebody do that?"

"That's the problem. We can see that the command was sent from Mission Control, but not who sent it. Or why."

"There has to be a way."

"Not from here," Ryker said from beside Zach. "The logs on the Gateway only log what's happening *on* the Gateway."

Cora sighed in defeat. "Who could even have sent the

command? Who would have had that kind of authority, I mean?"

"Your dad, for one," Ryker said, rolling a pen in his fingers, eyeing Cora. "He ran the place."

"What? No. He wouldn't have done that." Cora knew her father would never mess with the Gateway.

Zach leaned against the wall. He stared at the floor, deep in thought. After a moment, he perked up. "Wilford. Wilford was the Head of Communications. He would have had clearance."

"But why would he bother messing with the cryobay?" Cora asked. As far as she could remember, Wilford's role was limited to maintaining radio transmissions to and from the Gateway. While he may have been able to access the Gateway's systems, there'd be no reason for him to do it.

"I don't know," Zach said. "But I *do* know Wilford had copies of the logs on his laptop."

"Wilford had logs from the Gateway?" Ryker asked.

"No," Zach replied. "From Mission Control."

Cora's eyes went wide. "Please tell me you still have the laptop."

"No," Zach said. Cora deflated. Zach smiled. "But I can go get it."

AFTER RETRIEVING Wilford's laptop from his quarters, Zach placed the computer on the desk and flipped open the lid. A few seconds later, the screen flickered on, and OSE's logo appeared. Zach navigated to the logs he had found before their journey to Mars. "Yep. Here they are."

"We need the logs from August 26th, 2030," the programmer said.

Zach entered the requested date, but no logs labeled CB appeared. The only other entries from that day seemed to be routine checks of the Gateway's systems.

"There's nothing about the cryobay," Zach said and frowned. He looked at the Gateway's computer, double-checked the cryobay shutdown command, then looked back at the laptop. "It's not here."

"That's not possible," the programmer said. "Let me see." Zach stepped aside. The programmer squinted at the logs, then grunted. "Hmm."

"What?" Zach said.

"It's not here."

Zach threw up his hands and walked away.

The programmer opened a terminal and tapped out a few commands. He read the output, then shook his head. "It doesn't make sense. There's no way the Gateway received a command that Mission Control didn't send. Every command gets logged. It's all automated."

"And logs don't just disappear, right?" Cora asked.

"Right."

"So what does that mean?"

The programmer looked up at her with a troubled expression. "They've been deleted."

Deleted? Cora thought. A bad feeling began to brew in her stomach as she shifted her gaze to meet Zach's. "Is there a way to get them back?"

The programmer took a sip of his soda. "Maybe. This

laptop's ancient, though. I'm not sure I know my way around it."

"Just try," ordered Zach.

The coder puffed out a breath. "Yeah, okay. Give me a few minutes." He turned back to the laptop and began typing.

Zach, Cora, and Ryker stood in a small circle on the other side of the room, discussing. After about ten minutes, the programmer gave an exhale of victory. The three of them rushed back over to his side.

Zach leaned down to look at the screen. "What did you find?"

"Check it out." He pointed at the screen. Where there had previously only been one log, there were now two. The second was marked with a capitalized CB. The programmer opened the file. A sequence of commands appeared.

```
34°12'6.1"N 118°10'18"W
(OSE* #
## = Initiate Cryobay shutdown ## ;
access number: B59j4h7
authorization status # = Confirmed
(Proxy 67) ; 09/03/30
send location ^^ === Mesosphere **
Gateway Station
system failure stage + airlock ( 10 )
disable
1% gradual (-3) repeal; 6^
program initiate == CARVER, NICOLAS
```

Cora scanned the log until she reached the end. Carver?

What did he have to do with this? As she read it over again, she stopped again at the last line. *Program initiate.* Her stomach churned as the words registered.

Nicolas Carver had shut down the cryobay.

ZACH CROFT: 2053

Carver must have had a valid reason to justify shutting down the cryobay. He never did anything on a whim; he always had a detailed plan accounting for a thousand contingencies, anticipating every possible failure. It was the way he operated.

"There had to be something wrong with it," Zach said. "He must have done it to save us from something."

"Or to get rid of us." Ryker struggled to sit still. He beat his foot against the floor impatiently.

"We can't jump to that conclusion," Cora interjected.

"Why not?" Ryker replied, seething. "Cryo kills the Red Plague. We suspected that, even back then. If the cryobay had been open, Zach's father would have put everyone under before they got sick. And they'd still be alive!"

Zach understood what Ryker was getting at. He didn't like it one bit. "No. There's no way. Carver couldn't have known what would happen. He's a lot of things, but he's not a murderer." It was hard to even consider that Carver would have locked the cryobay, knowing it would end with the remaining colonists dead. Zach's *father* dead.

Staring at the screen, Cora approached the programmer and placed a hand on his shoulder. "Go. You've done your job. You don't need to be here for this."

"But—"

"Please. Don't tell anyone what happened here. If anyone asks, say the logs are still a dead end. Okay?"

After a moment, the programmer nodded hesitantly. "Okay." He took his stuff and left.

Ryker sat in the empty chair and rolled it up to the laptop.

"What are you doing?" Zach asked as he took a seat.

Instead of answering, Ryker went straight to the filter settings. He typed out a name, last name before first.

Carver, Nicolas.

"Let's see." Ryker landed on three entries, each labeled with Carver's name. The first was the cryobay shutdown command that they had just seen. Ryker clicked on the second entry, an audio log. A recording began to play.

It was an exchange between two men. One sounded like Carver, only younger, which made sense given the age of the tape. The other voice was familiar too, but it spoke with such desperation that it was barely recognizable. Zach felt sick listening to it. And he felt sicker when he realized who it was.

It was his father.

Quinton spoke in fragments, getting out little information at a time. He ranted about the Red Plague, leaving the sick colonists in Prescott, and people on the station growing ill.

Carver asked Quinton what they were doing to stop the infection, and Quinton shakily mentioned that he believed cryo would kill it. So, was the cryobay still working at the time of this recording? Zach looked at the bottom corner of the screen, seeing the date. It was less than a day before Zach and Ryker were put in the secondary pods. Less than a day before the cryobay was disabled.

With conviction, Quinton said that he could get the

survivors into stasis for the journey home, and all OSE had to do was be prepared. Suddenly, the connection to Mission Control was lost.

"Hello? Hello?!" Quinton called out.

The audio player closed. The screen returned to the list of logs, where only one remained unclicked.

Zach stared at the screen, struggling to comprehend what he had just heard. Carver had known that cryo was their only way to survive. Quinton had told him, clear as day.

Beside him, Ryker shook with rage. "You still think it's just a coincidence? That less than a day after this, he shut the cryobay down? He knew what he was doing! He was killing them!" Ryker shot out of his seat.

"Ryker, hang on—"

"Do you not realize he killed your father?" Ryker shouted. "Think!"

"Zach, we don't know that—" Cora tried to interject.

"He didn't kill him." Quinton had done that to himself. At the same time, he wouldn't have had to do it if the cryobay hadn't been locked.

He would still be alive.

"There has to be an explanation." Zach looked at the third entry with Carver's name, dated a month later. In dire need of an answer, he opened it and watched a block of data appear on the screen

```
EMERGENCY PROTOCOL
send location ^^ === Mesosphere **
Gateway Station
system failure stage + airlock ( 16 )
disable
pressurize maximum #
0.00006% gradual (13) repeal; 9^
re enable date "" NA
PROTOCOL initiate == CARVER, NICOLAS
```

Emergency Protocol?

Zach mentally replayed the events from the last day he spent on the station before going home. He remembered how they jettisoned his father's body out to space, how they went to the docking bay and boarded a dropship, and how Ryker ran off the ship just before a blaring siren sounded.

"EMERGENCY PROTOCOL ACTIVATED."

Then, the airlock closed. Zach was sent home while Ryker stayed behind. Had OSE known they were coming back?

"He..." Ryker trailed off, looking around the room with heavy breaths. "He left me here."

Zach had no clue what to say.

Ryker hurried on. "You were right. You were right from the fucking beginning. It was him." He stood and kicked a trash can at the wall. "It was him!"

"Ryker, wait," Cora said with conviction.

Zach recalled how effortlessly Carver had deceived him. *"You think I'd leave a kid up there if he was still alive?"*

Why had Zach been so quick to believe Carver? How could he have been so gullible? Zach thought of his plan to visit

Wilford in his search for answers, recalling that the cabin was on fire when he arrived. Could Carver have had something to do with that too?

No, there was absolutely no way. That would be outright murder.

"S-Something must have been wrong..." Zach stammered.

"Fuck something being wrong! He ruined my life!" Ryker appeared to hold back tears but masked them with red-hot anger. He drove his fist into the wall so hard his knuckles turned bloody.

Listening to Ryker's hand thud against the metal, Zach looked back at the screen. Realization hit him like a kick in the stomach.

"I wasn't supposed to come home either, was I?"

Carver had tried to kill Zach the same way he had with Ryker. To erase him from society, so whatever secrets were on the Gateway would stay there. The betrayal tore at Zach's chest. He had trouble catching his breath.

Carver had only pretended to be a father figure all those years because his plan to eliminate Zach had failed. So, what motivated Carver to look after him? Guilt? Concern? Fear of the truth—that Carver had killed the colonists—coming out?

He had used Zach, just like he used everyone. *You're like a son to me.* How many times had he said that? More times than Zach could count.

He said it, knowing very well that he had tried to murder his so-called *son.* Zach began to shake. Was that why Carver didn't want him to go to Mars? Because it would mean going to the Gateway, trying to use the cryobay, and finding out what Carver had done?

Cora quickly blurted out, "Zach, we still don't have all the information yet." She tried to comfort him, her voice breaking in the process. "Why would he want to leave you guys? Especially *you*, Zach. He cared about you."

Past tense. *Cared*. For all Zach knew, it could have *all* been a sham, a lie. An act to keep everything under Carver's control. If the evidence before Zach didn't make that clear, he wasn't sure what would.

"It was a mistake. It had to be," Cora said.

Ryker wiped his bleeding knuckles on his jacket. "People don't make mistakes like that."

"I don't think he would have left two kids to die on purpose." Cora tried to show reason, but nothing she said seemed to stick.

"There are too many failsafes installed to make a mistake like that," concluded Zach, the words bitter on his tongue. "That was a manual command."

"That son of a bitch," Ryker roared, then looked at Zach. "Where is he? And don't cover for him!"

Cover for him? Zach was *done* helping Carver. "I don't know."

"I'm going to kill him. I swear to fucking god I'm going to make him pay." Ryker moved for the door.

Zach stepped in front of him. "Hang on. Let's just figure this out for a second—"

"Get out of the way!"

"Just stop. I can help."

"I don't need your help!" Ryker shoved Zach hard enough that he fell back on the desk. "I needed your help when you left me here for dead! Where were you then?"

"Ryker, they told me you were dead. What was I supposed to do?"

"Use your fucking brain! That's what you were supposed to do. You knew I was alive up here. You knew it!" Ryker squeezed his eyes shut and gritted his teeth.

"Fine. You're right," Zach said sarcastically. "As a single, orphaned child, I could have done more to help."

"*Everything* that's gone wrong has been because of you. You think you're some saint helping everyone, but you're just a... a..." He attempted to find the right word. "A parasite! A parasite that latches onto people and fucks up their lives!"

"I was a kid! What did you expect me to do? Fly back and get you myself?"

"Okay, then what about on Mars? *You* made us go into that damn crater when we were kids! Or what about when the Emergency Protocol went into effect? *You* let me leave the dropship!"

"Me? I went into that crater because of *you*, because *you* were so upset about what happened to your dad!"

"I didn't want to go into that crater. You made me! You're always so ready to put other people in the line of fire as long as you don't get hurt!"

"That's funny coming from you. Have you ever considered that maybe *you're* the problem too?" Zach moved in on him. "That if you hadn't taken our stash of crystals and shown all your friends, maybe our parents would still be alive?"

Ryker laughed. "That's my fault? Your dad killed *himself*, for fuck's sake."

Zach punched Ryker in the face and was quickly met with an elbow to the nose. As he doubled over, Ryker turned for the door. "Maybe if you stopped worrying about everyone else, you'd realize you need the most help."

Coughing, Zach tried to stand up straight. "I'm sorry that I gave a shit about other people. But I guess that's not your strong suit!" He clutched his stomach. "We'd all be better off if you never came back!"

Ryker stopped at the doorway. "You'd all be *dead* if I hadn't come back." He stormed through the exit and slammed it behind him. Then, he did something Zach didn't expect.

He locked the door.

RYKER GAGARIN: 2053

The gun was easy to get.

With hundreds huddled in the living quarters, the armory was left unattended. Ryker slinked in, hands closed in tight, white-knuckled fists, and grabbed the first pistol he could find. As he made his way to Carver's new office, he thought of the ways he would make the bastard hurt. Hurt just as much as he had.

When he reached the entrance, Ryker cocked the handgun and threw the door open. Carver looked up in surprise, barely uttering a "what's going on" before Ryker grabbed him by the hair and slammed his head on the industrial metal table. A line of blood emerged from Carver's brow. He reached up to feel it.

"What the... what..." he stuttered.

Ryker pulled Carver's head back again and shoved the gun in the man's mouth. He wanted Carver to beg for mercy. He wanted him to feel every ounce of pain that Ryker had felt. It took all the self-control in the world not to blow his brains out right then and there. "Beg," Ryker ordered.

With his eyes full of fear, Carver tried to shake his head out of Ryker's grasp. "Are you deaf?" Ryker shouted. He pulled Carver's hair harder. "Beg for mercy!"

"Please! Please, I'm begging you, Ryker," Carver pleaded with a mouth full of metal. His voice was muffled nearly to the point of indecipherability.

That wasn't good enough. All the years Ryker lost because of this putrid excuse for a human, and that was all he got? He shoved the gun farther between Carver's teeth. "Tell me why you did it! Tell me why you fucking left me here!" The urge to pull the trigger ran through Ryker, but he quickly silenced it. That would be too easy on Carver. He pulled the gun from Carver's mouth and pointed it at his leg, deciding to start there.

Carver began to hyperventilate, looking around for someone to help. But there was no one to save him. "I— I don't know!"

Ryker pistol-whipped him across the cheek. "For once in your goddamn life, tell the truth!"

Suddenly, Zach burst into the room. Seeing the gun, he held his hands up, making a surrendering gesture. "Put the gun down, Ryker!"

"This isn't your fight," said Ryker.

"Just drop the weapon, and let's talk."

"He doesn't deserve to talk!" Ryker brought the barrel up, pressing it into Carver's neck.

"Do you want to be a murderer? Can you live with that?" Zach took a few steps forward.

"Is that even a question?" If becoming a murderer was

necessary to rid the world of this filth, Ryker would take that chance. And who was Zach to stand in his way? He had gone home and lived a happy life while Ryker was left alone. He knew *nothing*.

"This isn't you, Ryker. Please. Put down the gun."

"He tried to kill you too! How are you still defending him?" Ryker gritted his teeth. "He deserves to die!"

"Because we're not that kind of people." Zach shot a piercing look in Carver's direction and shook his head. "We're not *him*."

For a moment, Carver looked wounded. Then he quickly went firm again. "Please, just let me explain!" he shouted. "I didn't want the Red Plague to make it back to the ground! You know tha— that it would have killed everyone! But I never meant for you to get hurt, Zach. It—it wasn't even me that executed the command! I know it says my name, but Wilford was the one who did it! He logged in with my account unauthorized! And I've felt guilty half my life that we couldn't get you home."

"You're lying!" Ryker growled.

Zach studied Carver with a crinkled brow. "Why didn't you search for him? In twenty-three years, you never made a single attempt to get him back."

"I told you the truth when you came home. We found no heat signature, no signs of life—"

"Then how was I alive?" Ryker barked, pressing the gun so hard against Carver's throat that it looked like his jugular could explode. "You're a fucking liar. That's what you are! You tampered with the logs to make it look like you searched for me!"

He should unload the clip in Carver right now to get it over with before Zach found a way to stop him. Ryker didn't care what happened after, whether he was arrested or blasted out an airlock. It didn't matter as long as Carver was lying in a pool of blood.

"I'm sorry!" Carver begged. His dignity and composure broke down. "I wish we hadn't done it. I do! Please, please, *please,* don't kill me! *Please!*"

His eyes finding the floor, Zach spoke quietly. "We can't just execute him."

Ryker gaped at Zach in disbelief. "You want to let him off?"

"No," Zach said. "I want him dead too. But not like this."

"Like what, then?" Ryker couldn't believe what he was hearing. There were no laws or codes they had to follow anymore. Justice was justice. "He ruined my life!"

"Let's give it a minute. We'll lock him up, calm down, then figure out what to do. Okay?"

Shaking with anger, Ryker smashed the pistol into Carver's face, knocking him out cold. Carver's body dropped to the floor with a thud.

"Fine." Ryker tucked the gun into his waistband. "But I'm not gonna change my mind."

TWENTY-FIVE

NICOLAS CARVER: 2053

"I WANT HIM DEAD TOO."

Carver couldn't believe his ears. Those were words he would never have expected from Zach. While Zach had been quite disruptive recently—breaking Ryker out of custody, reaching out to Wilford, stealing the dropship from OSE—saying he wanted Carver dead was beyond the pale. After everything Carver had done for Zach, and those were the thanks he got?

The second Zach discovered what Carver had done, he overreacted in exactly the way Carver knew he would. He never stopped for a second to understand Carver's reasons, never considered that maybe Carver was doing the right thing, even if it was the hard thing, the messy thing. He could never understand that real leaders need to make tough choices. They don't always get to do what's popular. Sometimes they get none of the credit and all of the blame.

It was Carver who had gotten the last survivors—the *only* survivors—off that flaming planet, only to discover that the Gateway was gone. The Gateway would have been there from the beginning if Zach hadn't pulled his little dropship stunt. Instead, Carver had to maintain the sanity and morale of the survivors, rationing food and water in the hopes that the Gateway would return before they all starved to death.

Then, when Zach finally returned with the Gateway, Carver had again done the responsible thing and tried to put everything behind them. They had more important things to deal with than some petty disagreements from the past. But Zach's warped sense of morality couldn't just let bygones be bygones. Instead, he wanted Carver dead.

What an arrogant asshole.

Zach would have been nothing without Carver. He would have lived his life working some minimum wage job if Carver hadn't handed him an education and a top-notch job at OSE. Carver was there every step of Zach's life, watching out for him and constantly helping in any way he could. He should have let the kid rot.

Carver's eyes struggled to focus in the dim light of his containment vault. The unending machine hum ate away at his sanity. Metal ridges rubbed against his back and dug into his shoulder blades. *What a time to be alive,* he thought, conjuring enough willpower to sit up. Minutes seemed like hours. Hours, like days.

Despite his best efforts, Carver's mind turned again and again to the thought of what Zach might do to him. Would he leave him in the cell for the ride to Alpha Cen? Would they put him on trial? That didn't seem plausible, but Carver couldn't imagine Zach would just jettison him out to space. Or would he?

A few sharp beeps echoed outside in the hall, the sound of someone punching an access code into the control panel outside the containment unit. The door opened with a flash of white light. A silhouette stepped in.

"Get up."

RYKER GAGARIN: 2030

Why? Why did his mother have to go? As he looked at her through the quarantine glass, all Ryker could think of was what he could have done differently. Could he have spent more time by her side during her final hours? Could he have badgered the doctors to do more? No. It was pointless. It wouldn't have prevented her demise. There was nothing they could do.

He traced the hair on her head with his eyes. Her brownish-gold locks maintained little of their former beauty. Instead, they were coated in cold sweat and clinging sand. Ryker suppressed a sob.

"Ryker," Zach whispered from the tent's entrance. "It's time to go." His voice was soft, without the uneasy edge it had maintained over the last several weeks. But no amount of kindness could move Ryker from his current position on the dirty ground, staring at his mother's corpse.

Corpse. The realization that his mother had not just passed but had wholly and irrevocably died struck him. Ryker wished he could hear her voice one last time.

"Ryker," repeated Zach. "I'm so sorry." He hesitated before continuing. "My dad's waiting."

"I can't just leave her." She didn't deserve to be discarded by her only child, left for the elements. Left to rot.

Zach bit his lip and looked out through the flap of the tent. *"I'm sorry, but we have to go. They're leaving."*

Kayla's head drooped a bit against her pillow. *"Easy there, Ma,"* Ryker choked. *"Don't go falling over."* It was pathetic. He knew that. She was gone, and there was nothing to do but accept it.

When his father died, grief had led Ryker to the crater, to bringing back that irogen, and, finally, to the mysterious outbreak of the Red Plague. He didn't know whether it was his and Zach's doing, but the timeline was too coincidental. His sadness could have very well been the downfall of the colony. With that in mind, he calmed his nerves.

"Okay... Okay, let's go," Ryker said and slowly rose. As he walked toward the exit, he gave one last look to his mother, feeling that if he looked away, she would cease to exist altogether. He would forget her face, her voice, her touch. *"Rest easy, Ma,"* he whispered.

Then, he looked away.

ZACH CROFT: 2030

Quinton ushered Zach and Ryker through the empty streets of Prescott. The colony was deserted, deceased, broken. In the dead of night, even the buildings seemed sickly. Canvas doors and tents hung motionless. The few remaining street lamps flickered.

Zach couldn't believe they were leaving. It was astounding how terribly things had gone wrong. From the moment they touched down on the planet, they were doomed. It was as if *someone had cursed them. Any time the colonists experienced a period of relative peace, some other disaster upended their lives. Well, no more. Never again. It was over now. He was going home.*

The way Quinton had framed it, giving people the option to leave Prescott was a way to hedge their bets. Those who went home could gather help and develop a vaccine, while those who stayed could try to do something with the resupply ship scheduled for a few weeks out.

"We can't put all our eggs in one basket," Quinton had explained, "If we do, and we're wrong, we'll all die. This is our best chance for at least some of us to survive."

Zach didn't fully buy that explanation. It felt like his dad was trying to clear his conscience. Quinton wanted to leave. But by giving people the option to stay or go, he wouldn't be abandoning anyone; those staying behind would have chosen to do so. He wouldn't have to force anyone's hand. Everyone was free to make their own decisions.

As Zach and Ryker passed each dilapidated structure, Zach pictured the sickly people cowering inside them. He pictured their dead-grass hair, their bubbling skin, their tears of blood. He imagined what it would be like if he, too, was resigned to dying alone, with no one willing to be by his side for fear of contracting the illness.

Guilt pooled in his stomach as he thought about his hand in the situation. But before he could dwell on it too long, Quinton tugged him and Ryker through the last stretch of the town and into the sandy expanse beyond it.

In the distance, Zach saw the source of the muffled voices: a long line of people was assembled at the colonial airlock, fenced in by hip-height rails. The airlock was round and towering, bridging the gap between the colony and the long glass tunnel that jutted from it. At the end of the passageway, a dropship sat on the launch pad, steam swirling beneath its glowing thrusters. Small groups in twos and threes climbed its ramp and disappeared inside.

"What's the line for?" Zach asked Quinton.

"Security checkpoint."

"Security for what?"

"We can't risk letting anyone who's sick slip aboard."

Zach nodded. It made sense, but it was still a depressing thought, a grim reminder that so many people were forced to choose between saving themselves and leaving their friends and families behind or staying and risking almost certain death.

As they drew closer to the line, the muffled voices revealed themselves to be angry shouts. On both sides of the security line, enraged colonists yelled at the deserters, cursing them for leaving the sickly behind. The crowd surged against the security fences, seething with rage. They pointed fingers, shouted obscenities, and threw sand at the people in line. It was hard to believe that they had all been laughing and eating burgers together a few months earlier in Big Bear.

Zach looked up at his father. Quinton was staring at the chaotic scene, his eyes drained of all life. He gulped, took the boys' hands, and strode forward.

A guard in blue and black fatigues received the trio as they approached the line, placing his hand protectively on Quinton's back and leading him and the boys through the raucous crowd. "This way, sir."

Quinton looked nervously at the long queue of colonists. "How many people have boarded?"

"A little over a hundred."

Quinton nodded, but the uneasy look lingered on his face.

The guard led Quinton and the boys down the line, instructing the other colonists to step aside. As Zach passed them, he marveled at the guards' ability to tune out the vitriol being hurled at them from both sides of the line. They kept their eyes straight ahead, seemingly deaf to the shouts of the protestors.

Suddenly, a cup of dark liquid flew from somewhere in the mob and splattered on a man in front of Zach. He flinched as the deep purple fluid dripped from his jacket and suitcase.

"You can't just leave us!" the man who threw the cup yelled.

More voices shouted from the crowd.

"Fucking monsters!"

"We know you're not coming back for us!"

"Is there anything we can do about them?" Quinton asked the guard, motioning to the protestors.

"I'm afraid not, sir. We don't have the manpower to do crowd control right now. Who knows—maybe a few of them will wise up and get in line themselves."

"I can only hope—"

"Oh, and here's our brave leader!" one protestor hollered, pointing at Quinton and beginning a slow clap. Others joined in the ironic applause. Soon, the entire mob was shouting at Quinton.

"Look at him! Not even waiting in line to leave us all behind."

"Bored of your job, are you?"

"Jumping ship?"

Zach cowered from the protesters, tugging his father's arm for attention. "Dad—"

"Ignore them." Quinton squeezed Zach's hand and locked his eyes on some nonexistent object ahead of him.

"Are they going to hurt us?" Ryker asked.

Quinton eyed the escort's gun and shook his head. "We'll be okay."

At the front of the line, barricades had been set up to keep the protesters out and to regulate who got onto the ship. At least a dozen soldiers stood guard around the safe zone at various intervals, but only a few held guns. One man stood with a shaky hand over his holstered pistol, looking nervously from the line to his comrades. A thin sheen of sweat covered his forehead, and his foot beat anxiously against the sand. Zach noted the man's name tag, which spelled KENNER in bold white letters.

Where the security line met the barricades, two men in hazmat suits stood with tablets in one hand and flashlights in the other. They asked colonists their names, scanned their ID cards, then shone the light into their eyes to look for any signs of infection. If their eyes were clear, the guards sent the travelers to the dropship and prepared for the next few people.

When Quinton's group arrived, one of the hazmat-wearing guards quickly checked them for signs of illness, then sent them on their way.

As Zach passed through the barricade, he watched the next group of colonists step up for inspection. One of the men stood with a sleeping boy in his arms, leaning forward uncomfortably as one of the inspectors shined a light in his eyes.

"You're clear," the guard said. "Now, the boy."

The man glanced at his son, then cocked his head at the hazmat-wearing guard. "He's sleeping. It's the middle of the night."

"Sir, we need to see his eyes."

The frustrated line grumbled at the man, urging him to speed up. His lips curled into a nervous smile. "Come on. Aren't you a dad?"

"Not anymore. Show me his eyes."

The man turned bone white. After a beat, he reluctantly shook his son awake and whispered in his ear. The boy gave a confused look, to which his father returned one that said, "It'll be okay."

Impatient, the guard used his pointer finger and thumb to angle the boy's face toward his own, then shined a light in each of the boy's eyes. He paused. His arm fell gravely to his side as he shut off the light and took a few steps back. "Sir, you can't board."

"Please. I need to get him help," the man pleaded.

A few guards rushed over and took the man by the arms, guiding him forcefully away from the entrance.

"Please!" the man shouted. "Help us! Someone—" He struggled against the guards' grips, but they were too strong. Two men from the crowd hollered at the guards as he was pulled away from the line.

"He's a kid!"

"Let him go!"

Suddenly, a fist collided with one of the guard's faces. He faltered, grabbed his jaw, then returned a powerful punch. The attacker fell to the ground.

Infuriated, the protestors turned their string of profanities on the guard and moved to grab him. The guard pulled a baton from his belt and swung it at the crowd, commanding them to step back. Several men lunged at the guard, trying to overtake him. The baton collided with one of the men's faces. Blood spurted from his nose. More guards then charged into the fray, their batons swinging.

"Time to go," urged Quinton's escort. Strengthening his hold on Quinton's back, the guard hastily led him through the airlock and into the tunnel, tugging Zach and Ryker along for the ride.

Shouts pelted the trio from behind. As Zach looked over his shoulder, the queue and protesting crowds morphed into a single, outraged mass. In what seemed like an instant, the railings were knocked over. The angered colonists began stumbling over the barricade. The guards shouted at them to back up, raising their rifles to show they were serious. The crowd was undeterred, and they continued to shout at the guards as they advanced.

"What are you gonna do, shoot me?"

"Go ahead! We're dead anyway!"

Down the tunnel, several soldiers stood at the base of the dropship's ramp. As one noticed the party approaching, he ran over and looked to Quinton's escort for answers. "What the hell is happening out there?"

"The civs are getting rowdy. Get back to your place and stand guard." With that, the escort led the group the rest of the way into the dropship.

Once on the dropship, Quinton seated Zach and Ryker before being called off to another part of the ship. A tight circle of guards stood at the entrance. Some leaned against the frame of the blast door, making wild gestures at the colony. Others craned their necks to listen for news from their breast pocket radios.

A burst of gunshots rang out from somewhere down by the colony. Desperate calls for backup echoed through the walkie-talkies. The guards at the entrance reacted, unslinging their rifles *and running back down the tunnel. One of them ducked into the dropship.*

"Where's Quinton?" he yelled.

"He's in the hold down below!" someone answered.

A few more gunshots tore through the air, coming from what sounded like a single gun. Between the gunshots, the adrenaline-filled roars of the guards echoed in the distance, telling the gunman to hold his fire. But the voices were no longer coming through the radio.

They were coming from the tunnel.

"Goddammit, Kenner!" a guard called.

"Go! Now!"

Though the rest of the yelling was almost unintelligible, Zach could tell that the guards were pleading for the colonists to get back. A moment later, a blood-covered soldier limped up the ramp as fast as his legs would allow him and fell into the arms of the one remaining guard at the entrance.

"They're— they're coming!"

"Whose coming?"

"All of them! Everyone!" The guard fell from his comrade's arms and slumped on the ground, clutching his seemingly dislocated shoulder.

A moment later, Quinton emerged from the back of the ship and ran up to the entrance, pulling the injured guard inside.

"What do we do?" the other asked.

The tunnel was glass, so even from the dropship's elevated state, Zach could see the mob of hollering people rapidly approaching, filling the width of the tunnel with their staggering numbers. A few meters ahead, a line of guards ran for the ship as quickly as possible. One did so in a backward manner as he fired more panic-stricken shots into the crowd. He managed to land two or three before he was overtaken by the mob.

As his bullets met their marks, the colonists tripped and stumbled over their spasming neighbors, calling for the guards' heads. The crowd swallowed two more soldiers, leaving nothing but the men's desperate screams.

"What are you waiting for?" a voice shouted behind Zach. "Close the doors!" Zach turned to see a man he recognized as Councilman Faren unbuckling his seatbelt and rushing toward Quinton.

"We have to wait for the guards!" Quinton yelled.

"There's no time! We need to go now!"

"We can't just leave them."

"It's that, or we all die."

Quinton stared out at the tunnel, biting his lip as his eyes traced the guards' path. They were almost to the ship, but the mob was too. Seeing Quinton, a flicker of hope crossed the soldiers' faces. A few raised their hands as if to get his attention. One called out to him.

But then, someone in the crowd threw a rock at the man's back, and the soldier fell to the ground. The mob trampled him moments later. Faren tried to push past Quinton to engage the door himself.

"Quinton—"

Quinton pushed Faren away. He stared off into nothingness briefly before slamming his fist against the door frame and turning back into the ship. "Damn it! Close the door."

A moment later, the airlock shut.

A dozen frantic hands reached the blast door and began banging on it. Muffled voices plead for someone to open the door.

The pounding grew faster and faster until their muffled screams were drowned out, and two hundred other hands replaced theirs.

Quinton stared at the closed blast door in numb horror, his head slowly shaking back and forth. "How long to launch?" he asked, his voice sounding distant.

"Five seconds!" the pilot replied.

Five.

Four.

Three.

Two.

As the engines kicked on, Zach heard Quinton whisper, "I'm sorry."

ZACH CROFT: 2053

Zach glanced at Ryker as they passed a group of people in the hall. "I apologize for what I said earlier. Things got out of hand, you know?" Zach found himself replaying their fight and reached up to feel the bruise forming on the side of his head.

Ryker scrunched his face. "It's fine. Wasn't my proudest moment either."

"It's not just that. It's..." Zach took a breath, craning his neck. "I should have found a way to come back for you." They walked by the hydrofarm entrance. They saw lines of greenery sprouting from murky waterbeds through the glass doors. It was incredible the thing was still working after so many years.

"We were just kids," Ryker said. "There's nothing you could have done."

"I could have talked someone into it."

"Really? You're good, but you're not *that* good."

Zach nodded, cracking something barely discernible as a smile. "I know it sounds silly, but for the first few years after Prescott, I stared at the sky every night, hoping to see your ship fall from the brightest dot up there. Even though they said you were dead, I still did it."

Every night after dinner, he'd sweep his plate into the sink, grab his cheap telescope, and post up in the backyard. With the pool quietly churning beside him, he'd align the lens to the sky. Cora would come out periodically. Sometimes, she'd carry bowls of ice cream she had prepared for the two of them. Other times, she'd come bearing only the time. *"It's midnight. Mom says we have to go to bed."*

"Why?" Ryker asked. "Not to prod, but a dot in the sky isn't all that interesting."

Zach breathed a bit of laughter—the first bit he had in a while—and eyed his shoes. "I don't know. I guess I was hoping you were still alive. But," Zach sighed, "eventually..."

"You gave up."

Zach nodded. "I'm sorry."

"It's okay. I did, too, sometimes. A lot of times."

Over time, Zach stopped going outside. Sarina noticed. After all, he'd done it for years. She had been washing dishes when she asked him about it.

"Aren't you supposed to be on the terrace right around now?" she asked, dragging her hands across the embroidered rag.

Zach shook his head slightly. He walked over to the fridge and pulled out a grape soda. He was about to go back to his room when Sarina spoke again.

"Hey." She dropped the cloth into the drying rack as she

approached Zach from behind. "I know. I miss them too." She ruffled his hair. "We'll get through this. Trust me."

It seemed like a lifetime ago. So much had happened recently that Zach hadn't even given a second thought to Sarina or the fact that he never got to say goodbye. He also never got to thank her for taking him in when nobody else would. She didn't have to do it, but the better side of her told her it was the right thing to do. Zach sighed. At least she was with Victor now.

"How did you do it, Ryker?" Zach asked, coming back to the present. "Coping with so much loss, all by yourself?" He couldn't imagine what Ryker had gone through. To have nobody left to turn to *and* nowhere else to go? A normal person would have been crippled by it in a matter of months. But somehow, Ryker wasn't.

Ryker briefly looked at the line of windows beside him. "I told myself I'd make it back. No matter how long it took. And then I did." His eyes went glassy. "And now here we are. Right back where we started."

A voice crackled over the radio on Zach's belt. "Zach. Ryker. Did you guys release Carver?" Zach shot a worried look at Ryker and held the radio up to his mouth.

"What are you talking about?"

"His cell is empty. He's gone."

TWENTY-SIX

ZACH CROFT: 2030

ZACH FELT the fire grazing his face, coming so close that a sheen of sweat appeared on his forehead. He raised his sword to strike, preparing to bring it down on the brownish scales, then remembered it was only a book and snapped out of it.

But it wasn't just any book. It was the one Zach's mother used to read him. The one they pored over the night before she died. As he read, her voice sang, melodic and soft, through his head, bringing the words to life. How long had it been since he'd read it? It must have been years, but it was still one of the few things he brought with him on the mission. Despite it being amongst his only belongings, he never opened it. He never got past the title page until now.

With everything going on—all those people dead, abandoning the colony—he needed his mother's support. Zach felt her reading it with him. Not just her delicate voice reciting the words in his mind, but in a more physical form. As if her shape-

less spirit was hovering above his head. As if the breeze stroking his hair was her hand instead of the air from the vent in the wall.

He flipped the page and started the next chapter, though he didn't get more than a few words in before the bedroom light flickered on and Zach's flashlight went off.

"Time for bed," said Quinton, leaning against the doorway in a flannel button-down.

"Five more minutes?"

"I'm afraid not." Quinton sat down at the edge of the bed and ran his hand over the blanket. "We're going into cryo soon. It's best if you get some rest."

"Isn't that what the pods are for?"

"You'd think so, wouldn't you? But it doesn't put you to sleep. You're just... dormant." Quinton's brow furrowed with concern. He reached up to touch Zach's forehead. "When did you get that?"

Get what? Were there boils on Zach's skin? Was he infected? Zach dodged away from Quinton's hand. "What is it?" His mind sprinted to the worst possibilities. He had the Red Plague, and soon, he would feel nauseous and tired.

"A bruise, it looks like." Quinton clicked his tongue. "Does it hurt?"

Zach sighed in relief. He couldn't even remember getting it. "It's fine. Do you always have to be a doctor?"

"No, I suppose not," relented Quinton. "I'll just be your dad." He patted Zach's leg.

Zach fidgeted with a frayed piece of his blanket. "Can I ask you a question?"

"Go ahead."

"Do you think they'll remember us? On Earth?" Zach knew it sounded stupid, but it had been in his mind for days.

"What kind of question is that? Of course, they will. We're going to radio OSE as soon as everyone's settled. How's that sound?"

"What about the colony? What will happen to the people we left?"

"OSE will send a team to help everyone there. Trained professionals."

Zach wanted to point out that Quinton was also a trained professional—and hadn't been able to do anything about it—but only nodded. "Okay, Dad. Sounds good."

"Anything else you want to ask while you're at it? Why is the sky blue? What wiped out the dinosaurs?"

"What if I get sick? Because I went into the crater."

"We still don't know if that had anything to do with it. Besides, you'd be showing symptoms. Ryker too."

"What if—"

"You're okay. That's the end of it. Now, try to get some sleep, and we'll talk about it in the morning." Quinton turned the lights off on his way out, leaving Zach with his thoughts.

Zach realized how tired the last few days had left him. Clearing his mind, he turned over, wrapped himself in the covers, and allowed sleep to overtake him.

THE FOLLOWING DAY, footsteps beyond his door woke Zach up. He quickly pulled himself together, remembering the new ration schedule, and got dressed. He couldn't bring any clothes from the colony with him, so he had to make do with what was already on the station. That meant an oversized white t-shirt he had to tuck into his pants. After getting ready, he made his way to the cafeteria. His father and Ryker were already waiting at one of the tables.

Zach sat between them and waited for the meal to be served. When the two slices of bread and protein paste arrived, he stared at his plate vacantly. It didn't even look like food. Whatever. He wasn't that hungry. Ryker, on the other hand, dug in immediately.

On the far side of the cafeteria, Councilman Faren sat with a group discussing plans for Earth. Sweat coated his forehead, and he blinked hard every few seconds. Zach supposed he was under a lot of stress.

Eventually, Quinton noticed Zach avoiding the food and commented, "You haven't touched your rations."

"I'm not very hungry." He could at least count on a sandwich and juice at mealtime in the colony.

"You've got to eat something. We'll be fasting for a while in cryo." Quinton peeked around Zach. "Look. Ryker's got the right idea."

Ryker looked over clumsily. "I'm sorry."

"Don't be," said Quinton. "I could go for some ice cream right now. Why don't we get some when we get back to Earth?"

"I don't even remember what ice cream tastes like," Zach answered.

Suddenly, a high-pitched scream pierced the air, turning all heads to the end of the cafeteria. Something slammed against the ground. Immediately, Quinton shot out of his seat and ran over.

"Out of my way, everyone! Move!" He pushed his way through the cluster of people that had quickly gathered.

Zach and Ryker looked at one another before following everyone else. A flurry of questions erupted all around them.

"What happened to him?"

"Is he breathing?"

"Was there something in the food?"

Zach weaved through the crowd until he reached the front. He saw Quinton kneeling over Faren, his hands hovering just above the councilman's chest as though he was afraid to touch him. What was wrong? Only a minute ago, everything was fine. Faren had been eating, talking, and strategizing just as an ordinary, healthy man would.

But then, Quinton rolled up Faren's sleeve, revealing a cluster of boils.

NICOLAS CARVER: 2053

Carver closed his eyelids, attempting to shut out the blinding light. Purplish blobs floated across his vision.

"Good to see you're making friends," the voice of Rhea Vasquez said.

Carver rubbed his eyes. "Funny," he grumbled.

"I try. Why'd they lock you up?"

Carver hated that terminology. It made him seem like a criminal. He quickly concocted an explanation. "Zach decided he should be in charge, and I was in the way."

When he looked up, he found several faces peering down at him. They were not the faces of scientists and astronauts but of the workers. The grimy mechanics who spent their days fixing rockets and maintaining cruise ships.

"Nobody on this station is gonna go for that," Rhea said. She crossed her arms. "You saved us. Everyone knows that. Nobody's gonna let him stage a coup."

"That's the funny thing about coups, Vasquez," Carver replied. "It doesn't matter what people want."

"Well, our main priority is to keep you safe, sir," one of the mechanics said. "We owe it to you."

"I appreciate that. I do." Carver ran his fingers through his hair, surveying his surroundings. Stacks of supplies occupied dust-covered shelves all around them. "Do you know where Zach is now?"

Rhea shook her head. "I don't. But it won't be long before he finds out you're gone. We have to hide you somewhere."

"No. I'm not going to hide from him."

What good would hiding do? He couldn't stay hidden forever anyway. He supposed Zach could expose what he did to the cryobay, but so what? He'd committed no actual crime. He did what he had to. The Red Plague could have made it back to Earth and wiped out everyone if he hadn't. Anyway, he didn't think any survivors would genuinely care about a decision he had made decades ago, when many of them were still children. One way or another, they were alive today because of him. Because he took decisive action. Because he was willing to do what needed to be done to keep people alive, no matter the personal cost.

He never believed in the Exodus project, never wanted to go to Alpha Cen. But now that it was their only option, he was determined to make it work. They would start a new society, form a new government, and make fair laws. Rising from the ashes, they would do their best to avoid the mistakes of their past.

Mistakes like the ones Zach made.

Zach's arrogance had almost spelled the end of humanity. Carver and the others had fled the solar flares in the cruise ship, expecting to dock to the Gateway once in orbit. Instead, they were met with nothing but empty space. For two days, it seemed like all was lost. There was no room on the ship to sleep, so everyone just sat quietly as they waited for the air to run out. Thankfully, the Gateway had reappeared just before that happened. But if it hadn't? Well, Carver didn't like to think about it.

Zach was being reckless. And selfish. And closed-minded. He stood on principle instead of doing the right thing for the survivors. They were all that remained of the human race, and Zach couldn't let bygones be bygones. Therefore, he was a liability. But how could he be dealt with? Carver remembered the mention of the prisoner pods where Erik had been found and figured that if he could get Zach into one of them, then he wouldn't need to worry about Zach rallying people into a mutiny. But that seemed like a last resort. Perhaps he could try talking some sense into Zach first. He could allow Zach to stay awake as long as he agreed to keep a low profile. And if that didn't work, if Zach didn't agree to keep his mouth shut, he'd have to go into cryo.

Carver would have to meet with him somewhere secluded, with only one way in and out. That way, if things went south, he could have Zach arrested. God, he hoped it wouldn't come to that. Maybe Zach would remember all the things Carver had taught him—chief among them, the ability to back down when necessary—and come to some kind of agreement.

But Carver also knew that Zach was Quinton's son, and that came with strings attached.

"Sir? Are you okay?" one of the workers asked.

Carver blinked. "Yes. I'm fine... Would you do me a favor and get me a radio?"

NICOLAS CARVER: 2030

The whole thing was such a waste of money. Prescott. The Exodus program. Billions of dollars that could have been used to repair the magnetosphere. With perhaps the most advanced capabilities of any agency in the world, OSE should have dedicated its precious funding to saving as many lives as possible. Who could oppose that?

Carver worked his way down the hall. All these years he had spent trying to make the world a better place—or to continue to exist at all, for that matter—and what thanks did he get? None. Nil. OSE took half of its money and put it into Prescott. It was almost laughable how fast that had backfired, but Carver was determined to keep his resentment to a minimum.

They hadn't heard a peep from the colony in weeks, making it increasingly likely that it had been destroyed or severely damaged. Victor continued to deny it, insisting to his colleagues that the connection would be restored. He sometimes laid it on so thick that Carver doubted the man believed it himself.

It wouldn't be a surprise. After all, this whole fucked up mess was Victor's fault. Carver had tried to talk him out of the mission countless times. And did he listen? Of course not. Quinton was constantly chirping in his ear about irogen and how important it was for them to get to Alpha Cen. For that reason, Carver struggled to sympathize with Victor. He hated when people didn't take his advice, then acted like it was a surprise when it blew up in their faces.

Really, why hadn't they listened to him? Sure, he was younger than most board members, but didn't that say it all? He was the rare person able to climb the ranks with a quick wit and work ethic alone. He didn't have years of experience under his belt. He didn't come from money, like Victor. Or from a family already associated with OSE, like Quinton. Who knows? Maybe they were jealous of him. Or maybe he was doomed to be overlooked, to have his voice tuned out when all he made was sense. He consoled himself with the thought of one day having the opportunity to make a difference and help people when they needed OSE most.

Until then, Carver was forced to hear Victor whine about his failures while only half the money went to restoring the magnetosphere. It was better than nothing, he supposed. Still, seeing his prized project's funding go down the drain annoyed him.

People would never understand. No matter how often he warned them, pushing to stop the solar flares rather than escape them, they brushed him off. Why did he even work there anymore if they wouldn't hear him out?

He was almost to his office when a voice sounded behind him.

"Carver."

He stopped and turned around to see Wilford Owen approaching from behind. "Ah, Wilford. To what do I owe this pleasure?"

"We got a transmission from the Gateway."

Wilford led him to the Communications Bay and set him up at the computer. He pointed to the screen, drawing Carver's eyes to a bobbing frequency line. "Should I call for Victor?"

Carver ignored the question. "Are you sure it's them?"

"As sure as we can be. Comms are weak; only small bursts of information are getting through, but I might be able to home in—"

"How do I talk to them?" Carver didn't mean to snap, but this was an important matter. He could suspend his kindness for a bit.

"Here." Wilford grabbed a set of headphones hanging from a rack on the wall and handed it off. "Let me know if there's too much static."

Carver fitted the device to his skull, craning his neck. "Hello? Is anyone there?"

"Yes, yes! I'm here. Can you hear me?" a frantic voice sputtered.

"Loud and clear." Though it was a little spotty. "Who am I speaking to?"

"Quinton Croft. We're in trouble here."

"Trouble how?" asked Carver, glancing at Wilford.

Quinton went on to explain the events that had transpired after the landing. He spoke of a meteor that had struck the processing plant and rattled the ground so hard that most of Prescott collapsed. Then, some bacteria emerged and began killing colonists by the dozens. Quinton mentioned how they had decided to abandon the colony and set course for Earth, taking the hundred or so healthy colonists with them. But evading the disease, which Quinton called the Red Plague, had failed, and people were getting sick on the Gateway.

"Hold on, hold on. What is this disease? Where did it come from?" asked Carver.

"We don't know."

A mystery disease had sprouted in the colony and nearly wiped out most of the settlers, and now the rest of them were on their way back to Earth? That didn't sound like a good idea.

"We're quarantining for now," Quinton continued. "But almost everyone's already been exposed, and whoever hasn't will be soon enough. I have a theory, though. Putting people in cryo will slow—or even stop—the progression."

"All right, Quinton. Just hang on the line. Let me get some people together on my side. We'll see if we can help."

Carver took off the headset and handed it back to Wilford. "Keep him talking until I get back. I'm going to talk to Victor." He raced out of the room and didn't stop until he had summited the five flights of concrete stairs and opened the door onto the roof, where Victor often liked to hang out.

Today, Victor was perched on the outer ledge, eating lunch while looking over the city. As if sensing Carver's arrival, he commented, "It's a nice view, isn't it?"

"Beautiful," Carver replied. He approached with purpose and leaned his elbows against the rough stone. Victor wasn't kidding. From up there, you could see all of Pasadena. Back to the task at hand. "The Gateway radioed."

"What?" Victor exclaimed. "When?"

"Just now. The colonists are alive. Some of them, anyway."

"Some?"

"There was an outbreak of some sort. Quinton called it the

Red Plague. They don't know where it came from, but he said it's bad. A lot of the colonists have died. The healthy ones abandoned the colony. They're on their way back now."

"Oh, my god." Victor jumped down from the ledge. He rubbed his temples. "At least some got out. That's good. It's something."

"And he thinks cryo might kill the bacteria and get the survivors home safely," Carver said. "But... I'm not a doctor, but that doesn't sound like a good idea."

"Quinton's good at what he does. If he thinks that'll work, then it will."

"I'm not worried that Quinton might be wrong, but that he might be almost right."

"Why would that be a bad thing?" Victor smoothed out his hair as a breeze blew over the rooftop.

"Cryo might not kill whatever this thing is, but it could slow its progression enough to get the colonists—infected or not—back to Earth."

"And?"

"If that Plague, or anyone carrying it, gets to the ground, we could be looking at a pandemic. Then we'd have a real problem."

"We'll quarantine them, obviously," Victor replied.

"And if we can't?"

Victor gave an exasperated sigh in reply. "So, what are you proposing?"

"We can't let them come back to Earth."

"Then we'll go up to them. We'll send doctors, medicine—"

"No, you don't understand. Anyone we send becomes just as much of a liability as the colonists. They could get infected too."

"So, what? We just leave them up there to die?"

Carver was quiet for a moment. He knew what the correct answer was, but he was having trouble bringing himself to say it.

Victor's eyes narrowed. He seemed to be reading Carver's mind. "Nicolas, come on. You can't be serious."

Carver straightened his spine, then spoke quietly but directly. "We'll let them go into cryo. Once they're in, we'll disable their life support. It will be painless." He despised the idea of sentencing all those people to death, but it was their best option under the circumstances. Sacrifice a few hundred colonists, or risk a pandemic that could kill millions? The choice was clear.

Victor's mouth hung open. "Are you crazy? Even if I was considering it—which I'm absolutely not doing—we can't do that. We don't have that kind of control from here."

Carver's stomach turned. Victor was right. Mission Control could receive diagnostics from the cryo pods, but it didn't have control over the life support systems. Then another idea occurred to him. It wasn't as clean, but it would work. "We have control of the airlocks, though, right? We can shut the cryobay door before they get to it."

"Do you hear yourself?" Victor asked, his voice rising with anger. "We're not going to leave them to die up there. It's crazy."

Carver doubled down. "Here or there, they'll die no matter what. But if they die there, as terrible as it would be, it'll keep everyone here safe."

"Quinton knows more about this thing than we do. I trust him."

"He can't possibly know what he's dealing with! It's a completely novel xenobacteria. It could cause more harm than we can comprehend if it makes it back to Earth." Carver took a

deep breath, then changed his tone to be more contrite. "I hate what I'm suggesting. I really do. But it's the right thing to do."

"The right thing to do," Victor repeated with barely-veiled disgust. "This isn't about an outbreak, is it?"

"What do you mean?"

Victor walked back to the ledge. "You and Quinton have never seen eye to eye." And? What was he implying?

"Excuse me?" So Victor was, what? Suggesting Carver wanted to kill hundreds of people because of a personal vendetta? "I don't give a shit about Quinton! Millions could die if they bring the Red Plague back here!"

"You can tell yourself whatever you want, but you can't deny you would benefit."

"Benefit? That's crazy. How could I possibly benefit?" How could Victor even hint at that level of selfishness? Carver would never put that many people in harm's way for personal gain.

"Because Quinton would replace me if he were here. And you don't want that to happen."

That might have been true, but it had nothing to do with Carver's decision. "Do you think I'm that much of a monster?" He felt his voice rising. "I don't even know what to fucking say! Yes, Quinton being the head of OSE would be a disaster! His priorities are completely out of whack!"

"That's exactly what I thought you'd say."

"That's right. Because you know it's true. If Quinton was in charge, it would end with the solar flares burning up our planet until it turns to dust and blows away! But we'll be lucky if we even get that far, once he unleashes an alien plague on us. Do you know how dangerous that is? How much suffering that will cause? At least the solar flares would be quick!"

Victor fixed Carver with a cold gaze. "Quinton's coming back. And in a month, he'll be standing right beside me when I retire. And you better hope you even still have a job." Victor shook his head sadly. "I really thought better of you, Carver."

"Quinton just voted to leave hundreds of dying men, women, and children so the healthy could survive. Just abandoned them in the colony! How is that any better than what I'm suggesting?"

"I don't want to hear another word," Victor ordered. "Go. Get out of here. I'm going to talk to Quinton." Moving away from the ledge, he tried to walk toward the stairwell door. Carver got in front of him.

"Wait! Please. You're making the wrong decision."

"Get out of the way," Victor said evenly.

He tried to step around Carver, but Carver moved in front of him again. "I can't let you do this."

Victor gritted his teeth. "Carver, get out of the way." Carver didn't move. They stared at each other, eye to eye. "I want you out of here," Victor growled. "You're fired."

Carver's face went slack. "You can't fire me."

"The hell I can't!" Victor roared. "Now, move!" He shoved Carver backward.

That was the breaking point. All Carver wanted was to save lives, and Victor was trying to fire him for it? A blinding rage surged through Carver. He thrust his hands into Victor's chest, pushing him as hard as he could.

He barely had time to process what he had done before Victor stumbled backward and fell off the roof.

TWENTY-SEVEN

ZACH CROFT: 2053

"ZACH? ARE YOU THERE?" a voice said on the radio.

Zach shot a surprised look at Ryker. In a hushed voice, he asked, "Is that Carver?" as if confirming that Ryker had heard what he heard.

Ryker's lip curled. "Find out where he is."

Zach nodded, then spoke into the radio. "Yes. Carver. Carver, I'm here." Zach closed the door to stop anyone from hearing him. "Where are you?"

Another voice echoed behind him. Rhea, possibly? It sounded like her. Whoever it was, Carver quickly brushed her off and continued with Zach. "I want to talk."

"So, talk."

"In person."

Zach glanced at Ryker, whose eyes grew large at Carver's request. He shook his head as if to say, "Don't."

Zach thought for a moment, then responded to Carver. "Where?"

"Main loading bay. Ten minutes."

Before Zach could respond, the line went dead.

Ryker threw up his hands in frustration. "Are you nuts? Do you really think he just wants to talk? I almost blew his brains out! He's not gonna just let that go."

"What else can we do? Avoid him forever?"

"No. We can fucking kill him like we should have the first time."

"Everyone on the Gateway thinks he's a goddamn hero. He saved their lives. Nobody knows what he did to you, or to my dad, or to Prescott."

Ryker raised his eyebrows. "So, we'll tell them."

"Nobody's going to care! It's all ancient history to them. We kill Carver, and they launch us out of the airlock."

Ryker growled in frustration, then kicked the heel of his boot against a cabinet.

"Look," Zach continued, tempering his frustration, "last time, I wanted to talk to him, and you shoved a gun in his mouth. How about we try it my way this time?"

Ryker sighed. "Fine." He stood up and strode to the door. "But I'm coming with you."

ZACH ENTERED the loading bay with grim determination as Ryker lingered in the hall, just out of sight.

The bay was a cavernous space with multi-story racks of giant wooden crates and massive shipping containers. Varying sizes of forklifts were parked in neat rows along the sides, along with several loading cranes. An enormous airlock designed to accommodate supply ships from Earth dominated the space-side wall.

In the center of the room, Carver sat at a table waiting for Zach. He straightened his back as Zach entered. "I wasn't sure you'd show up," he said. "How are you?"

Zach approached the table warily. "A little tired."

"Well, please. Take a seat. Let's talk." Carver gestured to the seat across from him.

Zach claimed his chair at the table but kept one leg hanging off to provide quick means of escape if needed. "Start talking."

Carver pressed his lips together with a ghost of a smile. "You probably don't want to be talking to me, but hopefully, we can come to some kind of agreement here. I keep seeing myself in your shoes, you know."

"Seems like an odd thing to do, considering."

"Let me get right to the point." Carver's hand swiped at the air as if turning the page of a book. "I'm sorry. I should have listened to you. You were right about everything: the flares, how pointless rebuilding the magnetosphere was. Everything." He shrugged, his head dipping forward a bit in resignation.

"Excuse me?" Zach said with a mixture of confusion and disbelief. In all the years Zach had known Carver, the man had never admitted to being wrong. Not once. "What?"

"I should have listened to you. You're smart. Brilliant, actually. And I took that for granted."

No mention of Prescott, Ryker, or Quinton thus far. Zach nodded cautiously. "I warned you. Why couldn't you listen?"

"I believed what I wanted to believe: that I could save everyone. But I was wrong. And you were right."

"You *were* wrong."

"I should have authorized your Mars mission instead of forcing you to take it into your own hands. We'd all be toast if you hadn't. Getting the irogen... That was a big deal. I applaud you for it." Carver fixed the cuff of his jacket.

Zach could feel something off in Carver's voice, the unexpected warmth of his words. Carver wasn't one to layer on the compliments. "What do you want from me, Carver?"

Appearing a little offended, Carver coughed. "We all owe you for what you did. Truly. And I think it's time you sit back and reap the benefits yourself. Take a breather. Stop carrying the world on your shoulders."

"What does that mean?"

Carver leaned forward, rubbing his lip with his index finger and thumb. "The people on this vessel, they're OSE. That means they're my responsibility." He leaned back in his chair and gave a slanted, satisfied smile. "You don't have to worry about them anymore. I've got it."

"I'm confused... What are you asking me to do? Stop caring about what happens to us?"

"No, of course not. I mean, you don't need to keep trying to run the show. I'll handle it from now on."

Carver was sorely mistaken if he thought Zach would be content to fade into the shadows. "You want me to just sit back and do nothing?"

"Zach, I know you're angry. But we have to put the past behind us and move on. For everyone's sake."

"Move on?" Zach let off a slightly hysterical laugh. "After

what you did to Prescott? After you shut down the cryobay when my father told you it could cure the plague? You killed a hundred people!"

"Zach—"

"No. Don't try to explain yourself." Zach mimicked Carver in leaning over the table. "You tried to kill me. When I was a *child*. I only got home because something went wrong with your plan. So don't pretend like you give a fuck what happens to me."

"I never tried to kill you, Zach. But if the Red Plague had gotten loose on Earth..." He trailed off, allowing the implications of the statement to sink in. "I couldn't let them come home."

"So you killed a hundred sickly people? They needed your *help*, Carver." Zach pressed two fists against the table, baring his teeth slightly.

"Remind me again: why were they sick?" Carver cocked his head and raised his eyebrows. Zach went quiet. "Oh, that's right. Because *you* went into the crater when you were told not to. *You* brought back the Red Plague. *You're* the reason everyone got infected." He sneered at Zach with open disdain. "You're up here on your high horse as if you're any better than me when you were the reason they needed help in the first place!"

"I— I was a kid! What's your excuse?"

"I did what I had to." Carver folded his hands on the table, regaining his composure. "I wouldn't have done it if I didn't think it was the right thing to do under the circumstances. It was in everyone's best interest."

"Who are *you* to decide what's in everyone's best interest?"

"Zach," Carver said with a knowing look. "Come on. You do the same thing, and you know it. But you don't question the decisions you've *personally* made because you know why you made them. You chose to steal the Gateway, which nearly ended with the remainder of the human race starving to death on a cruise ship, and yet you haven't given it a second thought. Why? Because you know, deep down, that you did it for the right reasons. And I feel the same."

"That was different," Zach said. "*We're* different."

"Maybe we are." Carver nodded thoughtfully. "Maybe we're not. But do I wish I did things differently? Absolutely not. I made the best decisions I could at the time. But that doesn't stop me from thinking of Quinton whenever I look at you. He and I may have been at odds, but he was still my friend."

"Some friend," Zach sneered.

Carver's eyes turned cold as they gazed into Zach's. He shrugged. "Okay. I tried." He slowly stood, taking a long, deep breath. "I wanted to give you a second chance." He wiped his lip, pressed his eyes tightly shut, then said in a raised voice, "Rhea..."

Rhea stepped from behind one of the shipping containers, looking dazed and glassy-eyed, her mouth ajar.

"Rhea—" Zach started.

"Shut up." She blinked a few times. "Hands on your head."

"Rhea, you heard everything he said!"

"Be quiet. Do what I say. Now."

Far behind Rhea, Ryker lingered in the shadows, looking concerned. Zach wondered briefly how Ryker had snuck into the room with none of them seeing. Then, he returned his attention to Rhea. "Hey, look at me." Zach indicated his eyes.

He slowly rose to his feet. "Think for a minute. What do you really know about Carver?"

Rhea unholstered a handgun, pointing it at Zach. "I'm not going to tell you again."

"I have logs that prove all of it. Just lower the gun."

"Hands on your head!" She primed her pistol.

Detecting a glimpse of movement behind Rhea, Zach's eyes shifted a fraction of an inch from her face to a point over her shoulder.

Something about the slight movement of Zach's eyes must have triggered Rhea's military training because she spun around at the exact moment Ryker stepped from the shadows and lunged for her. He tackled her sideways, lowering his shoulder into her ribcage like a linebacker. The blow caused Rhea's finger to twitch on the trigger. A gunshot rang out. Zach ducked out of the way. He heard the gun clatter to the floor.

Despite being nearly a foot taller than Rhea, Ryker couldn't take her down. Instead, Rhea used Ryker's momentum to flip him over her hip and onto his back. She delivered a punch to his jaw and a sharp knee to his ribs, then dove to where the gun fell a few feet away. Snatching the gun from the ground, she rolled, leaped to her feet, and fired at Ryker in one smooth motion. The bullet ricocheted off the floor next to his head.

Ryker scrambled behind a shipping container, out of Rhea's line of fire. Zach, too, ran for cover, sliding behind the tread of a nearby forklift. Another gunshot echoed through the loading bay. Zach peered around the side of the forklift just in time to see Ryker race behind a shelf lined with propane tanks. Rhea fired at him as he ran.

Then, everything went white.

A series of powerful explosions erupted from the propane tanks as a stray bullet pierced one of them, setting off a chain reaction that caused them all to burst into flames. Rhea was thrown off her feet by the blast, slamming into the side of a shipping container and then slumping to the floor. She cradled her skull, eyes pressed shut in pain.

The sound of the explosion numbed Zach's hearing, replacing it with a persistent, high-pitched whine. Flames engulfed the loading bay. Smoke began to fill Zach's lungs. He looked up to find that the wall panels behind the propane tanks had been completely blasted away, exposing the flammable material behind them. Massive jets of flame roared from the gaps, whooshing in the air. As the fire spread behind them, more wall panels began to warp and twist in the intense heat. The wooden shipping pallets in front of the burning walls ignited, further fueling the fire. Another series of small explosions tore through the loading bay as whatever was inside the containers detonated as well.

Zach staggered to his feet, stabilizing himself with a metal shelf and wheezing in the poisonous air. Flames rolled across every surface. Burning crates lofted clouds of fire. Sparks flew from severed electrical conduits.

As he oriented himself, Zach frantically searched for Ryker but failed to locate him. Instead, he spotted Rhea stumbling across the deck toward the loading bay's inner door. She glanced over her shoulder at the destruction she had caused.

"Rhea!" Zach called out, praying she would be decent enough to turn back and help. "Please! We need help putting this out!"

But Rhea didn't turn back. She kept walking until she was

past the inner airlock and beyond the flames' reach. She paused for a moment, then exited the loading bay. The blast door closed behind her, the lock engaging with a solid *clunk*.

That bitch! Zach thought. How could she just leave them? Didn't she realize how dangerous it was to have a fire out of control on a space station? She was jeopardizing the entire Gateway, the entire human race. No matter how selfish Zach thought she was, he never would have expected her to be so *vile*. She was no better than Carver.

Carver, Carver. Where was Carver? He didn't appear to be anywhere—did that mean he'd already gotten away while Zach wasn't looking? How?

Zach dropped his head, a loud, involuntary moan emitting from his hoarse vocal cords. Ceiling panels began to plummet to the floor around him, landing with a whoosh of raw embers.

"Zach!"

Zach turned toward the sound of the voice. Ryker reached out to him from under a pile of collapsed shelving.

"Get this off of me," Ryker grunted as he tried to extract himself from the wreckage.

Zach rushed to him. Ryker was pinned under a fallen crossbar. Zach wrapped his arms around the rail and lifted with all his strength. It only moved a few inches, but it was enough for Ryker to slip out from under it. Ryker rolled away from the pile and climbed to his feet, hopping on one leg. "God damn it." He tried to put his weight on his injured leg, and it held. Thankfully, it didn't appear to be broken.

"Where is she?" Ryker growled.

"She's gone," Zach said. "She left us."

"And Carver?"

"I don't know." Zach wiped a layer of grime from his forehead. The air was hot, full of smog. He struggled to breathe as the acrid gas filled his lungs. "We've got to stop this fire."

"The sprinklers," Ryker said. "Over here." He limped to the far side of the loading bay, locating a red metal control box labeled *FIRE SUPPRESSION*. He tore the cover open, grabbed the thick handle, and yanked it down.

Zach prepared himself for a flood of water from the ceiling, a welcome relief from the boiling heat. Instead, the sprinklers sputtered, spitting out a few coughs of brownish liquid, then went dry. Ryker flipped the handle up and down. Again, the sprinklers released a quick spurt of water, then stopped.

"What's wrong with it?" Zach shouted.

"I don't know!" Ryker flipped the switch off and then on once again. "Come on..." Still no luck. "Fuck! It's not working!"

Zach coughed, his lungs tearing and his throat burning as he fought to breathe in the thickening smoke. He tried to think of what to do next, but his mind was cloudy from a lack of oxygen. "Is there any other water source? A hose, or—" Another coughing fit cut off the rest of his sentence.

Ryker shook his head. "No." He began coughing too. "Nothing."

Zach looked around wildly, searching for some other solution. There had to be something they could do. He couldn't imagine dying like this. After everything he had been through —everything they *all* had been through—surviving apocalyptic solar flares only to die in a fire was too terrible an irony to bear.

After a moment, Zach's eyes settled on the towering door of the exterior airlock, the one that opened into the endless vacuum of space. The *airless* vacuum of space. A realization hit him like the shockwave from the exploding propane tanks.

"We need to open the airlock!" Zach exclaimed breathlessly. Ryker stared at him in confusion. Zach continued, "Fire needs oxygen. If we drain the air, it can't burn."

"That'll kill us!"

"It'll kill the fire first."

Zach ran to the outer airlock, where a touchscreen command terminal was mounted to the wall. Perspiration ran down his back, and his head throbbed. "Hold on to something!" he shouted to Ryker as he quickly navigated the menus, bypassing all the warnings and confirmations until he reached the final flashing red prompt: *CONFIRM AIRLOCK RELEASE.* His finger hovered over the *CONFIRM* button. He looked over his shoulder, searching for something solid he could grab. He spotted a safety railing bolted to the floor nearby. It looked stable enough. Taking a deep breath, Zach jammed his finger onto the touchscreen, then ran for the railing and wound his arms around it.

Deafening klaxons sounded as the airlock opening procedure began. Swirling yellow and red emergency lights illuminated the smoke-filled air. The airlock depressurized with a tearing sound, exposing the loading bay to the vacuum of space. Smoke and flames were sucked from the bay, along with anything else that wasn't bolted down. Floor panels launched into the void, joined by piles of flaming debris and collapsed wreckage. Zach swung out of the way as a forklift sped past him, narrowly avoiding being crushed by the speeding machinery as it cartwheeled into space. Another forklift followed. Then another.

Zach felt himself being drawn toward the abyss. He held on with every ounce of his strength, his muscles threatening to tear from his bones. Still, he felt himself slipping. He squeezed his eyes shut, willing it all to be over. For a moment, a crazy thought crossed his mind: he could just let go. He'd fly out into the vacuum and have one hell of a view before his body imploded. It would be fitting death. Not easy, necessarily, but fitting. His corpse would drift through the universe for eons to come, just like the bodies of the other colonists who had perished on the Gateway. Just like his father.

But it also meant that Carver would win.

Zach opened his eyes. A surge of hope swelled in his chest at the sight of the flames beginning to thin. It was working. It was really working. He scanned the loading bay for Ryker, discovering him holding onto the frame of a loading crane. The entire structure of the crane was bending, leaning toward the open airlock. Ryker's face was contorted with strain, his lips blue from lack of oxygen. His eyes rolled in his head.

As the last licks of flame disappeared, Zach reached for the airlock's emergency closing mechanism. Opening the airlock had been a complicated process with multiple confirmations and authorizations; closing it was as simple as pulling the bright red lever on the wall. Simple was a relative term, though —the lever was several meters out of Zach's reach. In the panicked moments when he opened the airlock, he hadn't considered the distance between the safety of the railing where he clung and the lever he needed to pull.

He stretched for it, reaching as far as he could, but there was no way he could grab it. It was too far. There was only one thing he could do.

Jump.

If he missed the lever, he would be sucked helplessly into space. But he'd end up that way if he didn't try. His oxygen-starved brain would cause him to black out. He'd lose his grip on the railing, and ... well, it would end badly. For him and for Ryker. He couldn't bear the thought of failing his friend again. So, with the last bit of energy left in his body, Zach braced his legs against the railing, let go with his arms, and jumped.

His body hurled through the air far faster than expected, causing him to launch toward the lever like a rocket. Instead of gracefully grabbing the lever, he crashed painfully into the nearby wall. With nothing to hold onto, he felt himself being pulled back toward the abyss. He reached out blindly one last time, hoping to grab onto anything within reach. His fingers locked around something cold and metal ... and red. The lever. Zach's momentum caused the lever to swing downward, engaging the airlock's emergency closing mechanism. A different alarm began to sound, and a faraway voice announced, *"EMERGENCY AIRLOCK ENGAGED."*

Zach's eyelids fluttered as his consciousness began to slip away. He felt his grip on the lever loosen. The tug of space dragged his limp body across the floor toward the airlock. He flailed weakly, trying to grab onto anything that might stop him from being pulled into space.

Then, suddenly, he stopped.

The airlock closed.

Zach's ears popped as a great whoosh of air began to repressurize the loading bay. Gasping for breath, he crawled along the floor to a circulation vent nearby. A steady blast of oxygen whispered through it. Zach pressed his face against the grate, sucking in huge gasps of cool air. He hated the slightly metallic tinge of the Gateway's recirculated air. But at that moment, he thought it was the sweetest thing he had ever tasted.

Once he was breathing normally and his head was clear, Zach sat up and looked around the destroyed loading bay. He spotted Ryker sitting in the cab of the crane that he had been holding onto. His head was tilted back toward the ceiling. His eyes were closed, and his mouth was open. He looked like a workman who had fallen asleep on the job.

"Ryker!" Zach croaked. His throat felt like it was full of broken glass. "You okay?"

Ryker lifted his head and gave Zach a weak smile. "Never better."

Zach stood and limped across the loading bay to the inside blast door through which Rhea had fled. The metal was blackened with soot. Beside the door, the control panel was melted into a useless lump of slag. Zach wedged his fingers into the crack between the door and the frame and tried to yank it open, but it was pointless. The door weighed a thousand pounds. It was locked, and the control panel was the only means of disengaging it from the inside.

As Zach looked at the melted, deformed panel, he groaned and dropped to his knees in defeat.

They were trapped.

CORA KEATON: 2030

It seemed like just yesterday that the casket had closed. It was a cold Monday morning. The air was thick with fog. From all around, people in black clothing gathered to honor Victor Keaton, some of whom Cora recognized from the agency. It made sense that they'd be there. After all, Victor was a good leader. He had done things no other head of OSE had done before. But the stress of losing contact with Prescott had been too much for him, and, in a moment of desperation, he took his own life. Cora could only imagine the guilt he must have felt, as if he had failed the colonists, their families, the agency ... even Earth itself. So much was riding on that mission—every passing day without contact with the colony must have weighed on him more and more until he couldn't bear to go on.

The thought of her father leaping off the roof of a building, the very building he ran for more than a decade, made Cora want to cry and vomit at the same time. Cora had never been close to him, but he was good at his job—as the head of OSE and as a dad.

In the days after the funeral, Cora barely said a word. Sleep, eat, cry, repeat; that was her new life. Jason had come by a few times to see if she wanted to play, bringing water balloons or dart guns, but she always took a raincheck. Instead, she stayed in her bedroom with the blinds closed. Whenever Sarina came in and opened them, Cora would yank the covers over her head to block out the light. At night, her mother would try to coax her out of her room with her favorite foods: pizza, pasta, ice cream. But Cora couldn't even think of eating. Her throat was too raw to get anything down. She couldn't think of doing anything. Especially not school.

Cora didn't want to go back. As soon as she stepped through those dual glass doors, all eyes would be on her. She would be known as the girl whose father was too weak to continue living.

And with the Prescott colony gone silent, Cora didn't even have the comfort of knowing that Zach was okay. She didn't even know if he was alive. Nobody did.

Somewhere downstairs, the doorbell rang. Cora sat up in her bed and looked around with squinted eyes. Even the room was drearier. Grayer. Darker. The computer in the corner of her room was already collecting dust. She hadn't touched it in days.

Cora ignored the doorbell and plopped back against the bed. She burrowed the side of her face into the pillow and lay like that for another minute or two until the doorbell rang again.

"Mom! Can you get the door?" she shouted. Cora waited for a few seconds before calling again, "Mom!"

Sarina didn't respond, so Cora grunted and sat up. She swung her bare feet around until they hovered an inch above her hardwood floor, then set her feet down. An icy chill raced up her legs.

Cora wobbled as she stood. It felt like she hadn't walked in weeks. She approached her bedroom door, but stopped when she noticed a large ding in the doorframe. That happened when Victor bought Cora a microscope for her eighth birthday. He had accidentally swung the microscope against the frame while walking in to surprise her.

Cora sighed at the memory, then pulled the door open with a creak. The air in the hallway was warm, or at least the air in her room was much colder. She couldn't tell.

Over the wooden railing, the black outline of a person was visible through the front door window. Once she concluded her mother wasn't going to answer, Cora walked a little farther down the hall, then turned and went down the staircase.

She dragged herself across the marble floors of the front

room. At last, she came upon the door. It was tall, nearly double her size, with an opaque window in the center. A man was on the other side, his form blurred by the glass.

Cora's mother often told her not to open the door for strangers, but Cora didn't care. Hell, if someone snatched her up, would that really be so bad? At least she'd end up with her father.

Cora rested her palm on the door handle and turned it. A gust of air rushed in as she pulled the large door ajar.

"Mrs. Kea—" The man outside paused. "Oh, Cora. I'm Nicolas Carver. I'm the new head—"

"I know who you are," Cora answered. She had seen him at Victor's funeral. He was tall and sharp-looking, despite being only in his early thirties.

Cora realized she was wearing three-day-old pajamas. She was a little embarrassed.

"Great," said Carver. "May I please come in? I need to speak to your mother."

"Umm..."

"Cora?" Sarina asked, emerging from the kitchen with a dish rag in one hand. "Who's at the door?"

Carver looked past Cora at Sarina. "Oh, yes, Mrs. Keaton. I hope this isn't a bad time."

"Not at all," Sarina said. "Come on in. I've got coffee brewing." She looked at her daughter. "Cora, honey, please give us a few minutes?"

Cora trudged back up the stairs. What was he doing there? Did something happen? Cora ran through the possibilities as she approached her bedroom. But then Carver's voice stopped her.

"Before I give you this news, I first want to say... Your

husband was a great man. I only hope I can be a fraction of the leader he was."

Cora's mother sniffled.

"So, Mrs. Keaton, I wanted to update you on Prescott."

Cora's mouth fell slightly ajar. She walked back to the top of the stairs and leaned over the banister, straining to hear.

"Seeing as your husband invested so much time and energy into the mission," continued Carver.

Come on! Spit it out! Could he say it already?

"Of course," Sarina replied. "Why don't you sit down?" Two chairs scraped across the kitchen floor.

"I understand you've taken my husband's place at the agency?"

"Yes, at least for a little while," answered Carver. "And I assure you, I'll finish what he started."

"That's great. He was in the process of regaining communications with Prescott, right?"

Yes! That had to be why he was there. Come on, then. Say the colonists are okay! Say Zach's alive!

"That's actually why I'm here..."

Cora started to get excited. They were going to be okay. They had to be. Maybe they were on their way back, and Cora would get to see them. Oh, Zach and Ryker had missed so much. She had to tell them everything!

"In the days following Victor's tragic accident, we redirected some research satellites in Mars orbit to see if we could get photos of the colony..."

Stop stalling! Say it already! Say it wasn't all for nothing. Say that Prescott succeeded.

"I'm sorry, but... it's gone."

What? Cora's face fell, her shoulders dropping.

"Gone?" Sarina asked. She sounded as confused as Cora felt.

"Satellite images show a crater where the colony used to be. Something massive—most likely a meteor—must have impacted the area. It destroyed the dome, the mine, the hab units... everything."

"And the colonists...?"

Carver sighed. "I'm sorry."

The news hit Cora like an oncoming bus. Carver's voice receded into the background. It didn't matter what else he had to say. All that mattered was what Cora had already heard:

Zach was gone.

NICOLAS CARVER: 2053

Carver didn't see fleeing the fire as cowardly.

He had escaped just when Rhea started firing, crawling to the blast door and narrowly avoiding being hit himself. He hadn't seen what came after. Was Zach dead? Alive? Carver didn't know.

If Zach was alive and had somehow disarmed Rhea, then he still wasn't out of the picture. Even if Zach was dead, Carver now had Rhea to worry about too. She had overheard everything—she knew what Carver had done and surely wasn't happy about it. Would she come for him next? Would he be eating lunch when, out of nowhere, she put a bullet in his skull?

Carver paced the halls of the Gateway as he tried to figure out what to do next. "Confusing" was not extreme enough to describe the station's layout. The Works and the Spark seemed easy enough to navigate, consisting of only a few rooms each. But the Homestead was a labyrinth of interconnecting corridors that made the OSE lab seem like a studio apartment.

The lab! It was really gone. Though the entire planet was in flames, it had never quite registered that OSE, his kingdom, had fallen. Now, all that remained of it were the people. The workers. The brilliant scientists and engineers that Carver had handpicked from the ranks of elite colleges. A mosh pit of raw intelligence working toward a common goal: the continuation of consciousness in the universe. And they were succeeding. Things were running smoothly. Food was being rationed, water—however disgusting its origins were—was flowing from the faucets, and clean clothes were issued to everyone. Seeing everyone in Prescott-stamped garments made him a little uneasy, but there was nothing he could do about that.

Carver turned a corner, and ... who was that at the end of the hall? *Is that ... Rhea?* She looked like hell: burnt clothing, matted hair, and a crazed look. "You!" she yelped, then sprinted toward him. He tried to turn away, but she already had him by the collar of his shirt. "Don't you dare try to run from me!" She shook him back and forth. "Tell me! Was Zach telling the truth?"

"What? I... I..."

"Was he?"

"No, no, I promise he wasn't! He was just trying to get in your head!" Carver lied. "That was it. You have to believe me."

"Why should I?"

"Because he did get your father sick. That was on him. But he can't come to terms with it all, so he's pinning it on me."

"But he was so sure of it." Rhea loosened her hold on Carver's collar enough for him to breathe more easily.

"Prescott was Victor's show," Carver said as he calmly slipped from Rhea's grip. "Not mine. I had nothing to do with it."

"Then, why did Zach say all that?"

"Because—"

The ship suddenly lurched to the side, causing them both to stumble and lose their footing. Rhea landed on her hands, then began to stand. "What was that?"

"I don't kn—"

Another tremor knocked them back down.

"Something's wrong." Rhea sprang to her feet and limped down the hall.

"Where are you going?"

"The cockpit."

Carver tailed behind her, turning the next corner and confirming that everyone in the hall had felt the same thing they had. One engineer cupped a swollen forehead with a lump from hitting the wall. As Carver passed, he deflected the surge of questions for which he had no answer. After five minutes—and two more violent shakes—they crossed into the Works and continued until a door opened into the cockpit and allowed them entry. Rhea went straight for the pilot's chair, turned on the computer, and ran a diagnostics check. Then, her face, coated in ash and sweat, went stiff. "We're losing altitude."

"How?" Carver asked.

Rhea poked at the screen, bringing up a complex array of dials and readouts. "I don't know. It's like..." She leaned forward, squinting at the readouts and shaking her head in disbelief.

"Like what?

"Like ... like we're falling out of orbit."

"Then, do something about it!" She was the pilot, after all. Zach had asked her on his suicide mission for a reason.

"I fly cruise ships, not space stations." Rhea pressed her lips into a fine line. "I don't know anything about this thing."

"Try, goddamnit."

"Why don't you try? You know as much about it as I do."

Carver growled in frustration. No one else with flight experience had made it off the ground, short of two astronauts-in-training who hadn't even graduated past simulators. There was only Rhea. "You've gotta do something," he insisted. "You're the only damn pilot we've got!"

A look of realization spread across Rhea's face. "Not quite."

TWENTY-EIGHT

ZACH CROFT: 2053

WHILE THE FIRE may have gone away, the heat had not.

Zach's sweat-soaked clothes stuck to his skin, bringing back memories of summer camp before Prescott. Back then, there had at least been the relief of an icy cooler of fruit punch waiting for him in the bunkhouse. Now he didn't even have a decent glass of water.

He watched as Ryker tried to pry the melted control panel from the wall with a screwdriver, in hopes that maybe the electronics inside had survived the fire. The violent tremors that tore through the station had panicked Ryker in a way that Zach had never seen before. Ryker said he had never experienced anything like them in his twenty-three years on the Gateway. There was something wrong with the station. Something seriously wrong.

With a cry of victory, Ryker finally freed the control panel from the wall. He opened the housing to access the electronics inside.

"How's it look?" Zach asked.

Ryker tilted the housing toward Zach so he could see. The control board was a twisted curl of melted plastic. "Fried." He let it fall from his hand. It dangled against the wall, suspended by the remaining wires protruding from the hole where it came from.

Zach touched the blast door to check whether it was still hot, then pressed his ear against it for a moment, listening.

"What are you doing?" Ryker asked.

"Something's not right. Didn't anyone get alerted that there was a fire? Shouldn't there be alarms?"

Ryker flipped the screwdriver absently in his hand. "There should have been, yeah."

"Then where is everybody?" The floor rumbled again. The shaking was so intense that it caused Zach to stumble sideways. He braced himself against the wall. "That's not good."

Before Ryker could respond, the loading bay door slid open. Zach stumbled backward, surprised. Carver and Rhea stood just outside in the hall.

Ryker brandished the screwdriver and lunged for Carver, preparing to murder him on sight.

"Wait, wait, wait!" Zach pulled Ryker back. Ryker struggled to break free. Zach grabbed him by both arms and swung him away from Carver and Rhea. "Just wait a second!"

Ryker threw the screwdriver across the loading bay with a frustrated growl. He turned and sneered at Carver. "What the fuck do you want?"

"We have a problem," Carver began.

Ryker barked out a wild laugh. "You're fucking right, we do."

Zach held up his hand to silence Ryker. "What?" he asked Carver.

The ship swayed to the side again. All four of them stumbled off-balance. Rhea winced at the pain in her leg. The floor had a distinct tilt to it now—Zach found himself leaning to counterbalance against the incline.

Carver spoke quickly. He seemed uncharacteristically nervous. "The Gateway's falling out of orbit."

Zach and Ryker exchanged skeptical glances.

"Bullshit," Ryker said.

"This look normal to you?" Rhea asked rhetorically, thumping her foot on the tilting floor.

"We don't know why it's happening," Carver continued. "But it doesn't matter. We need your help." His gaze shifted to Ryker.

"*My* help?" Ryker just stared at him, dumbfounded. "You're kidding, right?"

"Stop being a child and listen," Rhea snapped.

"You just tried to kill us!"

Zach shook his head. "Space stations don't just fall out of orbit."

Ryker snapped at Zach. "Maybe opening a fucking door into space had something to do with it!"

Zach's stomach dropped. Opening the massive loading bay door had sent a powerful blast of air venting into space. But could it have been enough to knock the station out of a stable orbit? It seemed impossible, but ...

As if answering Zach's question, the floor rumbled again.

"You better take a look," Zach told Ryker.

Ryker's jaw dropped. "Are you serious? I'm not helping these people."

"Ryker, it's not just them. There are hundreds of people on this station. Including us."

Ryker glared at Carver and Rhea momentarily, then looked back at Zach. "Fine. Let's go."

AS THEY ENTERED THE COCKPIT, another thrash of the station sent Zach stumbling.

"You okay?" Carver grabbed his arm and steadied him.

Zach nodded. "Yeah," he replied as Carver released his grip. "Thanks." For a brief moment, it was like none of the last few weeks had happened.

Ryker rushed over to the control module and examined the altimeter. Sure enough, it was dropping. And fast.

Carver stepped up behind Ryker to look over his shoulder. Ryker turned and grabbed Carver by the front of his jacket, yanking him closer. "This is your fault," he muttered. Hot air whistled from his nostrils. His brow drew down. His eyes grew cold. He stared at Carver for a moment, then shoved him into a seat. "Buckle up."

Carver straightened his jacket, smoothed his hands over his hair, then buckled his seatbelt. He watched as Ryker began tapping and swiping on the control module touchscreen. "What are you doing?"

"Stopping this." Ryker navigated to a different screen. He glanced at Zach and Rhea. "You too. Strap in."

Zach and Rhea each took a seat and fastened their seatbelts.

"I'm going to engage the orbital thrusters." Ryker checked a series of boxes on a digital checklist, then flicked a few switches overhead. The Gateway convulsed again, nearly knocking Ryker off his feet.

"Why don't you take your own advice?" Rhea called out. Zach knew she didn't care for Ryker's well-being; she just didn't want their pilot to get injured. Ryker ignored her.

"Wait," Zach said, suddenly realizing, "how are you powering the thrusters?"

Ryker shot a look over his shoulder. "With irogen."

"What?" They barely had enough irogen to get to Alpha Cen as it was. If Ryker used it now—

Ryker must have recognized the panicked look in Zach's eyes. "Relax," he said. "We've got plenty. A drop of the stuff will put the engines on max power." Without waiting for another objection, Ryker cranked a lever on the side of the command module as hard as he could. "Engaging thrusters."

The ship responded with a sudden jolt. A green digital model of the thrusters appeared on the screen, confirming that they were engaged. Explosions sounded beneath the floor, reverberating one after another before harmonizing into a single, continuous blast. The sound overpowered Zach. The vibrations rattled his stomach. He felt the blood rushing from his head and pooling in his two aching feet.

For a few moments, it seemed the thrusters were doing their job.

But the station kept falling. Earth kept pulling.

Clenching his jaw, Zach peered out over the flaming ball he

used to call home. Eye-shaped clouds of fire and ash gazed upon the Gateway as Earth drew the station toward its fiery demise. The station creaked and groaned like a dying whale, gradually drifting into a nosedive.

The altitude reader on the control module flashed red as its numbers continued dropping. An alarm began to sound. Standing square in front of the module, Ryker pulled the thrusters' lever again as if they weren't already at full strength. But they were. Ryker's attempts were futile.

"They're not strong enough!" Ryker shouted over the roar of the engines.

Carver's eyes went wide. "But you said—"

"I know what I said!" Ryker planted his hands on opposite sides of the module and bowed his head in concentration.

"Are there other thrusters?" Rhea asked.

"No! No, there are no more thrusters!" shouted Ryker. He was quiet for a moment as he scanned the command module for an alternative. Then an idea struck him. "But we have a continuum drive."

"Use it," Carver ordered.

"Way ahead of you," Ryker said as he scanned through the continuum drive's preflight checklist. The glow of Earth's flaming surface illuminated his face with a flickering orange light.

"How long will it take?" Carver prodded. He shot a look out the window. "We don't have much time."

"It'll take a minute or so to generate a continuum bubble around us. After that, it'll be instantaneous."

Ryker's comment sent a shockwave of realization through Zach's body. "Hey, hold on!" Zach exclaimed. "It'll take half our irogen just to generate the bubble. We won't have enough to generate another to get Alpha Cen!"

"It's either that or we die now," said Ryker.

"Exactly," Carver said, seemingly almost surprised to find himself agreeing with Ryker. "So, let's just go now."

"To Alpha Cen?" Rhea asked.

"We've gotta go at some point. So, let's go."

"There's a planet in the way, Carver!" yelled Zach. He motioned to the window. "We're on the wrong side."

"So go around it!"

"We're too close," Rhea said quietly. She looked at Zach with a defeated frown. "Right?"

"Exactly," Zach said.

Ryker continued referencing the checklist as he poked at the command module to bring the continuum drive online. "We have to do this."

"Think about it, Ryker," Zach implored. "If we can't get to Alpha Cen, we'll starve out here! The cryopods are offline. The hydrofarm is failing. We'll be fucked."

Ryker left the control module and walked over to Zach's seat. He leaned over, hands together, as though he were praying. "In case you haven't noticed, we're *already* fucked. We're going to die. Right here. Right now." The station pulsed violently to the right, forcing Ryker to stabilize himself with the arms of Zach's seat. "This is our only choice. If we survive this, we'll have time to figure something out."

Zach pressed his lips shut and gritted his teeth. Ryker was right, and he knew it. "Fine."

Ryker returned to the command module and began the continuum drive initiation sequence. He turned a dial, tapped the touchscreen a few times, then watched as a confirmation message flashed on the screen. He tapped it. All the lights in the cockpit turned to a deep, dark blue.

On the screen, a diagram depicting the Gateway appeared. Surrounding it was a thin bubble that traced the contours of the station. A percentage bar was displayed above the diagram, beginning at zero.

One percent.

Five.

Ten.

A jacket of reentry smoke began to wrap around the cockpit windows as speckles of light flashed at their edges. Two modules turned red on another screen that displayed a Gateway schematic. Ryker noticed it and groaned.

Eighteen percent.

"What does that mean?" Carver asked, pointing at the flashing red modules.

"They're gone."

"Gone?"

Ryker slapped his palm against the command module's housing. "They're dead, Carver! Okay?"

"Which modules are those?" Zach asked.

"Maintenance decks." Two more in the Spark went red. The cockpit's lights flickered. "Energy processing units. It's okay, though. It's okay." His words lacked conviction.

Four more modules turned crimson. Zach couldn't help but wonder who was inside them. How unfortunate they were. How much damage could the Gateway take before the power grid went out? No power meant no air, no water, and no hydro-farm. And no hope of survival.

"We're still dropping," Rhea said, her voice shaking.

"We won't stop until the bubble's formed and we blink away."

Thirty percent.

The altimeter continued to plummet. The bright light of the burning Earth grew larger outside, seizing the ship in its hellish grip. Zach's heart thudded in his neck so loud and so hard that it seemed like it would burst through his skin.

The control module began to beep as the bubble reached fifty percent.

Fifty-four.

Sixty.

Zach realized the space outside the ship was beginning to distort. The flames of Earth wagged back and forth, spinning and stretching. Distant stars grew and shrunk as they ping-ponged between points in space. After another five seconds, the stars and Earth were so blurred and deformed that it seemed like Zach was looking at them from underwater.

Three more modules turned red onscreen, causing Ryker to curse loudly. He wiped his mouth and stared at the ticking percentage bar.

Sweat cascaded down Zach's back, gluing him to the leather seat. The ship thrashed to one side, the other, and back again.

Seventy-five percent.

Eighty.

Eighty-six.

An alarm sounded. The area connecting the Homestead to the Spark started to flash on the diagram.

"SECTOR SEPARATION IMMINENT," a monotone voice blared.

Ninety-two.

Ninety-six.

One hundred.

The space outside turned briefly white, blinding those in the cockpit. The station thrashed one last time, then went still. The brightness slowly dissipated. Zach uncovered his eyes and gazed outside.

In the distance sat a blazing Earth, only a fraction of the size it had been a moment before. The continuum drive had worked.

Zach let out a deep breath. He unbuckled his seatbelt, rose shakily, and went to Ryker's side. He clapped Ryker on the shoulder. "Good job."

Ryker swiped the sweat from his forehead and nodded. "Thanks." His voice was barely a whisper.

As Zach stared out the window at the now-distant Earth, he thought of their future. The hydrofarm couldn't support so many people for very long, and the cryobay was still inoperable because of Carver. Without enough irogen to get them to Alpha Cen, it was only a matter of time before they starved to death.

"Now what?" Zach asked.

"Now we figure out how to get to Alpha Cen."

Carver and Rhea rose from their seats and wiped the sweat from their foreheads.

"Take a team and check out the modules that went red," Carver said, directing Rhea toward the airlock.

"What do we tell everyone about what happened?"

"That's not important right now. Round up the doctors and figure out who's hurt."

Rhea sent a look Zach's way before nodding. "Roger that." She left, and the airlock thudded shut.

In the reflection of the control module's screen, Zach watched as Carver came to the center of the cockpit. He reached inside his black jacket and pulled something out.

"Now," Carver said.

Confused, Zach turned around to find Carver pointing a gun between him and Ryker.

"We weren't done with our discussion before," said Carver. "In light of what's happened, I hope you'll reconsider my offer, Zach."

"Are you kidding me? We just saved you!" Ryker yelled.

Zach kept his calm despite the growing pit of anger in his stomach. "What was the offer?"

"These people aren't your responsibility. They're mine." Carver tapped his chest a few times with the side of his pistol. "Either stand down or—"

"Or what?" Ryker mocked. He leaned against the control module casually. "What are you gonna do? Lock us up?"

"If it comes to that," Carver said.

Out of the corner of his eye, Zach could see Ryker's finger dragging across the control module, searching for something. To mask his actions, Ryker stood with both hands behind his back, his body blocking any movement of his fingertips. He subtly flicked the station-wide intercom switch. The light on the button turned green.

"Just put down the gun, Carver," Ryker said.

Zach realized what Ryker was doing. With the open intercom, anyone on the station could theoretically hear what was happening in the cockpit. It was a call for help. "Yeah," Zach added. "You want to talk? Let's talk. You don't need that thing."

Carver lowered the gun but kept it in his hand. "I'd hope not. But I can't let you keep causing problems for me."

"And I can't pretend you didn't just try to kill us."

"What does that matter, Zach?" Carver asked. "Do you think anybody cares?"

"Why don't we go tell them, then?" Ryker jeered.

"And then what? What are they going to do? They don't give a damn about you. These people owe their lives to me."

Zach wondered if anyone was on their way to help. What if the intercom wasn't working? What if nobody understood what was happening? Or, what if Carver was right? What if nobody cared?

Carver continued. "Like it or not, I'm in charge here."

Ryker spat out a laugh. "And why is that?"

"Because I'm the only damn person on this station with some sensibility! I worked my ass off to get to where I am today. I didn't have anything handed to me. I didn't cruise through life. I put my blood, sweat, and tears into becoming the leader of these people. And here I am!"

Zach scoffed. "You got *lucky*," he growled. "*That's* why you're in charge. My dad was next in line to lead OSE. If he hadn't died on the Gateway, you wouldn't have stood a chance." A plan was forming in Zach's head. His words were getting under Carver's skin. He could tell by how Carver's gaze darkened, flickering between anger and disgust.

"Hmm. That's interesting." Carver resumed a confident

mask, raising his eyebrows. "And why was your dad on the Gateway, Zach?"

Zach felt his face heat up. Carver was once again going to try blaming him for what happened in Prescott, for releasing the Red Plague. He opened his mouth to defend himself. "It wasn't—"

"As a matter of fact, why was he in Prescott in the first place?"

Zach cocked his head in confusion. Carver wasn't blaming him. But what was he getting at then? Carver knew why Quinton had left. "Because Victor asked him to go," Zach answered.

"Ah." Carver nodded, his eyes tightening into a squint. "I wonder where he got that idea. I mean, Quinton was an odd choice, wasn't he? Sending a medical doctor to run a mining colony? One with a kid. One who was next in line to take over OSE." Carver cocked his head thoughtfully. "Why would Victor have done that?"

"I don't..." As the pieces fell into place, Zach felt the world blurring around him. "You..."

Carver shrugged. "I didn't agree with the mission, but if it had to happen, Quinton was the man to go. It was nothing personal. He just wasn't the right person to run OSE. He would have cut funding to MagRes—"

"And he would have been right," Ryker jabbed.

"No, he would not have been—"

"Look outside!" Zach pointed at the window where the flaming Earth loomed in the distance. "You sent him away for nothing. And me too!" Zach stared at Carver in disbelief. "All those years you listened to me cry about what happened..."

"Because that's what a good person does. You needed me."

"I needed my dad!" Zach shouted. He scowled at Carver with a burning hatred he had never felt before. "You should've stayed the fuck away from me." Zach paused for a moment. His eyes narrowed. There was something about Carver's story that didn't add up. "What did you tell Victor?"

"About what?"

"He would've never let you disable the cryobay. He wouldn't have left us to die."

"I told him what was at stake. We couldn't let the Red Plague get back to Earth—"

"Oh, come on!" Ryker interrupted. "You didn't give a shit about the Red Plague."

"You don't know what the fuck you're talking about," Carver snapped.

Zach ignored the bickering. He was still thinking of Victor. "My dad was his best friend. He would've done anything to bring him home."

Carver turned back to Zach. "Well, it's a good thing he fell off the roof, then."

Zach stopped breathing. His knees felt like they might buckle underneath him. "Fell?" Zach said. His voice was quiet. He furrowed his brow. "I thought he jumped."

"Yes. That's right." Carver fixed Zach with a steady gaze. "He jumped."

Ryker's mouth hung open as he realized Carver's slip-up. "Him too?" Carver's eyes shifted to Ryker, but he said nothing. Ryker advanced on him. "You think you're so smart. But look at you. You're a failure. You're nothing." Carver's grip tightened on his gun. It trembled ever so slightly in his hand. Ryker kept his eyes locked on Carver's face. He continued walking forward. "The cryobay? You fucked that up. Leaving Zach and me to die on the Gateway? You fucked that up too."

"Ryker," Zach murmured.

"The magnetosphere? How'd that work out?" Ryker gestured to the burning planet in the distance. "Were you trying to make Earth look like Satan's asshole?"

Carver lifted his chin and straightened his shoulders. "I got my people off the ground."

Ryker scoffed. "Barely. And then what? What was your plan, exactly, without the irogen that *we* risked our lives to get? Which— oh!" He snapped his fingers and pointed at Carver. "You fucked that up too, didn't you? Zach asked you to send a mission to Mars to get the irogen. And you said no."

"Wilford," Zach said quietly.

Ryker glanced at him. "Wilford?"

Zach stepped up next to Ryker and said to Carver, "You killed him too, didn't you?"

"Wilford was a liar," Carver said through clenched teeth.

"Wilford's the reason we knew about the irogen in the first place," Ryker pointed out.

Carver's face clouded with confusion. "How?"

"Because *someone* fucked up," Ryker said with a bemused smile. "Guess who?"

Carver gaped at Ryker for a moment, then raised his gun. "On your knees."

Ryker chuckled. "I'm not—"

"Now!" Carver yelled and directed the barrel at Ryker's head. "Both of you. Get on your knees and put your hands on your head."

"Come on," Zach said quietly. He grabbed Ryker's sleeve and pulled him to the ground. "Just do what he says." Zach put his hands behind his head. Ryker reluctantly did the same.

As Carver approached them, he placed the gun in his belt, then removed a bundle of zip ties from his pocket. He walked behind Zach and fastened one of the restraints around Zach's right wrist.

Zach saw his opportunity. He drove his elbow into Carver's knee, then tried to stand. But before he could get to his feet, Carver punched him in the head. Stars exploded in front of Zach's eyes. He tried to catch himself as his body toppled forward, but his arms wouldn't respond. Instead, he fell face-first onto the floor, his face impacting the cold metal with a painful *clunk*.

At the sight of Zach falling, Ryker jumped up and swung at Carver. His fist smashed into Carver's jaw. Carver stumbled backward, then spat a web of blood on the ground beside Zach before delivering a blow to Ryker's stomach. As Carver attempted another punch, Ryker blocked his arm mid-swing and tackled him. The two locked against each other, Ryker roaring and Carver delivering a few solid punches to Ryker's midsection.

Carver's back collided with the wall. He grunted, then head butted Ryker and pushed him away. Dazed, Ryker stumbled back against the control module. Carver drew the gun from his belt.

Zach's brain cleared just in time to see Carver pointing the gun at Ryker. From the ground, he lunged at Carver, managing to knock Carver's arms toward the ceiling just as he pulled the trigger. The bullet exploded a light fixture, sending a shower of sparks down on them. Zach grabbed Carver's wrist and attempted to wrestle the gun from his hands. Carver pulled Zach closer as the two struggled for control of the weapon.

"Let... go!" Carver ordered.

Then, another gunshot rang out.

Zach froze. A piercing pain erupted in his chest. He let go of Carver's wrists. With shocked eyes, he looked down at the rose-colored bloom of blood spreading across his shirt. His mouth fell ajar. His breathing stopped.

As the gun tumbled from his hand, Carver whispered, "No..."

Then the world went black.

TWENTY-NINE

ZACH CROFT: 2030

STOP.

Stop.

Stop.

Make it stop.

Make the coughing stop.

No matter how much Zach pleaded to the universe, the painful wheezes and coughs of the family next door continued to shake his room throughout the night.

He sat in the corner of his tiny room, his hands wrapped around his knees as his eyes adjusted to the darkness. Shadows from the hallway slid through the sliver of light creeping under his door. He wasn't supposed to be awake, but how could he sleep?

Leaving Prescott did nothing to save them. Ditching the others did no good—it just trapped them in a tin can with the same problems they had on the ground. The only thing that changed was the gravity.

As the Gateway drifted back to Earth, its inhabitants grew sicker and sicker. How long would it be before Zach got sick too? Or Ryker? Or Quinton? They couldn't avoid the Red Plague forever. It was only a matter of time.

Suddenly, Zach heard his name. It came as a low whisper that could have been mistaken for air whistling out of the floor vents. He dismissed it.

"Zach."

The voice came again. Zach concluded it was coming from the hall and stood up shakily. His left leg had fallen asleep, a million tiny needles prodding at his skin. He ignored his discomfort and forced himself to hobble over to the door.

"It's Dad. Open up." The door handle rattled a bit.

Zach cracked the door open to peek outside. Quinton opened it a little more and pulled his son out.

"What's happening?"

Quinton squeezed Zach's arm firmly. "Don't say a word. Just follow me." They started down the brightly-lit hallway. Zach squinted to dull the throbbing in his eyes.

Every time they passed someone, Quinton would sweep Zach to the side closest to the wall, away from the person. Halfway down the hall, they stopped in front of another living quarter.

Ryker's living quarter.

With nobody left alive to share it with, Ryker was left alone. Zach had asked his father if Ryker could stay in the room with him—it would be like an extended sleepover—but Quinton didn't want to take any unnecessary risks with the Red Plague.

Quinton tapped on the door with a knuckle. "Ryker, buddy. You in there?"

Bed springs squeaked. Feet shuffled across the floor, and the door inched open. A face shrouded by a shaggy bedhead revealed itself. He wore a loose gray shirt with sleeves that hung farther than his hands. He looked between Zach and Quinton with tired eyes. "What are you guys doing here?"

"Get some clothes on. We've gotta go."

"Where?" questioned Zach.

Quinton flicked a glance at Zach, then back at Ryker. "Hurry."

Ryker stood confused for a moment, rubbing his eyes, before receding into his room. "What time is it?"

"Just get ready."

"Okay..." Ryker threw on a sweatshirt and some slacks. Zach could hear the sink running as Ryker pushed back his messy hair and appeared back at the door. He slid the G engraved ring onto his finger. "Did I oversleep for breakfast or something?"

"No. Come on." Quinton urged Ryker out of the bedroom and shut the door behind him. Ryker shot a look down the hall, still half asleep.

Quinton led them past the cafeteria. The semi-sweet smell of rations wafted toward them, though the sharp odor of antiseptic and bleach soon replaced it. A man stumbled out of a nearby living unit. He scratched at his forearms.

"Doctor Croft," he said in a raspy voice.

Quinton pushed Zach and Ryker away from the sickly man. "I'll be with you in a second. Cover your mouth and report to the medbay. And don't touch anything."

The man nodded and passed them by. Quinton exhaled in

relief. He got Zach and Ryker back in front of him. "Go, go. We're almost there."

Reluctantly, Zach and Ryker kept walking. It was obvious that Quinton didn't want anyone else to know where they were going. That scared Zach. What could be so bad that the leader of Prescott couldn't let his people know?

Quinton ensured nobody was looking, then led the two boys into a storage unit. He immediately went to the center of the room and dropped to his knees.

"What are you doing?" Zach asked with more intensity than before.

"You're going into cryo."

Zach gave Quinton a confused look. "What? Why?"

"I was experimenting with infected cells and dropped their temperature to cryosleep levels. The damaged cells burst, leaving only the healthy counterparts."

"So, you found a cure?" Zach asked hopefully.

"I don't know. Maybe. Or maybe cryo will slow it down long enough to get us back to Earth. Or maybe it's nothing. But regardless, I'm putting you two under. I want you out of harm's way."

"Then why are we here?" Ryker asked. "Why aren't we in the cryobay?"

Quinton pulled up on a floor panel, revealing a control board beneath it. As he pressed a button or two on it, an audible click sounded, followed by a whoosh of escaping air. Several panels on the far side of the room then rose a few inches and slid back into the wall. Two cryopods appeared in place of the panels. Ice crystals and nitrogen gas clouded their glass shells.

"Whoa," Zach said. He and Ryker exchanged a surprised glance. "What're those for?"

Quinton ignored the question. He pressed a button on each pod, causing the lids to slide open. "Come on, get in."

Following Quinton's instructions, Ryker climbed into his pod. Zach hesitated. "What about you?" he asked Quinton.

Quinton smiled warmly. "Don't worry about me. When you wake up, I'll be right here waiting. I promise."

ZACH CROFT: 2053

Zach's eyelids fluttered open.

He was lying on his back, staring at a polished metal ceiling. But before he could figure out where he was, a cloud of exhaustion descended on him, and he fell back to sleep. In his dreams, he saw Alpha Cen. It was a vibrant world, with lush fields spanning far into the horizon under impossibly blue skies. Laughing children played games in the forest while adults built cabins on a nearby river bank. It was paradise.

As he dreamed, Zach was vaguely aware of being wheeled in and out of rooms and put through various machines. Periodically, someone peeled his eyelid open to shine a flashlight beam into his pupil. It was uncomfortable, but he was too tired to complain. A woman—Cora, maybe?—approached his bed and rested a hand on his leg. "Do me a favor and live, okay?" The voice sounded choked up.

By the time he regained consciousness, the bump on his head was no longer sore. And while a dozen layers of bandage shrouded his chest, a morphine drip dulled the sharp edges of the pain. He couldn't remember what had happened—his brain was still too murky, wavering between reality and the fictional Alpha Cen he had concocted. But he was in what seemed like a recovery room, stripped bare of any supplies, consisting of only the bed and a map of Earth on the wall.

He felt a hand clamp around his wrist and saw Mabel standing beside his bed with a large, hypodermic needle. Was she giving him antibiotics? More sedative? He couldn't—

"Oh, my god." Mabel's face appeared over his. "Zach, can you hear me?" The needle clattered against a tray.

Zach forced himself to nod. He started to sit up, tugging at the tubes connected to his forearm, but Mabel stopped him. "No, no, don't move," she said frantically. Her voice caught in her throat, and her eyes glazed with tears.

"I'm fine. I'm fine."

"Hang on. Let me help..." Mabel adjusted Zach's bed to a sitting position. "I didn't think you were going to wake up." She consulted one of the monitors connected to Zach, pausing to watch the numbers climb upward.

"What happened?" Zach asked drowsily. "Where am I?"

"You're in the medbay," Mabel answered. She disconnected a series of electrodes taped to Zach's skin.

"Why?"

Mabel hesitated. "Carver shot you."

Carver shot me? As Zach strained to remember, Carver's terrified face materialized in his mind. He could almost hear the gun clack against the ground as Carver looked on in shock. But that was it. That was all he remembered.

"Where is he now?" Zach grabbed onto Mabel's arm.

"It's okay. He's in a prisoner pod. Rhea too."

"Like where we found Erik?" Zach asked.

Mabel nodded and smiled. "Exactly where we found Erik."

Zach relaxed, relieved that Carver was finally out of the picture. "What happened after I blacked out?"

"Carver tried to save you. He and Ryker both did. They carried you to the medbay. Then, the guards showed up and took Carver away."

"He let them?"

Mabel laughed. "Well, he didn't go quietly, that's for sure. But he didn't have much choice. Nobody would let him get away with what he did to you. Or anything else." Zach gave her a puzzled look, unsure of what she meant. Mabel recognized his confusion. "The intercom. We heard everything."

A memory flashed through his mind, a brief image of Ryker's fingers flipping the intercom switch on the command module. Zach couldn't believe it—Ryker's stunt had worked. He silently thanked his friend in his head, resolving to thank him in person as soon as he could.

"Everyone was shocked by what Carver did," Mabel said, wiping her eyes. "They refused to go under until he was punished."

"Go under? What do you mean 'go under?'"

Mabel hesitated, seemingly unsure whether she wanted to answer the question. "We put everyone in cryo."

"How?" The cryobay door was disabled—Zach remembered that. That was why they had confronted Carver in the first place.

"One of the OSE devs managed to hack past the code that locked the doors. Took him like a week."

"A week?" Zach asked. "How long have I been out?" Mabel's sudden silence cut deep.

"You have no idea how hard it was to save you. There were only so many real doctors that survived." She rested two fingertips on his chest. "The bullet missed your heart by two inches."

Zach winced. "You said everyone's in cryo. But you're still here." He reached out and placed his hand on hers. "Thank you."

Mabel squeezed Zach's hand. "There are a few of us still awake. Me and you, Erik, Cora, and Ryker. Erik's checking on the pods, but the others are in the cockpit."

"Can I see them?"

CORA'S EYES lit up when Zach and Mabel entered the cockpit. She glanced at Mabel in confusion, then rushed over and pulled Zach in for a hug. Then, she withdrew and looked at him with a smile. "You just can't seem to die, can you?"

In a scratchy voice, Zach replied, "Apparently not."

Ryker walked up next. He tugged Zach into an embrace, patting him firmly on the back.

Zach ignored the jab of pain in his chest and questioned, "How are you doing?"

"I'm alive, thanks to you," Ryker said.

"Thank *you*. You saved us with that intercom."

Ryker waved off the praise. "I just didn't want to get shot by that fucker." He laughed and pointed at Zach's bandages. "Does it still hurt?"

"A little," Zach admitted. Ryker led him to a seat and pulled him down. "What are you guys all doing here?"

"We... um..." Ryker exchanged an awkward glance with

Cora, and the joy seemed to drain from the room. Everyone looked down, either fidgeting with their hands or analyzing the rivets in the floor.

"What's wrong?" Zach pressed.

Ryker gave an exhausted sigh. "The irogen."

"What about it?" Really, why was Ryker acting so solemn?

"What else do you remember, Zach?" Mabel asked. "Other than the shooting."

Hmm. Zach put some thought into it. "Something with the airlock. A fire, maybe? Then, um..." He bit his cheek. "I don't know. Why?"

Ryker exhaled and cocked his head to one side. "We had to use half of our irogen to stop us from falling out of orbit. It's gone."

"Gone?" Zach asked.

Ryker nodded solemnly. "Not all of it, but... too much."

"Then, how do we get to Alpha Cen?"

"We don't." Ryker rubbed his eyes, walked over to the pilot's chair, and sat down.

"What do you mean, 'we don't?'" Zach asked. He looked at Ryker, then at Cora, searching for an explanation. Cora averted her eyes. Nobody answered, so Zach continued. "What do we do, then? What's the plan?" There must have been some contingency they'd thought of while he was asleep. Cora sat down next to him. She draped her hands over her lap and waited for Ryker to continue.

"We don't have many options," Ryker said quietly. "The hydrofarm is screwed. Even if it wasn't, it was never designed to sustain so many people for so long. No hydrofarm means no food. It would only be a matter of time before people begin to starve. We could all go into cryo to conserve resources, but... for what? There's no one to wake us and nowhere to go when we wake."

Zach waited for Ryker to continue, but he seemed to be struggling to form the words. "Or..." Zach prompted.

"Or," Ryker said. He traded solemn glances with Cora. "Or, we can cut the oxygen to the cryopods now, and everyone can go peacefully in their sleep."

Zach's jaw went slack. "What?" He pivoted to Cora as if to confirm what he had just heard. She cast her eyes to the floor, answering Zach's question without having to open her mouth. "You can't be serious," he said. "You want to kill everyone?"

"We don't *want* to do anything," Cora snapped. Her tone softened. "We've got no other choice."

How could she be on board with this? "There's got to be another—"

"There's not!" Ryker barked. "You think we haven't been trying to come up with a solution? We've been talking about this for weeks. Our best option—our *only* option—is to... to slip away."

Zach turned to Mabel for support. "Mabel, come on. You don't want this, do you?"

"Of course not," Mabel answered. "But I also don't want to starve on a space station. Under the circumstances, I think it's for the best."

No. Not Mabel too. She was the reasonable one, the overly cautious one. And this was the motherload of batshit insanity! How was she okay with it?

"We just made the decision this morning," said Ryker.

"Why did you save me, then? If you were already going to

kill everyone." Nobody said anything, though their silence brought back the image of Mabel standing over his bed, holding a needle. A sickening realization turned his stomach. He looked at Mabel. "The needle..."

Mabel covered her mouth with her hand. "I'm sorry," she whispered.

Cora stepped forward. "We wanted you to go peacefully."

"That wasn't your choice to make, Cora! None of this is!" Zach stood and slowly backed away from her. "I don't care what any of you say. We're not taking the coward's way out. No way."

"Nobody will feel anything," Cora insisted. "They won't even know it happened."

"That makes it worse! They went to sleep thinking they'd see the light again, and you want to take that away? I'm assuming you didn't run this little plan by anyone before they went into cryo. Am I right?"

"We didn't know," Cora said. "Until today."

"Listen," Ryker said in a calmer tone. "I know what it's like to live up here with no hope, waiting to die. It's terrible. So bad that I'd rather end my life than spend another minute alive in this place."

"Ryker—"

"No."

"Come on, man. This is just... just..." Zach pinched the bridge of his nose in thought, shaking his head. "How do you know it will be painless?" he asked. If they were to do this, there was no way he'd let those people suffer any more than they already had.

Mabel came to the center of the room. "We'll gradually

lower O2 levels in the pods until the inhabitants are no longer breathing. The cold suppresses the nervous system, so we can rule out discomfort. It'll be peaceful."

"It's like Prescott," Ryker gathered. "Your dad chose to leave the colony. He didn't want to, but it was his best option. This is the most merciful thing we can do."

Was it really? Zach thought. There was always another way. When one door closed, another opened. So, what was the alternative? What was behind the other door? Starvation? Madness? What was the right thing to do?

As a kid, he struggled to understand why Quinton abandoned the colony. At the time, he found it barbaric, leaving hundreds behind on a barren world. But now Zach understood.

"You're right. It is no different than Prescott," Zach said quietly. "We killed them all too."

ZACH CROFT: 2053

Knowing it'd be the last time he ever saw the man who raised him, Zach thumbed through the stack of his father's old photos slowly and thoughtfully.

The pictures were worn and grainy, creased and dirtied around the edges, but he handled them like precious artifacts. In some ways, he supposed they were: the final relics of a lost civilization. He pressed his lips shut, flashing back to those chilly winter days spent bundled up inside with a cup of hot cocoa and Quinton by his side. His father would stay home from work, and they'd watch movies all day, eventually ordering a pizza for dinner. The smiles were genuine, spanning ear to ear, and infused with laughter. They were snapshots of a happier time.

Ryker had given him the photos earlier, claiming he found them in a storage room years ago and had always wanted to return them to Zach. "Hope they help," he said, handing Zach the crinkled envelope and walking off.

Zach didn't look through the photos then but felt that now was the proper time. That way, his loved ones' faces would be clear in his mind as it shut down for good. A few pictures had his mother—his beautiful mother—but they were few and far between. Most showed her holding Zach when he was barely older than a newborn.

She used to tell him stories of what a strong-willed baby he was. Constantly climbing out of his crib, scaling the dresser to grab an out-of-reach toy, or trying to cajole them into giving him solid food from the table. The stories used to make him laugh, but seeing her tired eyes in the photos now made him feel guilty.

Why did the universe have to take her away? She was kind and pure. "A real gem," as Quinton had described her. It went both ways. They were kindred spirits, and when she passed, it was almost like Quinton had absorbed her goodheartedness and merged it with his own.

Putting aside the photos of his family, Zach picked up another stack of pictures about six inches high. Splashes of color dabbled the edges. They were pictures of Earth. Cities. Forests. Oceans. Stuff to help them remember the planet now that it was gone. He had imagined the photos appearing in history books as his descendants went to school in the new world. Maybe they'd learn about Prescott and everything OSE did to get them there. Or maybe they'd choose to forget their ancestors' mistakes, forging new paths for themselves. But that wasn't going to happen. Zach sighed.

"Hey," Erik said, walking up from behind.

"Hey," Zach put the photos down next to him. "What do you need?"

"Mind if I sit?" Without waiting for a response, Erik claimed the seat next to him.

Zach bit down so that his jaw muscles clenched. He just wanted ten damn minutes to himself, his *last* ten minutes.

"You scared?" Erik asked.

"I don't know." Zach shrugged. "You?"

"Nah," Erik replied. "I'm going to give my daughter a big hug."

"Sounds nice." Zach rubbed his temples. "Why are you here, Erik?" He didn't mean to seem so abrasive, but the clock was ticking.

Erik was quiet for a moment before answering. "I just... I haven't been entirely honest with you."

"About what?"

"About why they arrested me." Erik hesitated. "It wasn't for stealing food."

Zach wasn't surprised that Erik had lied, but it hardly mattered under the circumstances. "What are we talking about, then? Murder?"

"No, definitely not that. I... I went into the crater. Right after the meteor hit. The council ordered us not to, but I couldn't just leave it alone." Zach had heard *that* before. "The crystals had already multiplied so much in the tunnels that I had to see them myself. I smuggled a bunch back to my quarters, and when the council found out about it, I was shipped up here for cryo."

"Why are you telling me this?" Zach asked. "Why now?"

"Because I want you to know that the Red Plague wasn't your fault. It was mine."

Zach shook his head in disbelief. Was Erik serious? "That can't be."

"It is," Erik confirmed. "Ryker told me you and he went out there together. I was out there a week earlier, at least. My brother was the first to get sick, after I showed him the crystals. He was a mechanic in the rover garage?" He phrased the last part as a question, as if asking if Zach might have known him.

Rover garage, rover garage. Zach remembered meeting the man in the garage, the one with the strange bumps on his arm, right after Ryker had been there learning how to drive. Zach always thought Ryker had transferred the Plague to the mechanic, despite not being sick himself. But thinking about it now, it made no sense that the mechanic would have shown symptoms mere minutes after exposure. That meant Ryker hadn't given the Red Plague to patient zero.

Erik had.

Zach's mind swam with uncertainty. He thought back to Prescott, replaying the timeline in his head. He and Ryker had taken the crystals, then the first victims had shown up virtually overnight. It happened so fast. Too fast. But now, it made sense. Erik unknowingly gave the Red Plague to his brother, and *that* started the outbreak. Maybe Erik had the Plague too, but his containment in the prisoner pod had killed it.

Part of Zach wanted to shout at Erik, but he couldn't bring

himself to do it. The guy had made the same mistake Zach had. He wasn't trying to harm anyone. He didn't understand the consequences. It was an innocent mistake. An innocent, fatal mistake.

"Anyway," Erik said and stood up. "I just thought you'd want to know." He walked to the door, then stopped. "You're not a killer, Zach. You're a survivor. But not a killer."

THIRTY

NOTHING BUT SLEEPING, soon-to-be-dead faces here.

Zach dragged his hand along the lids of the pods, feeling the icy droplets on his palm as he moved silently through the cryobay.

Each chamber was fully frosted over, other than a small circle in the center that showed the person inside. As he walked, all Zach heard was the low hum of the cryopods and the clacking of his shoes. One by one, he went down the lines of pods and picked out the ones of those he knew. Their faces were so peaceful. It was a small consolation considering what Zach and his friends were about to do, but it was better than nothing.

Down the line, Zach spotted Cora. She loomed over her pod, wearing a tank top undershirt, with her face twisted in despair. Wasn't she eager to do this? It sure seemed like Cora

414

Keaton was 100% on board, but one look that this fragile, kind person would say quite the opposite.

He approached her and rested two comforting hands on his friend's shoulders. "Hey."

She touched one of his fingers, then returned to the chest-level bed. "Hi."

"Do you need help?" Zach asked.

Cora pushed her hair behind her ears and adjusted her shorts. "No... no, I'm fine. Can you sit with me for a little while, though?" She raised her eyebrows, and a bit of her former self surfaced.

Zach smiled. "Of course. Here. Sit." Even though the walkway between the two rows of pods was only about four feet wide, they sat beside each other with their knees pulled in close. Cold radiated from the chambers behind them. "I'm not going anywhere." Zach draped an arm over Cora, and she leaned into his shoulder. He had to stay strong, no matter what. If he broke down, Cora could only follow suit. Not because she was weak—hell, Cora was about the strongest person he knew—but because he knew she hated to see people cry.

Cora propped her chin on his arm and gazed at him with those ocean-blue eyes. "Remember spring break, '41?"

Zach strained for the memory. "Junior year of college, right?" He had gone to Harvard while she went to Cornell. Whenever they got time away from school, they'd spend it together.

Cora nodded. "Senior for me, though."

"Yeah, I remember. We..." Zach smiled. "We flew to

Pasadena, then took your mom's car to Oregon. We went thirty above the speed limit and got arrested."

"I forgot about that!" She definitely hadn't. "Carver bailed us out."

"Yeah. He did." Zach fell silent, thinking of all the times Carver had gotten him out of the most difficult scenarios. "Did you ever see the darker side of him?"

Cora drummed her fingers as if playing the piano. "Honestly? Yeah, I did. But you guys were so close..."

"So you kept it to yourself?"

"So I kept it to myself," Cora echoed. "I thought we were supposed to be talking about happy things. Like... what happened when we got back from Oregon." She perked up.

"Your mom charged us both the bail price as punishment. How'd she even find out, anyway?"

Cora mulled it over. "Carver, probably."

"Damn snitch," Zach joked, and they both laughed.

The short-lived happiness died out as reality set in.

"Thank you, Zach. For everything." Cora tugged him in closer.

Zach patted her on the arm. The list of thank yous he could make was too long to count. "You too. For keeping me out of trouble."

"Never for very long. You're too damn stubborn!" She mock-punched him in the stomach, and he pretended to double over.

"FIVE MINUTES TO SHUT DOWN," the system called out. That meant air, heating— basically everything—was about to go into the shitter. Cora gave one last dimpled smile and stood back up. She hopped into her pod, laid down on the cool sheets, and wiped away a tear that streamed down her temple.

"It's going to be okay," Zach comforted, but his voice lacked conviction. The truth was, they weren't going to be okay. This was the end. The bitter close to their lives. "Are you ready?"

Cora hesitated, then nodded before any more thoughts could sway her otherwise. She reached out and grazed Zach's hand quickly, then went rigid. Zach pressed the activation button, stepped back, and waited. A glass lid emerged from the wall, Cora's pod slid back, and they met in the middle. The edges clicked into a place. A second later, the supercooled gas was pumped in, and temperatures dropped.

Zach watched as ice crystals began to climb around the edges of the pod, sprouting all around until only the tiny oval around Cora's face was visible. Then something struck him. A realization.

His mind traveled back to Mars. To the irogen mine. There were just so, so many crystals. Before the meteor, Prescott had struggled to find just a few, and even those were underground. An entire mining operation was dedicated to digging them out of the rocky Martian dirt. But when Zach returned as an adult, the crystals were *everywhere*. Where had they come from? There must have been something different about them. But what?

An idea struck him like a bolt of lightning from the gods, hitting him with such force that it took his breath away. He leaned forward against Cora's pod, resting both hands on the cool glass as he tried to control his breathing. Then he shouted out, "Gateway! Stop the shutdown!"

FOR THE NEXT HOUR, Zach pored over every file he could find in the Gateway's computers related to irogen. Research papers, computer models, charts, graphs, and even an animated video made for a kids' science class on Prescott. Then he radioed Ryker, Erik, and Mabel and asked them to meet him in the cafeteria.

"What's going on?" Mabel asked, concern in her eyes. "Is everything okay?"

"Maybe," Zach said breathlessly. And he meant it. For the first time since discovering Earth was lost, he felt something resembling hope.

Ryker leaned against a table, his arms crossed over his chest. "Why'd you stop the shutdown?"

"I have an idea. It may be nothing, but it may be worth a try." The others exchanged skeptical looks. Zach didn't blame them. They had spent countless hours trying to find a way out of their situation—what were the odds that Zach had suddenly thought of some brilliant solution they hadn't considered? Probably next to zero, but Zach didn't care. "I was thinking: why was there so much irogen when we returned to Prescott?" He turned to Erik. "Any ideas?"

"Not really," Erik replied.

"Come on, you're a geologist." Zach tapped his temple. "How did the crystals grow in the first place? They didn't just magically appear, right?"

"Of course not. You can't create something from nothing. It just comes down to chemistry. If you combine the right elements..." He trailed off, thinking.

"You get where I'm going?"

Erik nodded. "The raw materials for irogen. Right. But I don't know. We didn't go to Mars to *make* irogen—we were getting what was already there out of the ground."

Mabel stood and began pacing, her mind clearly working on the problem. "The elements would have to be on Mars, though. So, that narrows it down a bit."

Ryker rolled his eyes, "If you're suggesting we go back to Mars again..."

"No, but think," Zach said. "Prescott was a mining colony. We had to *mine* the irogen. It wasn't easy to get at, was it?"

Erik snorted out a laugh. "No, not quite."

"Except when we went back to Prescott, it was. It was *everywhere*. There was so much there that we had to move it out of the way to get into the mine. The question is: why? What changed? Why was there suddenly so much?" Zach didn't have any answers. He was just spitballing, fishing for any hint of a solution to their problem. If they could figure out how the irogen multiplied, maybe they could get it to multiply for them. And if they could do that, they could make enough to get to Alpha Cen. It was incredibly unlikely, but Zach still had to ask.

Erik nodded thoughtfully. "Well, the meteor hit. That was a change."

"Come on," Ryker said, maintaining his skeptical attitude. "A meteor full of irogen hitting an irogen mine? That seems *kind of* unlikely."

Mabel stopped pacing. "What about the heat? Or the pressure? Like when coal turns to diamonds or whatever. Could that have done it?"

Zach suppressed a small smile. She was spitballing too, which is exactly what he wanted. He needed her brainpower to help figure this out.

"Even if that was true, how does that help?" Ryker asked. "Does anybody have an extra meteor in their pocket? No?" He stood up and shoved a chair against the table, causing the legs to screech along the floor. "You're wasting your time. We've been through every possible option—"

"So? What does it hurt to try?" Zach asked. "We literally have nothing else to lose."

"Because we're just delaying the inevitable! It was hard enough to make this decision in the first place, and now you want to go back to where we started."

"The Red Plague," Erik interjected. "That's another thing that changed."

Ryker threw up his hands. "So? What does that have to do with anything?"

"Yeah, I'm not sure if that's relevant," Zach agreed.

Mabel drew in a sharp breath. "Actually, maybe it is." Zach and Ryker both looked at her doubtfully. She rolled up the sleeves of her blue sweater as she explained. "Have you ever heard of biomining?"

Zach and Ryker shook their heads. Erik's eyes widened. "Ahh," he said as if beginning to understand.

Mabel continued. "Some colleagues from my graduate program worked on it a few years ago, for a computer company."

"Why would a computer company be doing biomining?" Zach questioned.

"There are certain types of microorganisms that consume

metals for sustenance. My friends would feed them mother-boards, circuits, anything with high concentrations of precious metals. And in return, the organisms would filter out all the impurities from the metals, turning them back into their original form. It was phenomenal."

"Of course, that makes sense," Ryker quipped. "Bacteria that shits metal."

Zach tapped his fingers against his lips in thought. "So, you're saying the Red Plague created irogen?"

"I'm saying it's possible."

"No, it's not," Erik countered with a downtrodden sigh. "Irogen was there long before the meteor. Probably millions of years before."

Zach deflated. Erik was right. It wasn't like the irogen had started growing after the meteor hit. It was already there. There was just more of it.

Grabbing a water bottle from the cooler and taking a swig, Mabel wiped her mouth and asked, "That's true. But how sure are we that the Red Plague arrived on the meteor?"

Ryker held out his hands as if explaining something obvious. "Well, that's when everyone got sick."

"But that doesn't mean the plague came *on* the meteor. For all we know, it was already on Mars."

"But wouldn't people have been getting sick before?"

"Not necessarily. It could have been dormant," Mabel suggested. "Frozen, maybe? Then when the meteor came..."

Zach nodded slowly. "The heat could have thawed it out." Mabel pointed at Zach as if to say, "exactly."

"Let me see if I follow." Ryker looked at the ceiling and ran down a list in his head. "An alien bacteria first created irogen millions of years ago but then froze in permafrost. A meteor shows up, murders my dad, then reanimates the crystal shitters. Irogen production picks up again, starts multiplying, and we bring some back to the colony, with a little Red Plague along for the ride. But then why did people get sick from it?"

"That part's easy," said Mabel. "We had no immunity. It's like European settlers coming to the Americas. They brought smallpox, which the Natives hadn't been exposed to, and that killed millions of people. The same thing could have happened in Prescott."

Zach turned to Erik. "Let's say Mabel's right. Whatever caused the plague still can't make something from nothing, right? So we're back to the question of elements. What did it have?"

"Whatever was in the ground," Erik answered. "Iron, mostly. That's the most common element on Mars. It's everywhere."

Zach extended his hand to Mabel. She passed him the water bottle. He took a swig, then asked. "Is this something we can test?"

Ryker resumed his position leaning against the table. He looked fed up. "What, exactly, do you want to test?"

"That the Red Plague can turn Martian dirt into irogen."

Ryker closed his eyes and pressed his fingers into his temples. "This is crazy."

Mabel cast her eyes at the floor. "Even if it was possible to test, we don't have any rocks from Mars. And thank god we don't have the Red Plague..."

"We might," revealed Ryker. "There's a door in the Science Center with a biohazard sign."

"What's in there?" Zach asked.

"I don't know. Biohazards? I never bothered to look."

"If there were going to be samples of the Red Plague anywhere, that's probably where they'd be," Mabel confirmed. "We should check it out."

"Even if there are samples, we don't have the dirt," Ryker said.

"Yeah, we do." Everyone turned to look at Erik in surprise. "At least, we might. My brother constantly complained about how the sand on Mars stuck to everything. So, what about the dropship? There's gotta be some dirt stuck somewhere."

Zach nodded. "On the landing gears. Or the ramp. Or—"

"Okay, hang on," Mabel interrupted. "One thing at a time. Let's figure out if we've got samples of the Plague first. Then we'll worry about the dirt." She strode for the door in the direction of the Science Center. As she exited the cafeteria, she shivered, clutching her arms. "Oh, and someone turn the damn heat back on!"

ZACH CROFT: 2030

The cryogenic gas had only begun to clear when Zach searched for his father's voice. A friendly "you're awake" or "how'd you sleep?" Wasn't that part of the promise? That he'd be there when they awoke? That he would pull them back to reality?

Zach sat up and immediately climbed out of his pod, reaching out for Quinton, wherever he may be. But all that greeted him was the railing of a nearby shelf. Gaining his composure, Zach rose to his feet and helped Ryker do the same.

Bits of the room had shifted from the last time they saw it.

The lines of metal racks had been arranged in a labyrinth, possibly to hide the pods? They were largely picked clean of any supplies they once held.

Zach peered between the shelves, trying to see whether Quinton was amongst them. He wasn't. So, where was he? Was he running late? As far as Zach knew, there wasn't an exact time of day the pods were supposed to open. Only that they'd disengage when the Gateway reached Earth.

Earth! They were back! Quinton had gotten them home.

"EARTH ORBIT STABILIZED. FURTHER HUMAN GUIDANCE REQUIRED," the intercom instructed.

"Should we go find your dad?" asked Ryker.

Zach looked around a moment longer, then agreed. They stepped out into the hall. The air was chilly, almost icy. When Zach exhaled, his breath hung in the air as if they were in the arctic. He clutched his biceps, teeth chattering.

The corridor was deserted. From end to end, not a single person was visible. Where was everyone? Zach briefly considered that it could be mealtime. Still, it was odd that there weren't at least a few stragglers in the hall. But there was no one.

No one at all.

The lights overhead flickered off, drawing a gasp from Ryker. After a moment, they turned back on. A few seconds later, they went off again. The cold, the lights... Was something wrong with the power?

"Hello?" Zach called out.

"Stop, stop. Do you hear that?"

Zach listened intently, searching for the noise. It was a whistle, like the sound of a balloon slowly deflating. They walked in its direction. The lights flickered several more times before they reached a burst steam pipe on one of the walls. "No one fixed it," Zach observed.

Now, he was getting scared. What was going on? Where was everyone? Could they have gone to the ground without Zach and Ryker? Had they forgotten them? No. Quinton would never let that happen. But what if something had happened to him?

They approached a nearby door and knocked on it. When no one answered, Zach slowly pushed it open and stepped inside. He didn't know whose living quarters it was, but the two beds were strewn with dirty sheets piled with clothing. Everything was still there. If the colonists had gone to the ground, they would have taken their stuff. Wouldn't they?

A gushing sound filled Zach's ears. He turned to see Ryker in the bathroom, hunched over the sink. "Running water," said Ryker. "That's good."

"But that's not." Zach indicated the mirror above the faucet. It was shattered. The floor and the counter were spotted with blood.

As they stepped back into the hall, Ryker reintroduced the 'left behind' argument, to which Zach assured him, "My father wouldn't let them do that."

"I don't know, Zach. There's no one here..."

This reminded Zach of something. What was it? "Roanoke..." he whispered, remembering the story of the early American colony where the settlers had mysteriously disappeared. He silenced the thought. "We don't know that yet. I'm sure they're around somewhere."

The following rooms they inspected didn't provide much solace. Besides some packed suitcases, most everything remained right where Zach would expect it to be. Shirts still hung on racks. Soap sat deformed in the showers. Even as they entered the cafe-

teria, plates covered the tables. A few held rotting food. On the bright side, yellow distress lights illuminated the common area when the main lamps flickered. At least the emergency backup systems were working.

There was also something about the air. As Zach inhaled, his nostrils burned. That couldn't be a good sign. "They're not here, and they're not in most of the rooms. Where else might they be?" Zach left it open to suggestions.

"We should check to see if all the dropships are still here."

Zach stopped at a window when they reached the hallway leading to the docking bay. Through it, he could see the outside of the dock and all the dropships attached to it.

At least that told them something. The colonists hadn't gone home. They had to be somewhere on the ship—all Zach and Ryker had to do was find them.

One corridor was particularly unsettling. Sheets of plastic hung from doorways in some attempt to, what, quarantine? The entrances themselves were ajar, and the flats behind them were bare. The ground was littered with articles of clothing, trash bags, and papers.

There was blood splattered on the wall, dried and brown. When Zach saw it, he immediately steered clear. It didn't look like a handprint or the by-product of a gunshot wound. From a cough, maybe?

Ryker noticed the blood too. "Do you think it was the Red Plague?"

Zach hated to admit it, but he was thinking the same thing. After all, people had been dropping like flies when he and Ryker went into cryo. Quinton had said he'd try to cure them, but what if he failed? But if he had, where were all the bodies? It made no sense. The colonists couldn't have died in the tight confines of a space station and suddenly evaporated into thin air. They had to still be alive somewhere.

"Let's get out of here," said Zach. They walked to the next hallway over.

"We've checked half the ship and found nothing. We're alone!" Ryker burst out. He kicked a trash can, then calmed himself by rubbing the ring on his finger.

"We don't know that."

By early afternoon, they had covered eighty percent of the Homestead and were discussing whether to check the Spark when a subtle alarm grabbed their attention. It was quiet, almost impossible to hear if not for the silence of the corridor. Where did Zach recognize that from? Oh, it was a watch. That was it. A watch alarm.

They followed the noise and came to the entrance of the Science Center. The two swinging doors were slightly parted in the middle, allowing them to peek into the room. There were microscopes. Desks. Lab coats. Research devices scattered across the tabletops. Where was the watch?

Zach stepped inside fully and identified the sound's source. In the back of the room was a long, angled desk that rounded the left corner of the lab. Black shoes stuck out from behind it. A few hesitant steps forward brought the ankle cuffs of black pants into view.

"I don't want to go in there," announced Ryker.

"Be quiet." Zach walked several more steps until he was in the center of the room. He shot a look back to the door. Ryker hesitantly entered. The tail of a dirty lab coat now came into Zach's view. The sight hit him hard. He felt a hammer pounding his *chest. A wrecking ball smashing into him. A million punches to the gut. "No..."*

He ran to it and nearly stepped in the dried blood puddles around the corpse's wrists. Zach paused as he was about to touch the man's head, to pull him up and reveal his identity. He wasn't sure he wanted to find out who it was. But he had no choice. He held his breath and pulled the head up a few inches.

He felt his grasp on reality loosen when he saw the face.

It was Quinton.

"He... he promised." Zach dropped his father's head and scuttled back across the floor. "He told us..."

Ryker noticed the body. He slid down next to Zach and wrapped his arms around him. "I'm so sorry."

Quinton told them he'd be there when they woke up! How could he lie about that? And it clearly wasn't the Red Plague that got him! At least not entirely! One look at the puddles of red surrounding his hands and the scalpel dropped beneath the table nearby could tell you that. No, he meant to break the promise. It was his choice.

"Why don't we get out of here? Okay?" Ryker asked, trying to pull Zach up.

But Zach resisted. "I can't just leave him." His anguish was momentarily replaced by anger. His father had abandoned him. He left the world knowing his son was still in it. What kind of person did that? Certainly not someone like Quinton—good, selfless Quinton. Then, why was his body here, left for Zach to find like some twisted treasure hunt? What were they supposed to do now? There were no signs of anyone else, and, well, Quinton would be of no help. How would they get home?

"Is that broken glass?" Ryker asked, pointing at clusters of tiny shards in Quinton's red splotches of blood.

"I— I don't know. I don't know," Zach stammered.

"It's okay. You're going to be okay." Ryker tightened his grip on Zach and pulled him up. "Come on."

As Ryker tried to lead Zach away from his father's body, Zach spotted a handwritten note on a torn piece of paper on a nearby desk. He broke away from Ryker, picked up the letter, and began to read.

Dear Zach,

He recognized Quinton's handwriting immediately.

I'm sorry that I had to do this. I'm sorry that I broke my promise to be there when you woke up. I'm the only one left. Everyone else is floating with the stars now.

Floating with the stars? What did that mean? Did they jettison the Red Plague's victims out to space? That would explain why there were no bodies.

I wish it didn't have to end this way. That we could go home and return to our daily lives. Go out for ice cream after school.

Then, why did he kill himself?

I need you to know it's going to be okay. You can

go on without me. If you're reading this right now, that means I was right. Cryo did kill the plague. I considered putting myself under, but I'm already too far gone.

If you're awake, you made it. When you look outside, you'll see blue and green. That's Earth. Don't contact the ground for help. I know it sounds strange, but you've got to trust me.

Take a dropship. The power button is beneath the control module. From there, go to Navigation. It has autopilot. All you need to do is initiate that, and the dropship will do the rest. It might seem difficult, but you're smart and strong, Zach. Ryker is too. You can make it.

Wait. Hold on. Quinton wanted them to fly a dropship? They were just kids!

I love you, Zach. More than you'll ever know.
— Love, Dad

ZACH CROFT: 2053

Zach didn't want to be in the Science Center any longer than he had to be. Most of the Gateway held some horrid memory, but this sterile, quartz-white room was the worst. It was where he found his father, bloodied and lifeless, with a handwritten suicide note beside him. Part of him felt like Quinton was a coward for taking the easy way out, for abandoning them, when he could have gone into one of the prisoner pods and survived. But another part of him was sure that Quinton had no choice. He never would have done it otherwise.

Perhaps he was worried he'd give the Plague to Zach upon waking up. That must have been it. Quinton felt that if cryo had given Zach and Ryker a second chance, he didn't want to risk them getting infected upon their return to Earth. And the only way to avoid contaminating them was to die. As the last person on the Gateway who had the Red Plague, killing himself meant the Plague died with him. Weirdly, it was the noblest thing he could have done.

Zach's chest felt on the verge of splitting open as he entered the room. He noticed the desk in the corner, the same desk under which Quinton had died, and tears welled in his eyes. But he forced them back down. "Let's get this done fast."

Zach tried to walk forward, but Ryker pressed a weak hand into his chest. "I'll tell you what: Mabel and I can do this. Why don't you go help Erik with—"

"I'm fine. Really." He joined Mabel toward the center of the room. "Where's the door, Ryker?"

"This way." Ryker led them down a hallway that broke off from the back of the lab, pointing to the end of it. There, a door marked with a biohazard sign caught Zach's eye. A shred of caution tape dangled from the brass knob. A hazmat suit hung from a rack beside it.

Upon reaching the door, Zach found that the entrance practically radiated cold. Zach rattled the doorknob, but it didn't budge. Of course. Why *wouldn't* it be locked?

"Do we need a key?" Mabel asked, trying the knob herself.

"Looks like it." Zach thought about where the key could be.

In a drawer? Filing cabinet? Upon further thought, that wouldn't be particularly secure, so one of the scientists would probably carry it.

Ah, fuck.

Quinton would have had it, but his body was halfway across the galaxy by now. And even if he was still here, Zach couldn't imagine looting his corpse. There were still some lines he wasn't willing to cross. "I need something to break the handle." Zach retreated to the main lab and began rummaging around in a cabinet.

Ryker followed him. "Are you sure we should go in there?"

"What's it matter? We're dead anyway." Zach found an old, worn-out microscope with a broken lens and tested its weight in his hands. "This will work." He went back to the door and slammed it into the knob.

Once.

Twice.

On the third, it came clean out of its socket, bouncing off the floor. Zach used his shoulder to force the door open. A burning blue light filtered out. *UV?* Zach thought, putting his arm over his eyes. It made sense—UV light was used as a disinfectant.

As he entered the biohazard unit, the dirt and dust peppering Zach's clothes glowed in the blacklight. He approached an octagonal machine, about waist height, that resembled a stockier cryopod. While the glass was frozen, a slight heat seemed to radiate from behind it.

"It's keeping it at just the right temperature," Mabel observed, dragging a finger gingerly over it. "Brilliant. So it doesn't freeze, but also doesn't grow."

Zach wiped away some of the ice on the outside. He could make out a few canisters of grayish sludge under the glass. Next, he wiped the metal edges, clearing them of any dust. With the sheen of grime gone, the words *DO NOT OPEN* could be seen. Promising. Real promising.

"This is a horrible idea," Ryker said

"We've done worse." They were no strangers to messing with things they shouldn't. The crater, the irogen, the dropship, the Gateway. What was one more thing? Zach pressed his fingers around the lid to find a release. His fingers grazed a switch, and the covering retracted into the wall. Decompression jets pumped out a warm gas, dispersing its cryogenic counterpart. Ice crystals clinging to the glass jars melted back into water droplets. They slid down and pooled on the inner floor.

"Gloves." He motioned to a box on a nearby shelf. Ryker pulled out a pair of blue nitrile gloves and tossed them over. Zach slid them onto his trembling hands, then reached in and clutched one of the jars. It felt slippery, and he was careful not to drop it as he raised it into the blue light. Thawing air bubbles rose to the top of the alien fluid.

"We'll make sure this is it, then get the rest." With his free hand, Zach closed the pod. He walked back into the lab, then placed the glass beside an intact microscope.

Mabel sat at the desk, flattened out her pants, and searched for something. "Can one of you get me a petri dish?"

"Sure." Zach began to scan tables for the basic equipment but couldn't see one anywhere. The hunt brought Zach to a set of filing cabinets. They were unlocked. Inside was a collection of documents stored in hanging file folders. Out of pure curiosity, he pulled one out. It was signed with the name QUINTON CROFT.

Zach peeled open the cover. The first several entries had no useful information; they were simply an angered Quinton stating how he had no fucking clue what was going on.

But on page nine, article three, something drew his attention. It was an autopsy report dated a week after Zach and Ryker went into cryo. Zach began to read.

> *The subject's symptoms began two days ago: coughing up blood, bruising all over the body, and numerous points of swelling. Today, while in quarantine, he passed away in his sleep. Upon further investigation, we discovered strange formations within his bloodstream. We don't know what they are yet, but the crystalline structures seemed to have ruptured the blood vessels, causing the abnormal bruising. We can assume that a similar phenomenon is affecting the others in quarantine. I'll try my best to keep this journal updated.*
>
> *More soon, Quinton.*

Zach stared vacantly at the last three words. *More soon, Quinton.* He knew the handwriting. He felt his father on that page. "Crystals," he said under his breath, turning around.

In the time it took to read the file, Ryker had already found a petri dish and given it to Mabel. She peered into the microscope's lens.

"What did you say?" Mabel asked as she studied the sample.

"Crystals. They were forming in the colonists' bloodstreams. The infected ones."

Mabel nodded thoughtfully. "Interesting..." As she adjusted the petri dish beneath the scope, something else occurred to her, something important enough to pull her eyes up to Zach. The realization was so powerful that it made her gasp. "Iron. Iron in the blood."

"What?" Zach asked.

"It was biomining them," she said with quiet fascination. "It was extracting the iron from their blood and turning it into irogen."

An image flashed through Zach's memory: his father's body lying still with two lakes of dried blood beneath his wrists. He remembered the shards in Quinton's blood. He had thought it was broken glass. But could it have been irogen?

The idea sickened him.

Zach tried to imagine what that was like for the Red Plague's victims, what it would feel like to have thousands of tiny shards rushing through every artery, every vein. He pictured the blood vessels in his eyes bursting. The feeling of barbed wire sliding through his jugular. The agony of irogen crystals forming in his heart, in his lungs, in his liver. It explained the bleeding eyes, the oozing bruises, the coughing and vomiting of blood. The Red Plague was crystallizing people from the inside out.

Mabel pulled on a pair of gloves and looked back into the lens. "I can see something moving around." She zoomed in. "A lot of somethings, actually."

"May I?" Zach asked. Mabel slid her chair aside, allowing Zach to gaze at the petri dish. Circles were beginning to stir. The first few awoke from their decades-long slumber and shot across the surface like oil in water. They bumped into a few others. Those woke up too, and the process continued until the microscope's lens looked like TV static. "There's a lot of them, all right. I'm surprised they're still alive."

"Aren't we gonna get infected, being this close to it?" Ryker covered his nose and mouth as if it would make a difference.

"It's not airborne," Zach said as he returned the microscope to Mabel. "That's one thing my dad did know about it, even back in Prescott. We all would've been infected way sooner if it had been."

Adjusting the lens to her liking, she smiled. "They're all awake. And assuming this isn't the only surviving batch, I'd say we've got plenty to work with."

"Great." Zach picked up a scalpel off the table and pricked the tip of his finger. A round globe of bright red blood emerged from the wound.

"What're you doing?" Mabel asked, alarmed.

Zach brought his hand over the petri dish and allowed a drop of blood to fall into the sample. "Testing our theory." He squeezed his finger until another few drops splashed into the dish.

Mabel stared into the microscope for what seemed like an eternity. Finally, a small smile curled her lips.

"Well?" Zach asked. "Is it working?"

She pulled away from the eyepiece and slid aside again. "See for yourself."

Zach peered through the microscope. The drops of blood

looked like giant red islands in a sea of squiggling bacteria. The microorganisms seemed drawn to the blood by some form of magnetism. Then, abruptly, they pounced, extruding siphons only a few nanometers thick into the plasma. The siphons turned red, followed by the bodies of the bacteria themselves. As more and more bacteria consumed the blood, tiny crystals of blue and purple began forming on the liquid's surface.

And as the new irogen grew, Zach's hope grew with it.

THIRTY-ONE

ZACH CROFT: 2053

WALKING past a line of rumbling generators, Zach came to a slanted trap door fenced in by low metal rails. He knelt and tugged it open, groaning nearly as loudly as the unoiled hinges of the hatch.

Ryker stepped through the trap door and positioned himself on the ladder's top rung.

"Do you need a light?" Zach extended a bright LED lantern.

Ryker waved it off and tightened his goggles. "I'll let you know once I get down there."

With the grim determination of a coal miner, he descended rung by rung before being swallowed by the darkness entirely. The echo of his boots thudding down the ladder lingered for Zach and Mabel to hear. Then, Ryker jumped to the bottom. His heavy landing echoed up the maintenance shaft.

"What do you see?" asked Zach.

"A big machine. Looks like an elbow," Ryker snorted,

knocking a fist against something metal and hollow. "Some pistons. A bunch of tubes."

"Hydraulics," Zach commented.

Mabel shouted into the darkness. "Any dirt?"

"Not here. Still looking, though." Ryker stepped in what sounded like a puddle of water, muttering the word "gross."

Zach contemplated joining Ryker in his search. They would need a lot of dirt to make enough fuel. "What are the odds we'll be able to produce enough irogen?" he asked Mabel.

With a frown, Mabel shook her head. "Better than no chance."

"Guys, it looks like there's nothing down here," interjected Ryker. "We're gonna have to—"

CRASH!

Ryker screamed, prompting Zach and Mabel to lean over the edge of the hatch.

"What happened?" Zach called down. "Are you okay?"

No answer.

Zach feared that the landing gear had collapsed on his friend. But then a cough sounded from below. Zach turned on the lantern and shined it down, its bright light cutting through the dusty air.

At the bottom of the ladder, Ryker stood covered in red sand. It clung to his hair, his clothes, even his face. He made eye contact with Zach and coughed again. "Found some."

"GIVE IT HERE." Mabel took the bucket of dirt from Zach and walked to the table where she had laid out the jars of bacteria.

"I'm going to need some sort of container." Zach found one in a closet and handed it to her. "That'll work." She emptied some dirt into it and smoothed it into a thick, even layer. With her finger, she made a few divots. "Jar," she said like a doctor in surgery.

Zach gripped a container of gray sludge with both hands and held it over the Martian soil. "Should I pour?"

"Yes. Into the craters," Mabel answered. "Just be careful."

Zach drizzled the liquid into the container. The first divot filled up, and he moved to the next. Then, the next. And the next. Once they were all full, he set the jar aside and exhaled in relief.

"How's it looking?" Erik said, stepping into the room. He rolled up his sleeves and assumed a position next to Mabel. "Is that...?"

Mabel nodded.

"How long's it supposed to take?" Zach asked.

"Your blood only took a few seconds." Mabel slid the microscope across the table, then took a spoon from the shelf. She drove the metal into the soaked soil, scooped out a small amount, and placed the sample beneath the lens. Peering through the eyepiece, she frowned. "Hmm. No reaction yet. Let's give it a bit."

After several excruciating minutes of waiting, the worry began to set in. Maybe they were wrong about the soil. Zach bit his fingernail and asked, "Why isn't it working?"

"I don't know," Mabel said through clenched teeth. "Just wait, okay?"

But no matter how long they waited, nothing changed. Periodically, Mabel checked the microscope for crystals, then stirred the mixture more. "Is there something missing?" she asked rhetorically, pinching her brow with her index finger and thumb.

"You tried Zach's blood, and it worked," Erik said. "So, maybe the iron has to be liquid."

Mabel poked the inside of her cheek with her tongue. "That would make sense if the dirt had been liquified on Mars. But it wasn't. There's no water there at all."

"Maybe not, but we said the Red Plague might have been in permafrost. If the meteor melted the ice, that could have supplied the water it needed."

"Could be," Mabel admitted. "Here. Someone get me a bottle."

Ryker walked to a sink against the wall and filled a large flask. He handed it back to Mabel, who poured its contents into the soil. She stirred it with a glass rod until the dirt mixed with the water and bacteria sample, turning it into a thin red slurry.

Then, they waited.

After what seemed like an hour, Zach cursed under his breath.

Ryker sighed, walking a few feet from the table with his hands on his hips. "What else can we do? Feed it floor panels?" he asked facetiously, thumping his heel on the metal floor.

"It's unlikely anything up here is made of iron," Mabel said.

Ryker gaped at her. "That's the stupidest thing I've ever heard."

"No, the stupidest thing would be launching a ship made of iron into space. It's too heavy."

"Well, we know for sure that blood works," Zach said, stopping the argument. "What if we wake up ten or fifteen people at a time and have them donate blood?" The hydrofarm was on its last legs, but it could still indefinitely support a small crew of people.

"Or we could just use Carver," Ryker suggested.

"Stop," Zach snapped. "Everyone on the ship can donate a pint. If we still need more, we'll let people recover and do another round of donations. We can keep that going until we have enough."

"How much would we need?" asked Erik.

"As much as we can get. It wouldn't hurt to—"

"Hey!" Mabel interrupted. "Check it out." She used the stirring rod to point to the edge of the container, where the reddish mud met the glass. A small cluster of blue and purple crystals had begun to form.

"What's that?" Zach asked. His heart began to race.

"What do you *think* it is?" Mabel exclaimed.

"Are you sure?"

"Look!" She brushed some dirt out of the way to confirm what she saw. As she did so, another cluster of blue and purple materialized in the sand. Her face lit up with a giddy smile. "And there's more!"

Erik rushed to the table and shoved in next to Zach so he could see. "Holy shit." He stepped backward and rubbed his hands down his face. "We did it. We fucking did it." He grabbed Zach's shoulders and shook him a little. Zach laughed in disbelief.

"No," Ryker said, staring at the crystals. "This doesn't make any sense."

Zach deflated a little. "Why not?"

"Everything that *could* go wrong *has* gone wrong, every single time, for my entire goddamned life." He looked at Mabel. "And you're telling me it's working?"

Mabel gestured to the container, where new clusters of irogen crystals were sprouting from the mud with increasing speed. "I'm not *telling* you anything."

She didn't need to.

They could see it with their own eyes.

TIME PASSED FASTER AFTER THAT. Every day, more and more irogen formed, consuming their soil stores but getting closer to the required amount so quickly that they didn't care. A few times, Zach visited the cryobay to speak with Cora through the glass. He knew she couldn't actually hear him, but he didn't care. He chatted up their success with producing irogen, giving her credit for the discovery. After all, Cora's pod freezing over gave him the idea.

Night after night, their weariness dissipated. Zach had less trouble sleeping. Walking by windows still unsettled him, though the fiery light of Earth had dimmed to a dull, muddy brown. And while it sucked to see his home planet so lifeless, he was relieved they had escaped it in one piece.

On the fourth day, Zach was awoken by Mabel pounding on his door. Did she ever sleep? She woke the others and led them to the Science Center, where a large vat had been erected. It was filled to the brim with irogen.

"We have enough." With gloved hands, Mabel picked up

one of the crystals like a diamond and studied its translucent surface. "It's beautiful, don't you think?"

Oh, it was beautiful for a lot of reasons. Chief among them... they were saved! They would live to see Alpha Cen and have the privilege of starting new lives. And this time, it wasn't just a far-off dream. It was reality.

They carted the vat of irogen to the Spark's engine room and deposited it into the irogen processing unit, watching through a glass window as feathers of heat melted away the crystals and boiled the liquid inside. A collective breath was held in fear of it not working. Of the Gateway rejecting the work they had done. Of their last hope for survival diminishing.

But when they ventured to the cockpit and loaded up the control module, Ryker gave them all a happy but astonished shake of his head. "We're golden."

"No, no, not yet. I'm not celebrating until I see that continuum bubble," Zach said. "Get us on our way."

"Glad to say goodbye to this place once and for all," commented Ryker as he powered on the continuum drive. He sat back in his pilot's chair, taking in the window with squinted eyes. His knuckles turned white as he gripped the armrests in anticipation.

Over the next thirty seconds, the space outside began to twist and stretch, just as it had when the Gateway escaped its fall out of orbit. Stars boomeranged back and forth, some coming so close to the ship that Zach worried they'd be burned. But then, he remembered nothing could hurt them inside the bubble. It was merely space working its way around the station.

The distant Earth distorted like a piece of putty, a wad of chewing gum. But there it lingered, not bouncing as the stars around it did, not coming close to the station, and not growing farther away. It simply watched them. Studied them. Said its goodbyes.

As the continuum bubble continued to form, Mabel asked Zach, "What do we do if this works?"

"*When* this works," Ryker quipped.

Zach had put so much energy and time into getting them to this moment that he hadn't even considered what they would do next. Luckily, the answer was simple. "We go into cryo."

"And then?" Erik prompted.

Zach was surprised to feel a smile forcing its way to his lips. "And then we're at Alpha Cen."

Erik smiled, too, then nodded to Ryker. Ryker gave a slight nod back. It wasn't a smile, but it was the most they would probably get at the moment.

When the continuum bubble was fully formed, the station appeared suspended in an orb of liquid water. The stars had diminished to hazy, wavering specks of light. The darkness seemed to tumble over itself as if it were not a void but a collage of somersaulting balls of smoke. Still, Earth glared at them.

"Gateway," Ryker called out. "Set course for Alpha Centauri."

"*SETTING COURSE FOR ALPHA CENTAURI,*" the intercom blared.

The floor started to shake. The space outside pulsed and vibrated. Then, with a high-pitched whine of the station, Earth shrunk to the size of a golf ball. The darkness of space began to brighten into a brilliant white light.

Zach realized he had been holding his breath. He exhaled, then smiled again. "*Now*, we're golden."

ZACH CROFT: 2030

Seeing his father's body drift through the vacuum of space left an emptiness in the pit of Zach's stomach. He knew nobody was watching him. Still, he tried his best to keep the tears at bay. He wanted to look away, but he couldn't. It was like watching a train crash or a building collapsing; horrifying but fascinating. Plus, this was the last time he'd ever see his father, even if all that remained of him was a stiff, bloated figure growing farther away with every passing moment.

They should have put him in a body bag. It would have been the respectful thing to do, but Zach couldn't stand being around the corpse any longer than he had to. He could still feel the dead weight as he and Ryker dragged it through the halls on a sheet, headed for the main airlock. As they struggled with the body, Zach wondered how long it had been in the lab before he found it? A day? A week? A month?

As hard as it was for Zach to believe, he was now an orphan. They both were: him and Ryker. They were scared, hungry, tired, and, worst of all, alone. Alone forever.

What would happen to them on the ground? Certainly, OSE hadn't a clue that any of the colonists were still alive; as far as Zach knew, the Gateway had never been able to get through to Mission Control. What would people think when two children showed up on a spaceship with no adults? Zach could imagine the shock on their faces, their jaws falling open as they realized Zach and Ryker had arrived alone.

He inhaled a weak breath of recycled air, zipped up the dark green sweatshirt he'd found, then shivered. He heard footsteps behind him and turned to address them. "Where were you?"

"I wanted to give you time to say goodbye," Ryker answered.

"Yeah. Thanks." Zach looked back at the glass airlock, searching for his father. Quinton's body was an insignificant black speck against the vibrant blue backdrop of Earth. "None of this seems real..."

"I know." Ryker nodded. "What do we do now?"

Zach reached into his pocket and felt the crumpled note from Quinton. "I guess we go home."

Home. Such an arbitrary term. First, it was Pasadena, then the Gateway, then Mars. Zach wondered if they had a home to return to, being two orphaned children.

They made a pit stop in the pantry to grab some protein packets for the trip, then trudged to the docking bay and opened the blast door.

"Which one do we take?" asked Ryker, looking at the series of airlocks leading to the dropships.

Zach had no idea. The whole process was a mystery to him— getting a ship online, navigating to autopilot, then what? Just sit back and enjoy the flight?

Zach approached the dropship labeled with the number 5 above the airlock and pressed the door open.

There were so many seats. Hundreds that should have been filled with people were now painfully empty. He and Ryker were all that was left. Zach's pulse thumped in his temples.

He had to do this. If he couldn't resurrect his father, he could at least follow his instructions. Don't radio. Activate autopilot. Go to the ground. Simple.

The control module loomed above him, dozens of flashing buttons fighting for his attention. He recalled the letter's content, remembering the power button was somewhere beneath the command block. "Sit down," he said to Ryker. Ryker didn't move. "Come on. Sit."

"I will." But Ryker stayed behind him as Zach got onto his knees and reached under the control module.

He slid his fingers across the panel, felt a switch, and pressed it.

ZACH CROFT: 2054

Zach shot up with a start, waving away the icy gas swirling all around him. Shivering, he swung his legs out of the cryopod and jumped down.

"ARRIVAL AT ALPHA CENTAURI WAYPOINT IN T-MINUS THIRTY MINUTES," the intercom boomed. *"PREPARING TO DISENGAGE CONTINUUM BUBBLE."*

Zach snagged his t-shirt from the floor and pulled it over his torso. Then he rubbed his heavy eyelids and replied, "Gateway. Time passed?"

The station informed him that eleven-and-a-half months had passed, and they were currently transiting past the gas giant ACB-FOUR. Zach recalled the hazy images that OSE space telescopes had gotten of the planet, no more than a luminescent sphere. It would be fantastic to see it in person.

Ryker's hand clamped on Zach's shoulder. "Cockpit?"

"Go ahead. I'll catch up." Zach scanned the rows of survivors emerging from their cryopods until he spotted Cora. She leaned against the edge of her pod with a confused look. Her eyes bulged as she saw Zach weaving his way toward her. He raised a finger to his lips in a *shh* gesture. "Come with me." He took her by the arm and led her into a small room adjacent to the cryobay.

As soon as they were out of earshot of the other survivors, Cora whispered, "We're at Alpha Cen?" Zach nodded. Cora let out a surprised laugh. "How?"

Zach explained everything, from seeing the ice crystals on her cryopod to using the Red Plague to produce a new batch of irogen.

Cora stared at him in disbelief. "That's crazy."

"I know," Zach acknowledged. "But it's true."

"So... we're alive?"

"Yeah. We're alive."

Cora's face morphed into a broad smile. She hugged Zach, squeezing so tightly that he could barely breathe. She laughed, released him, and apologized. "Oh, I'm sorry! I didn't mean to hurt you." Then, she tugged him back in. "But this is just so great!"

"Okay, okay. Now, listen. I need you to help get everyone out of cryo safely. Have them go to the cafeteria so I can brief them, then come get me in the cockpit."

"Of course. Anything."

ZACH ENTERED the cockpit to find Ryker staring down at the control module. He could tell from how Ryker was chewing on his thumb that something was amiss. "What's the matter?"

Ryker looked up at Zach, then gestured at the screen. "It looks like we've been running off the backup generators since we left," Ryker explained. He rolled his chair away from the computer and came to a smaller rig against the wall, accompanied by a long array of command buttons. He pressed two of them, his brow pinched tight, and a model of the Spark flickered onto another screen.

"Why would we be on backup?" asked Zach.

Ryker pointed at the corner of the diagram. "Two of the power processing modules are down."

"Why?" Zach leaned over Ryker and squinted at the screen. "We were in a continuum bubble."

"It happened before we left." Ryker gave Zach a grim look, then rolled back to the other computer. "When we fell out of orbit." He tapped the computer's display, which now showed the model of the station. He dragged his finger across the diagram before stopping on a crimson part of the Spark. He glanced over his shoulder at the other rig and remarked, "The shoe fits."

Zach looked at the model of the Spark, noting the location of the red modules, then looked at the diagram of the entire station. "Shit," he murmured, wiping his eyes of any remaining sleep. "How much time do we have?"

"They're designed to last a year, but..."

Zach finished the thought for him. "That's how long we've been in cryo."

Ryker replied with a solemn nod, then angled his face to

the ceiling. "Gateway, how long before the backup generators die?"

"FORTY-EIGHT HOURS, THIRTY-SIX MINUTES, TWELVE SECONDS."

Ryker sighed. "Fuck, okay. That's cutting it close, but it should be enough time, right?"

"Should be, if we begin our descent as soon as we're in orbit around Alpha Cen. But we've got a lot to do before then."

"Well, let's go, then," Ryker said as he stood. "Clock's ticking."

STANDING upon a makeshift platform Cora had set up in the front of the cafeteria, Zach looked at the mass of people before him. The cafeteria was large, but even then, the more than eight hundred survivors stood shoulder to shoulder as they conversed with the people around them. Some wore spare Prescott sweaters salvaged from a supply room. The outfits gave Zach an eerie sense of *deja vu*, as if he was a kid on his way to Prescott for the first time. He pushed the thoughts out of his mind and focused his energy on the present day.

"I know this hasn't been easy," he said, pacing across the stage with the microphone. "But I'm happy to say that the announcement you heard on the intercom was right. We're almost at Alpha Centauri." The crowd buzzed with excitement, prompting smiles and hugs between people that may have only been strangers on Earth.

Zach took a moment to bask in their relief. After all their hardships and pain, they were almost to their new home.

"Look!" someone called, pointing at one of the many octagonal windows. Beyond the ship, the blank white of interstellar travel faded into darkness as the distortion of the continuum bubble dissipated.

A brilliant kaleidoscope of colors painted the space outside. Purples, pinks, blues, and oranges intertwined in distant explosions that seemed frozen in time. The crowd pressed toward the windows, standing on tippy toes, climbing on tables, and craning around colleagues to glimpse the vibrant cosmos. The light illuminated their faces with swirling colors, and a glimmer of hope Zach had not seen before their home's destruction appeared in their eyes. A mixture of joyous laughter, relieved sobs, and expressions of awe rippled through the crowd.

"Look, look, look! There!" Another person pressed their finger against the glass. Zach followed it, leaning against his elbows against the pantry railing as a colossal planet appeared in the corner of the window.

It was ACB-FOUR, glowing and vibrating, with auroras swirling through its atmosphere. Long, winding neon stripes streaked across the outer layer of the gas giant. They pulsated, casting a greenish light on the Gateway that made Zach's eyes water. The planet's beauty was overwhelming. Would they be able to see it from Alpha Cen? Oh, that would be stellar. To look up at the night sky and see that gleaming orb alongside the moons. Things got better by the second.

Soon, ACB-FOUR passed out of view. There was an idle moment in the cafeteria as everyone savored what they had just seen. Then, the usual buzz resumed.

"All right, everyone! Listen up!" Zach said, bringing the

crowd's attention back to himself. "We're almost to Alpha Cen. I need volunteers to take whatever we can from the supply rooms," Zach pointed at the doors behind him, "and load it all into the dropships. Food, medical supplies, clothing, anything you can carry. We're gonna need it all."

"What about shelter?" Cora brought up from below.

"Good question," said Zach. "There are some leftover building supplies from Prescott, some spare hab units and tents, plus the dropships we'll fly down on. It'll be a challenge, but we'll make it work."

"And clothes?" a woman asked. "I don't want to wake up one morning and see Larry's bare ass prancing through the streets." She elbowed the man beside her, who gave a mock-ashamed smile as he fielded laughter from all around.

"Yes, yes. The clothes too. There's more than enough in the living quarters, plus more in storage. All right? All right." Zach clapped his hands. "Let's go, people. Divide into groups and pack up anything you think will be useful. We're not coming back here, so get your affairs in order and prepare to go home."

A few whoops sounded as Zach descended the stage and headed for the supply room, accompanied by a dozen others eager to help. "Boxes are there, and canned goods are on the higher shelves," Zach said once inside.

For the next fifteen minutes, Zach put himself to work. Over and over again, he loaded nonperishables into boxes and deposited them against the adjacent wall. He didn't stop until a muffled voice in the cafeteria below called for him.

"What's the matter?" As he emerged from the pantry, Zach found that a crowd had formed around the windows again. But unlike last time, they were silent, their forlorn expressions seemingly cast in stone. The excitement was long gone, replaced by a fog of eerie uncertainty that hung over the room.

The assembled crowd blocked his view, so Zach could not see out the windows until he was deep into the mob. He pushed his way through, ignoring the unanswerable questions that bombarded him. What was the matter? They were almost to Alpha Cen, right?

Just as he reached the windows, he was blinded by a hot flash of lightning.

"WHAT THE HELL IS THAT?" Ryker yelled, waving a hand at the cockpit's front window. His cheeks burned red with frustration.

"A storm," Zach answered simply, though the reality was anything but. It was no ordinary storm. The entire planet—all of Alpha Centauri—was covered in thick, tumbling purple-gray clouds, with miles-long bolts of lightning pulsing through the atmosphere. The lightning cracked the clouds like old porcelain, multiple bolts colliding in blinding white flashes that lit up the inside of the cockpit. Spirals of clouds resembling Earth's hurricanes spiraled across the surface. The remaining murk drifted across the planet from left to right in long, billowing waves.

"A *storm*?" Ryker fumed. "What kind of storm looks like that?" A vein in Ryker's forehead materialized. "Are we even in the right place?"

For a moment, Zach considered that the autopilot could

have taken them to a different planet. "Gateway, where are we?"

"*ENTERING ORBIT AROUND ALPHA CENTAURI.*"

"No, we're not," Ryker growled in denial. "You can't tell me this is it; this is your utopia? It's a fucking nightmare."

"It's a storm. It doesn't say anything about what's on the ground below. Besides, we knew storms like this could happen. OSE studied them for years."

"You knew about this and didn't say anything?"

"I didn't know about *this*!" Zach moved his arm in a fast, circular motion that traced the planet's edges. "We knew that Alpha Cen had some wild storms. But they only formed once every few decades, and it's not like we had a whole lot of advance notice—"

"Well, what *do* you know?"

"We sent a probe to the surface during one of them, but..." Zach trailed off.

"*But?* But what?"

Zach closed his eyes and pinched the bridge of his nose. He suddenly had a massive headache. "It didn't make it."

"It didn't make it," Ryker repeated. He gaped at Zach in disbelief, then sighed. "All right. So, we wait for the storm to pass. We've got plenty of stuff to do in the meantime."

The headache pulsing in Zach's ears threatened to split his skull in half. "We can't," he said, his voice barely audible.

"Say again?"

"We can't," Zach said, louder this time. "The storms last for weeks." The bitter taste of bile rose in the back of his throat.

Ryker dropped his arms. He sat slowly in a chair, then rested his elbows on his knees and lowered his face into his hands as he absorbed the implications of Zach's words. After a moment, he looked up at Zach. "So, we're fucked."

"We're not fucked," Zach replied. He hoped that saying the words out loud would help him believe them. It didn't.

Ryker laughed incredulously. "Or, what? You want us to fly through that?" He pointed at the storm outside the window. Another flash of lightning illuminated the cockpit. "You think that shit's survivable?"

"What choice do we have?" Zach exclaimed, his voice rising. "Once the backup generators go, we've got no power. No power means no water. No food. No air." He looked out at the roiling storm. "We have to try."

"Zach," Ryker said, trying to sound reasonable. "If we fly through that storm, we're dead."

Zach fixed Ryker with a steady gaze. "And if we don't?"

THIRTY-TWO

NICOLAS CARVER: 2030

AS HE EMERGED from his new office, Carver remembered how he had gotten there. For a month, he'd hardly been able to sleep, eat, or function in any significant way.

Because of Victor.

Victor, Victor, Victor.

Carver still felt the shock that forced his legs into motion, carrying him to the roof's edge to determine Victor's fate. He spotted Victor's body crumpled and twisted far below, lying in an ever-expanding pool of red. His ears picked up the piercing screams of those closest, the pounding feet, the calls for ambulances. He couldn't catch his breath. The world spun around him.

He had stepped back abruptly, collapsed next to the ledge, and rubbed his eyes while he tried to comprehend what had just happened. Victor was dead. And Carver had killed him.

It was self-defense, though, right? Victor pushed him first—

all Carver did was shove back. If anyone questioned him, he would explain that he had been defending himself.

Carver went on autopilot, stumbling through the roof exit and down the stairs while everyone else was distracted by the mess in the courtyard. Still numb with shock, he returned to Wilford and ordered him to lock the cryobay before the colonists went under. He would have to deal with what happened to Victor, but he also couldn't ignore what was happening with Quinton and the Gateway. Wilford had questions but eventually gave in to Carver's insistent commands. One click of a button, and that was it. The cryobay was locked, inaccessible to anyone without explicit authorization from Mission Control. The colonists would never return to Earth. They would die on the Gateway, and the Red Plague would die with them.

Over the next several days, Carver sequestered himself in his house, staying away from OSE and even skipping Victor's funeral. He felt like all eyes would be on him, even though nobody knew he was the reason Victor was in a casket. The incident had been written off as a suicide. Nobody suspected any foul play. There were no witnesses, nothing that could link Carver to the time and place of Victor's death. As far as anyone else was concerned, Carver was dealing with his grief in his own way. It wasn't entirely untrue. Whenever Carver closed his eyes, Victor's face was the only thing he could see: the look on Victor's face as he lost his footing and tumbled over the ledge.

Carver wondered why he wasn't as disturbed about what he had done to the colonists on the Gateway. After all, he was just as responsible for their deaths as he was for Victor's. There were hundreds of them—that surely should have haunted him more. And yet, for some reason, it didn't. Maybe it was because he and

Victor had been such close friends. Carver may have disagreed with him sometimes, even reviled some of his decisions, but a friend was a friend. Plus, Carver had killed Victor directly, with his own bare hands. With the colonists, it was less personal. There was a distance to it, literally and figuratively. He wouldn't see it happen. He would never witness the expressions on their faces as they took their last breaths. Technically, he wasn't even the person who closed the cryobay—even though it had been on Carver's orders, Wilford was the one who had sent the final command.

Despite his guilt and grief, Carver couldn't deny that some good would come from Victor's death. With Victor and the colonists—specifically Quinton—gone, Carver had assumed the role of head of OSE. Control of the agency meant Carver could finally devote all their funding to a solution to the solar flares. The real solution. With Prescott in the past, the agency could move forward with MagRes, his project for restoring the magnetosphere.

"Carver!"

Carver was broken from his memory by a voice behind him. He turned to see Wilford approaching quickly with a panicked expression. It felt like history repeating itself.

"What's the matter?" Carver asked.

"One of the Gateway's dropships activated," Wilford whispered quietly enough that no one else could hear.

Carver scoffed. "That's impossible." Quinton had claimed that, without cryo, the colonists would be dead in two weeks. It had been a month. There was no way anyone was alive up there... unless Quinton was wrong. Who would be left then?

Could it be Quinton? If so, Carver would be fucked. Quinton was the only person—besides Wilford—who knew what Carver had done to the cryobay. Who knew what he'd say? If he had somehow survived, Carver would be finished. No, it had to be a malfunction. "Relax," Carver said with a calming gesture. "Something must have caused the dropship to disengage from the Gateway. A software glitch. Or a mechanical systems failure. Something—"

Wilford shook his head insistently, interrupting Carver. "No, you don't understand. The command is from the dropship itself. It was activated manually. Someone's alive up there."

ZACH CROFT: 2054

"We're not seriously talking about this, are we?" Cora paced to the window and stared at the thick storm clouds below. "I mean, Christ, Zach! Look at it!"

"We've got less than a day," Zach said. "There's no other choice." They had spent the previous 24 hours trying to repair the power grid but to no avail. The damage was too severe, and they didn't have the parts, the tools, or the specific expertise to fix it. The Gateway was dying. All life support systems would shut down in a few short hours. Water filtration. Heating. Oxygen scrubbers. A descent to Alpha Cen through the raging electrical storm was, for better or worse, their final option.

"Cryo!" Cora blurted out hopefully. "We can go back on ice. Wait out whatever... clusterfuck is going on out there." Her hand indicated the storm swirling around Alpha Cen.

"The power's going to shut down regardless. The pods will defrost. Anyone in them will suffocate."

"Fuck, man." Cora pushed her hair back, then massaged

her tired eyes. "There has to be something we can do. There's *always* something!"

Zach sat in the corner of the cockpit, his face falling into his palms. "There's not. Not this time. It's over."

"The hell it is!" Cora sat down across from him and flicked his forehead. "Stop it. Let's put our heads together and actually do something for once!"

"It's the flares all over again."

"Keep it together. If not for me, then for everyone else. Okay?" Zach wiped his nose, nodding. Cora continued. "Great. Now, what's the problem? With the Spark."

"The modules that process energy from solar. They were damaged when we fell from orbit."

"Define 'damaged'... what does that mean?"

"Damaged," Zach said, lifting his fingers to make air quotes. "They were destroyed. There's practically nothing left to repair."

"So, what about the backup systems? Maybe there's a way to recharge those?" Cora's eyes lit up as an idea struck her. "Oh, my God. We can use the irogen!" Her excitement dissipated when she saw the pained look on Zach's face. "No?"

"That's just not how it works."

"So? We'll make it work. I mean, you figured out the biomining thing, and that was *way* more complicated. This is just an engineering problem. And this place is loaded with engineers."

"Maybe if we had more time. But we don't." Zach grasped Cora's hand. "I appreciate your optimism, Cora. I really do. But there's nothing we can do."

Cora pulled her hand away. "No. No, we're not launching

those dropships into a global electrical storm! It's crazy. We'll never make it through."

"Maybe." Zach stood and walked over to the window to look at the storm. "But we have to try."

ZACH CROFT: 2030

The screens flickered on, and Zach shielded his eyes from the light.

A chime echoed through the intercom, informing him that the dropship was online. A prompt appeared on the screen, asking him to choose a directive. He scanned the list of commands.

[Engines]
[Fuel]
[Navigation]
[Comms]

How was he supposed to recognize any of this? He was a child—not remotely trained or qualified to operate a dropship. But his father had said Zach could do it, and Zach believed him.

"He said something about autopilot," Ryker said. "Maybe you should check navigation?"

Zach did, and another menu was displayed on the screen.

[Manual]
[Override]
[Autopilot]

There! Autopilot. Zach selected it, watching as a map of the U.S. popped up. A red crosshair scanned the landscape, first settling on Florida—OSE had a launch facility there—then moving to Texas, then to California. The crosshair flashed green, zoomed in, and revealed a satellite image of Pasadena. More specifically, OSE headquarters.

"DESTINATION SET," the system said. "TWO MINUTES TO DEPARTURE."

"Strap in." Zach moved for a seat, draping the restraints over his chest. Ryker did the same, then stopped. "What's wrong?" Zach asked.

Ryker ran his hands over one another, eyes widening. They moved to his jacket pockets, then to the crevices in his cargo pants. "My ring! My dad's ring. It's gone." He jumped out of his seat and bolted for the exit.

"Wait!" Zach shouted. He rushed to unbuckle the restraints and followed Ryker, grabbing his arm right before Ryker reached the airlock. "Forget it!"

"I can't!"

"We don't have time." No way was Zach about to mess this up. They were finally going home. It wasn't worth risking it all for a ring.

"It's all I have left of him." Ryker pulled from Zach's grasp and crossed the divide into the station. "I must have dropped it somewhere out here."

Ryker left the docking bay and ran into the corridor. The sound of his footsteps got weaker the farther away he went. Would he be able to get back in time? Zach shot a glance at the control module. Ninety seconds until launch. "Do you need help?" he called.

A faint voice, quickly getting louder, responded, "No. It's fine. I'll find it." But he didn't sound too convinced.

In the meantime, Zach stared through the dropship window at North America: the blues and greens, the yellows and browns. God willing, he'd never see the world from this angle again. From a spectator's point of view. Like he was an alien surveying worlds in the same way critics judged art or food. What kind of rating would he give Earth? Hmm. Compared to Mars? Five stars. Ten out of ten.

Zach tapped his foot nervously against the ground, having not heard from Ryker in over thirty seconds. They were really cutting it close now.

Ryker ran back into the docking bay frantically. "I can't find it. It—" Something caught his eye on the other side of the hundred-foot room: a glint of metal under the farthest airlock. As he started to run for it, all the lights in the dock suddenly turned red. A siren tore through the air, followed by an urgent voice blaring from the intercom.

"EMERGENCY PROTOCOL ACTIVATED. CLOSING ALL AIRLOCKS. PLEASE STAND CLEAR."

The airlock began to shut.

Ryker looked back at Zach, then at the shining bit of silver on the other side of the docking bay. The ring. He turned in its direction.

"No, Ryker!" Zach cried. "Get on the ship!"

The countdown read thirty seconds. The airlock was a third of the way shut.

Ryker sprinted as fast as he could, pumping his feet against the metal. As he crossed the room, he slid to the floor on his knees and stopped in front of the ring. He snatched it up, then turned and scrambled to his feet.

The blast door was halfway shut now.

Ryker's legs shot back into motion, propelling him toward the dropship. Zach waved him on from just inside the ship. "Come on! Hurry!" The gap in the airlock was nearly too small for Ryker to fit. If he didn't get there immediately, it was over.

Ryker stumbled, then regained his footing. "Wait! Don't—"

But it was too late.

Ryker's words fell short as the airlock closed completely. The inside of the dropship went silent. Ryker crashed into the other side of the blast door. He pressed his face against the glass, his eyes wide with terror. Then he stepped back and pounded on the door, yelling for Zach to let him in.

"Ryker!" Zach knew his words would go unheard, yet he couldn't stop himself from calling to him. Tears spilled from his eyes. He turned and looked at the countdown. Ten seconds.

Zach ran to the command module and pressed every button he could. "No! No! Stop! Stop the launch!" He slapped his palms against the complicated array of screens and switches.

Nothing worked.

The dropship began to rumble as it prepared to detach from the Gateway. Zach rushed back to the airlock, where Ryker was still pleading for entry.

"Please! Zach!" Ryker mouthed. "Don't leave me!"

Suddenly, Zach was thrown against a row of chairs by the force of the dropship's launch. His head collided with a heavy plastic armrest. His vision went blurry. Zach lurched back toward the blast door, fighting through a haze of confusion. The Gateway was already receding into the distance, but Zach could still see Ryker's face framed in the bright circle of the airlock door.

Ryker was still shouting.

Zach couldn't make out most of his words, but even from a distance, one phrase was clear.

"Come back!"

THIRTY-THREE

NICOLAS CARVER: 2030

PRESCOTT WAS FINISHED.

It was a long, hard-fought journey, but one that was finally coming to an end. As Carver stepped into his new office with the last of his boxes, he realized it was true this time. It was done.

Even more importantly, Earth was safe from whatever the colonists had contracted on Mars. Initiating the Emergency Protocol ensured that the dropships would be sealed off, preventing anyone left alive on the Gateway from bringing the Red Plague back home. Everyone was quarantined on the station, where they'd eventually succumb to the illness. It was a tough decision, but Carver was no stranger to tough decisions— he had made his fair share of them in the last few weeks. They were for the best, though. He was sure of that.

As he set down the cardboard crates, he kept his eye on the office window and awaited the imminent fireball streaming across the sky. Since the launch command had already been issued, the dropship would fly to the ground regardless of the Emergency Protocol lockdown. But nobody would be on it. OSE would have to explain how it launched—a glitch, probably— then he'd order the agency to destroy the thing. It wasn't worth taking any risks.

Carver picked up the nameplate from his new desk. It was an extravagant thing, engraved in real silver. "NICOLAS CARVER," it read in bold capital letters. Then, below, "Director, Organization of Space Exploration." Carver was the youngest man to ever lead OSE. Of course, Congress hadn't officially approved him yet, but that was just a formality as far as he was concerned. He was the obvious pick. The best pick. Until then, he'd fill the role in an interim capacity.

He wished his father could see him now. Mason Carver, the narcissistic scumbag who never gave a damn about his family. Never gave a damn about his wife. His kid. Never showed up to any parent-teacher nights or ice cream socials. Wasn't there to teach Carver how to shave, drive, and file taxes. Half the time, he wasn't even home. Carver never really knew where his father went. He was probably gambling away what little money they had or passing out in the bathroom of some musty bar. Thank God he at least wised up enough to jump off the Golden Gate Bridge.

When the news of his father's death reached the house— Carver was only ten—his mother descended into a sobbing mess. Her reaction never made any sense to him, even back then. With his father gone, Carver and his mother would be free to live without someone breathing down their necks or extinguishing cigarettes on their skin. There would be no more late nights waiting for the inevitable knock at the door, followed by two police officers depositing his father, bloodied from some pointless bar fight, on the threadbare couch. There would be no more shouting. No more cursing. No more bloodied mouths or blackened eyes. His mother wouldn't need to spend an hour applying makeup every morning to conceal her husband's rampage from the previous night. They were safe.

After Mason died, it took a while for Carver and his mother to bounce back. Money was tight, but every night Carver would remind himself how lucky he was that his father was dead and gone. The world was a better place without him.

A loud boom startled Carver out of his memories. He could see the streak of light he'd been expecting through the window. It broke through the atmosphere and plummeted toward the ground, headed for the landing pads adjacent to the OSE headquarters. With the autopilot working as expected, it would be on the ground in minutes.

While he waited for news of the ship's arrival, Carver unpacked his boxes. He placed a photo of him and his mother on the shelf, one taken at his college graduation. Next to it, he put a picture of himself with Victor, God rest his soul. On the wall behind his desk, he hung an oil painting he had created a year prior.

Just as he finished arranging his belongings, a woman bounded through the door. "Sir, thank god you're here! We need you in the landing bay."

"Why? What happened?" Carver slid his charcoal blazer back over his white dress shirt.

"There's a kid."

"What kid?"

"On the dropship! There's a kid on the dropship."

Carver's stomach plummeted. A kid? Whose kid? And how was that even possible? The Emergency Protocol should have prevented anyone from boarding before the ship took off. "Are you sure it's a kid?"

"Yes, sir," the woman answered. "We've been speaking with him on the radio. He said he's ten years old."

"Did you get his name?"

"His name is Zach." The woman glanced at her paper. "Zach Croft."

ZACH CROFT: 2030

The air was chilly in the quarantine room. It wasn't as cold as on the Gateway, but somehow it cut deeper. Zach's expression was empty, lacking any emotion. What was he supposed to do, smile? Be grateful he was back on Earth with other people? Something about that didn't feel right. His father was dead, and Ryker was trapped on the Gateway. Should he be sad, then? No, that wasn't right either. He certainly was glad he had made it home after all he'd been through.

Through the glass, Mr. Carver—that was his name, right?— tapped a stack of paper into alignment. He surveyed Zach with a sympathetic look, then spoke into a microphone.

"I'm sorry we've had to keep you here for so long."

Zach shot a look around his small isolation room. The bed. The bathroom next to it. After a week locked in a sterile hellhole, he only wanted to feel the sun on his face. Or his father's hand interlocked with his own. But that wasn't going to happen.

"It's okay," Zach said. "I understand." In truth, he didn't. He obviously wasn't infected. Otherwise, he'd be dead. So why was he

being quarantined? "Can you at least tell me if my friend is alive?"

Carver took a deep breath, then gave a sad, sympathetic smile. "I'm so sorry, son. It doesn't appear so."

For the first time since returning to Earth, Zach lost control. Tears welled in his eyes. "How can that be?" Zach asked. "I was just with him!"

"We checked every system we could," Carver replied. He flipped through the papers in his hand. "Security cameras, motion sensors, thermosensors, microphones."

"That's impossible."

"If he was alive up there, we'd know. He'd show up in at least one of those systems. But there's nothing. No signs of life." Carver sighed. "He didn't make it."

"But there was nothing wrong with him! He was fine." Zach replayed his last moments with Ryker in his head. Ryker banging on the airlock. The ship leaving without him. The terror in his eyes.

Carver turned as someone walked through the door, approached, and whispered something in his ear. "Really? So soon?" asked Carver.

"The doctors say he's clear." The woman shot a look at Zach, sizing him up.

Carver got out of his seat and strode toward the door of Zach's quarantine room. Zach could hear the beeps of the keypad on the wall, then the door slid open, and Carver stepped inside.

Zach instinctively got up and moved over to his bed, putting as much distance between himself and Carver as possible.

"It's okay, Zach. You're not sick." Carver walked up to the

mattress and squatted in front of Zach. "You remember Sarina Keaton?"

Zach squinted at Carver, puzzled. "Cora's mom?"

"Yes, that's right." Carver nodded. "Well, Mrs. Keaton has agreed to take you in for now. She's waiting outside."

"I'm going to live with Cora?" It didn't seem real. Cora was a good friend, but he couldn't imagine living in the same house as her.

"Come on." Carver stood and gestured for Zach to follow him. "I'm going to help out too. Me and your father... We were good friends. I'm terribly sorry for what happened to him." He squeezed Zach's shoulder and looked him in the eyes. "If you need anything, I'm here for you."

"If you're here for me, then check the Gateway again. Send someone up there. Bring my friend home."

Carver released his grip on Zach's shoulder. "He's gone, son. I'm sorry.."

"Just try. Please."

Carver placed his hand on the small of Zach's back and tried to guide him toward the door. "Let's get you home now, okay? Sarina's waiting."

People moved aside as they walked down the halls to allow them to pass. Zach couldn't tell if that was because Carver was the head of OSE or because he was the only remaining Prescott colonist. A survivor.

Light spilled into Zach's eyes when the two stepped through the giant glass doors that acted as a gateway into OSE. The brightness should have made him wince, but he welcomed it. Martian sunlight was dim and red. But here on Earth, the sunlight was pure, silky gold. Zach gazed off into the distance *at the rolling green hills just beyond the buildings of Pasadena.*

They walked through the courtyard and to the asphalt parking lot. A black SUV pulled up with Sarina Keaton in the driver's seat. The back door suddenly sprung open, and a little girl jumped out. Her smile seemed impossibly wide.

"Cora! Come back," Sarina said.

Cora ignored her, running as fast as she could up to Zach and wrapping her arms around him. "I'm so happy you're home." She closed her eyes as she rested her head on his shoulder. "I'll never let anything bad happen to you again."

Then, Zach did something that even surprised himself.

He smiled.

ZACH CROFT: 2054

It started with a jolt, a snap, as the dropship separated from the Gateway. Sweat poured down Zach's face, but he made no effort to wipe it away.

He replayed his last conversation with Ryker before they parted ways. They had just collected Carver and Rhea from the prisoner pods and loaded them onto Dropship One. After getting the two prisoners strapped in, they returned to the docking bay. Zach knew they should be rushing to depart, as everyone was already loaded up, but he couldn't move away.

"I guess this is it," Zach said. His voice felt thick in his throat. He could feel his body shaking despite his best efforts to conceal it. "Are you sure you're up for this?"

Ryker moved forward and hugged Zach. "Definitely. I'll get them down there safely."

Zach nodded, pressing his chin into Ryker's shoulder. "Thank you for coming back to Earth. We'd be dead if you hadn't." They really would have been. His return had led Zach to Wilford, to discovering the vast supplies of irogen in the colony, to Mars, and, finally, to Alpha Cen. Ryker had started it all.

"Yeah... You definitely would be." Ryker patted Zach on the back, then released him.

"Okay. Okay, you've got this," Zach said.

"Damn right, I do." With one last smile, Ryker walked past Zach and into his dropship.

As the airlock shut between them this time, no tears were shed. They weren't slamming their fists against the divide, begging for it to open. They only exchanged a brief nod as Zach mouthed, "See you on the other side."

Zach looked at the dropship beside his own and prayed they would be okay. The turbulent orb in front of them held little promise. But, he reminded himself, they had no choice. They would die if they stayed on the Gateway. They were probably still doomed trying to fly through the storm, but maybe less so. They still had a chance, no matter how small.

Zach leaned back in his seat and shut his eyes. He wanted so badly to disappear. To fade away into the sunset, never to be seen again. But he couldn't do that. The survivors depended on him. He had to get his people to safety.

His people.

When had he started thinking of them like that? He never considered himself much of a leader, but the last few weeks had left him feeling responsible for everyone. With Carver out of the picture, people had started looking to him to make decisions. He didn't love doing it, but someone had to. It just so happened to be him.

After tugging on his restraints to ensure they were secured, Zach asked the pilot to hand him the radio. It was patched through to the other dropships. "Dropship One here. Is everyone ready?" he croaked. Of course, they weren't ready. They never would be. Neither would he.

Ryker responded with, "Two here. We're all good. Three?"

The pilot for Dropship Three's gravelly voice cut through the air. "Ready as we can be."

Zach glanced out the window. "Okay." He took a deep breath, trying to keep his words steady and commanding. "All dropships, engage thrusters."

"Engaging," the other two said in succession.

The next few seconds were surreal. Those on his ship released a collective gasp as the floor began to rumble. The sound built into a roar, then they were off. The dropships blasted forward, the darkness of space disappearing around the windows' edges, only to be replaced by an endless gray. Zach felt his breathing hitch as they sliced through the top layer of the atmosphere. Unease gripped his throat, squeezing tighter and tighter.

Tendrils of flame ascended up and around the glass, framing the scene before them. Clouds buffeted the ship. But there was no lightning. Not yet. Where was it?

The fire of reentry—or just *entry*, he supposed—was thinned out by water in the clouds.

Then, the first bolt of bluish lightning flashed outside, accompanied by an immediate boom. Reflexively, Zach recoiled back. Others did too. But miraculously, the bolt didn't hit them, nor did the next few.

Zach clutched the sides of his seat so hard that his knuckles felt like they might burst through his skin. His stomach tightened with a powerful sense of *deja vu*—it was like his first descent to Mars as a kid. The shaking, the terror, the flashing lights. It was all happening again. As frightening as the memory was, he reminded himself that he had survived that descent, and he would survive this one too. The thought calmed his nerves a little. But just a little.

Another bolt of lightning blazed outside. Then another. And another. Zach glanced at the side windows, a baseball-sized lump appearing in his throat. Through the layer of fog, he could see the outlines of the other two ships, each maybe five hundred yards from his own. At least they were still intact.

The deeper they went into the storm, the more violent the lightning got. The dropship bounced and tilted on its side, sending Zach's heart lurching into his throat before the pilot managed to get his bearings and get the ship back on course.

Suddenly, Dropship Two veered to the side. "Everything good over there, Ryker?" Zach asked into the radio.

"Just peachy," Ryker answered breathlessly. His ship drifted away from the rest a few times, but he always managed to get back in line. It was surprising how good of a pilot he was. All those years of killing time in the simulator on the Gateway had really paid off.

"Hey, we're... we're having some troubles over here," the pilot for Dropship Three said in a trembling voice.

Zach looked to his right, studying the ship. Nothing

seemed too out of the ordinary from what he could see. "What's the problem?"

"I— I don't know. One moment, I have control, and the next, I don't!" He pulled in a shaky breath. "We're slowing. I... I..." The astronaut, who had only been a trainee back on Earth, stammered for something to say.

"Hold on. Just keep calm and focus. You hear me?" Zach assured him. "You're going to be fine." But his voice lacked conviction. Dropship Three continued to fall behind, sputtering like a car running out of gas.

"I can't— I don't—" the pilot said. He cursed at the dropship as he struggled to maintain control. "Come on, goddamnit!" Suddenly, a blinding bolt of lightning struck the ship. It tore a flaming hole through the heat shield, setting off a series of explosions around the hull. When the fire reached the fuel cell, the whole ship exploded in a brilliant ball of fire. Thick, black smoke followed the wreckage as it plummeted toward the ground. Plates of sheet metal peeled off the flaming wreckage. Debris spilled from the gaping chasm in the back of the craft. Bodies, too—some dead, some alive.

Oh my god, oh my god, oh my god, oh my god. Zach stared in horror at the disaster unfolding before him.

"Fuck!" Ryker roared through the radio. "Do you read, Three? Do you read?"

"DROPSHIP THREE DISCONNECTED," the intercom blared. The monitor above the control panel, which once displayed black outlines of the three dropships, now only showed two. The third flashed red, with a label above it reading: *OFFLINE.*

Zach felt a bubbling wave of bile rise up his throat. Three

hundred people were gone in a split second. And it was his fault. He made them launch. He knew not everyone would make it, but he gave the order anyway.

"Do you see that?" Ryker cried, and a whoop of joy followed.

The sound obliterated the guilty thoughts flooding Zach's mind. He looked out the window to see what Ryker was shouting about. Outside the glass, flashes of greens, reds, and blues had begun to emerge between the roiling storm clouds.

Zach couldn't stop himself from smiling. An irrational burst of laughter spilled from his lips. He had never been so happy to see anything in his life.

Ryker's gleeful shouting continued. Zach could practically hear him bobbing up and down in his seat. "Let's fucking go! We made it! We—"

There was a flash of light. A burst of fire. An ear-splitting crack of thunder as Ryker's dropship was practically cleaved in half by a massive bolt of lighting.

"Ryker!" Zach yelled.

The blast sent Ryker's dropship spinning in circles, detritus rocketing from the craft in all directions. The ship dove, shedding plates from its heat shield as it fell. Its roof tore open, exposing everyone and everything inside to the violent winds of its spiraling descent.

"We— ca— ar—" Ryker's voice, detached and grainy, rasped through the radio. Then there was another explosion at the back of the ship. The voice turned into a scream.

"Ryker!" Zach yelled again. "Ryker, can you hear me? Answer me! Come on! Please! Please, respond!" He strained to hear anything; a yelp, a groan, *something* to show Ryker was alive. But there was nothing.

One thruster on Ryker's ship tore free and rocketed toward Zach's dropship. Zach's pilot swerved out of the way, slamming everyone to the side. A sudden pain in Zach's upper arm screamed for Zach's attention, but he ignored it.

With that final maneuver, Zach's dropship sliced through the last layer of storm clouds and emerged into a sky as clear and bright as Earth's best day. The planet below was a lush world filled with green trees. Red grass. Mountains. Hills. Lakes.

But the jaw-dropping display of beauty did nothing to distract Zach from the horror in the sky beside him. Ryker's dropship continued to break apart, charred metal plates curling and twisting as debris spewed from a hole in the back. With the ground drawing near, the ship disappeared behind a tall mountain range. A deafening boom and a smoke-filled, fiery explosion followed.

"Ryker!" Zach's voice morphed into a loud cry. Then something rattled beneath him, and the pilot announced the reverse thrusters had kicked in. Zach's chin fell to his chest.

A moment later, a heavy thud rattled his teeth.

They had landed.

ZACH RELEASED his restraints and staggered to the front window of the dropship, leaning against it for support. In the distance, towers of oily smoke billowed from behind a mountain range, reaching high into the sky. The clouds overhead looked peaceful—the lightning couldn't be seen from the ground. If Zach didn't know any better, he'd think it was a pleasant spring day with some light rain in the forecast.

Cora's voice snapped him back to reality. "You're hurt." The next thing he knew, she was bandaging up the deep gash in his arm. The gauze wrapped around his bicep, pulled tight to stop the bleeding. Some soaked through. But Zach wasn't thinking about his arm—he was picturing Ryker lying dead in a pile of flaming wreckage. Or no, worse, already incinerated. How could Zach have let that happen? If he'd forced Ryker to go on Dropship One with him instead of allowing him to pilot Dropship Two himself, his friend would still be alive. Instead, Ryker's blood was on his hands. Zach squeezed his fingers into fists to stop them from shaking.

Cora hugged him from behind. "Listen to me. It's okay. It wasn't your fault," she said. But it wasn't okay.

Somehow, seeing Ryker go out like that was harder than when Carver told him Ryker was dead when he was a kid. But why? The simple answer was that Zach hadn't seen Ryker die back then, so he always held on to a tiny hope that he was still alive. But this time was different. Zach had seen Ryker's dropship explode, first in the storm, then in one last boom behind those mountains. The evidence was in that massive pillar of smoke right in front of him.

"He could still be alive out there," Zach said quietly. He didn't believe it but couldn't bring himself to say otherwise.

Cora put her hand on Zach's cheek, turning his face away from the window and toward hers. "Maybe. But *we're* alive right here." She gestured to the shell-shocked passengers starting to rise from their seats. "Let's take care of them first. Then we'll go look for the others. Okay?"

Zach nodded. He knew Cora was right.

For the next half-hour, the pilot monitored outside conditions through the dropship's external environment scanners to ensure the air was safe to breathe and the temperatures weren't too extreme. Meanwhile, Zach instructed a group of passengers to assemble supply packs that could be distributed to everyone as they disembarked. By the time everyone was ready, plans to send a rescue party toward Ryker's ship had been hammered out, and the survivors were doing their best to line up at the airlock. Mabel quickly stepped in and announced, "Zach should go first."

All gazes turned to him. He looked to the floor. "Thanks." Silently, he approached the blast door, feeling Ryker's spirit with him. As incredible as it seemed, it had been barely a week since they were reunited—not accounting for cryo. One short week. That was all they got. After twenty-three years apart, struggling with the trauma of the past, their only reward was a dangerous few days which ended with Ryker dead.

Zach reached up to grab the release lever, then pushed it down slowly. The airlock hissed, then slid open. The ramp descended.

Rays of golden sunlight cut into the ship, making Zach shield his eyes. When the ramp thudded against the alien ground, he dropped his hand and marveled at the sight before him.

Their dropship had landed in a field of bright red grass that stretched for about a hundred yards before it met a dense tree line. Each blade of grass was nearly up to Zach's knees. The trunks of the trees in the distance were shrouded with moss-like growth that filled the deep ridges that rippled across the bark. The trees' branches looked more like vines than wood, with colorful, prismatic leaves sprouting along their lengths. The hues of the foliage seemed to shift with the angle of the light.

Further toward the horizon, jagged mountain peaks jutted straight into the air, higher than any mountains Zach had ever seen. Then, there was the sky. It was a deep greenish turquoise, smooth as silk, with orange-tinted clouds. Sunlight sliced through the sky like god lights.

Zach couldn't believe his eyes. He didn't deserve a place this breathtakingly beautiful after all that happened. He felt a tingling in his nose and slight pressure in his eyes. As he breathed in, he realized he could taste the air. It was sweet, almost like cotton candy, leaving a heavy feeling in his chest that he couldn't explain. It wasn't bad, just ... different.

As Zach gazed at the landscape, two brown, fur-covered animals scurried across the grass, weaving together in a zigzag. The grass crunched under their tiny feet as the animals let out quiet cries like birds chirping.

"My god..." Cora said from the dropship. She smiled, her teeth gleaming. "They're beautiful."

For a few moments, Zach took it all in. The forest beyond the clearing seemed to go for miles, and... what was that? Zach could just make out a group of figures emerging from the trees at the edge of the grass. Although they were silhouetted by the bright sunlight, Zach could still see their basic outlines.

They looked human.

A broad smile formed on Zach's face as he realized who it

must be. It was people from Dropship Two. Survivors! Zach ran back into the ship and began delivering orders immediately.

"Everyone! There are people from Dropship Two out there! Mabel?"

Zach searched the crowd for her. Mabel pushed her way through the group, waving her arm at Zach. "Here!"

"We need to be prepared to treat anyone who's hurt. Medical supplies, surgical gear. Whatever you've got."

"On it!" Mabel motioned to several other doctors in the crowd. They disappeared back into the dropship to assemble whatever supplies they could find.

"Water," Zach said to Cora. "Clean water. How much do we have?"

They didn't have much, but it only had to last them until they found another source on Alpha Cen. Given the trees, grass, and foliage, something was bound to be nearby. But they needed water *immediately* to help the injured.

"Okay," Zach said. He took a deep breath, then exhaled. "I'm gonna go see how many there are. Have everything ready as soon as possible!"

Zach felt hope swell in his chest as he headed down the ramp. If there were survivors, then Ryker could be among them. He could have made it. He could still be alive.

Zach reached the sea of red grass, then suddenly stopped. He felt his stomach drop. First, confusion set in. Then, fear.

The figures that had emerged from the trees were barely thirty feet away now. They were spread out in a half circle around the dropship. None of them were injured. And none of them wore the torn and tattered clothing the survivors had been wearing when they left the Gateway.

Instead, these people were clad in leather-like armor and hammered metal helmets. They wielded handmade spears with long, menacing blades in their right hands.

All except for one.

A woman wearing a long white gown with embroidered flowers stepped forward from the front of the pack. Her long black hair fell over the front of her shoulders in two thick sheets, extending almost to her knees. She held no weapon. With a wave of her hand, the people in armor stood at attention, their chins pointed high.

What the fuck? Zach thought. *What the actual fuck am I looking at?*

He had to be dreaming. Or dead. Yeah, he was definitely dead. How else could he explain what he was seeing? He had a million questions. A billion, perhaps. But he could only muster one.

"Who are you?"

The woman ignored his question.

"Welcome to Eden," she said instead. Zach opened his mouth to speak, but the woman cut him off once more. "We've been expecting you."

TO BE CONTINUED...

ACKNOWLEDGMENTS

Thank you to my father for being there every step of the writing process. You believed in me when I said I wanted to write a book and did not doubt for a second that I'd be able to. You helped me outline the story, brainstormed with me when I ran into worrisome plot issues, and proofread my final manuscript before pushing it through publication. *The Forgotten Colony* would truly be a different book without you. My original draft was terrible, but having the ability to bounce ideas off of you gave me the means to make it into something I'm proud of. It took a long time. Many late nights were spent talking about the plot, character arcs, and twists. I'll admit, the many times you urged me to delete and rewrite my favorite scenes were rough. But I knew you only wanted the best for me, so I always took your advice and gave it another go. I know I'll never be able to repay you for what you did, though I can only hope that I've made you proud by staying true to the promise I made at twelve years old: that I was going to write a book.

Thank you to my mother for bringing me into this world and keeping my life running smoothly while I worked on this novel. You picked me up from school, took me to doctors' appointments, and did any favor I asked of you without complaint. You spent many nights on your own as my father and I worked out the specifics of the book. You could have grumbled about it, but you knew what we were doing was important, so you sacrificed time with your husband so he could spend it with his son.

Thanks to Justin Lancaster for designing *The Forgotten Colony*'s cover. For more of Justin's work, visit his website at studio1126.com and follow him on Twitter at @_byeforever_.

Thank you to Sonnet Star, Noor Mujahid, Camilla Rojas, Harshitha Sree, and Poppy Scotchmer for being a part of my Acknowledgments contest on Instagram and TikTok. The videos you created really brightened my day and made me very hopeful for the future of *The Forgotten Colony*. I would also like to thank everyone else who has supported the release of this book with your comments, fan art, videos, and other creative contributions. Your encouragement, enthusiasm, and love mean so much to me. I truly cannot be more grateful. You have all been so kind, and I can't wait to interact with more of you in the future.

ABOUT THE AUTHOR

J.B. Ryder is a teen author from Southern California. *The Forgotten Colony* is his first novel and was published when he was a sophomore in high school. For more information, visit jbryderauthor.com.

instagram.com/jbryderauthor
tiktok.com/@jbryderauthor
x.com/jbryderauthor

Made in the USA
Las Vegas, NV
26 November 2024

12672709R00288